VIVA!

a novel

Graziela Pimentel & Mark Fortier

Charlotte House
Toronto
2012

To my parents

— Graziela Pimentel

For Charlotte and Julia

— Mark Fortier

CONTENTS

PART ONE

Chapter One   1

Chapter Two   19

Chapter Three   43

Chapter Four   69

Chapter Five   93

Chapter Six   115

Chapter Seven   131

Chapter Eight   165

Chapter Nine   181

PART TWO

Chapter One   199

Chapter Two   227

Chapter Three   249

Chapter Four   265

Chapter Five   289

Chapter Six   311

Glossary of Portuguese Words   333

PART ONE

Chapter One

São Miguel, Açores, 1918

Gabriel Aguiar's daughter-in-law, Maria de Conceição, died two days after going to bed with a headache and fever. By then everyone in the village was afraid of the sickness taking so many lives—children, young people, middle-aged, and old, no one could know who would be next. In Agua d'Alto José *dos Mortos*, the coffin maker, couldn't make enough coffins for the dead: Maria de Conceição was to share a casket with her third cousin.

Gabriel was climbing the path up the hill to his son's house. At this time of the morning, before the sun rose, the blackberry bushes along the stone walls on both sides of the road were wet with dew. He picked a few berries and threw them into his mouth; he wasn't hungry but he knew it would be the only thing he would eat until dinner, which would be reheated *caldo azedo*, the soup Maria de Conceição had made the day before she took ill.

He came to João and Maria de Conceição's house, small, unpainted, mostly mud with a little cement, two of the walls buried against a dirt hill, green and pink with wild lilies and hydrangea.

1

They had lived there since their wedding, at first with her parents while they were alive, and then by themselves with their only child, Maria de Deus. His granddaughter, looking puny in her mother's oversized black dress, her head covered in a black kerchief, sat by her mother's body laid out in the coffin and whimpered into her white embroidered handkerchief. João was in the kitchen, squeezed into his dark suit, the one he had worn fifteen years ago on his wedding day. He was grumbling to the men who had come to carry his wife down to the church.

"What's going to happen to me? I'm thirty-seven with no sons, only a daughter to help me. I should have gone to America with my brother." João's voice was a fitful whine.

"Don't despair," consoled a man with a thick lips whom everyone called *Beiços Grossos*. "You can still get married again and have a son."

João went silent at the sight of his father.

"We should start down to the church. It could be a while at Ana's house," advised Gabriel.

The procession of six men with Maria de Deus following behind made its way down the hill, watched in silence by neighbours who came out of their houses to pay their respects. Some lined up behind Maria de Deus and fell in step with her. The procession stopped halfway down the hill and the box was carried inside a whitewashed house where Maria de Conceição's third cousin, a woman in her forties, laid waiting for her share of the coffin.

Two more men joined the pallbearers. By the time they had descended the hill the procession was a chain of fifty. At the bottom they turned to the right, where the road widened, and the houses on either side were built large and on high ground, with balcony windows covered in French lace. At the crest of the road cement steps rose to a wide courtyard in front of a white church trimmed with basalt stone around the edges, facing the green mountains.

Gabriel had been blessed with two grown sons; Rosa had given birth to four but only two had survived. When João and Manuel were boys Gabriel had hoped someday to buy land where the three of them would grow crops to sell at the market in the city, *Ponta Delgada*. He had worked long hours, six days a week, but had never managed to buy any land; he had barely managed to feed his family. Nor did the three of them work together for long. Manuel, his younger son, had one day announced he was going to emigrate to Brazil. Now he had been away for over ten years; after a few years in Brazil, he had gone to America. Once every few years, they received a letter from him, from places Gabriel could not imagine—São Paulo, California, Massachusetts. It had broken Rosa's heart that her son had gone so far away. Lost to her forever.

In the village he had been known as Manuel *Lindo*, Manuel the Beautiful.

"He had such a beautiful face. Green eyes. Hair the colour of wheat. My Manuel! He could have married any woman in *Agua d'Alto*. Even one from a rich family." Rosa cried for years after he sailed away.

She never stopped talking about him. When she lay sick and dying she murmured his name over and over again. If only Manuel had come back, or never gone away, then Rosa might have lived longer. But he hadn't come back, and his mother had died.

Gabriel had always been confused by his younger son; he was too good-looking to be a boy, his features were delicate like a girl's. He had made a strange sight working the soil with the other men. But he had been a hard worker, just as strong with the hoe as the rugged-looking ones. But Gabriel had never understood how he could have left his mother, his home, his island, for strange places.

There was pain too when he thought about his older son, although there was far less confusion. João was never going away anywhere. He was rooted in the land like a heavy rock: hard and in the way. João was the first to work with Gabriel for the village *patrão*. At twenty he married Maria de Conceição. Maria de Deus was born barely nine months later. Maria de Conceição and João's union promised abundance. Then Gabriel had noticed a couple of missing teeth in

João's mouth, and not long afterwards João's face was bruised and gashed from another man's blows. Gabriel began to hear the village whispers: temper, drunk, brawl.... The village women stopped talking at the sight of Gabriel. Maria de Conceição miscarried in her second pregnancy. It was then that Gabriel first noticed her bruises.

Soon she was pregnant again.

One night Gabriel had arrived at João's house to find Maria de Conceição and frail little Maria de Deus, hiding behind her mother's skirt.

"*Pai*, your blessing?"

"God bless you. Where's João?"

"Out, sir."

Gabriel looked at her face, the right eye swollen and grey blue, her cheek puffy and red, her lips the colour of a blackberry stain.

"Did he do this to you?"

"I fell."

"Don't lie to me. I can see the mark of his hand. What kind of man beats the mother of his unborn child?"

She sobbed uncontrollably and the little girl started to cry, clutching her mother's skirt in her small hands.

"Calm down. This won't happen again. I give you my word. Now answer my question: how often does this happen?"

"It used to be only every couple of months. Usually on my arms and legs but lately it's been all the time."

"You and the girl go up to bed."

"He'll want his dinner."

"I'll take care of him."

"*Pai*, your blessing?"

"God bless you."

They climbed the stairs to the attic, like mice scurrying to hide.

Gabriel went up to the window and removed the stick from the shutter and laid it beside his chair. He sat down and waited.

Gabriel dozed off. He awoke when the door banged open. João

stormed into the house.

"Where's my dinner?" he growled.

"It isn't dinnertime," answered Gabriel. "If you want dinner you should be home at the right time."

João, drunk, stumbled when he saw his father in the shadows.

"*Pai*, your blessing."

Gabriel did not answer.

"Where's Maria de Conceição?"

"In bed."

"I want my dinner."

"You need to learn to eat when it's dinnertime like everybody else."

"This is my house. I can do what I want."

"This house belonged to Maria de Conceição's parents. You disgrace their memory in the way you treat their daughter. Never forget that I'm still your father."

Gabriel stood with the stick in his hand. He looked at his son with shame and anger and started beating him. João didn't resist as the blows came down. He crumbled under their power.

"You're my son, but may God forgive me, you're an animal and I beat you like one. No man hits a woman. Don't think when I'm gone you can hit her for what I've done to you. If you ever hit her again, I'll kill you. Don't think you can hide it from me. I'll know. Even if she doesn't tell me. Even if she covers the marks. I'll know by the fear in her eyes and I'll come here and kill you like a dog. May God forgive me."

The beatings stopped but Maria de Conceição miscarried anyway. The years passed; Maria de Conceição's eyes and belly had been full of emptiness a long time when she died.

The village priest, in his white tunic and chasuble embroidered in gold filigree, sprinkled the coffin with holy water. Gabriel folded his earth-stained fingers, knotted and twisted with arthritis, and prayed that things might someday be well for his family.

"Children of God," spoke the priest, "I know how you suffer.

Why are you losing your parents, your wives, your husbands, your children, your grandchildren? I have no explanation to give you. But in this difficult time we must trust in God and take comfort in believing that life on this earth is just a short passage to a better one."

Gabriel couldn't imagine a life not of the earth; every day, as he always had, he dug his fingers into the soil, sowing seeds and pulling up roots. He had buried his wife deep and dark inside the earth, and someday he too would be planted there. Although he was pious and upright, Heaven meant little to him. Gabriel was not an ambitious man or a man of great understanding or imagination. He had never been to school. His sense of the world stopped with his family and his village. Even the people of the city on his own island seemed foreign to him. His life on the land was a hard life but he was certain it was the only life for him. He was reliable and hard working. When the men spoke together in the fields, he listened but had nothing to say. Sometimes they spoke of things that went over his head; sometimes, when they spoke of things that were down to earth, he had an opinion but kept it to himself.

And yet for some time now Gabriel had been fascinated by stories from Fatima, where the Blessed Virgin had appeared to three children, children who were very much like the child he himself had been. The idea that into a life such as his, into the hills of a world very much like his own, something miraculous should come struck him with an awe and excitement almost sexual in its power—like when he was an adolescent and someone had shown him a photo of a naked woman: that such wondrous bodies existed right here under the drab dresses of the women and girls of the village took his breath away. A heaven elsewhere he could not imagine, but heaven coming to these simple children in their own fields struck him with excitement and awe.

Once he imagined Rosa appearing in brightness beside his bed in the middle of the night.

Gabriel was not usually a man to be carried away, but he had furtively followed the story anyway he could—listening in to talk in the street or in the square or after Mass, attending on those who read aloud accounts in the newspapers or summarized what they had read.

Fatima, Portugal

The people of Fatima, although far away and on the mainland, were much like the people of Gabriel's village and saw the world in much the same way. During the war everything had gone crazy. No one had bread. Money was worth nothing. One government quickly followed another, with elections, conspiracies, coups, strikes, riots, bombings, and assassinations. The army was off dying in France and in Angola. Once Lisbon was bombarded by its own mutinous ships. At the university the students shouted slogans, slashed the portraits of the kings, tore the robes off the backs of the professors, and threatened to torch the place. Where was there any order?

In the city people no longer believed in God. There was even divorce. The cardinal carried a gun to defend himself. Those who had bread stuffed their faces and didn't bother about those who had none. Many, like Jacinta's brother, were sent off to die in the war. Lucia's brother was supposed to go too, but his godfather spoke to the examining doctor who was from the country and understood these things, and the doctor wrote down that the young man was in poor health even though he wasn't. Lucia's mother was grateful to God for that.

Lucia's mother, Maria Rosa—named like Gabriel's Rosa—was a saint. When people were sick they came to Maria Rosa for help. Everyone said she was worth all of her daughters put together. When the new priest said it was a sin to dance, Maria Rosa stopped dancing, even though it was her only pleasure. Her husband didn't like this, and when the new priest told him he shouldn't drink so much, he stopped going to church. Maria Rosa had much to bear. Her husband couldn't manage money because he drank and God wanted to punish him. When Lucia was seven she had to go out to watch the sheep at *Cova de Iria*, a bowl of dry, rocky earth, so that her older sisters could work in the fields or hire themselves out as servants. Maria Rosa could read, but none of her children could. She taught them all their catechism at home because if the priest had asked them at Easter and they had been unable to answer, she would have died of shame.

Lucia always remembered everything she was told. She loved to tell her younger cousins, Francisco and Jacinta, the stories she had learned from her mother about Jesus and the Virgin Mary. On feast days her sisters would dress her up like an angel, white wings strapped to her back, and she would walked in the procession, with solemn footsteps over the flower-decorated road, her eyes fixed on the summer-blue sky. Lucia knew her catechism so well she was able to make her first communion when she was only six years old. The parish priest disapproved of a child her age taking communion, but he allowed it as a special favour to Maria Rosa, who was a saint, and because she suffered so much and was in poor health.

When they were old enough Francisco and Jacinta were sent out to watch the flock with their cousin. Every morning the three of them would gather the sheep together and take them out to the rocky hills where the olive trees grew. Francisco went along with whatever the girls wanted to do. People said he wasn't very bright. Jacinta had a pretty face. She liked to stand with her hand on her hip. Lucia thought her spoiled. She wanted her own way all the time and when she didn't get it she pouted. Lucia had a flat face with dark protruding eyes that gave her a permanent scowl, but Francisco and Jacinta loved her.

When they were on the hills around *Cova de Iria*, Lucia would tell them stories about Jesus and Jacinta would kiss the crucifix over and over. They sang hymns, "Hail Noble Patroness" and "Virgin Pure."

They liked to make their voices bounce back from the far hills. Of all the words the one that came back clearest was "Maria."

One day when they were getting ready to take their flocks back home, right after they had finished saying the rosary as they always did, skipping a few "Hail Marys" to make it go quicker, they saw a flash of lightning in the blue sky above the sandy hills and the squat holm oaks.

That night Jacinta told her mother what had happened to them even though Lucia had made them all agree that they wouldn't. It wasn't long before everyone knew, including Maria Rosa.

Maria Rosa didn't believe a word of it. This wasn't the first time. Two years before, when Lucia had been with other children, they said they had seen a figure wrapped in a white sheet walking over the tops of the trees. The other girls had told their mothers, but Lucia, just like this time, had said nothing. Now when Maria Rosa questioned her there was the same evasiveness.

"What did you see?"

"We saw a Lady."

"And what did this Lady say?"

"She said that we should say the rosary."

"It's a sin to lie."

Lucia didn't want to say anything else, but Jacinta let everyone know that the Lady had said she would come back the next month. The village hummed with the story. Maria Rosa took her lying daughter to the parish priest.

"What did the Lady say to you?" The priest pursed his thin lips.

"She asked us to pray for the world." Lucia's voice was as faint as her breath.

"And did she tell you to go to your priest?"

"No."

"Then this can hardly be the work of God. Dona Maria Rosa, you'd better pray your daughter is lying, because if she isn't, then this has all the marks of the work of the devil."

Maria Rosa wished her daughter had never been born when she heard the priest's words. What could be worse than to have a child who was the devil's instrument? When they got home, Maria Rosa demanded that Lucia admit she was lying and beat her with a broom handle. Lucia let herself be flogged in silence, her arms hanging at her sides.

"You're lying! The devil is going to take you to hell!"

Lucia went to bed with her arms bruised like apples, spotted and mushy, but she would recant nothing.

Now when the three children went into the fields together they thought of ways to sacrifice for the Lady: they gave their lunches to beggars, sometimes they fed morsels of their cornbread—their precious bread—to the sheep and ate unripe olives or acorns; they poured the water in their canteen onto the ground and drank from the stagnant pool where the sheep drank. They told no one. Jacinta was sorry that she had let others know in the first place, especially since Lucia was the one to suffer for it.

"If only my parents would beat me too," she wished. "I could offer the sacrifice to Jesus."

A month after the first time, on the thirteenth of June, fifty people followed them into the rocky hills. Most believed, but some mocked the whole thing.

Afterwards Maria Rosa took her daughter back to the parish priest.

"He'll force you to tell the truth. I don't care how he does it. Let him punish you. Let him do whatever he likes with you, just so long as he makes you tell the truth. Then I'll be satisfied."

"After all the troubles I've been through, Senhor Padre, and now this. Please help me, Senhor Padre," she begged.

But Lucia would not admit to lying.

After that the local administrator demanded to see the children and their parents. Francisco and Jacinta's parents refused to submit their children to an interrogation and went to answer for them. Lucia's parents did not feel the same way.

"As for Lucia, I'll take her myself," said her father. "Let her answer for herself. I don't know anything about visions from God."

"If she's lying," said her mother, "it's a good thing that she should be punished for it."

Francisco and Jacinta cried when Lucia was taken from them; they were afraid of what would happen to her. When the administrator saw that only one child had been brought, he scolded Francisco and Jacinta's father and threatened to have him imprisoned. Then he demanded that Lucia be left alone with him. Her parents obeyed in silence.

First he asked what she had seen, then suggested that it was all a girlish lie.

When she wouldn't agree to that, he threatened to boil her in oil.

She would not change her answer.

When they arrived back home, Maria Rosa beat her daughter and tried to make her confess.

Lucia dreamt that the devil had deceived her and came to carry her off to hell. People mocked her on the street. Anarchists and atheists came around to preach against her, and the priest said nothing to defend her. Still she believed. At the same time, on Sunday, after mass, people who were sick or poor, or who had sons in the war, came up to her and begged her to ask the Lady for help. On the thirteenth of July, over two thousand people walked the rocky hills to wait with the children.

After that the children were more secretive than ever, though priests were sent to talk to them and men in suits came from the city. Whenever someone called for them, or whenever they saw strangers, they would run into the hills to hide.

When the thirteenth of August came around, the local administrator sent his men out to kidnap them, so that there would be no one there for the Lady to appear to. He locked them in jail and threatened to kill them. When the children knelt to pray, some of the prisoners, murderers and thieves, knelt to pray with them. When they returned home, they went back into the hills, six days late. The crowds trampled over the fields and destroyed the year's crop. Maria Rosa was furious. Sometimes she refused to give Lucia anything to eat.

"Go ask your Lady for food," she taunted.

Lucia said nothing. She would bear hunger along with the beatings. The three children began to mortify themselves. They hit themselves with nettles and tied ropes around their chests until they couldn't breathe and passed out. They talked about the things they had seen and about hell and all the people who would burn there. Once Francisco saw a devil who chased him up a hill.

The parish priest was angry when he found out that people were leaving money in the hills and not giving anything to the church. Some people tried to give Lucia money so she would intercede for them, but she never took any. Her mother didn't believe this and demanded to know where Lucia was hoarding it.

There were pious women who, whenever they met Lucia in the street, would kick her, because they knew her mother wouldn't mind. There was a drunken woman who did the same thing. Lucia wished her mother were protective and kind, like Jacinta's mother, but she felt no resentment.

The government sent men around to chop down the holm oak where the Lady had appeared. When Lucia heard this she was terrified and ran into the hills. When she got there she saw that they had cut down the wrong tree. She told no one.

In September they were told they shouldn't tie ropes around themselves any more when they went to bed.

Everyone knew that October was supposed to be the last visitation. There would be a miracle. The night of the twelfth was full of rain and gales, but the next day people stood shoulder to shoulder in the mud.

When the children left their homes, their parents went with them. There was talk that the anarchists would explode a bomb, and Maria Rosa said if her daughter was to die she was determined to die with her.

"How wonderful," whispered Jacinta, "if we were granted the grace of going up to Heaven with Our Lady!"

And now the two little ones, Jacinta and Francisco, had died of the influenza just like children in Gabriel's own village.

São Miguel, Açores

Gabriel couldn't hear the voices but he sensed people were saying things about his family once again behind his back; the women at the windows stopped talking and gave him fake smiles whenever he passed by.

"Good day, neighbour!"

"Good day, ladies." He lifted his cap and continued walking, feeling their secret words hot on the back of his neck as he walked away.

The men didn't say anything, but he could feel their holding back when he smoked with them Sunday afternoons in the square across the road from the church. What could it be this time? He knew it had to be something bad that João had done. Maybe it was a particularly bad fight with another man. He searched João's body for new bruises. He looked for the marks of João's hands on his granddaughter. She always looked pale and sickly, when he visited in the evenings, but he couldn't see any signs of João's handiwork. Maybe when there was more to eat for everybody then Maria de Deus would grow healthier and find herself a man. She would be better off married than staying with her father. It crossed Gabriel's mind that the kind of trouble that João was in had nothing to do with violence this time. He might have gotten some woman in trouble. It made Gabriel warm with fear. It was better he not know. If João had gotten a woman in trouble, then it would be better that she be married. If she were clever, she could pass off the child as her husband's. Gabriel prayed that his son would not dishonour him anymore.

Gabriel waited in the darkness of the harbour, his eyes fixed on the prick of light that slowly flickered toward shore. He was standing with a dozen others who had come to greet the passengers on the boat, waiting for his younger son, Manuel, who was coming back after many years abroad. Maybe this was the answer to his prayers. Manuel was still young, in his mid-thirties, with a lifetime to make things better. Maybe he would bring money, and uprightness. Gabriel leaned on his cane as the light moved closer over the waters.

"Who are you waiting for?" asked the man beside him, whom Gabriel recognized as a farmer from *Vila Franca do Campo*.

"My son."

"My son's coming back from California. Been gone for three years."

Everyone squinted at the boat as it approached, searching for the faces of their memories. Gabriel's tired eyes followed the passengers as they walked across the plank that was laid from the boat to the pier. There were many men about his son's age. Around him he saw the clasping of bodies and kisses as families claimed their kin. He shifted his weight from side to side, moving his cane from one hand to the other, thinking that perhaps Manuel wasn't on the boat after all. He had borrowed his neighbour's horse and cart for nothing; he would make the trip back to *Agua d'Alto* alone. Gabriel had given up searching the faces when he heard a voice nearby call out to him.

"*Pai*, your blessing." The voice belonged to a slim, still handsome, man.

Gabriel held back the embrace he had been saving for his son and instead clutched his cane. His son looked much the same, except that his skin was stretched less tightly across his face. Gabriel's heart was divided. If only Rosa had lived to share this moment!

"Ask your *avô* for his blessing," Manuel told a boy standing beside him.

"Is this, is this...?" Gabriel stammered.

"My son!" Manuel couldn't hide his pride.

"I didn't know. You never wrote us anything. I didn't know you had married."

The older man bent his arched frame and covered his grandson with a hug and kisses. The boy stiffened.

"Does he speak our language?" Gabriel asked.

"He speaks Brazilian Portuguese. English too. His name is Gabriel."

"Gabriel!" The old man was touched and there was a tear in his eye. "You never wrote us anything. His mother was Brazilian?"

Manuel nodded.

"And she died?"

"Not as far as I know. I'd guess she's still alive."

"Let's get your things. It'll take over an hour to get back home." Gabriel was weary.

They picked up a heavy old trunk tied with rope, carried it along the pier, and hoisted it onto the carriage. The men sat in the seat, with the boy between them, and started along the twisting coastal road in the silent darkness.

The next morning Gabriel sat on his chair in the backyard, drinking a bowl of barley coffee, looking at the green mountains behind the village and waiting for his son to awake. Manuel hadn't said much, but Gabriel thought him pleased to be home, sleeping in his own bed after all these years. It must be hard to travel so much, especially when you were not as young anymore and had a boy to take care of. The boy lacked the kindness that came with a mother's touch, but Gabriel would love him just the same. If Rosa were alive, she would have smothered him with kisses and filled his belly with sweets. From the looks of things, Manuel had brought no money with him. No matter: he was a good worker and such men were always wanted. It might be embarrassing for him at first, coming home with his tail tucked between his legs, but that would pass. But there was one thing wrong.

When Manuel came down, Gabriel gave him a bowl of coffee and some bread.

"Why did your wife allow you to take the boy away?" Gabriel's voice broke the morning stillness.

"I wanted to see America."

There was silence from Gabriel, demanding more.

"A boy should be with his father. It was for his own good. He's been to America. Maybe someday he'll want to go back there."

Gabriel folded his hands into a hump in front of his stomach, his coffee turning cold.

Manuel dug his hands into his pockets and waited for his father's response.

"Did your wife consent to this?" He looked straight into his son's eyes.

"I didn't ask her."

Gabriel searched his son's face for remorse.

"Do you think that was right?"

"It's done now. I've looked after the boy."

"But he doesn't know his mother."

"When he's older, I'll tell him and then he can go see her if he wants."

"We're not waiting until he's older and it's not up to him whether he wants to see his mother or not. It's up to me. There will be no more shame. You must do what is right."

"I'm not letting him go."

"I'm not asking you to give up your son. I'm telling you to write to your wife and tell her to join you."

"She has a big farm outside São Paulo. She's not going to leave that and come to a place in the middle of nowhere."

"She will come here if she loves her son."

"I don't even own a house," argued Manuel. "I have nothing to offer her. She has money."

"My grandson's mother has a home here and a family if she wants it. That's what you have to offer her." Gabriel's eyes were dark with disappointment and anger. "You've always been a good son, Manuel, don't disappoint me now. I expect you to do the right thing for your family. Write to your wife and tell her where her son is."

Gabriel stood up to signal the end of the conversation, finished his cold coffee, and left Manuel staring at the green mountains.

A little over a month later Marina Teresa Xisto Caçador Aguiar wrote that she would sail for São Miguel as soon as she could. She thanked her estranged husband for letting her come to see their son. Nothing could make her happier. Nothing would keep her away.

Chapter Two

Porto, Portugal, 1890

There had been rain most of the night, and when the rain stopped it left behind a thick fog in the streets. At one o'clock there was silence; at two there was the crowing of roosters. At three there was shouting in the *Campo de Santo Ovidio*.

"Long live the Republic! Long live the army! Down with the monarchy!"

The Ninth Hunters' regiment had gone into formation. The Tenth was in two circles on the opposite end of the field. The Sixth Cavalry, which had left by the back gate, came at full gallop around to the front of the barracks. There was more shouting. Loudest and most jubilant were the students and civilian supporters who had somehow gotten wind of what was taking place. They made no formations but embraced, held each other by the shoulders, and raised their fists.

"Death to the Braganças!"

The Eighteenth was still inside the barracks. Everyone was waiting for them to come out, calling to them, encouraging them, certain of them. Everyone believed that something critical and irrevocable was happening.

Quietly in the fog the Municipal Guard had taken up positions in the streets leading out of the *Campo*. At first no one noticed them, then word passed through the crowd, and people stared anxiously at the obscure, grey shapes in the distance. It had been the Municipal Guard that had charged on the people during republican demonstrations in September. Many in the crowd had been injured. Those in the square knew that if there was to be any opposition this time, it would come from the Municipal Guard. The students especially hated the Guard, but their hatred was cut with fear. Some thought of shouting "Death to the Guard," but for the moment no one dared.

Slowly out of the thick air came an officer on a horse. It was the Deputy-Chief of the Guard. He was a tall man, and from the top of his horse he towered over everyone. He came up before the first platoon of the Tenth and cast a slow, sweeping glance over the assembled soldiers.

"Who is in command?" he asked calmly.

"I am," said a young lieutenant.

"Lieutenant, do you know what time it is? Let these poor men go back to bed and get some sleep."

"I'm afraid that's impossible. I have orders from my captain. We have left the barracks and are in revolt." The lieutenant's voice was young and thin, self-conscious and arrogant.

There were a few nervous shouts. "Long live the Republic! Down with the Braganças!" The Deputy-Chief acted as if he didn't hear them. He stroked his thick moustache and took a slow deep breath. Then he said, "Where is your captain?"

The lieutenant pointed down the line towards the second platoon. The Deputy-Chief tapped his horse, which moved with measured steps.

"Captain, call in these poor people before you've utterly compromised them."

"No one is leaving. The die is cast. We are seeing this through to the end."

The Deputy-Chief looked at the captain for a long moment, as if expecting him, sooner or later, to change his mind. Then he said, "Are there any other officers with you?"

"There is a lieutenant with the Ninth."

As the Deputy-Chief moved down the line into the miasma, the students lost sight of him. They couldn't hear what was said. But evidently the lieutenant with the Ninth stood firm, because a few minutes later the Deputy-Chief ambled back to his men and there were excited, exalted shouts from the rebel troops behind him.

"Viva this!" and "Viva that!"

The Municipal Guard broke ranks and retreated quietly into the fog, and the streets into the city were open. The students were the first to move, enthusiastically, without discipline: some of them even embraced the soldiers, who tried to fend them off and keep their dignity. The soldiers were drawn up four abreast to march out of the *Campo*. They came around behind the barracks where the Eighteenth was still strangely silent. The gates were locked, but two men began chopping at them with axes. One of them was Miguel Verdial, the famous actor and republican. When a hole had been hacked in the door, he made a heroic gesture and climbed through.

The gates were opened from inside and everyone rushed into the courtyard.

"Long live the army! Long live the Eighteenth infantry regiment! Down with England! Down with the monarchy!"

Everyone was certain now that the Eighteenth would follow them. They left the barracks and marched quickly down the steep *Rua do Almada* toward the *Praça de Dom Pedro*, the main square of Porto. The students and civilians ran along and in front. All along the way people were leaning out of their windows. Men were shouting "Viva!" and those in the street shouted back. In silent exuberance women waved their handkerchiefs, which looked like wavering patches of dense fog, and clapped their hands.

There was already a crowd in the square. As the marchers poured out of the *Rua do Almada*, even the soldiers lost whatever order there had been. There was no room for them to take formations, so they dispersed among the people. Some of them tried to retain a military bearing; some whooped and yelled with the students; and a few even fired their guns in the air. The cavalrymen tried to keep their horses from stepping on anyone.

Some people began to sing the national anthem:

Às armas, às armas!
Sobre a terra, sobre o mar,
Às armas, às armas!
Pela pátria lutar
Contra os canhões marchar, marchar!

No one knew what should be done next.

Among those who had come to the square was Edmundo Caçador, a recent graduate from the University of Coimbra. Edmundo was a republican sympathizer. He had taken part in the demonstrations in the fall, was a loyal reader of *A República Portuguesa*, the republican newspaper, and often sat up late in the Swiss Café arguing about the future. He had marched with the Patriotic League of the North to greet Antero de Quental, the great socialist poet. An hour before a friend had hastily called for him with excited rumours of what was happening. He was very excited. But like everyone else he was slightly confused and disoriented.

Edmundo saw one of his friends in the crowd and they leapt forward to embrace each other.

"Long live the Republic!"

"Is it really happening?"

"Yes, Edmundo, yes!"

Not everyone in the square supported the revolt, but those who didn't were keeping quiet. When Edmundo spotted Pereira, Clara's father, looking stiff and displeased, he felt a sudden revulsion and fear. Pereira approached him.

"Let's go," he said. "This is no place for people like us."

"I couldn't agree with you less, sir." Edmundo suddenly hated Pereira as he never had before, hated his assumption, his proprietorship, as if Edmundo were one of his precious barrels of wine, to be locked away and aged. Pereira seemed so insidious here, as if a great lethargy and defeat were emanating from him. For some reason Edmundo suddenly despised Clara too.

"Long live the Republic!" he shouted, and then, because he knew that it would particularly gall Pereira, "down with England!"

Pereira said nothing, but looked at him with a stern and indomitable disapproval. Then he turned and walked away. Edmundo felt a little afraid of what he had done.

"What are they going to do now?" someone asked.

Everyone was wondering the same thing. The soldiers appeared confused and almost lost. People were wandering back home. Was there a plan? Was there someone who would take the lead? Edmundo wondered what would happen next and what his own role would be. Could it possibly fall to someone like him to take a leading part, or was he to be just one of the crowd of onlookers? Should he leap up on the steps and make a speech? What should be said? What was to be done?

The fog had begun to lift, and those on the north side of the square, where Edmundo stood, could now see that several men had appeared in the window of the municipal chambers. Edmundo recognized João Chagas, the Brazilian *caboclo* who was editor of *A República Portuguesa*. There was also Miguel Verdial, the actor, always at the heart of the show. At the front was a third man, older, heavier, whom many didn't recognize, but they knew he must be important. He had taken out a piece of paper, an envelope, and had begun to read something that was written on it. But his voice wasn't carrying, and the people couldn't make out what he was saying.

"Louder!" someone shouted; but the man kept reading in the same way.

Miguel Verdial suddenly snatched the envelope and waved it above his head.

"Dr. Alves da Veiga, civil leader of the revolt, wishes to announce to you the members of the provisional government of the Republic!" There were cheers, and Verdial read out the names with dramatic flourish. Even Dr. Alves da Veiga, who had at first been affronted when Verdial had taken away his envelope, was pleased with the effect the actor was having on the crowd.

Not everyone bothered to listen. After all, it was just a list of names. "Take a stand!" someone shouted. Edmundo was slightly bored and disappointed for himself. He longed to leap up onto the window, take the envelope from Verdial, and make a speech that would inspire everyone. But instead whatever was happening seemed to be happening without him. Was there nothing for him to do? He drifted about the square through the thinning crowd. Some of the soldiers had noticed that the Eighteenth had still not arrived. They wondered what this meant. Edmunto listened to them talk and felt troubled. People were wandering up the streets that led out of the square. On the *Rua do Santo António*, a street of shops at the southeast corner of the square, they found that the Municipal Guard had reformed. Word spread quickly through the crowd.

It was full daylight now. The fog was gone. The captain of the Tenth took some men up the street to investigate. Some fiscal police and many civilians accompanied them. The Guard had formed before the *Igreja de Santo Ildefonso*. Their guns were held in readiness across their chests. The Deputy-Chief sat quietly atop his horse.

Edmundo had come up the street too. He could see the Guard on the church steps. He remembered the night in September when they had charged into the crowd on horseback and sent the demonstrators into flight. But this time the soldiers were with them; this time the

Guard would be unable to stop what was happening.

Someone threw a rock. People were shouting, "Down with the Guard!" Two members of the fiscal police, who were undisciplined, fired their guns in the direction of the Guard, but the captain ordered them to stop. There were members of the Sixth on their horses in the crowd and it was becoming hard to move.

Then the Deputy-Chief ordered his men to fire. With the volley everyone screamed and people ran, colliding with each other. Someone knocked Edmundo down and he lost his glasses. He reached across the stones for them. A man on a horse jumped over him and he felt the hoof graze his shoulder. When he put his glasses back on, he saw a man lying in the street with blood spreading across his chest. The Guard fired another volley. Soldiers were shooting back at the Guard, but they were in the open street and the Guard was sheltered by the church steps. Edmundo stood up and tried to run, but he had hurt his knee in the fall. A door near him opened from within and Edmundo and several others rushed inside.

"What is it?" a woman asked.

"The Municipal Guard is firing on the people."

From the hallway they stood listening to the shooting in the street. Edmundo felt ashamed of the way he had panicked, although everyone else had as well. He wished he had stayed in the street, taken the gun of a fallen soldier and carried on with the battle. But he knew nothing about guns. When he looked down he saw that his trousers were torn and he was bleeding.

"You're hurt," the woman said, kneeling before him. "Are you shot?"

"I fell. It's nothing."

She ordered a pretty servant girl to bring water and cloth, then she cleaned and dressed the wound. It was soothing to have her do this, but Edmundo felt ashamed when he thought of the people dying in the street.

A young man went up to the second floor of the house to look out a window, and when he returned he reported that the soldiers had retreated into the square.

No one spoke much. Many of them had been up all night and were numb with weariness. A series of impressions ran through Edmundo's mind. The dampness, the horses, and the guns. He remembered the man he had seen bleeding in the street, and he remembered that hope rested on the Eighteenth coming forth from the barracks. He began to fear that the revolt might have failed, and that wrenched his stomach and made his knee hurt more.

The shooting was over by nine o'clock. The troops returned to barracks, and the bodies were picked up from the cobblestones. The tram rumbled down *Rua do Santo António*.

Edmundo started home. His leg had stiffened up and he was limping. The run-off from the rain rushed ankle deep down the steep streets to the river. The pain, weariness and disappointment made him feel sick.

He was thinking about Pereira. Pereira had won. Life would go on in the same way. There would be no war with England, and Pereira could continue to sell them his wine. Edmundo would marry Clara. He would never be free. Pereira had seen to that. Portugal would never change. What might have been accomplished if men like Pereira didn't exist would never be.

And yet there was more. He had been part of the failure. Why hadn't he been able to do more? Why hadn't those with the right views been able to rise in triumph? Why was Pereira successful, why had Pereira always been successful and why had he and people like him always failed?

He had come to the great metal span of the new *Ponte Dom Luís I*. Above was the low grey ceiling of unbroken cloud cover; far below, below the great black arch, was the dark, swirling water. Edmundo instinctively secured his glasses to his face whenever he came up here. He had to cross the river into *Vila Nova da Gaia*, where his family lived, where the wine merchants had their storehouses. His father, like Pereira, was a wine merchant, and might have been just as anti-republican if his business had been so dependent on the English. But his father traded mainly with Brazil and Argentina, where people aped English manners and had developed a taste for port wine. He also imported coffee.

Edmundo's parents were waiting for him anxiously. When he came in his mother threw her arms around him.

"*Filho!*"

"Edmundo!"

"I prayed to God that you would be safe!"

He looked at them with weariness and shame. They didn't understand what had been lost. They could see that he was upset and didn't know how to comfort him. Then his mother saw his knee.

"Your leg!"

She fell to the ground and embraced his leg.

"It's nothing!" he said, flinching petulantly. "I fell when I was running away." He threw himself into an armchair. "All is lost. Portugal is lost. We are all lost."

His mother stroked his wounded knee with gratitude. She was grateful to God for having spared her only son.

In the evening there was word that martial law had been declared.

All that winter life seemed very bleak. In February it rained every day. The leaders of the revolt were allowed to go into exile. *A República Portuguesa* and other republican publications were suppressed. There was no one in the Swiss Café. When his knee was better, Edmundo went for long walks late at night. Sometimes he thought about his country, about its failure, and how unfortunate he was to be born into such a degenerate age. If only he had lived during the Reconquest, or during *Os Descobrimentos*, when Portugal was the greatest nation in Europe, or if only such greatness could come to the land again. But the glory had been waning for three hundred years. There was a continuous shrinking: of power, of empire, of imagination, of heart. Today Portugal was no more than an English puppet, owned by English money, bullied by English might. Even here in Porto most of the great wine merchants were English, or German. Men like his father were an exception—masters in their own house. And this was the world he had to live in. Backwater, backward, superstitious, medieval. Even the small hope of Republicanism—that it would carry Portugal belatedly into the nineteenth century now that it was almost over—had come to nothing. Progress was impossible here. There was something in the soil that killed it at the root.

It was almost a year since he had graduated, almost a year of stagnation. Everyone expected him to go into business with his father. No one understood why he was hesitating. A life had been mapped out for him. But Edmundo loathed the idea. He didn't know what he wanted, but he knew he didn't want to be a merchant. And yet he had no other plans, had done nothing to create an alternate possibility. He had dabbled in the politics of revolt, but mostly the revolution had come and gone without him. At heart politics bored him as much as business did. The meetings and squabbles and nitpicking left him listless. Even the speech-making was not all it was cracked up to be.

Sometimes he wished that he might be a great poet, but he never felt more than a fleeting inspiration, could never muster the energy to beat his thoughts into lines. Besides, what inspiration was there to be had? How could anyone be a poet in a country whose soul was so deflated? He sometimes felt very ambitious, superior in some undiscovered way to everyone around him; but he had found absolutely nothing he cared to accomplish, nothing which could set his great ambition in motion. The only activity for which he had inexhaustible enthusiasm was reading. He read philosophy and sociological treatises, but mostly he read novels, French novels, and poetry. His favourite author was Stendhal. Once he had shocked Clara by reading her passages from *De L'Amour*.

Sometimes his thoughts wandered over the past. He remembered his brother Jorge, who had drowned, who should have been the one to go into business with his father. When they were boys, Jorge, Edmundo, and Clara's brother Daniel had been inseparable friends. But Jorge was dead, and Daniel was like a stranger. Daniel had never been much of a student, had never been interested in reading or thinking. When they were young it didn't matter. But Edmundo remembered the day he had shown a new book to Daniel, a book that excited him tremendously, and he had seen that the book meant nothing to Daniel, and Edmundo had suddenly felt very disappointed in his friend. Edmundo had gone off to school for five years, and now when he saw Daniel he could hardly speak to him.

When he was a boy he had never given a thought to Clara, Clara who had just been Daniel's sister, little Clara who was always in the way. But somehow over time she had made herself big in his life, and now everyone expected him to marry her. She had waited for him to finish his education, so that now she was over twenty and still unmarried, and people had begun to talk. He had never promised anything to her, but now if he didn't marry her, just as if he didn't go into business with his father, he would have committed a grievous affront.

The Moorish blood was strong in Clara. She was squat and dark. Her will was silent, patient and unswerving. But she had no dreams, no ideas, no spirit. She had no interest in the things that interested him. She never read anything, not even romances like other girls. She didn't listen when he tried to tell her about the ideas and dreams he had. She never questioned the life around her. She knew he didn't want to be a wine merchant, but she didn't care. She didn't care if he was happy. He knew he could never love her. He doubted that she loved him.

Like everyone else, Edmundo had once been to a prostitute, but she had been so coarse and brazen, the experience so disgusting, that he had never gone back. Once in Coimbra he had been with a gypsy, and he often remembered her. Sometimes, when he could no longer stop himself, he masturbated, and then he felt sickened by himself. He often dreamed about someone still very vague whom he might come to love, someone very different from everyone around him. He longed for a love pure and carnal at once, although in his own heart he had as yet no way of making such a reconciliation. When he thought of marrying Clara and being with her, he felt revulsion as strongly as when he remembered the prostitute.

Every Sunday Edmundo went to the Pereiras' house for dinner. There would be Clara, Daniel, Pereira, and Pereira's widowed sister, who was very devout.

Pereira hadn't yet forgiven him. He had become offensively smug and overbearing. All republicans were fools or hooligans, he said; the Braganças were the glory of Portugal and ruled by the will of God; the university had become a dangerous institution, questions of philosophy and morality should be left entirely in the hands of the church; socialism was a form of Satanism; the French were a decadent and feminine race, really Portugal had nothing to learn from them. Daniel would sit blithely accepting all this, as if none of it concerned him. Pereira's sister would nod and add an occasional platitude, which only showed that she had no idea what century she lived in. Clara would be sitting at her embroidery, without looking up. Edmundo knew that she was angry, not with her father for saying these things, but with Edmundo himself, on account of his unspoken thoughts.

Edmundo said nothing. He knew that every word Pereira spoke was a challenge directed at him, that Pereira was testing him, breaking him, forcing him into a submission from which he would never be able to escape. Sometimes it was almost unbearable to keep silent; sometimes he thought that unless he spoke he would no longer be himself. And yet again they had put him into an untenable position, so that no matter how much he was provoked, if he were to speak he would be the one in the wrong, the transgressor.

One Sunday there was an extra guest at dinner. Pereira had invited

Mr. Hastings, an English wine merchant. The English in Porto tended to be standoffish and rarely went into the houses of the locals, but in the face of the recent tensions, efforts were being made to recreate a friendly atmosphere. Still Edmundo felt certain that Pereira had done this merely to insult him.

Pereira and Hastings talked about the recent strain between their two countries, a strain that had arisen over their rival claims in Africa. Both men made an effort to be polite and obliging.

"The whole affair has been poorly handled," Hastings said. "By both sides I believe. Really Salisbury's ultimatum was quite unnecessary, and I can see why you Portuguese would take it as a slap in the face. But this sense of outrage only obscures the issues, which I believe should have been rationally debated. I know that your people feel that England has taken from them their rightful possessions, but you know, in London the man in the street has a completely opposite view. Who's to say who's right? Really, such jingoism is quite counterproductive. After all, there's land enough in Africa for everyone, isn't there?"

"Yes of course," said Pereira. "The whole issue has been overblown. Here it has served as an excuse for fanatics to express their discontent with the government. What they fail to understand is that Portugal is a Mediterranean nation with Mediterranean traditions. To change those traditions would be an aberration. I for one will be happy to see everything back to normal. Don't you agree, Edmundo?"

There was a brief pause.

"On the contrary, I disagree with every word you've spoken in the last three months."

Everyone was silent. Clara looked up from her plate. No one was sure what was happening.

"I fail to see," said Pereira, "how a true Portuguese could disagree with anything I've said."

"Pardon me, sir, but I fail to see how a man who supports a foreign power against his own nation has any right to say who is a true Portuguese." Edmundo turned to the Englishman. "Mr. Hastings, the sentiments you express are very noble and reasonable. I have nothing against you personally—although I do resent the ownership of Portuguese industry by foreigners. But I consider that the government of your country has acted against my nation in the manner of a pirate and a bully. You forget that we are a proud people, a European people, with a past as glorious as your own. You're not dealing with a subjugated race. That our government has given in to you and allowed you to insult us in this way is to the everlasting shame of our country. I know it is rude of me to speak this way to you, but my opinion was solicited, and I have decided to speak the truth."

Clara was yelling at him with her eyes.

"You are a very foolish young man," said Pereira coldly.

"Why? Because I refuse to bow down before the forces that have been crippling my nation for three hundred years?"

"It's obvious you are confusing the good of your country with your delusions of grandeur."

"I have no delusions. I see the truth around me. I am ashamed to live in this country as it is now governed."

"Then go! By all means go!"

"Father!" exclaimed Clara. "Don't say that!"

"No, let him go! Let him find some place more to his liking. I'll even pay for his ticket. I wash my hands of him."

"Senhor Pereira," said Edmundo coldly, "this is the best advice you have ever given me: I intend to follow it."

"Magnificent!"

These events caught everyone by surprise, Edmundo included. But he refused to change his mind. At first he thought of rushing into exile at Madrid with the leaders of the revolt; but he wasn't really one of them, and he didn't believe that he deserved to be among them. His father at first tried to talk him into staying and patching up his differences with the Pereiras, but after a few weeks, when Edmundo still insisted that he had to leave Portugal, his father began to talk to him about Brazil, where there were business connections he could presume upon, people who might help a young man get started in a new place. When he thought about it, Edmundo was attracted to the idea. Brazil was a country he found politically attractive: the slaves had been freed; there had recently been a revolution—a successful revolution in which the emperor was deposed; and the new republic had taken as is motto a phrase from the great positivist Auguste Comte: "Order and Progress." Here was a nation that had gotten up off its ass!

He also thought of jungles and heat and strange colours, of bizarre plants and animals, and exotic, almost frightening people.

So Edmundo's father wrote a letter to a Senhor Xisto in Rio de Janeiro. Xisto was originally a peasant from Braga who had emigrated to Brazil and made good as an importer-exporter. The Caçadors sold him wine and bought coffee from him in return. Senhor Caçador asked if he would be willing to take Edmundo in his charge and see if a suitable opportunity might be opened for him. Then they waited for a reply.

Coimbra, Portugal

There was no moon. The river was black and quiet. The clock tower of the university rose above the town.

A month had passed. At last there was a letter from Xisto, who would be glad to do whatever was in his power to help. Edmundo could leave as soon as he wished. Already he had misgivings. He wasn't at all certain that this was what he wanted. Brazil was so vast and unknown and far away. He was frightened by it. And suddenly he had begun to realize how Porto was his home, how its ways and sensations, his family and his life there, were the only things he had ever known, how he loved them and needed them in spite of himself.

But how could he back down? How could he not leave now? He didn't know what he should do.

He had come to Coimbra, ostensibly to say goodbye, but really for a moment of escape. He realized how much he would rather go backward into the life he had known here than forward into the unknown future which faced him. He remembered other nights here along the river, alone with his dreams, or with wine and loud friends, their black capes riding behind them, a guitar, a fado, cigars. Then he had been free to dream; he had never had to face what the future would actually demand of him. It had only been a year since he had known that life, it was still almost close enough to touch, to breathe in, but he could feel it slipping away like the waters of the river, like distant footsteps retreating down a long hallway. He wanted to be very still and listen as long as he could.

He had spent the evening with two old school friends. Furtado was now a lawyer; Oliveira had a position in a ministry. They had talked about old times, and about the future.

"You know, Edmundinho," Furtado had said, "you've surprised us: in spite of all your protestations, we always believed that in the end you would go into business with your father, and become a seller of port."

Edmundo hadn't said anything, but he felt insulted. So that was how others saw him: as a dreamer, doomed to capitulation, incapable of action. They had no faith in him. And he felt ashamed, because he knew that part of him would indeed rather be a seller of port than face the demands that an uncertain future might put upon him. But once again he felt that he had no choice. How could he turn back now, now that he knew what his friends really thought of him? He realized that he had never been close to his friends, that none of them had ever been like a brother to him. He had visited places and asked them to yield to him the joy of his own past, but now he realized that there had never been any real joy, just dreaming and expectation. He had never been happy.

If only time could have stood still at this moment, if he could have been left in the dark of the river forever, and never have to step into the daylight again. A line of poetry passed through his mind:

To cease upon the midnight with no pain.

English poetry.

But it was time to go back. On principle he had eschewed the Hotel Bragança where he normally would have stayed, and had taken a room at the Hotel Mondego near the train station. He had to go back across the river.

He was standing on the terrace of the *Convento de Santa Clara-a-Nova*. He turned around and took a last look at the convent. This was where the body of Isabel, the sainted queen of the great King Dinis, had lain uncorrupted for six hundred years. There were many legends about her, about her goodness and holiness. Once she had been caught smuggling bread out of the palace against the king's orders in order to feed the poor. When the king confronted her and ordered her to open her cloak, God had turned the loaves into roses. His mother had told him that story when he was a boy, but it had never really moved him as his mother had intended it to. It was too pious a tale for him, and there seemed much more exciting ambitions than providing the people with bread. Besides, he was a progressive young man with little regard for religion and he found it hard to believe in such fairy tales.

He started down past the old convent, *Santa Clara-a-Velha*, which had been flooded for centuries. Here he remembered other famous tales from the past. This was where Pedro and Inês had lived. Pedro had been heir to the throne. When his first wife died, he married Inês de Castro, one of her maids in waiting. Inês was very beautiful, and they had been deeply in love. But the relationship was disapproved of at court, and one day when Pedro was away, the king came with his nobles and allowed them to slaughter Inês while her children watched. The king died and Pedro came to the throne. The murderers were captured in Spain and returned to Coimbra. Pedro had their hearts ripped from their living bodies. Then he assembled the entire court and set upon the throne the corpse of Inês, four years dead. Everyone there had been made to kiss her hand. Edmundo didn't like this story either. He found it a depressing tale, macabre and out of touch with the sense of progress and reason he prided in himself. And yet when he thought about it, he could almost feel the dead hand at his lips. Suddenly he was afraid, afraid of the dark like a child in bed at night, afraid of a ghost or something like it, and he rushed on ahead toward the bridge.

In the middle of the bridge he caught something out of the corner of his eye and startled, turned his head to someone leaning against the parapet. It was a man, a tall, lean man standing very still, almost lost in shadow. There was something in his stance, a twist, a strain, which made Edmundo think that he was in some pain. Edmundo hesitated, then stopped and spoke to him.

"Excuse me, are you alright?"

The man said nothing. He didn't move. His head hung over the water. Edmundo wondered whether to speak to him again; but then the man turned slowly toward him, and his long, pale face came into the frail light.

"Yes, I'm fine. Thank you for your concern."

In the moment the man turned, Edmundo recognized him. Again, he wondered whether he should speak.

"You're Antero de Quental. I was in the crowd at Porto last year, when you were made president of the Patriotic Alliance of the North. It is truly a great honour for me to meet you. My name is Edmundo Caçador."

"My pleasure."

Antero de Quental was the most famous poet in Portugal—Edmundo's favourite—and one of its leading social reformers. Edmundo knew all the details. He had been at Coimbra in the seventies, one of the renowned Group of Five. In 1871 he had taken part in the First Socialist International and arranged socialist conferences at the Lisbon casino, which were eventually suppressed by the government. In 1879 he had run as a socialist candidate for the house of deputies. He had been of the greatest importance in the introduction of progressive French ideas, Comte and Proudhon, into Portugal. Once he had said to the Italian prince, Umberto, "We have come to welcome you not as the son of King Victor Emmanuel and heir to the throne, but as the friend of Garibaldi." Edmundo remembered the night the students had marched with torches and Venetian lanterns to where he was staying in the *Rua de Cedofeita*, and he had spoken to them from the balcony. "You must not believe in yesterday," he had said. "Believe in today." It was rumoured that Antero was very ill.

Edmundo was so bold as to move up next to him against the stone.

"Are you a student?" Antero asked.

"No. I used to be."

"And what do you do now?"

"At the moment nothing."

"Nothing? That's not good. You must have work."

"I'm going away soon."

"From Coimbra?"

"From Portugal. I live in Porto. I've just come here to say goodbye."

Antero turned to look at him.

"We have something in common then. I too have come to say goodbye."

"You are leaving? Where are you going?"

"To the Azores."

"Good heavens, why! Have they exiled you?"

Antero laughed aloud.

"No, no! It's of my own free will, I assure you. I was born there. It's time for me to go back"

"Excuse me. I hope I haven't insulted you. It's just that it seems such an unpromising place to go."

"I suppose it does. And you? What promising place calls you?"

"Brazil."

"A young country for a young man. And what will you do there?"

"I don't know yet. My father has business connections."

"Well, I wish you luck. So tell me, what memories of Coimbra will you take with you?"

"Oh many. I've just been by Santa Clara."

"The new or the old? What interests you, the saint or the lovers?"

"I have no interests in saints."

"Then the lovers?"

"Yes and no. It's a morbid story."

"The truth usually is."

"Why do you say that? Actually the one who interests me most is Isabel's husband, Dinis. I would like my own life to be as worldly and as fruitful."

"But what if it isn't?"

"It can be, if reason prevails."

"But reason very rarely prevails. You know it has often struck me that the story of Pedro and Inês is very much like the story of Auguste Comte and Clothilde de Vaux. Here is a man, the father of positivism, renowned for his reason, and yet he writes letters to a dead woman. One would have thought such things happened only in Portugal, but you see, the French do it too."

"What are you saying? That reason will never triumph? That all revolutions are doomed to failure? Do you believe that?"

"No. I believe that there will be a revolution in Portugal. I don't see how they can stop it. Certainly not in my lifetime. Maybe not even in yours. But causes are relatively easy to manage compared to an individual life. Forgive me: I'm not well, and sometimes my illness makes me unduly pessimistic. I sincerely hope that life will be kind to you. Which way are you headed?"

"Back into town. Can I help you?"

"If I could just hold onto your arm."

Edmundo walked the poet back across the river. The next day Edmundo sought him out to speak with him further, to come away with a less gloomy impression, but Antero had already departed.

Edmundo booked his passage for the end of April. So he was really going. He still didn't quite believe it. The rain had let up and there was bright spring sunshine every day. He felt good, almost confident; but he wished that these last warm days at home could have gone on a little longer.

He had to say goodbye to Clara. He dreaded it. He felt embarrassed, uneasy, guilty, almost dishonourable. He had never meant to hurt her, but now he had humiliated and abandoned her. What would she do now? Who would marry her? Pereira would have to buy her a husband. He was afraid of what would happen when she saw him again. Would all her composure be gone? Would she fall at his knees begging him to stay? Would she be feverish and wild?

He didn't want Pereira to be there. That would be too much for him. So he picked a time one afternoon when he knew Pereira would be away. The maidservant, Ana, let him in and announced him to Clara; then, since there was no one else at home, Ana sat down discreetly in a corner so as not to leave them alone together.

"You've picked a strange time for your visit, Edmundo," said Clara. "We haven't seen you in a while."

"No. I've come to say goodbye to you."

"Goodbye? Where are you going?"

"I think you know, Clara, that I'm going to Brazil."

"People have told me, yes. I suppose I had forgotten. One can't remember everything."

"I'm leaving at the end of the month. I've purchased my ticket."

He saw Clara flinch, but she instantly regained her composure.

"Well, *bon voyage*, as the French say."

He could see that she was forcing herself to be flippant. Half of him wanted to say goodbye quickly, to escape before her mood changed. The other half wanted to force an honest response out of her, even if it were unpleasant.

"You know, Clara, I really am going."

"Are you, Edmundo?"

"Yes. You act as if you don't care. Or don't believe me."

"Well, I must say I find it all quite ridiculous and absurd. If you could only see yourself, it's quite funny. You're really not the type to go exploring; you seem to believe that you're the new Vasco da Gama. People know you better than that. I'm surprised at your father, that he has allowed your charade to go this far. Among your friends you've become something of a joke."

"I can't understand why you would ever have wanted to marry a man for whom you have so little respect."

"I respect you, Edmundo. I respect you for what you are: the child of a wine merchant, just like I am. What am I supposed to believe, that you are the type of man who could run away and forsake all his responsibilities, that you could deny all the obligations you have toward me!"

"I'm sorry, Clara. I wish you the best. I wish you'd never known me."

"That's not enough!" She was openly angry now. "You owe me more!"

"I'm sorry. I promised you nothing. But I knew there were expectations and I did nothing to correct them. I accept my share of the blame. But I never could have married you, Clara, even if I had stayed. I don't love you, and I don't think that you really love me."

"Don't talk to me of love! What do you know about love? Nothing! You've proven that. So you never would have married me? How flattering of you to tell me so! Or perhaps you are trying to console me: I had forgotten how thoughtful you can be."

"I've told you that I'm sorry. There's nothing else for me to say. I think I should go."

"May God punish you for this."

"If He's the kind of God you believe he is, he probably will."

Edmundo got up to go. Ana had been sitting in the corner pretending not to hear a word. He quickly closed the door behind him.

The day the boat was to leave, Edmundo's parents rode with him down to dock where the launch was being loaded. Everyone was quiet; they had said all there was to say, and yet no one wanted to let go and allow the future to unfurl. The moment approached when Edmundo would go five thousand kilometers away. They waited beside the launch for a few minutes more, delaying the goodbye, even as the sailors subtly showed their impatience to be off. It soon grew too boring and uncomfortable to stand around any longer. Edmundo shook hands with his father, then embraced him hard. There were quiet tears in their eyes. When he embraced his mother, who had been calm the whole time, she burst into tears, and eventually her husband had to pull her gently away. Edmundo could see them standing together on the quay, holding on to one another, as the launch moved down the river. Then they were gone from sight.

So he had done it. The hum of the engine in the planks, the railing in his hand, the sea breeze: they were all real. He could not go back now even if he wanted to. It would be many years, if ever, before he returned. He had begun a new life, a life which would be full of things he couldn't imagine. He was nervous, but for a moment no longer afraid. He would make the best of it, of this strange, new place, Brazil.

Chapter Three

The ship steamed toward the bay. The Sugarloaf rose on one side of the strait like a great human head. There were long green tresses of vegetation, and the ridge was hunched up behind it like the body of a sphinx. The morning sky and the sea were a clear deep blue; the waves rolled gently white upon the light sand. Then the ship was in the bay, and Edmundo could see the city, slipped into the pockets of flatlands here and there between the mountains, unfold pocket by pocket before him. Then the city centre gleamed before the bow, white and green. He had never yet seen anything more beautiful.

When the ship docked Edmundo was anxious to get ashore. The voyage had not been uncomfortable, but he was eager to leave the confines of the ship and to stretch his legs in his new land, to start his new life. He quickly found a porter and led him down to his cabin to gather his trunk. He hoped that Xisto would have someone there waiting for him. But before the porter could get the trunk out of the door, a young man appeared in the cabin.

"With your permission, sir, are you Senhor Edmundo Caçador?"

"Yes, I am."

"How do you do! Welcome to Brazil! I am Julio Xisto. My father sent me to meet you."

The young man beamed a smile. He was dressed most handsomely, in a fine linen jacket and a bright satin vest. He wore a velvet bow tie and French cuffs and collar. In the top pocket of his jacket was a handkerchief, which reeked of cologne. He carried a cane with a gold tip and on his head at a rakish angle sat a derby hat. His hair was black and wavy with a sheen of coconut oil; his beard was shiny and thick, his skin the colour of wet sand. He was of mixed race.

He extended his hand and shook Edmundo's warmly.

"I have the carriage waiting. Is this all you have? You travel light. We've been so looking forward to your arrival! Unfortunately, father is away till tomorrow, but we have everything set for you at home. How was your trip?"

"Fine. The seas were quite calm."

"Excellent. When we get home we'll prepare a bath for you, if you'd like—or you can eat, or nap, whatever."

There was a grace about Julio, a natural charm, which was instantly striking. First it was in his smile, his wide, infectious, full-toothed smile, and then in his sparkling dark eyes, and in his voice which was musical and gentle, and in the way he carried himself, light and gay. Edmundo liked him. Things were off to a good start.

On the dock, Edmundo found that he had as yet no land legs, so Julio took his arm and helped him keep his balance as they walked. The carriage was drawn by two handsome black horses, freshly brushed and cleaned. The young black driver jumped down smartly to help with the trunk.

"Edmundo, if I may—let's be friends, you must call me Julio—this is Carlos, our driver. Carlos, this is our guest from Portugal, Senhor Edmundo Caçador. He's still a bit unsteady on his feet so he'll need you to help him up."

"Of course, sir."

Julio tipped the porter and they were on their way through the heart of the city. Palm trees lined the avenues; the fronds waved in the breeze. The side streets were narrow and shaded. Everywhere dark-skinned people appeared—mulattos, blacks, mestizos. He saw a handsome black woman, in all her finery, riding in a carriage.

"This is *rua do Ouvidor*. The shops here have the finest clothing from Paris. Simply magnificent things! My sister buys all her dresses here. Unfortunately, she's in Paris at the moment. She'll love to meet you. She's a marvelous girl. She's coming home in September. Of course you'll still be here, what do you think?"

"I don't know. I haven't made any set plans."

"Of course. You've just arrived. I'll show you everything. I can tell we're going to be great friends. Don't you think?"

"I don't see why we shouldn't be. You're making me feel most welcome."

"Good! Look over there. You can just see the top of the Sugarloaf."

They drove through the tiled streets. Over the top of the buildings they could see the sky, so deep and blue it seemed almost like a coat of wet paint.

"What a beautiful morning you've picked for your arrival!"

"Yes. It's wonderful."

Carlos stopped before an iron gate. He called out and an old black man appeared from within. He opened the gate and Carlos brought the carriage inside. The old man rushed over to help the two young men step out.

"Thank you, Gilberto," said Julio. "Edmundo, this is Gilberto, our butler. Carlos is his son, and his wife Graça is our cook."

"A pleasure to serve you, Senhor Edmundo."

"How do you do." Edmundo extended his hand, but Gilberto was already folded over in a bow.

"I do hope that Nanette has that bath ready for you!" said Julio. "Gilberto, you and Carlos carry the trunk to Senhor Edmundo's room."

"Yes, Senhor Julio, at once."

Julio took Edmundo into the house. It was arranged much as his parents' home had been: a warehouse and offices on the first two floors; family quarters on the higher floors. A blonde servant girl met them on the third floor.

"Nanette, Senhor Edmundo has arrived!"

"Welcome, Senhor Edmundo! We've been quite anxious to meet you."

"And how about that bath? Is it ready?"

"Yes, quite ready."

Ah Nanette! You're so marvelously efficient!"

Julio showed him to his room.

"Here you are! Bathe, nap. I'll have Nanette call you before supper. Tonight we'll see how you feel. If you're up for it, we'll go out together and I'll show you our cafés. Now I'll leave you, my new friend."

Nanette brought him towels and began to put his clothes away into hampers and laid out a fresh outfit on the bed.

She was quite pretty, small and delicate, demure—especially in contrast to Julio. She was wearing a simple black gown and a starched white apron.

"You are from France, Nanette?"

"Yes, sir. From Marseille. Do you know it?"

"No, I've never been to France. Although I admire your country greatly, of course. Your family is still there?"

"I have a brother. My parents died when I was quite young."

"And how have you come to be in Brazil?"

"Dom Ernesto, Julio's father, advertised for a maidservant when he was in Marseille, and I was fortunate enough to be given the position."

She was standing beside the bed, her small face flushed from activity. A lock of her blonde hair had fallen out of place over her forehead.

"Will that be all, Senhor Edmundo?"

"Yes, Nanette, thank you very much."

When he was alone, Edmundo undressed and climbed into the

great wooden tub. What a strange world he had come to! He had never seen a blonde woman before, except on the stage. He had never seen a black, or a mulatto. And what a strange social order where the blonde woman was the servant and the mulatto the master! It would take getting used to. And yet he liked it, he liked this strange world where everything vibrated with colour. He liked Julio, liked him immensely. Back home he would have been leery of someone like him, so unreservedly friendly. But this was a different country, with different ways. The old ways didn't matter anymore. It was a good start. He was happy.

After his bath he lay down on the bed. The room was cool and dark with fine slivers of light coming through slits of the shudders, and he fell fast asleep going over the details of his arrival. He was awakened when Nanette knocked on the door and told him that Julio would meet him before dinner in the turret. Edmundo realized again, as she stood in the doorway, how attractive he found her.

She took him up to the tower. Julio was there waiting for him, smoking a cigarette.

"Edmundinho! How did you sleep? Are you refreshed?"

"Yes, quite, thank you."

"What would you like? A cigar? A cigarette? Something to drink? Port—your father's best? Cognac? Vermouth?"

"Whatever you're having yourself."

"Cognac then."

The room was circular, with huge bright windows framed with heavy damask curtains. Along the walls were benches, covered with satin cushions, and scattered throughout the room French tables and desks. The walls were covered with yellow paper and decorated with holy pictures. In a gold-plated cage sang two bright-coloured canaries.

"Come here, Edmundo. Come see our wonderful view." Julio led him to the window and they looked down together over the property.

"That's the servants' quarters, and there are the stables. Look, you can see Carlos."

"Yes." Edmundo skipped over the roofs of buildings out to the blue bay.

"And down there is the garden. Tomorrow I'll take you for a tour. We had a French gardener lay it out for us and Gilberto has done a marvelous job of keeping it up. We have roses, beautiful red and pink roses, camellias, orchids, and carnations. And we have orange and lemon trees. And, of course, a fish pond."

"It's quite impressive. Your father has done well by himself."

"Oh yes! He has a real head for business, that old man. Unfortunately, I haven't inherited it. Money doesn't interest me—or rather having it does, making it doesn't. I handle the correspondence for him, because I like writing letters, and my father frankly has a hard time writing his own name—but don't tell him that to his face or he'll become quite angry at you."

"I'm anxious to meet him."

"He's a fine man. You'll like him immensely."

"I hope so. I'd be happy if I could like everything about Brazil. So far I have."

"I'm so glad."

"I'm anxious to hear about this new constitution. Tell me, what do the people think of it?"

"We're all very happy. We're going to have a President, just like the Americans. Very progressive. Very chic. But I'm afraid, Edmundinho, that I don't have much of a head for politics either. Emperor, President, what difference does it make? But does it interest you very much?"

"Yes, very much indeed."

"Oh well, then I shall have to find someone else you can talk with. You and I will talk about art and life and beauty. Do you like to read?"

"Very much so."

"And who do you read?"

"Stendhal, Flaubert."

"Yes, yes! Les Dumas, Jules Verne. You must talk with my sister. She reads constantly. Have you been to Paris?"

"No. Have you?"

"Yes. I went there to study, but I wasn't a very diligent student. And poetry, do you read poetry?"

"Yes. French poetry, and some Portuguese poetry. Do you know Antero de Quental?"

"Yes, of course, a little."

"I've met him."

"Have you! Marvelous. Tell me about him."

"He's a very sad man."

"But a great poet."

"Yes. But I wouldn't want to be that sad, even if I could be a great poet."

"Well, in Brazil, no one is sad. It's against the law."

For supper Edmundo was treated to the local cuisine, which didn't resemble anything he was used to eating. Julio saw how his new friend drew back and moved to reassure him.

"This is *feijoada*," he said. "It's our national dish. There are black beans and fish and rice and manioc and eggs. And on top of it we pour plenty of hot pepper sauce, like this. That's how I like it, nice and spicy."

Edmundo was given a plateful and put as little hot sauce on it as he thought acceptable. "Well, what do you think?"

Here was his first negative impression of Brazil. The taste was very strong and unpleasant. His stomach proved an organ much less open to new experiences than his eyes had been earlier in the day: the meal stayed with him all afternoon and in the evening he had cramps and told Julio that he would be unable to accompany him to the cafes. Julio gracefully expressed his regret: there was always tomorrow.

In the morning Edmundo felt much better. Nanette brought him a cup of strong sweet coffee and a plate of English biscuits. Her presence continued to excite him. Julio took him down into the cool garden and then on a perfunctory tour of the warehouse and offices. At noon Xisto returned home amid a flurry of activity and told of Edmundo's arrival the previous morning, sent for him and greeted him warmly like a son.

"Welcome, welcome! How is your father? How is your family? I hope Julio has been keeping you entertained!"

"Yes, he's been most hospitable."

"Good, good."

Xisto was a true Portuguese peasant, a type Edmundo was quite familiar with: short, stocky, with harsh, strong features and hair that had turned steel grey, but would never, no matter how long he lived, turn white. It was hard to imagine that Julio was his son. But the old man too welcomed Edmundo with his own genuine warmth, a warmth that was brisker, and less gracious.

With them was a third man, a man about thirty, lean and hawkish.

"This is my manager, Luis de Fonseca, my right hand man."

"How do you do."

"Edmundo is a *doutor*, he's received his degree from Coimbra. But he has no taste for his father's wine business. So I'm going to find something more suitable for him."

"Frankly, Senhor Xisto, I'm not sure if I'm interested in any form of business. I really don't know what I want to do."

"The important thing is that you've got a head on your shoulders. So consider what I do for you as a continuation of your education. I'll help you get to know the country and in time you'll come across something that interests you."

"I don't want to burden you too much."

"Not at all. There's nothing more useful than having bright young men around. Believe me, I'll get more out of you than I can possibly return. Where to begin? I suppose I should keep you here with me at first and let you see what I do. How do you feel about coffee? Do you like it?

"Yes, but I like port too. That wasn't enough to keep me at home."

"True. Coffee is 'king' right now. A lot of people have made money with it. If prices continue to rise as they have been, by next year they will have doubled in five years. But this doesn't interest you, I'm sure. Luis and I were just in São Sebastião, dealing with plantation owners, and you know, now all the talk is rubber. Rubber is going to be the next 'king'. If I knew more about it, that's where I might guide you."

"Where would one grow rubber?"

"It grows wild, up the Amazon. Now that might interest you. Are you an adventurer? What do you say, Luis, maybe I should send you all up to the Rio Negro?"

"I would want to know much more. And one would need a great deal of capital. After all, I'm merely a hired hand; I haven't made the profits that you have, sir."

"You've done well for yourself and you know it. I've shared my know-how with you, which is worth something extra. All of you, listen. You too, Julio, my son. I'm an old man, I won't be around forever. You've all got to make plans for yourselves."

"Papa, you're as strong as a horse. Tell me, Edmundo, this pessimism, this fatalism, is it a Portuguese trait? I simply don't understand it. Papa, you know the moment you die, I will sell the business and Imaculada and I will go to Paris to live."

Xisto laughed indulgently.

"You see, Edmundo, my son is a dandy. He has no interest in work. And I've spoiled him. He takes after his mother."

"Which, from what I've seen," said Edmundo, "is another kind of virtue. Julio is one who loves life."

Julio smiled at him.

"See, Papa, Edmundo and I are true friends already."

Xisto smiled. Edmundo smiled.

That evening he went with Julio to the International, and Julio introduced him to his friends. They were all preened and fashionably dressed, although none was quite as handsome as Julio; they spoke of Paris, of the latest social gossip, of actresses and plays. Edmundo had known such cliques at home, but he had never been part of them, moving in a more bohemian, intellectual circle. He couldn't help disapproving of them slightly, of finding them trivial and feminine. And yet they were amusing and their high spirits were infectious. One of them was a poet and at Julio's insistence recited something for Edmundo. Edmundo praised his effort, but really it was quite amateurish.

While they all sat drinking and laughing, into the café came a group of officers and took a table nearby. Julio's group became strangely quiet. A strained, angry look gripped the young Xisto's face.

"Is something wrong?" Edmundo asked him.

"It's time to go."

"Are you alright?"

"Yes, it's time to go."

And without even saying goodbye to his friends, Julio got up to leave, Edmundo following behind him.

"What is it, Julio? What's wrong? Are you alright?"

Julio had almost regained his composure and forced himself to laugh.

"It's nothing, Edmundinho. Just a little too much cognac. I felt a little bit faint. But now I'm fine. The air has done me good. It's nothing, really."

Every day he went into the offices with Senhor Xisto and Luis, and occasionally Julio. When Xisto was occupied, or when there were details to be gone over, he was left in the hands of Luis. Luis was extremely competent, with a mind like a clock. He was by nature wary and uncharitable, but he seemed to hold for Edmundo a grudging respect. Still, he seemed pleased whenever Edmundo made a mental mistake, or failed to understand something. Edmundo didn't like him, and yet he also felt a grudging respect.

Sometimes when they broke for coffee or dinner, Luis would talk with him. At first Luis was all questions. He was eager to size up the new arrival and so be better prepared to put him in his proper place.

In return he offered a few curt details about himself. He was from the south of Portugal, near Portimão. His father was a government clerk. He had lived in Brazil for ten years. What did he think of it? It was "a land of great opportunity," he said with a mean, sly smile.

He sometimes expressed political interests—although his observations seemed cynical and reactionary when Edmundo drew him out. He asked about the revolution. Had it been bloody?

"Not at all! The emperor had no support. No one was willing to die for him. You know what they called him? Pedro Banana. No one respected him, not even the army and the Church. And the nobles were angry with him for freeing the slaves. You know what his problem was, he wasn't enough of an Emperor. There was nothing regal about him. His father—there was a man! There was an emperor. No, there was very little blood. You know the only ones to defend him? The niggers! The slaves he had freed. You should have seen it, it was really quite absurd. These niggers in the streets with their knives and clubs. Have you ever seen them fight with their feet? They call it *capoeira*. It's quite a joke. So any way, the Republican militia simply aim their rifles and boom, there are dead niggers all over the place. People were shooting at them out of their windows with revolvers. It was really quite a bloodbath. They learned their lesson.

"The niggers, you know, are the number one problem this country has to face. What are they going to do with them now? Now that they've freed them. Slavery will come back to haunt us. It would have been better in the long run to have done without them. My view is, no matter what the expense, it would be best if right now we gathered the ships together and sent them all back to Africa. If they stay here, they are going to impede all progress, like a blight. You can see the way they corrupt things. Have you noticed the way people speak? The way they mispronounce words, slur things together? Even Xisto does it now. That started with the niggers. They were simply too stupid to speak the language properly. And they multiply like rabbits. What are they going to do with them all? And syphilis is everywhere because of them. They're like animals. You're a progressive minded young man, like many others, but there will be no progress with this weight around the neck of the country. You will find that Brazilians like to think of themselves as a European nation, but really, European nations are white."

After this outburst Luis seemed a bit uncertain, as if he had been indiscreet and made too many assumptions about his audience. But when Edmundo said nothing, Luis relaxed.

Edmundo felt very uncomfortable listening to all this. Part of him was ashamed that he hadn't immediately denounced the scoundrel to his face. He wanted to believe that he had come to the best of all possible worlds, a world that had freed itself from the yokes of the past. Luis was a despicable man, and what he said about blacks and mulattos was foul and detestable; and yet he was willing to tell him things that everyone else hid from him.

Another time Luis opened up to Edmundo about the Xistos.

"Xisto is a hard worker, and quite smart, for a peasant. This is a land of great opportunity for someone like him, and he's made the most of it. Back home what would he have? A few hectares? Maybe an ox, if he was lucky. I take my hat off to him.

"His family, of course, has been quite a disappointment to him. But he has no one to blame but himself. It was foolish to marry a nigger, he knows that. I'm sure he was desperate, alone, he wanted a woman. But that's what whores are for. There is no shortage of whores in Rio. Go to the *rua do Sabão* and you can see them hanging half naked out the windows. He regrets it now. Especially with the way his children have turned out. They're mulattos—what do you expect. They're very handsome, I give you that, but brittle inside, like glass. Look at his son: a good for nothing really. Incapable of work. And Xisto has spoiled him. And his daughter, of course, that's been a total fiasco. Do you know that story? You don't know why they shipped her off to Paris? It was a nice little scandal, pitiful really. She met this nobleman, de Bettencourt, who became infatuated with her, was almost ready to marry her. These mulattos have a certain charm, especially in bed. They can't get enough of it. I can attest from personal experience. But I prefer European women. If you're interested, someday I will take you to the *rua do Ouvidor*, to Susana's. It is very expensive, but worth it. Have you heard of Susana? She sleeps with women. At any rate, this de Bettencourt was almost ready to marry her. She's a beautiful woman, I have to give her that, as beautiful as someone who's half nigger can be. But de Bettencourt must have been a fool to think of marrying her. Anyway, when his mama found out, of course she put her foot down. No son of hers was going to marry the daughter of a slave and that was that. De Bettencourt went scampering away with his tail between his legs."

Edmundo continued to listen in silence. Part of him didn't want to know the Xistos' family secrets; it made him feel embarrassed to do so, as if he had been caught eavesdropping or reading someone's private correspondence. Another part of him was a creature of curiosity. And he was excited by some of what he heard—the sexual allure and insatiability. He restrained himself from asking questions or soliciting information, but he allowed himself to listen to anything Luis volunteered to tell him.

Luis told him more about Xisto's daughter, Imaculada. She was sixteen. Quite spoiled, quite unthinking and flighty. She had a certain charm, but Luis seemed particularly loath to admit it. It almost seemed he bore her some grudge.

"She used witchcraft to lure de Bettencourt," Luis claimed.

"What do you mean?" asked Edmundo.

"She served him witch's coffee," snickered Luis.

Edmundo still did not understand.

"She put her woman's blood in the coffee."

A few days later Luis shocked Edmundo with another disclosure. Nanette was Xisto's mistress. This unsettled Edmundo. He had taken a fancy to Nanette and had even begun to contemplate what intentions it would be honourable for him to hold for her. He had assumed she was virtuous. To think of her with Xisto repulsed him. Somehow it also made him think worse of Xisto, whom he genuinely liked. But he told himself he was being naive and foolish. Everyone had a mistress, everyone had needs. Why should Xisto be any different? He himself wasn't. Of course he told himself he must never think of Nanette again.

One evening when he found himself alone with one of Julio's friends, Edmundo asked about the night at the International when Julio had acted so strangely.

"Don't you know? De Bettencourt was with them! Julio refuses to be in the same room with him. He won't even allow you to mention de Bettencourt's name in his presence. He's really quite rabid about it!"

He was also told that Luis had once proposed to Imaculada, and she had turned him down.

By the end of the winter, Edmundo could write his family that he had become well acquainted with Xisto's business. He found that he didn't need to put his heart into it, that his head was enough, and that he was quick at grasping the way things worked, even if— he refrained from telling his family this—it seemed to him like an empty game.

One day Xisto proposed the next step in his education. There was a plantation near *Paraíba do Sul* owned by a Senhor de Figueiredo, whose son was unfit for business—'Much like my Julio, pity'—and he needed someone to help him manage this year's crop. It was a large plantation, though not as big as some. Xisto felt certain Edmundo was ready to handle the work. It would be good experience.

"When would they want me?"

"As early in the spring as possible. Not after the end of September."

Edmundo saw no reason to turn the offer down. He decided to delay his departure till the last possible moment, so that he would be there when Imaculada arrived home from Paris. Both Xisto and Julio wanted him to meet her, and he was anxious to see for himself who had painted the closer portrait, Julio or Luis.

Early in September Edmundo read upsetting news in the newspapers: Antero de Quental had shot himself. Edmundo, feeling sick to his stomach and feverish, sought out all the news reports he could find and pieced together in his imagination his own personal account of what had happened, an account resonant with his own blackest feelings.

São Miguel, Açores

The high summer day broke hot and humid, the sky somber and heavy with clouds. The poet hadn't slept again. He had walked, then returned to his room and lay listening to "the tragic, hoarse voice" of the sea: "a howl, a groan, and nothing more." It was endless, like the pain, like the sadness. There was nothing good to look forward to any more. He no longer had hope of getting away, of escape, of change. He felt oppressed and caged, walking the same streets every day, seeing the same faces, and having the same dull, painful conversations. There was always the same scorching wind and blank sky, and the same monotonous sea. The melancholy had come back, stronger than ever. The pain was unrelenting, and he had no more faith in cures. The doctor in France had told him it was in his head and recommended hydrotherapy, which did no good. The doctor in Lisbon suggested that he could avoid the vomiting by having his food in a series of small meals, but he only vomited more. He found himself thinking about all the causes that had ruled his life, the mad love, the infatuations, the social issues. Nothing had come of them. He had nothing to show for them. His hands were empty. There was little solace even in his poems, his life's most important accomplishment.

We strive in vain. Like a thick fog
The uncertainty of things enwraps us.

The soul, while it grows and transforms itself,
Is snared in its own web.

He lit a cigar and sat wearily by the window. What was he to do? What could he do? He was forty nine. That wasn't so old, not as old as it felt. What had he been doing ten years ago? Twenty years ago? He couldn't remember. Had he felt younger? Had there been more hope? Yes and no. He had spent his life in anxiety, expectation, and disappointment.

He went down into the parlour and a friend came in. Antero looked at that dull, healthy face twisted into its familiar smile, like animated bread dough. He could no longer enter into this man's sense of life. They had breakfast. They talked about the weather and the news from Lisbon while the coffee turned cold and insipid. When he was alone again, he went out for a walk, dressed in black despite the oppressive heat. He went down toward the harbour and sat on a wooden bench. There were boats bobbing listlessly on their moorings. At the horizon the grey sea met the grey sky, 'in the immense extension where the immortal unconscious hides itself.' The afternoon had become almost unbearable. There was no escape. What was he to do? Was there any reason to go on? The sea told him: no, there was none. So he had decided then? Yes, the time had come. Wasn't he in his heart dead already? Really all he would be doing was saying farewell to the dust and nailing the lid of the coffin shut. He had been reluctant to do so, but it was time.

In the ironmonger's shop he told the clerk he was a farmer and needed a revolver to shoot rabbits that were eating his lettuce. He asked the clerk how to use it and the clerk showed him where to put the bullets and how to cock it. It was very simple. He asked the clerk to wrap it in brown paper.

Now that he had decided he realized there were those he wanted to see, those he wanted to say his goodbyes to. He visited friends. They complained about the heat. He no longer felt it. They asked after his health. He was fine now. They suspected nothing. He visited his cousin Pedro and his sister. Neither asked about the package. At his sister's he forget to take it with him, and she called him back for it. Fate had decided.

It was dusk. It was time. He found himself in the *Praça 5 d'Outubro*, near the *Igreja do Senhor Santo Cristo dos Milagres*. There were benches along the wall. Above them was a tile plaque; a blue anchor, and the word '*Esperança*.' It was as good a place as any. His heart was racing. He was afraid. He had never wanted this. The soul was not meant for this. The soul is a hymn to light and freedom and full fruit. But the soul is always in agony, in dissatisfaction and emptiness. It longs. It longs.

What is this anxious wish that tortures?

He broke the string and opened the paper wrapping. He loaded one bullet, then another and another until the first one came round again. His heart was beating fast, as at the end of a race. He picked the gun up in his hand and held it awkwardly. He had never held a gun before. It was a strange, hard thing to have in his hand. He slipped the barrel up into his mouth. The end had come. He was afraid. He pulled the trigger.

The bullet ripped up through his nose, and near his eyes. The pain! Then he knew he was still alive. He could feel the pain, the consciousness. His head had fallen back against the wall. The gun was in his hand on the bench. He was still alive, he was in agony. He would have to lift up and shoot again.

When they found him he was still alive. His eyes were open. A doctor came and tried to communicate with him. There had been two shots. Was the one to the back of the head the first or the second? Antero was unable to speak, but he held up two fingers. What did it matter? The bleeding couldn't be stopped.

They carried him to the hospital. There was nothing to be done.

After an hour he went into convulsions, which were so strong two men couldn't hold him still. He died for some reason with a smile on his face.

For two weeks Edmundo was at a loss. He was too susceptible to feeling that life—his life at least—was meaningless, futile, bound to come to nothing, and the suicide of this man whose soul and sensibilities he found so worth cherishing threw him down into his own blackest doubts. If this was all that life had offered a Great One, then what could he—no more than a useless worm—expect from it? Maybe he should never have left home. But would things be any different there? Was there anything about his existence which hadn't been utterly pointless? Julio sympathized with Edmundo's sense of loss, but Edmundo knew that he had alarmed the household with the depth of his sudden despair.

Imaculada arrived home to the highest, gayest welcome of the household. Julio and Xisto couldn't keep themselves from leaving ridiculously early to meet her at the boat; the servants, who seemed to have a genuine affection for her, fussed with the smallest details of her homecoming. Even Luis groomed himself more thoroughly than usually and offered a bow and a "Welcome home, Menina Imaculada."

She was unmistakably Julio's sister. She had the same dark skin and dark flashing eyes, the same wide cheekbones and immense smile, yet each feature softened and feminine. There was the same vivacity spilling over from her eyes and smile, and the heaving of her bosom.

"Tell us about Paris!" cried Julio.

"Let her catch her breath first," complained Xisto. "And let us introduce Edmundo!"

"Edmundo, Edmundo, excuse me! Imaculada, my dear, dear sister, this is my great new friend Edmundinho who has come all the way from Portugal just to meet you!"

"Is this true, Senhor Edmundo?" she said, laughing at him, coyly, warily.

"Far be it from me to contradict my friend Julio."

Julio laughed too.

"Well said! Well said! Non committal! So now: Paris? Did you get to the Salon?"

"Oh yes, of course! All Paris was up in arms! And we saw La Duse and Sarah Bernhardt. Magnificent! And we met Jules Verne!"

"And what about the Eiffel Tower? Did you see it?"

"How could you miss it?" she said, with a disapproving scowl.

"Is it as big as they say it is?"

"Yes, of course. And twice as hideous, isn't it Ida?"

Imaculada's former governess, now traveling companion, was a big, blunt German woman who took a spot beside her charge on the sofa. She seemed neither pleasant nor unpleasant, but neutral somehow, dull witted and stolid, incapable of either gaiety or hatred. Julio and Edmundo sat in arm chairs on either side of the sofa. Luis sat far to one side in a straight chair, and Xisto quietly to the other.

"I was afraid that it was about to fall over on us," said Ida.

"Let it fall over! It would be for the best, absolutely."

"But you enjoyed yourself?" Julio asked.

"Of course! How could I not enjoy Paris? If not for you and Papa I never would have wanted to leave, would I have, Ida?"

"She was happy, Dom Ernesto."

Xisto walked to the sofa and took his daughter tenderly by the hands.

"I'm so glad. But I'm even happier to have you back."

When she had gone up to her room with Ida to rest, Julio turned to Edmundo excitedly.

"What do you think of her? Isn't she beautiful?"

"Yes, very beautiful."

"And such a charmer. I'm so proud of her."

Edmundo couldn't say what he really felt. Yes she was very charming and gay, but it seemed to him that her gaiety was more strident than her brother's, more forced and high-pitched, false, as if there were nothing underneath it, no joy, as if it were merely the pose of a woman who knew how to act in society. These views she expressed so strongly, so exuberantly, Edmundo knew they were not her own. They were things she had heard someone say, and now she said them too, as if she were fashion's parrot. She was shallow. He didn't believe that he would like her as he liked Julio.

But maybe he was being too much of a Hamlet. The recent death of Antero had caused him so many dark reflections and the clouds hung on him more than they should and coloured the world with vanity. Maybe he was being too harsh on her? Maybe he was wrong?

She made him feel something else too and it made him uneasy. She had aroused him, in spite of, or because of this façade she had mastered. She made him feel as if he were in the presence of a great courtesan. Of course he couldn't tell Julio any of this.

That Saturday there was a party to celebrate Imaculada's return. All the doors were thrown open to provide space for dancing, and an Italian was engaged to play the piano. The best cask of port was opened, and there was, at Imaculada's insistence, champagne.

Imaculada did not descend until the guests were already spilling through the rooms. She came down on the arms of Julio and her father, and as if on cue everyone broke into applause for her. Edmundo stood off to one side, watching her. Her smile was so bright, so spectacular, that he was almost able to believe that it was real. She was indeed stunning: her face, her eyes, the delicacy, grace, and brittleness of her gestures. She was dressed in blue silk, like a robin's egg, cut low at the bust where her flesh slid into it. Her hair was turned and pinned into the most elaborate movements, and there was an ivory comb and a red rose to crown it and keep it in place. She wore long kid gloves and carried a fan painted and inlaid with mother of pearl. There were embroidered satin slippers on her feet with *Louis Quinze* heels. She was the most beautiful and extravagant woman he had ever seen. She attracted and repelled him.

Now the dancing could begin. First Imaculada danced a waltz with her father, and then "the lancers," the most aristocratic of dances, with Julio. They were incredibly handsome together, incredibly graceful.

Julio came over to Edmundo, flushed and happy.

"You must ask her to dance!" he said.

"But really, I dance so poorly," Edmundo protested.

"Nonsense! Besides she wants to dance with you. She's told me so."

She was sitting out an energetic, undisciplined polka, fanning herself about the bosom and long neck. She looked up at him as he approached, watching him, studying him, and smiling at him. He bowed before her.

"Menina Imaculada, may I request a dance of your excellence?" he asked stiffly.

She laughed and entered his name on her card.

He retreated and watched her dance while he anxiously, nervously awaited his turn. She danced with a handsome young friend of Julio's, and coolly with Luis.

At last his turn came. She was waiting for him, smiling, he felt, right through into his exposed heart, mercilessly.

"I believe this dance is mine."

"I believe you are right."

It was a waltz again, and he took her in his arms, afraid to pull her too close. She kept looking right into his eyes, smiling, letting nothing he felt escape her.

"My brother is very fond of you," she said.

"And I of him."

"Do you think I will be fond of you?"

"I hope I will do nothing to make you dislike me."

"Not to dislike is different from to be fond of."

"Yes."

He couldn't say any more. She had aroused him, and he was deathly afraid somehow she would notice. The dance seemed to take forever and was over all too soon.

There was a bit of a hubbub when some of the guests began dancing the *maxixe*.

"What's this!" exclaimed Julio to Edmundo. He explained that the *maxixe* was a popular dance of African derivation, which was considered in better circles to be crude and vulgar. Julio was afraid that his sister would be upset.

"She can't stand anything base."

They hurried off to see after her, but found her serene and distant, looking over the dancing like a disinterested goddess.

"Let them be," she said.

At midnight Xisto made a drunken impromptu speech to welcome his daughter home. It was disjointed, maudlin and somewhat embarrassing, but people knew he really loved her. She smiled through the whole thing and then let him embrace her.

When the speech was over the servants brought out trays of refreshments: papaya, guava and passion fruit, quince and pineapple, coconut and Brazil nuts and imported raisins, figs, and prunes. When it was one o'clock everyone looked tired and sloppy, except for Imaculada, who was like an orchid picked that very moment.

The next day was Sunday, and the family all went to church together—except Xisto who was hung over in bed. Edmundo was no longer in the habit of attending Mass, but this time he made an exception.

Imaculada insisted that she wanted to go to the *Igreja da Glória*, her favourite church. They arrived early and there was time for a stroll.

"Isn't it beautiful?" she said. "It was the favourite church of the Emperor."

This seemed to impress her. Edmundo less so.

"Do you know the story of the two angels?" she asked. He didn't. "This was once the place where a hermit had his shanty. One day two angels came to him and helped him make a statue of Our Lady. The statue was so beautiful and so lovely that when it was lost in the ocean it miraculously came ashore."

"Hmm," said Edmundo.

"Don't you believe in angels, Edmundo?"

"I've grown skeptical. I remember when I was a boy in bed at night. I would think of Jesus or Santa Maria appearing before me in my room, and I was so frightened by the idea that I would pull the covers over my head and pray for them to choose someone else."

"How strange! I used to plead for them to come to me. I had long speeches composed that I could recite to them depending on which one it was."

"But they never came."

"No, and I was so unhappy."

She didn't look unhappy. She looked coy.

Edmundo hadn't been to Mass in a long time and he had forgotten how boring it could be. He forced himself to kneel when it was time to kneel, but he declined to take communion.

Afterwards they strolled through the French park nearby. Imaculada smiled wistfully and said she missed Paris already.

Julio walked ahead with Ida; Imaculada walked with Edmundo behind. She looked at him; he tried to stare in front.

"I like your moustaches," she said. "That's how men look in Paris now. Here everyone, as you see, still has a long beard. I must get Julio to cut his off. But I must warn you, Brazilians aren't used to men who shave. They'll think you effeminate. I'm surprised no one has said anything to you about it. They must be mocking you behind your back." She smiled at him playfully. He said nothing.

"Must you always wear your glasses?" she continued.

"Only if I wish to see."

"How unfortunate. They make you look very distinguished, but without them I believe you would be positively dashing."

Did she really mean this? If she did, wasn't it immodest of her to tell him?

Julio had suddenly stopped. Coming toward them was a handsome young officer with a pale young woman on his arm. Edmundo watched Imaculada. Her face went blank for a moment, as if she had fallen asleep with her eyes open, and then, immediately, she recovered her composure.

The officer stopped before them.

"Hello," he said, to Imaculada presumably, though his eyes darted from face to face.

"How are you?" asked Imaculada dispassionately.

"Well, and yourself?"

"Well. And your mother?"

"Well. And your father?"

"Well. May I introduce Senhor Caçador, who has recently come from Portugal? Edmundo, may I introduce Lieutenant de Bettencourt."

"How do you do."

"How do you do."

"And may I introduce my fiancée, Menina Dina."

"How do you do."

"How do you do."

"At any rate, it was very charming to see you again," said de Bettencourt.

"Yes. Give my best to your mother."

"And mine to your father."

"I will."

"Goodbye."

"Goodbye."

De Bettencourt gone, Julio, who had been unable to bring himself to utter a word, took his sister solicitously by the arm.

"Are you alright?" he whispered anxiously.

"Yes, of course, Julio, I'm perfectly fine." And she seemed to be. "Don't be a ninny."

The walk continued without incident. Edmundo kept behind them with Ida and watched brother and sister.

"He cares so much for her," Edmundo thought. "He is so protective, he doesn't see how impervious she is. She doesn't feel the things he thinks she feels. Only he feels them. She is like ice."

Edmundo laid down for a Sunday afternoon nap, but he couldn't sleep. He didn't know how to take her. There was something immensely attractive about her, not only in her features, but in her manner, in her very soul. She was beautiful and of a noble nature. But she was cold and heartless and shallow, he was convinced of it. He felt such contradictory things and he was sick to feel he had betrayed his true friend Julio to think such negative things. He was anxious to get away from her, to leave for his position in *Paraíba do Sul*. Spring would be there. The air would be fresh and clean.

Rather than toss in bed he decided to read. The light was poor in his room so he picked up the volume of Antero de Quental that had been his companion for weeks and went towards the turret.

He stopped suddenly at the foot of the stairs.

Imaculada lay fallen on the landing above, as if she had collapsed. Ida knelt beside her, holding her. Edmundo stepped back out of their sight, but stayed close enough to see and hear.

"Why did we come back?" Imaculada said. "I knew what would happen."

"We couldn't stay away forever," said Ida. Her voice was flat, but to Edmundo it no longer seemed dull, but calm and knowing. "Your father needs you. Julio needs you."

"I'm no good to them. They just worry. And I can't overcome my sorrow, not even for them. Really, Ida, it would be better if I were dead." She said this without self-pity or petulance, with great cold resolve. "I really mean it, Ida."

Ida stroked her dark hair.

"I know, *querida*, I know."

Chapter Four

When he arrived at the plantation, to amuse himself and pass the time, Edmundo began to keep a journal. Who knew? Someday he might even write a novel.

Monday, September 29

Arrived in the afternoon to a minimum of fanfare. Warm, bright day. Spring. Having crossed the equator I missed a summer, or had it delayed for six months—although it makes little difference in such a tropical place. Except maybe to the spirit. Perhaps one reason why I have felt so oppressed lately. But now that spring is in the air and in the heart, I might feel more cheery. Hope so. It is dusty here.

First impressions. People are gruff, rustic, have neither the grace nor sophistication of the Xistos. Was met by a foreman who hardly spoke to me at all. Carried my own bag. Given a dark, damp room, unornamented except for a crucifix, a monk's room. Plantation itself is very large, like a small town. The big house is set in its own walled enclave. The top of the wall embedded with glass shards to keep out intruders—I suppose boys who would steal a banana or a pineapple. Within the enclave live the de Figueiredos, their horses, their pigs, their chickens, their household servants. There is a garden and a fish pond, an aviary, a fruit orchard. Outside the walls are the coffee trees, thousands of acres of them, and the workers' quarters. The workers are mostly Italians. There are some Portuguese, even some Germans. I have been given a place set slightly apart from them. Was shown the bookkeeping office, which it seems, is where I will be working. I protested that I hoped to be able to spend time in the fields, and was assured that would be the case. There is also a bakery and a saw mill, even a brewery. The Negroes live in a shanty town down the road. Was told the men are all drunkards and the women all whores.

The spring makes me think of home, for it was on such a day that I left. Strange, but I hadn't been homesick until now. Suddenly I feel lonely and afraid again, like a child sleeping in a strange room for the first time. The Xistos have been so friendly, have made me feel so welcome, that there was no place in my heart left to long for home. I miss Julio already. And Xisto. I even miss Luis.

Haven't been able to stop thinking about Imaculada and Ida on the stairs. What is it about me that so misjudges character, until some force of circumstance reveals the secret heart of a person to me? Why am I so stupid in that way? I so misread her, so misread them both. I rightly saw that she had put up a facade, but blind and insensitive as I am, I couldn't see what was behind the façade, and assumed there was nothing. With Ida, her quiet dignity, her understanding completely escaped me, and I thought her an oaf. I am the oaf.

She loves him, like the Portuguese nun loved the chevalier. He is unworthy of her. He is a fool to turn his back on her. How could he leave her for anything, especially for that little blonde mouse we saw him with? Why does she stoop to love someone like him? But like the nun, the love she bears him ennobles her, though the beloved is unworthy, inconsequential, irrelevant. Can't she say to herself, "My emotions are centered on the false idol I have built myself?" But again, what do I know? How can I judge de Bettencourt? Would she love someone so unworthy? If she loves him, shouldn't I respect that, respect him? She has chosen him. To her he is singled out from the rest of the world, where all the oafs are gathered together.

Thursday, October 1

Have now been introduced to the business of a coffee plantation, a plantation which, I am told, is large, but not nearly as large as some.

There are 2600 acres of orchard, or about one million trees. On a really large plantation each administrator would be in charge of a million trees. The trees yield fruit in their sixth year, and continue to produce for fifteen to thirty years more. At which time the orchards are abandoned. Harvesting takes place in May, which to someone like me having come from another hemisphere, still seems strange. Each of the workers will be given a thousand to fifteen hundred trees to harvest. They will begin at four in the morning and work till seven in the evening, with breakfast at six, lunch at twelve, and dinner served in the orchards at four. Each tree yields 3 to 4 pounds of unhusked berries, each acre 400 to 500 pounds, the entire plantation almost four million pounds. A good crop might bring in 300 to 400,000 *escudos*.

The berries are stripped off the branches by hand and put into bags. The weather must be hot and dry. Each day, for a month, the berries are laid out in the sun to dry, and each night raked into piles and covered with canvas. When the berries are thoroughly dry they are beaten by hand with a mortar and pestle in order to open them and release the beans. They are winnowed on large round screens, sorted, graded, sacked, and sent to Rio.

I have been introduced to Dom Ignacio de Figueiredo, who took one look at me and asked why I didn't have a beard. I was tempted to answer that it was because I shaved it off, but I just said that moustaches were the fashion where I came from. He said that all the men he knew had beards, otherwise one was a woman. (And I thought Imaculada had been joking!) I didn't know whether to laugh or challenge him to a duel. I let it go. If I'm to work here in peace I might have to let my whiskers grow.

He says I must meet his son, whom he calls "a stallion."

Sunday, October 4

Met the stallion. He was lying in a hammock being deloused by his mother, Dona Alma, and a Negro servant girl. Very petulant, uncouth, lazy. His great passions are horses, cockfighting, and, from what I've gathered elsewhere, whoring. His name is Clement. Somewhat fat and soft looking. But the face is mean and dazed, as if he had been hit by a shovel. (Similar expression seems to run in the family. I see it when I look at them unawares.) The only person he shows any deference to is his mammy, a pompous overbearing Negro woman of perhaps fifty. She is the only one who is able to make him listen. Occasionally he talks to her in baby talk. To his own mother, on the other hand, he adopts the cold, severe tone of his father, the patriarch.

Mammy has most peculiar views on slavery. Laments its passing. Thinks of it as a noble institution, better for Negroes than freedom. She's very overbearing and it would be impossible to argue with her. The de Figueiredos don't bother. In fact they give the definite impression they agree with her.

The mother is fat and magnificently obtuse—if I may, after my misreading of Ida, venture to judge, but this time I'm sure I'm right. She puts up with her son's rudeness by failing to notice it. She notices nothing. Seems devoid of thought.

There are daughters from what I hear, but none were outdoors. There is a brother to the patriarch, a priest, Padre Jesus. Same dullness of expression and speech. He has no parish, but administers to the spiritual needs of the family. Very convenient. I'm sure he'll get the whole lot of them safely, slowly, to heaven. There is also, I gather, Dona Alma's widowed sister, whom I have not met, and her two young sons, whom I think I saw running about. No one to talk with. Miss the Xistos.

I should have brought more books. There is nothing to read. The nights are lonely.

Sunday October 11

Invited to dinner at the Big House. The family gathers around an immense dark mahogany table; at the head, in a chair larger and more ostentatious than any other, sits Dom Ignacio. The meat is brought in and set before him. He serves himself first, taking the choicest portion. One has the impression that if another were to attempt to serve himself ahead of the patriarch, there would be bloodshed, as among baboons. The food is horribly spicy, worse than in Rio. Much is made of manioc meal.

The patriarch dominates the conversation. His daughters don't dare to speak. The eldest, Beatriz, has the same dull, blunted look as the others, but one can also see that she is terribly unhappy and discontented. She is thin, shriveled, prematurely withered. The others are so shy and frightened as almost to be devoid of personality. Dona Alma and her sister, Dona Graça, speak only in the most meaningless and punctilious phrases, almost always either to agree with de Figueiredo or to chide one of their offspring. The nephew, a boy of eight, is treated with the utmost harshness. It seems everyone has license to scold and beat him for the slightest offence, real or imagined. I believe it wouldn't have raised an eyebrow if I'd hit him myself. The second son, a child of four, is on the other hand pampered to distraction.

De Figueiredo talked to me of slavery, about which he is very bitter, although he readily admits that the Italians are more efficient workers and that he would have eventually replaced his Negroes in any case. He seems to see emancipation as an affront to his honour. Like Mammy, he claims that the Negroes were better off as slaves. He says he always dealt with them fairly, with their best interests at heart. Even allowed them to work holidays for pay to earn their freedom. Claims he never sold a child under fifteen away from its mother. Says it was mostly the same everywhere, although he admits that a planter in dire economic straits, or trying to get established, might work his slaves too hard, but that, he said, is understandable. Of course I found this brutal nonsense, but said nothing. Now he is quite hateful. Traces the beginning of the end to the slave revolts of 1835—before his own birth—when a number of slave owning families were massacred. He says the masters could never look on the slaves with the same affection after that. Hence the walls topped with glass shards. The bitterest day of his life was May 13, 1888, when he had to set the last of his slaves free, with work still to be done on the harvest. Tremendous hatred of the Emperor for allowing this to happen.

After dinner I was shown Dona Alma's altar to her 'angels': the children she has born who died in childhood. There are lighted candles and locks of their hair. Seems to love them more than the ones who are living, almost worshiping them. She tells me she prays here every morning and night. Why? Let us turn our backs on death and embrace the living.

As I was leaving I passed by a servant girl sitting with the two boys in the dusk. There was a gentle breeze coming in off the fields and a deep red glow in the west over the black trees. She was telling them, in a dialect I could barely recognize as Portuguese, about something called the *Quibungo*, a boogie man, who would come and eat them alive through a hole in the back of his head. She sang to them, in a deep, scary voice—or as deep and scary as she could make her own sweet tongue:

Whose house is this
Here by the way?
Do I eat a child, do I eat a child,
Do I eat a child today?

The children clung to her, and she put her arms around them to protect them from the darkness. I think she believed it as much as they did.

At dinner everyone commented on my moustache. The men sneer and the women giggle. I'm really afraid I shall have to give in.

Thursday, October 20

I raised with Dom Ignacio the question of installing steam huts to speed the drying of the berries, which I've discovered is done in some places. But he had no patience for the idea. I also asked why he waited so long to replant old orchards. "You don't understand this country," he said. "You come from a small, worn out country where everyone looks to the past. Here we all look to the future." I assured him I was looking to the future, and he said, "The future takes care of itself."

Perhaps he's right. I'm out of place. What am I doing here? Sometimes I feel in love with Brazil, especially when I think of Rio. Sometimes it appalls me. Everything, the glories and the sins, are written in bright blue and green. Everything seems bottomless, the wealth, the land, the future. It frightens me. I don't know what to make of it. Am I alone? Don't they see how monstrous this land can be? How bottomless the pit? Am I wrong? Do I see things in the wrong way? Perhaps I am part of an old world, a world full of doubt. Here everyone is certain, certain that the world lies before them for the taking, that it will always be so, for that is what it means to have a future.

I can't stop thinking about Imaculada. I feel afraid.

Monday, October 26

I have begun to go bathing with Clement in the mornings. His body is white and plump like a turkey. He seems to be fond of me, in his own way, with a sort of leering, teasing respect. He talks incessantly of the most disgusting matters.

He had syphilis at the age of fifteen, but claims to have gotten rid of it by giving it to a Negro girl of thirteen, a virgin. Every night, and often during the day, he is to be found in the shanty town, for he has an insatiable hunger for Negro women. Indeed he has known no others, and shudders at the thought of touching a white woman, for they make him quake with awe. The only other partners he has ever had are animals or inanimate objects: dogs or watermelons. He claims that the fruit of the *mandacaru* is just like human flesh. He offered to provide me with one, but, of course, I declined the offer. He also invited me to accompany him to the shanty town.

His speech is riddled with obscenities, and his manners are nonexistent. He takes delight in farting, always taking pains to telegraph the event ahead of time. Also picks his nose.

Yet somehow he fascinates me. Strange how I am drawn to such creatures, like Luis, whose manners and hatred totally appall me. Is it really that I seek the truth, or do I seek something more disgusting? Perhaps in my heart of hearts I am not so different from them.

Sometimes I disgust myself.

Friday, October 30

I have been asked to dinner again. The others think this a rare honour, but I find it onerous. Feel very stultified, smothered when I sit with them all around that massive dark table.

Have received a letter from Julio. He reiterates the family's invitation that I come for Christmas. Have already accepted, but will write him again and tell him how much I am looking forward to it, which of course is absolutely true. So much so, I can hardly stand waiting.

He says in the letter that Imaculada is well.

Wednesday, November 11

Just had a disturbing experience. After dinner I was walking by the big house when I came upon Beatriz beating a young Negro girl with a stick. The girl was crying and covering her head with her hands and begging for mercy. Beatriz seemed almost in a frenzy, almost mad. I quickly stepped between them and pleaded with her to stop.

Suddenly she seemed to come to consciousness and looked at me, the stick frozen above her head. She was embarrassed, ashamed, I supposed, because I had seen her lose control of herself; but there was in her the indignation of the slave master that I, an employee, should keep her from doing whatever she liked with one of her Negroes. She stood glaring at me, without lowering her weapon.

"Senhor Edmundo," she said, "this doesn't concern you, please step aside."

The girl lay broken and sobbing at my feet, clinging and terrified.

"I beseech you, Menina Beatriz, you have punished her sufficiently for whatever she has done; as a favour to me, please let her be."

"Please step aside."

I wouldn't move. She didn't dare to strike me. It had now become for her completely a question of her honour. I was disgracing her.

"Please Menina Beatriz," I said, trying to mollify her. "You have punished her sufficiently. Grant me this small favour."

But I could see the outrage and shame in her eyes. Suddenly she lowered the stick and rushed off into the house.

I helped the girl to her feet and examined her head and shoulders. There were bruises, but I don't believe she had been seriously injured. She couldn't stop crying. I think she was afraid that Beatriz would come back, so I stood with her for a time until she became calm. Then I told her to go to her room.

I fear I have made an enemy. What will she do? If she tells her father, he'll of course side with her. Everyone, of course, would believe that she had every right to beat the girl to death. They might disapprove, but no one would deny her the right. And yet I did the only thing I could have done. But what would I have done if I had come across de Figueiredo himself beating a servant? I suspect my courage would have failed me. I'm afraid of him.

How am I to deal with this cruelty? It is everywhere. I have seen young Alfonso kicked and beaten for nothing, as I wouldn't treat a dog, and he one of their own blood. Why didn't I step in then? Or when Clement took me to his precious cockfight? These men intimidate me, these stern, hairy creatures with their hunting knifes always at their sides. Dom Ignacio speaks of the paternal kindness he always shown his slaves, and yet I have seen what remains of the stocks and shackles and branding irons. Is this the real face of the new world, the face of the future, of progress? Why am I here if I can't stop these things? To take part? My very soul rises against it. And yet, if not, why am I here?

Friday, November 13

Rotten luck. Have been asked to dinner again. Will have to go. I must suppose Beatriz hasn't told her father about our confrontation. Why? Could it be I frighten her?

Spent the afternoon with Padre Jesus and was terribly bored. The man is truly dim-witted, a real priest (although Clement assures me that his housekeeper does more for his bed than just make it). He asked me questions about myself, my family, my beliefs, my ambitions. I tried to be circumspect, I don't know why. Felt stifled by his dusty, chalky cassock.

Sunday November 15

Dinner passed without incident. Beatriz averted her eyes the whole time. Happy when it was over.

Friday November 20

Relieved. Not invited for Sunday.
Christmas approaches. Can't wait to see the Xistos.

Friday November 27

Invited to dinner. Devastated.

Sunday December 6

Went to dinner again at the Big House. Beginning to suspect a plot: Clement has told me things about his sister. She is eighteen, which is an overripe age for marriage. I've also learned that the family has been searching for a suitable match and turned up no one in the vicinity. They are loathe to have a spinster on their hands, for fear that she will, in her baseness, do something to disgrace them. Hence they keep her locked up in a windowless bedroom, a virtual prisoner. There has been talk of sending her to a nunnery. Once, when her father suggested this, she dared tell him she wouldn't have it, and he struck her with his cane. His code of honour tells him he has complete authority over her, even to the point of life and death. If he were even to suspect her of being unchaste he could shoot her and no one would lift a finger against him. The family is desperate for a solution.

I fear I am being groomed as their solution, hence the dinner invitations. Clement—who is somewhat reticent on this, which is totally out of character—has told me that a son-in-law would be offered management of the estate and almost the status of a son after Dom Ignacio's death. All this for accepting the shriveled fruit of their blood.

Clement has assured me that Dom Ignacio has no cause to worry about his daughter's chastity. She is a virgin and is too well watched to become otherwise. And yet she has the heart of a whore. Clement tells me she likes nothing better than to take the Negro girls who have been deflowered, sometimes when still children, and have them confide to her the most intimate details of everything men have ever done to them. In this way Beatriz has become a true aficionada of lust, familiar with the tastes and textures and smells of the basest acts. And this is the woman they would have me take for a wife! Far better that I had taken Clara Pereira! I cannot allow this to happen to me. I refuse to give my life away to them. Slavery is no more in this country, I refuse to be mastered.

Monday December 14

Was invited to dinner for Sunday and of course I had to accept. But Sunday morning I sent word that I was sick and would have to stay in my quarters. They sent a servant girl to ask about me. I felt ashamed, but there was nothing else to be done.

Next Sunday, thank God, I leave for Rio. Which means that I have till January to figure a way out of this. Longing for the warmth of the Xistos.

Of historical note: word has come from Paris that Pedro Banana is dead. No one seems to care one way or the other. Here the past dies quickly, is buried, and instantly returns to the earth.

Saturday December 19

Had occasion to visit the shanty town for the first time.

The huts are huddled together on a barren mud flat that has no other possible use. They are made of bamboo and grass with thatched palm roofs. The floors are the bare earth, which is often wet and muddy. The outhouses are placed beside the wells. There is dysentery everywhere.

These are the people who used to harvest Dom Ignacio's coffee, or what's left of them. Some of the younger ones have gone to the cities in search of work. Those left behind have an aimless existence, abandoned like refuse. Their lives are a ridiculous emancipation, an unintentional mockery of plantation activity. The old men lie in their makeshift hammocks, like Clement, as if they were so wealthy that they never need lift a finger. I saw a woman sitting proudly while her daughter deloused her—as if she were Dona Ana herself. I saw a woman dressed in rags, barefoot—as everyone is—but with an old French hat upon her head, a hat that had been once fashionable and sat on the head of a rich white woman fifteen years ago. I saw a man naked except for old flannel pants cut off at the knees and a worn out frock coat. Freedom baffles them. They have no idea what to do with it. They either continue with their slave ways, the women whoring, the men aping their masters, or they return to the wild, to the African ways they have kept alive somewhere inside them. Perhaps Luis is right. It would be better if they were all sent back.

Better for them especially. Here they are a waste. There is nothing for them. To the whites, who have built their fortunes with them but now have no more use for them, they have become a new species of pest, like cockroaches or rats. There is no dignity here and little hope. They will never be able to raise themselves up out of this mire.

To think that Imaculada's mother was one of these people, that their blood is in her.

Monday I leave for Rio.

Thursday January 1

Been too busy to write. The holidays are almost over. Tomorrow I return to the plantation. Wish I could stay here forever.

When I arrived Julio was there to meet me at the station. Because of the heat he was wearing white duck trousers, and looked most dashing. We embraced and he laughed and told me how anxious everyone was to see me. If only he could have known how anxious I was in return to see them, more anxious by far, I am certain.

Carlos was there with the carriage and we greeted each other warmly. Already I was feeling relieved and almost joyous.

"Imaculada is having her hair done," said Julio. "We'll go together to pick her up. While we wait we can go have a drink together at the *Globo*. How's that?"

The *Globo* was bright and vividly active. It made me realize how a farm boy must feel when he arrives in the big city for the first time. We sat at a table with Julio's friends, familiar, festive faces. They all greeted me warmly and welcomed me home.

We drank gin fizzes and Julio asked me about my work. I smiled sourly and told him I wasn't meant to live in the country. He said he was exactly the same and didn't know how I could stand it. Everyone was talking about the opera and the latest indiscretions of Madame L. (with Dr. H., the cabinet minister). It was very trifling, and very amusing, but I felt inside me an overwhelming anxiousness and found it hard to pay attention.

When it was time to go, we bid everyone adieu, and my heart was racing. We drove in the carriage through the shady streets, the high sky bright over the roofs of the buildings, like the ceiling of a celestial cathedral. Julio talked incessantly, and I smiled to indicate that I was listening. I suddenly felt more alive, more at home than I ever had in my life. Everything seemed to exist just for me.

Carlos went in to fetch her and I sat with Julio for those interminable moments in the carriage. Then I saw her. She hurried with Ida and Carlos over to us, her step light, light.

"What's that on your face!" she exclaimed, first thing, with light, playful laughter.

I felt ashamed, and offered to shave on the spot if a razor could be found.

She laughed again. I was much too serious. The beard, she said, looked handsome on me. But I had already made up my mind to be rid of it.

"And my hair!" she said. "What do you think of my hair?"

She beamed while we admired her. It was a coiffure of infinite elaborateness, labyrinthine, delicate, graceful and tentative, the product of a dedicated, futile care, like writing in sand before the sea. I felt it made her look foolish somehow, but beautifully, deliciously so. Julio praised her effusively. I told her it was quite becoming. She took my arm when she mounted into the landau.

"Do you know why I've had it done?" she asked.

I told her I didn't.

"Because Julio and I are taking you to the opera tonight!"

I protested that I would make very dull company, but they, in the highest spirits, insisted, and I allowed myself to accept their invitation, most contentedly at that.

When we arrived at the house everyone was there to greet me. Dom Ernesto embraced me like I was his own son. Luis shook my hand, and I felt that he was actually glad to see me, if only to have someone who was willing to listen to him talk. The servants were smiling, and Nanette wanted to shake my hand, but I kissed hers instead.

I went to my old room to rest, but I could hardly sit still. There was a letter from my parents which had just come for me. They are well, they miss me—especially at this time of year —of course, there is always the unwritten sadness of my brother's death so long ago. They have never gotten over the loss. They implore me to write more often. My father says Pereira continues to treat him coldly and that Clara has become a recluse, and that everyone jokes about her. I'm sad to hear this. I wish she would marry someone suitable. I never wanted to hurt her. But to tell the truth, I was only distracted by all this for a moment. I was looking forward to the opera.

To appear at such an event with Imaculada on my arm, beautiful Imaculada, dressed in the finest, most dreamlike of dresses, with orchids at her bosom and the smell of jasmine in her hair. To look over and see her smile. This was all I could ever hope for. It was clear to me now—my excitement was so inordinate and undeniable—that nothing, no one, mattered to me now but her.

The theatre was bustling joyfully. It was almost Christmas and the soprano had a large, devoted following. The students in the upper balcony stamped their feet and chanted her name. Everywhere there was the movement of people in and out of their seats, and it all made me feel that I was at the centre of the universe, the place where what really mattered was carried out.

Imaculada was gay and talkative. Julio somewhat less so. We sat in our box, overlooking those below. I could see the expectation—or nervousness—in their eyes and I knew they were each wondering if they would see de Bettencourt—after all, it was a gala event, it was most likely that he would be there. However, we saw nothing of him. I couldn't tell if she was relieved or disappointed. At any rate, it made me feel inconsequential. But I would have been contented to be there, to play my part with her, even if I had been no more than a petal on one of her flowers. All I wanted was to be near her.

Her façade was as perfect as ever. I would have almost believed that she was happy, empty-headedly happy. Her smile, her eyes were as fluid as ever—except perhaps for an almost imperceptible new stiffness, like the first autumn ice on a stream. But I knew how she really felt, how savaged and bleak was her soul. I had been privileged to steal that knowledge from her—or an inkling of that knowledge— and now I would never doubt her or be fooled by her again. Julio knew it too, somehow, though I was sure she hadn't told him. If he had hoped that she would have returned from Paris with a mended heart, he had been bitterly disappointed. And he had taken it badly, he loved her so. The infectious gaiety was gone from him. Now it seemed forced and strained and made for discomfort. When he took me to the *Globo* again, I made a point to ask one of his friends about him and he told me that Julio, far from letting his hatred for de Bettencourt subside, had actually become steadily more vehement.

The celebrations on Christmas Eve began when Dom Ernesto and Luis came up from the offices after work. Nanette was there, Julio and Imaculada, Ida, and I. There was punch and sweets and everyone was smiling and trying to be gay.

Imaculada and Ida told Nanette how charming she looked, and she did, with her blonde curls and blue eyes and delicate features like a doll. Nanette smiled.

"Thank you, "she said. "But I am just a pale little thing when compared with you."

Imaculada's smile was suddenly harsh and pained.

"Not at all," she said, "I would gladly change my appearance with yours. You see no matter how expensive my clothes or lavish my jewels and hair, I am still dark and ugly, but you, no matter what, are always soft and fair."

Ida took Imaculada's hand. Julio rose out of his seat, nervously.

"Dark and ugly!" he cried. "What nonsense."

"I am."

"You're not! You're the most beautiful woman in Brazil."

Imaculada laughed derisively. I wanted to tell her that I thought she was the most beautiful woman I had ever seen, or even imagined, that she was so alarmingly beautiful that when I was in her presence I felt myself in danger.

"I hope that when you marry," said Nanette, "your husband agrees with your brother."

"Oh, but I will never marry," said Imaculada, still smiling.

Xisto was slumped in a chair, looking at her, with great sadness in his eyes.

Julio was losing his patience.

"Of course you will marry!" he said. "You have to."

"But why? Marriage is too much work. I am a lazy woman. I prefer to pass the rest of my life doing nothing, with you and Ida and papa."

Everyone was uncomfortable now, and no one spoke. I watched her. I wanted to do something for her, but she was so strong, and so unhappy, what could I do?

"But let us talk about something else," she said at last. "Julio, show us your impersonation of the tenor last night. He was really quite comical, and Julio has captured him completely."

"I don't want to."

"You must. Julinho, it's Christmas Eve, we can't be unhappy. We must celebrate. Please, just do it once."

"No, I can't."

But Luis, in a rare charitable moment, brought on by I don't know what, came to the rescue and carried the conversation forward.

"I heard that this tenor is quite ridiculous," and he let his eyes dart around the room before finishing with a snicker, "that he's a fag."

"Yes, I've heard that said too," Imaculada answered. "But I really don't know. Perhaps it is just a rumour. After all, quite virile men may occasionally be suspected of femininity, may they not, Edmundinho?"

She smiled at me the most playful, teasing smile, and I had to smile back.

"Only if they shave," I answered. And she forced me to tell everyone about my conversation on this matter with de Figueiredo. I did so happily, for all I wanted was to serve her in any way I could. Everyone was amused at my predicament. And although Ernesto and Luis and Julio all have full beards and would never think of shaving them, they all agreed that I had every right to go about clean shaven.

And so the conversation passed on to something else, and even Julio allowed himself to be coaxed out of his funk. But of course deeper down everyone was just as miserable as before.

I too was miserable, afraid, sorry for these, my dearest friends. I wished nothing more than that they might be happy. And although I was overjoyed to be near her, to be able to watch her, to look at her all evening long, and even to talk to her, I was still so afraid of her, afraid of what she made me feel. She is a saint, a goddess, and all I want is to worship and serve her. Why then, do I feel the most shameful urges? Desire the most hideous and unimaginable things? Why, even in the moments of my greatest admiration for her, do I find myself staring at her, at her bosom and her waist and her long slender arms? Why must I pollute what I feel for her? If ever she were to know! I would be so ashamed that I would have no recourse but to shoot myself, like a dog.

Now it is early in the morning of the first day of this new year. At midnight we drank a toast and went to the open window to hear the city's revelry. There was shouting and singing and the clanging of pots. Her face glowed softly in the moonlight. I was looking at the nape of her neck, for her hair was pulled up off of it and it was exposed. I felt that if I didn't turn my eyes away that very moment I would lose control of myself and put my lips there. She turned to look at me and smiled, a tender, knowing smile. I hated myself.

Tomorrow I return to my exile. Such begins a new year. What will it hold? How will I ever be happy away from her? And yet what can

I hope from her? She says she will never marry. And I believe her. What vanity would lead me to believe that, even if she were to marry, she would marry me? I am nothing to her. She is de Bettencourt's, even though he has thrown her away.

Paraíba do Sul
Wednesday, January 7

Incredible heat. In the mornings, already sopping with sweat, I meet Clement at the river and we swim together. The sun is already high and merciless. The trees glint in the fields. All day I am loathe to step out of the shade. In the evening, sunset brings small relief. Clement takes a bottle of whiskey and heads for the shanty town.

When I returned with my cheeks shaven, Dom Ignacio was visibly taken aback. I don't believe anyone has even so indirectly defied him before. He said nothing, however. He is still hoping I will marry his daughter. But once the harvest is in, and the crop has been sold, I hope I never see this place again.

Already I miss Rio, and Imaculada. At night I can't help but think about her. The heat overpowers me. My blood boils. Why must I do this? Why can't my love for her be as pure as I wish it to be? I have no right to debase her, even in my imagination, as if she were no more than the fruit of the *mandacaru*.

Perhaps I should learn to scourge myself, like a priest, until such feelings subside. For it is as her priest that I must love her.

Saturday January 10

Have just returned from the shanty town with Clement. Why? Why? Why! I have done something unspeakably shameful.

Clement came by before sunset. He had been drinking. He was

going for a woman, he told me, and as always he asked me along. I had been having the most uncontrollable thoughts all day long, in the sun, in the shade, in the cool of dusk, and then alone in my room. He saw how I hesitated.

"So," he said. "Are you coming this time then?"

I asked for his bottle and took a long burning drink.

"Yes, I'm coming."

We walked along as night enveloped us. We had no lantern, but Clement assured me that his nose would lead us to what we wanted. I felt as if I were walking into another world, or over the black edge of this one. My heart was racing, I was short of breath, and I was covered in sweat. And yet my organ was erect, painfully erect and yearning.

We walked for twenty minutes, and I asked Clement two or three times to drink from his bottle. He could feel how anxious I was.

"Calm down," he said. "You've had a woman before. What are you afraid of? They'll do anything you want them to."

I wanted to turn back but I couldn't, or didn't.

When he arrived at the mudflats the moon had risen over the trees and he brought me to a hut near the well. He called someone's name in the darkness and there was an answer and stirring inside. We went in.

There was an old man lying on the ground smoking a cigarette, and two girls, one perhaps eighteen, the other younger. Clement sat down beside the old man on the dirt floor. I remained standing in the doorway.

"I've brought a friend," Clement said. Then he turned to me and said, "You can have her"—meaning the younger one—"she's new, practically a virgin." Then he offered to pay for me and took out some money to give to the old man.

"I'll pay for myself," I said.

"As you wish."

I gave the old man what he asked for, and stood there alone, in a state of desire and fear.

"Well," said Clement, "take her, she's yours."

"Here?" I asked.

"My friend is shy," he said to the girl. "Take him with you into the back."

I followed her into a small space in the shack that had been partitioned off. She sat down on the floor and looked up at me. She was pretty, young, unspoiled, too young for me to be with her like this. She didn't yet know how to be a whore, she didn't come to me, or encourage me, she just sat there for me to take her, like a victim. And, to my everlasting disgrace, I did. I laid her down in the dirt and entered her. All the while I felt like the pig I was, all the while I could hear Clement swearing and sputtering a few feet away, all the while I was carried away by my own horrible desire, and all the while, God, if he exists, cannot forgive me for this, I was thinking of Imaculada—even as the lust ran out of me. And all the while the girl said nothing, had not even raised her hands to touch me. When it was over, there was nothing but shame, and I could no longer even understand what had driven me to do this. I felt nothing but the drink that had gone heavy and shameful in my head.

When Clement came for me I was sitting on the floor, leaning against the wall, and the girl was sitting up staring at me, fearlessly, like a wondering child. I wanted to ask her to forgive me, but I said nothing. I looked so unsatisfied that he asked me if I had done. I told him yes and we went out together.

I was silent for a long time walking back in the blackness. He whistled and sometimes belched. I was glad he didn't talk to me. When we came to my room he stopped and looked at me.

"You want to go again?"

"No."

"Suit yourself."

"I have a question. She was scarred down there. She'd been cut. Why?"

"They do that to them. They cut them and sew them up so when they marry her husband would have to cut her open and he'd know she was a virgin. That's what they do in Africa."

"But she's a whore. She doesn't have a husband."

"They do it anyway. I was there when they cut that one open."

There was nothing more I wanted to know.

"Goodnight," he said.

"Goodnight."

Early in February Edmundo discovered a chancre on his penis. But it went away, and he was relieved to be able to forget about it.

Chapter Five

Edmundo was back in Rio at Carnival time. He had been invited, and though Dom Ignacio frowned and tried to discourage him, nothing could have kept him from going to the Xistos.

He wanted to speak to Xisto about his future. Plantation work held no interest for him. Was there something else he could try? Something that would tie him to the city? He no longer really hoped to find work that would stir his soul, but if he could keep close to Imaculada, that would satisfy him now. But when he arrived in Rio he discovered that Ernesto had once again been called out of town unexpectedly, and there was nothing for him to do but enjoy the company of Julio and Imaculada, which made him feel uneasy and guilty, as if he were living a lie.

Julio and Carlos met him at the station. It was very hot and he was perspiring. They embraced in the warm shade, and smiled big summery smiles. Edmundo felt grimy and wanted a bath.

Carnival was to begin at noon. Blacks had already gathered in the streets; there would be sambas and dancing and practical jokes.

"You must be careful," Julio said. "They will throw flour and water on you and turn you into a cupcake. You can die that way, if they plaster your nostrils."

For respectable people there were masked balls. The Catete Palace had one. Julio and Imaculada had their costumes. They were to be Louis XVI and Marie-Antoinette.

"If you had a costume, you could come with us," said Julio.

"Yes, but it must be too late."

"Yes, alas."

When he arrived at the Xistos', Imaculada put her arms around him and gave him a kiss on the cheek.

"Edmundinho, wait till you see my costume! Too bad you can't come with us. Maybe you could go as yourself, do you think people would be impressed?"

"Hardly."

After supper Edmundo provided them with their first audience. Imaculada came in on Julio's arm. She wore a great white wig, which rose over her head and tumbled around her neck in curls, a red satin gown that pushed the tops of her breasts together and rustled around her on the floor, and a small bejeweled lorgnette which she held before her eyes. She had her nose in the air and a mock-pompous look on her face.

"Let them eat cake," said Julio.

Imaculada slapped him playfully.

"That's my line."

She restruck her regal air and looked down her nose at Edmundo.

"So, what do you think?"

"I think if Marie-Antoinette had looked like you, they never would have dared to touch her."

"Really. How perceptive of you to say so."

"And me?" said Julio, acting neglected. "What do I look like, a livery man?"

"Not at all. Like a king, a true king."

It was good to see them so happy again, even if it was just for a moment, even if it were false and superficial. "The capacity for joy has not died in them," Edmundo thought. "Perhaps it is foolish of them to be carried away by a ball, perhaps it shows that they lack *gravitas*. But I love them for it. Even now they have moments in which the joy, the joy of worldly things, bursts forth from them."

As foolish as it was to wear a silly costume, he regretted that he wasn't going with them.

Just then they brought out of hiding a third costume, which they had been keeping for him all this time. A bright and outlandish musketeer, right out of Dumas *père*!

"But really! I couldn't. Besides, what if it doesn't fit?"

"Hurry and put it on or we'll all be late!"

He rushed to his room with childlike excitement and when he was finished he looked at himself in the mirror. He was afraid he looked quite ridiculous. What was he to do with his spectacles? If he took them off he wouldn't be able to see: not only would he feel uncomfortable, but he would see nothing of Imaculada all evening. He decided to wear them.

He went sheepishly in to display himself. They giggled with delight.

"Le Chevalier de Caçador!" exclaimed Julio.

"No, no," said Imaculada, "he is my Cyrano de Bergerac."

Edmundo looked at her questioningly.

"Is my nose that big?"

"No, Edmundo," she said, smiling tenderly, "I was speaking of your heart."

She had never said anything like that to him before.

"I want to tell you something," said Edmundo. "I don't deserve friends like the two of you. But I am forever grateful for everything you've done for me. I feel closer to you than I do to anyone else in the world."

And she kissed him once again on the cheek.

"But the glasses must come off!" she said and reached up to remove them.

"No, really. I'm quite blind without them and I become quite nervous."

"Just for one night. We will guide you everywhere. You'll be in good hands."

And he consented to let her slip them up from behind his ears, gently fold them in her hands, and slide them delicately into his pocket.

As they rode in the open carriage through the warm and festive evening, Edmundo could hear music and laughter coming from the dark blurred streets around him. Blind, disoriented, joyous, he felt as if he were being carried away in a dream.

They took him by the arms and led him up the stairs into the great bright palace. He could see nothing but shapes and movement; the figures who passed close by had the vagueness of an Impressionist painting. He could feel Imaculada's hand in the crook of his elbow and hear the floor swept beneath her dress.

Many people came up to greet them, and soon Imaculada's dance card was filled, but the first dance was for Edmundo. The rest of the world slipped away into mist, and there were just the two of them, together. This was the moment he had longed for, this was the moment that all his life had mysteriously and unexpectedly but inexorably led him to. Nothing else mattered except in its relationship to her. He was almost trembling. He wanted her, and feared her, and she was like water or air in his hands, and he felt how impossible it would ever be for him to possess her as something human and familiar and mundane. Every moment, even as he held her, her spirit was slipping away from him. This was all he could ever hope for, her partial passing presence, but even this was so wonderful that it was almost enough.

When the music stopped and they stood facing each other in their costumes, he felt the outside world stumble in between them and knew he would never be able to speak to her from his hidden heart.

While she danced with others, he was silent. Although he couldn't see her, he observed her, observed her when she was taken away onto the dance floor, imagined her talking and laughing, and caught his breath when she appeared again out of the chaos and stood near him. He could tell that she was happy, excitedly happy, but not because of him. He was just an accessory to her joy.

Even Julio was happy: dancing and laughing, half the time away somewhere across the room. It was at such a moment that someone dressed as Napoleon stepped up before Imaculada and bowed to her.

"You have promised this dance to Lieutenant Cortazar, but he has been called away. He has allowed me to beg of you that you give me the honour of taking his place."

Edmundo knew, though he could not see, by the voice and the carriage and turbulence in Imaculada's heart, which he could feel as surely as he could feel his own, that it was de Bettencourt.

He felt everything she felt: the hesitation between longing and horror, the questioning, the chaos opening before her, the cruel inscrutability of de Bettencourt's expression, the sudden presence of fate. He didn't want her to go with this man, but he knew she would. She disappeared with him.

He needed his eyeglasses. He had to see her. He fumbled for them, and slipped them on. The room came clear before him. There she was. De Bettencourt was talking to her, casually, easily. She was smiling, but her smile was strained and alarmed.

What if Julio saw? Edmundo looked around quickly and saw him. He had seen. He was staring at them.

The dance was anxiously long, and Edmundo was afraid that Julio—or one of them—would do something rash. But when it was over de Bettencourt brought her back, bowed to her, and went away.

"You're wearing your eyeglasses," she said distractedly.

"Yes."

Once again, he realized, he had been mistaken about her inner life. Her hope was not dead; it was as acute and painful and unrealistic as ever before. It was just such a hope that swelled inside himself.

"She's strong and stubborn enough to go on this way," Edmundo thought. "So am I, no matter how painful and wearying. But what of Julio? He was made to be happy. How will he live with her sadness?"

Time passed almost unobserved. For a vague period Julio seemed to have disappeared, but then he was there again, calm, strongly and strangely calm.

"How are we all?" he asked. "Everyone enjoying themselves?"

Imaculada danced with the partners she had written down on her card, smiling at them automatically as they led her away. While she was dancing, Julio leaned close to Edmundo and spoke to him quietly.

"I have challenged de Bettencourt to a duel."

"What!" Edmundo laughed.

"Will you be my second?"

"Julio, this is madness!"

"You won't be able to dissuade me. I ask you as my dearest friend to be my second."

"But why?"

"You know why. Must I ask someone else?"

"No, don't."

"Then you agree?"

"Let me think."

"There isn't much time."

Imaculada's partner was leading her back.

"We'll talk later," said Julio quickly. "Don't tell my sister." And he hurried away.

Imaculada came and stood beside him.

"Are you enjoying yourself?" she asked him.

"It's marvelous."

He looked at Julio in the distance. He didn't know what to think, what to do, how seriously to take this business. It was not surprising, in retrospect, that Julio would do something like this, but it was hard to imagine that he would have the bleak strength of will to carry it through to the end. Edmundo wondered whether to speak to

Imaculada, but he decided against it. First he would talk to Julio and see if he could reason with him.

They were there another hour. Edmundo saw de Bettencourt leave. He watched Imaculada, and knew she saw too. Shortly thereafter Julio came back to them.

"I feel tired suddenly," he said. "Shall we leave soon or would you two rather we stay?"

No one objected to leaving. Imaculada made apologies to those she hadn't yet danced with.

In the carriage everyone was silent. Carlos drove on through the warm, unquiet night. The brother and sister seemed to hear nothing, they were so closed in their own thoughts. Edmundo alone heard the obtrusive revelry. It made him feel alone, like a child abandoned by his playmates.

Carlos let them out and went to put the horses away. Imaculada went up to her room and Edmundo met Julio in the turret.

Julio offered Edmundo cognac and a cigar and after Edmundo declined he poured out a glass for himself and began to smoke. Both men were silent until Julio sat down on the sofa.

"Well, have you decided? Will you be my second?"

"I have decided to talk you out of this."

"You won't be able to, I told you that already. You know, Edmundo, I am stronger than you realize. You think I'm rather weak—no need to deny it, everyone does. It's the way I present myself. But I'm not weak."

"If I did, I certainly never thought you mad. It seems I was wrong on both counts."

"Perhaps."

"Do you know anything about shooting?"

"No. Do you?"

"I'm afraid I make as poor a second as you do a duelist."

"How fitting."

"Not at all. Be serious for a moment. De Bettencourt is a soldier.

They know all about these things. You're no match for him."

"No, I'm not. Neither is my sister."

"Ahh!" said Edmundo in exasperation. "If you're doing this for her, I don't see what good it does."

"Edmundo, please enough. My mind is made up. I need a good night's sleep. So answer me, yes or no. Will you be my second? If not, I will have to find someone else."

Edmundo sighed.

"Very well. What am I supposed to do?"

"Thank you. I realize that this is painful for you, and I appreciate how great your friendship for me must be. I do not ask you in order to hurt you, but because I love you. You must go back to the ball and make arrangements with de Bettencourt's second. His name is Cortazar, Lieutenant Cortazar. He is expecting you."

Edmundo looked at him. They were both still wearing their costumes and Julio's wig was slightly askew.

"Very well."

He had decided to tell Imaculada. She had to know, even if there was nothing she could do. When he left Julio, he went down the stairs and quietly to her door. He knocked gently.

She opened the door and looked out at him. She had put on her nightgown and let her long thick hair fall free.

"Edmundo, what is it?"

"I must talk to you."

"Now?"

"Yes. I don't wish to compromise you, but you must let me in."

She knew he was in earnest and she let him in and closed the door behind him.

"I'll come straight to the point. Julio has challenged de Bettencourt to a duel."

"But he can't be serious!"

"I'm afraid he's quite serious. At first I thought he had merely lost control of himself and would soon see reason, but I've tried to talk him out of it and I've gotten nowhere."

"Well then I'll talk to him."

"No, he told me not to tell you. If he finds out it will make him angry and harder to reason with."

"Then we must talk to Marco."

It hurt to hear her call de Bettencourt by his first name.

"I will go to him," she said.

"No." He was almost angry with her. "Do you realize how that would compromise you? Julio would have every reason to demand satisfaction. If anyone is to speak with de Bettencourt it must be me."

"Yes, of course."

"I have agreed to act as Julio's second. I am to go back to the ball and speak to de Bettencourt's second. I'll insist I call on him and beg him to withdraw. You believe he will?"

"He must."

"We shall see."

She paced impatiently before him.

"Why has Julio done this?"

"He feels he has no choice. You know he's been troubled for a long time."

"Yes, but I never thought it would come to this. You must stop it! Promise me you'll do everything you can."

"Of course I will. Even if you hadn't asked me."

"Yes. Forgive me."

"I have tremendous affection for your family. I can think of no higher duty than to see that no harm comes to any of you."

She was only half listening to him now. He started to walk to the door.

"I will call on you when I get back."

"Yes, the moment you return."

From her room he went to knock on Carlos' door, but there was no answer. He knocked a second time and then went in. The bed was empty; no one had slept in it. He sought out Gilberto's room.

Gilberto opened the door and stood before him in his nightshirt. He had a startled look in his eyes from being suddenly awakened and he looked timidly at the musketeer who had disturbed him.

"I must go out again," said Edmundo. "I can't find Carlos."

Gilberto's wife, Graça, had appeared behind him in the door way, peering out from the darkness. Neither of them spoke.

"Do you know where Carlos is?" Edmundo asked.

"Forgive him, Senhor Edmundo," said Graça, but Gilberto turned on her to make her hush.

"I will get him for you, Senhor Edmundo," said Gilberto. "Carlos is a good servant. He will come right away. He doesn't want any trouble." And he hurried away nervously.

Graça stood hesitantly in the doorway, then slowly closed the door, as if afraid to offend Edmundo. But she didn't shut it all the way and when her husband had disappeared around the corner, she opened it again.

"Forgive him, Senhor Edmundo," she said. "Please don't tell the master. He is young and she is such a pretty woman, with her blonde hair and white skin."

Edmundo looked at her. He was angry with her, although he knew he had no reason to be.

"This doesn't concern me," he said curtly. "Go back to bed." And the timid old woman obeyed him.

In a few minutes Gilberto returned with Carlos. Carlos had in his eyes a certain fear, and a certain defiance. He said nothing.

"I must go back to the Catete Palace," Edmundo said.

Carlos looked at him then nodded.

"Yes, Senhor Edmundo, very well. I will get the carriage."

Edmundo went out into the moonlight to wait. The air was warm and clear and thin. He could hear noises coming from the sibilant distance and near by the rustling of leaves and things creaking gently in the breeze.

This latest episode had irritated him beyond its importance. He would rather not have known that Carlos had begun to spend his nights with a fair blonde woman—who could only be Nanette. He would rather not have been concerned with this distasteful, petty lust, this commonplace betrayal of master by servant, which drew him in and made of him either accomplice or stoolpigeon. There was too much on his mind already, and this only made his thoughts muddier and baser. When Carlos brought the carriage around, Edmundo climbed in without speaking.

They rode through the city, which was still unnatural with revelry. Once Carlos had to rein in the team when someone jumped out suddenly in front of them. Once Edmundo saw someone looking at him from behind a strange African mask.

At the ball Edmundo sought out Lieutenant Cortazar. He was a pudgy, pompous young man with slow, sleepy eyes. He was dressed as Pierrot.

"How do you do," said Cortazar. "You have come to make arrangements for your man?"

"Yes."

"Are you familiar with the English rules of dueling?"

"No."

"You should be. As a second it's your duty to stand up for your man's rights."

"Which are?"

"As the challenged party, my man has choice of ground and time of meeting. He has instructed me to inform you that he will be on the beach at Copacabana tomorrow morning at five thirty. I assume that is acceptable."

"Yes, I suppose."

"You suppose? Either it is or it isn't."

"I said it was."

"Alright then. Do you have pistols?"

"No, I don't believe so."

"Well, can you get some?"

"I don't know. I'll have to ask Julio."

"I have some. We can use mine, if you suppose that would be acceptable. But you should try to bring some anyway. It is customary to have a second set."

"I'll see what I can do."

"Don't strain yourself. You will of course want to bring a doctor."

"Yes, of course, I hadn't thought of that."

The lieutenant laughed derisively. "Shots will be fired, my friend, someone may very well be hurt."

"I'm quite aware of that. Is there anything else?"

"Your man has the choice of distance, depending on how serious he sees the matter."

"I see. Anything else?"

"As seconds, we have a duty to attempt a reconciliation."

"Yes. I want to speak to de Bettencourt."

The lieutenant laughed again.

"That is quite out of the question. I am his second; you should talk to me."

"I'm afraid that's not good enough. Where is de Bettencourt? I insist on speaking with him."

"He has retired for the night."

"I want his address."

The lieutenant hesitated, then in a huff asked for a pen and wrote the address on a slip of paper.

"This is highly irregular," he said, handing the paper to Edmundo. "Obviously you have never been a soldier. You lack the necessary discipline."

"No doubt."

"*À demain*," said the lieutenant, with a brief, cocky bow.

"*J'espère que non*," said Edmundo and strode away.

When he stepped into the carriage he handed Carlos the slip of paper, then sat down silently. He wished that he could have been spared this duty. He wished that he were asleep in his bed. He knew, but he found it hard to feel, that he was engaged in a task of the gravest importance.

Carlos took him to a large, dark, silent house. Edmundo removed his wig and stepped down into the street. He waited a long time for someone to come to the door. He said he had urgent business with Lieutenant de Bettencourt and gave his name. The old man went away suspiciously, closing the door behind him. When he returned, he took Edmundo inside and guided him through the dark house to a small room on the third floor. De Bettencourt had thrown on some clothes and was sitting waiting, smoking a cigarette. He motioned Edmundo to sit down and sent the old man off to bed.

"Senhor Caçador, how are you? Forgive me for entertaining you in such a bleak little room, but I must keep this business from my mother. Can I get you a brandy? A cigar?"

"No, nothing."

"I assume you've come on behalf of Julio Xisto? You are his second?"

"Yes."

"You've spoken with Lieutenant Cortazar?"

"Yes."

"Is something wrong? Something doesn't suit you?"

"I have no complaints."

"Good. Then may I ask what brings you here?"

"I've come to ask you not to take part in this duel."

De Bettencourt took a long drag of his cigarette.

"I see. What exactly do you propose for me to do?"

"Not show up."

"And what of your friend? Does he intend to show up?"

"Yes."

"And you ask me not to?"

"Yes. I appeal to your reason. Nothing good can come of this. No purpose will be served. What can it hurt you to refuse to take part?"

"But there is the question of my honour, is there not?"

"You are the better marksman. I don't see how anyone could question your courage. You would be bringing more honour upon yourself by avoiding bloodshed."

De Bettencourt laughed, but not unkindly.

"I'm afraid that is not how one's honour is judged. People would not see the situation as you do. You are a reasonable man, a good man, a man with progressive ideas. I admire that in you. No, really, I do. Under different circumstances we might have been friends. But with all your reason, you must see the position I am in. I am a soldier and a gentleman. Certain things are expected of me. One cannot always act as one pleases, or as one may think best. You are an idealist, perhaps, and I may sound cowardly and false to you. But in your own life, if you search hard enough, I am certain that you too have done just as I have done."

De Bettencourt lit another cigarette.

"This entire affair is most unfortunate, almost ridiculous, I'll admit. I even accept part of the blame. It was foolish to ask her to dance, but I thought it a harmless gesture."

"Perhaps not so harmless."

"No, perhaps not. But was it ill-intentioned? I cannot say to myself that it was. Under other circumstances nothing would have come of it. But as I say, it is an unfortunate situation."

"Not for you alone."

"No, not for me alone. No doubt you have heard talk of me, from your friend, and you disapprove of what I have done. I am not without guilt, but who is? I made no promises, I broke no vows, I did nothing dishonourable. If I have done anything harmful, it was only in trying to extricate myself from the situation. And believe me, I have been as gentle as it was possible to be. Let me be quite frank with you, Senhor. The girl is most charming. I was quite fond of her. Inasmuch as I am capable of love, I loved her. I have no reason to want to hurt her. I have no quarrel with her family. But I made no proposal of marriage to her. I have ambitions. I am young. I consider myself intelligent. No doubt you yourself have things you wish to achieve. We all do. We are men of talent, you and I. You think I am flattering you, but I can tell by the way you carry yourself that you have something upstairs, something extra. So anyway, such a marriage would have ruined me. I have nothing against the girl. But I must think of my future. Under different circumstances, who knows?"

"Her father has money. He would have helped you."

"Ah, Monsieur, I am not a seller of coffee! What is money to me? I am a soldier. A gentleman. I don't intend to spend my life peering into account books. There are greater tasks in the world. Don't you think?"

Edmundo looked at him, and couldn't hate him. "This man is no better or worse than I am," he was thinking. "Perhaps he is more certain of himself, less plagued by doubt, handsomer, more graceful, in some ways more courageous, in some ways less so; perhaps his conscience is slightly more indelicate, but all in all he has done no worse than I have done. It is wrong of Julio to hate him. But is it any less possible for Julio not to hate him than for her not to love him, or for me not to love her? Fate has driven us all to this. I look at him and wonder what she loves in him? Is it his looks, his bearing, his aristocratic air? Does she love something she only imagines him to be? Or does she see him as I see him and yet still love him? Why does she love him and not me?"

Edmundo suddenly realized he had sat in silence for some time.

"She still loves you," Edmundo said.

De Bettencourt's eyes became sad and almost watery.

"Does she? Did she tell you that?"

"She didn't have to."

"Well, I am sorry for her then. Under different circumstances. I am not a scoundrel. It hurts me to be taken for one. I really have no desire to harm her brother. Tell him I regret having offended him and offer my sincerest apologies. If that satisfies him we can call this whole thing off. You must realize that an apology from me is no small thing. But unless you send word that he accepts my offer, it will be necessary for me to show up in the morning as arranged and go through with this business."

"Thank you. I am hopeful that your apology will suffice."

Edmundo had gotten all he could expect from coming here and stood to go.

"Tell me, Senhor," asked de Bettencourt, "you are more than a friend to her, are you not?"

Edmundo was caught off-guard and didn't know how to answer.

"Anyway. I wish you all well. You know, we might have been friends. It would have made me happy to have a friend like you. But perhaps some things are not meant to be. In any case, it is very late, and I have nothing more to say."

As he rode home, Edmundo felt a need to say something to Carlos.

"Carlos," he said, "I don't approve of what you have done and I would advise you to leave the woman alone; but although Dom Ernesto is my friend, I don't intend to say anything to him in this regard. It would only pain him more. So don't worry. But I must tell you I am profoundly displeased with you. When we get home I advise you to go back to your own bed and get a good night's sleep."

Carlos didn't speak for a few moments. Then he said, "Thank you, Senhor," and that was all.

Edmundo went to Julio's room and woke him.

"I have taken the liberty of visiting de Bettencourt," he said. "He has offered his regrets and made his apology. So now there is no need to go through with this."

Julio sat on the edge of his bed. He said nothing for a moment, and then he spoke.

"I am sorry you have troubled yourself in this way, without my approval, and disturbed my sleep for nothing. There will be a duel."

"Why? What do you want? The man has apologized."

"Yes, and that makes everything right, does it?"

"What else can he do?"

"Nothing. It is too late for everything. There will be a duel."

"Julio, you are my friend, but I must tell you, you are in the wrong now. He has been generous in this."

"Oh yes, it must be quite humiliating for him to apologize to a mulatto. You see that is the essence of this affair, its *raison d'être*. 'Come now, Julinho,' you say. 'The lieutenant has apologized to you. No matter that he thinks your sister unworthy of himself, you should be thankful that he treated her almost as fairly as he would have treated a white woman. Really Julio, do you expect the lieutenant to take this duel seriously, with you? Whose mother was a slave? You, an empty-headed, bright-smiled, dark-skinned dandy? We have received you into society out of the goodness of our hearts, but don't presume that we really think of you as an equal.' Isn't that what I should be thinking, my friend?"

"You know I have never thought those things, Julio. There is no one I love and respect more than you and your sister."

"Forgive me. You are not my enemy."

"De Bettencourt is not your enemy either."

"But you see I have no choice but to treat him as such. Because I can no longer go on without an enemy to face. It could have been another. It could have been the one who took my mother when she was twelve years old and gave her syphilis. It could have been one of those who laughed at my father for marrying her. It could have been one of the thousands who have talked behind our backs, or slighted us in the street without even knowing us. It could have been almost anyone in Brazil. But de Bettencourt is the handiest."

"I didn't know about your mother."

"No, we keep our dark secrets hidden away, you see. We are supposed to smile all the time, in light of our good fortune. But I can't smile for them any longer."

"What good will this do?"

"I want to be a man of honour on their terms. They might respect that."

"But he will likely kill you."

"*Tant pis*! My life is not important to me anymore. The gesture is the only thing. Perhaps it is trivial, even ridiculous, but it is all that I am capable of. I would like to be a black stain on the lieutenant's conscience."

"And what of your sister? She will suffer more than he does. Do you realize that she still loves him?"

"Yes, of course, I realize it! She is a woman. Women have no pride. She doesn't care what her humiliation does to me. She loves him for despising her, for mocking her. She has played right into their hands. She does his suffering for him. She would prefer that I leave things as they are. She is like the slaves who rail against their own emancipation. It is most ironic, don't you think? Well, I've had enough. I won't allow her to go on enslaving herself."

"You will be dead, and she won't be any freer than she was before."

"Probably."

"I have spoken to her and told her of the duel."

"I wish you hadn't, but I suppose you did what you thought best."

"If you insist on going through with this, I will go to her immediately and talk with her again."

"I respect you for that, but I won't change my mind. Are you still my second, or must I replace you?"

"I'll be your second, if only to have more time to dissuade you."

"Good. Did you see his second?"

"Yes. He said we should bring a set of pistols and a doctor."

"A doctor I won't need. As for the pistols, I believe João da Silva has a pair. Do you remember João?"

"Yes."

"Marvelous fellow. Tell me, have the time and place been set?"

"Yes."

"So…?"

"Maybe I shouldn't tell you."

"If you don't, I'll just have to go ask Cortazar myself and find another second."

"Copacabana. This morning at five thirty."

"That sounds alright. What do you think?"

"I think this is madness."

"I don't believe it is. But anyway, I must get another hour's sleep, and you must run to my sister, mustn't you?"

"Yes."

"Anything else?"

"Nothing that I haven't said already."

Julio said one last thing: "Don't be so glum; maybe I will shoot him."

Imaculada had been lying in bed awake and had had plenty of time to consider the gravity of the situation and work herself into a state of high tension. Edmundo could see the anxiety in her eyes.

"Did you see Marco?" she asked.

"Yes."

"And what did he say?"

"He agreed to offer his apology. But Julio won't accept it."

"What do you mean? You've talked to Julio?"

"Yes. He refuses to call off the duel. He wants to die."

"We can't let him do this!"

"There is nothing else I can do. I've spoken to them both. There is an impasse. There is no way to bridge it."

"Then I must speak to him. He will listen to me. Don't you think?"

"I think you must speak to him, but I don't think he will listen to you."

He followed as she rushed to Julio's room. Julio opened the door and let them in. He sat on his bed and Imaculada sat down in a chair with a show of prim calmness. Edmundo stood near the door

"So, Julinho, what's this I hear?" she said in her haughtiest, falsest manner.

That, in spite of everything, almost made Edmundo laugh.

"I don't know," said Julio. "What is it you hear?"

"I've heard that you've challenged Lieutenant de Bettencourt to a duel, and when he offered to apologize, you refused his regrets."

"That's more or less the size of it, yes."

"Well, that's a bit ridiculous, don't you think?"

"Most ridiculous."

"Then what do you intend to do about it?"

"Nothing."

She lost her composure and stood up to raise her voice at him.

"Nothing! I haven't asked you to defend my honour. Frankly I don't feel that my honour needs defending. If anyone has made me appear ridiculous it's you. There's not going to be a duel."

"Please, don't yell at me, I am very tired."

"But I must yell at you! You are acting like a madman, or a baby. I won't allow you to go through with this! I'll tell Carlos not to let you out of the house!"

"Carlos will do what I tell him to do."

"Then I will stop you myself."

"How will you do that? With words?"

"I will get a knife! I will get a gun! I will shoot you if I have to!" She had lost control of herself. "I won't let you kill him!"

When she realized what she had said she stopped suddenly and looked at Julio, then at Edmundo. There was a look of shock and shame in her face, but Edmundo couldn't hate her, for he knew that it was true, that she would rather have killed her brother than let de Bettencourt be harmed, and he knew that there was nothing she could have done to make herself feel differently.

Julio looked at her too, as if he wanted to hit her.

"You've said enough," he said, barely controlling himself. "Go back to your room."

She stood looking at him for a long moment, deciding. Then she rose, and turned with her head bowed, speaking softly before she went out the door.

"Forgive me, dear Julio, as I forgive you."

There was silence for a long time. When Carlos arrived home with the pistols, it was time to go.

It was just before dawn. There were still remnants of revelry in the streets, but slow and heavy. They didn't speak to each other until they were well on their way.

"Edmundo, have you ever been with a prostitute?" Julio asked.

"Yes, of course."

"Didn't you find it a distasteful experience?"

"Once I was with a gypsy, and it wasn't bad."

"I always found it distasteful. I've only been when my friends insisted that I accompany them. Really, you know, women don't fascinate me so much. Do they fascinate you?"

"Yes. Sometimes the feeling overwhelms me completely."

"Does it? I think they are distasteful creatures. No good comes of them. But you don't agree?"

"No."

"I think they are distasteful creatures."

They were silent again for a moment, then Edmundo asked, "What should I tell your father if anything happens to you?"

Julio thought and said, "Nothing; there's nothing to say."

The beach was a dumping ground for garbage, and there was a stench in the morning air. The sea was calm and blue. De Bettencourt was already there with his second. There was a physician with them, but he remained at a discreet distance.

Just before they stepped down out of the carriage, Edmundo asked Julio one last time if he wouldn't change his mind, and Julio said no.

The parties bowed to each other curtly.

"You haven't brought a doctor with you?" asked Lieutenant Cortazar.

"No," said Julio.

The lieutenant laughed his mocking laugh, and said, "You're very confident, Senhor."

"It is my understanding," said Julio, "that it is my right to choose the distance from which we will shoot."

"That is correct."

"And the minimum acceptable distance is?"

"Ten paces, but I hardly think that advisable."

"Ten paces it is."

Cortazar laughed and looked at de Bettencourt, who was alarmed and uncomfortable. De Bettencourt spoke to Julio.

"I should tell you that I intended to fire my pistol into the air, but at ten paces I will be forced to treat this as a serious matter."

"By all means, it is a most serious matter, and I advise you to take it as one. I should also tell you that if neither of us is hit on the first shots, I intend to demand that we fire again, and again after that if necessary."

Cortazar laughed again.

Then he took Edmundo aside to load the pistols.

"Everything is acceptable?" he asked when he was finished.

"If you think so," said Edmundo. "You know more about this than I do."

"You and your friend come here and demand to shoot at ten paces, and yet you don't bring a doctor and don't even know how to load a pistol. You realize this is almost insulting to men in our position."

"That really doesn't concern me right now."

Julio and de Bettencourt were stood back to back on the sand and given their weapons.

"Do you want to give the order to fire?" Cortazar asked Edmundo.

"I'd rather not."

Cortazar called out and the two men began walking away from each other. They took ten slow even steps, then stopped and turned to face each other. Edmundo's eyes shifted back and forth between them, as if (the thought slipped through his mind) he were about to watch a tennis match.

"Fire!"

Chapter Six

Marina was on edge the whole time aboard the ship. She kept her young son very close to her. Julio was small for his age, almost puny, and cradled himself against his mother's body when they lay in their berth. She whispered him to sleep and, hours later, awake:

"We're going to see your brother. Yes, my darling, we're going to be a family. You'll be so happy!"

Then she would bury her face in his soft hair which smelled of soap and feel the anguish in her heart. She never let him see her face in those moments but soothed the little boy with plans for the future.

"Your brother will play with you and look after you, won't that be nice? You'll have a new father."

Julio's huge soft brown eyes studied his mother's face. He was full of questions he didn't know how to ask.

"One more thing, Julinho: from now on when anyone asks how old you are, you must tell them you are six, not five."

"Why?"

"Because no one will like you if you are only five. You must be a big boy and be six."

"Why won't anyone like me if I'm five?"

"That's just the way it is, *querido*. You must do as I tell you. How old are you?"

"Six?"

"Not five?"

"Six."

She rewarded him with a birthday party in the dining hall; the women kissed him, and the men shook his hand, and there was a cake made of chocolate and candy.

While Julio slept in her arms, Marina's heart was filled with anticipation and longing for the son she had not seen in six years. Gabriel, she said the name softly to herself, although she had always secretly wished that he had been named after her own father and not Manuel's. She kept the letter and photograph of a young boy she no longer recognized pinned to her undergarment close to her bosom. When Julio lay softly sleeping she would pull out the letter, moist with her warmth, and read it to reassure her troubled heart:

Querida Marina,

You'll probably be surprised to hear from me. It has been more than six years since Gabriel and I left Brazil for the United States. You would be proud to see our son. He has grown tall and handsome. I am sending you a photograph for you to see for yourself.

I decided to come back to my island of São Miguel because I didn't like life in America and Gabriel needs a family. My father asked me to write you to ask if you would consider joining us in São Miguel. I know that it was wrong to leave you and to take Gabriel, but I believed that it was best for him to be with me. I still think it was good for him to go to America with me. He's learned to take care of himself and to be a man. I ask you to forgive me and I hope you consider coming here, not for me, but for the sake of our son.

I did not save much money when I was in the United States. I do not have a house or land here. Gabriel and I are living in my father's house. If, God willing, you decide to come, you'll need to bring money. We could buy land and build a house. You know I'm a hard worker and would do my best, especially when I have Gabriel's future to think about.

I hope this letter finds you in good health and that you'll consider coming to São Miguel to reunite with Gabriel.

   Your husband,
   Manuel

Near São Paulo, Brazil, 1907

Early on Marina had been anxious to know about the world and the life he had come from, and Manuel had been charmed that she was interested. He told her how he worked another man's land with his father from dawn till nightfall, how they cut and ploughed and cleared the fields. It was very hard work and often by midday they were already dead tired but they always carried on and finished out the day.

"Farm work is the same everywhere," Manuel had told her.

"But it's different when you're the *patrão*, isn't it?"

It was in the spring, when they manured the fields, scattering the moist, heavy dung by hand from a burlap pouch hanging from the cord that kept up their pants, and Manuel was preparing to leave. At dusk, as they walked home, Gabriel and Manuel walked in a procession of men who lived in their village. The dirt road rose and dropped, giving the men glimpses of the grey Atlantic that stretched in all directions.

Manuel was immigrating to Brazil in a few weeks. The other men were sceptical about his plans.

"You'll be back in a year," they jeered.

"Never!" insisted Manuel.

His mother was clearly heartbroken at her son's imminent departure, but Manuel was not to be dissuaded. Wages and dignity were next to nothing on the island, and he was bound to prosper in a big country like Brazil. Some day he might come back home, triumphant, with money in his pockets, and he would build a big house, but not for a long time.

When they arrived home, the house smelled of grilled fish and boiled potatoes. Father and son washed their hands in the fountain outside. Berta Aguiar had warmed up the week-old corn bread and sliced it into thick pieces. Manuel loved the bread.

"You'll have to come back soon so I can cook your favourite meals for you," his mother said.

"Hmm," was all Manuel said.

They ate in the small, dark kitchen, lit by a candle. There were no windows, only a door that opened onto the yard.

"I finished knitting you a sweater, Manuel, a nice red one," Berta smiled at her son.

"It's hot in Brazil," he told her.

"It must get cool in the evenings," she said in a disappointed voice.

Manuel turned to his father.

"I should be able to get work all year round." He always gave work and money as his reasons for leaving the island. He never talked about feeling humiliated and suffocated in such a small place. There was also a certain disgust.

"I won't end up like him," he promised himself, looking at his father's tired face in the candlelight. "Old and finished at fifty. Working until I die, collapsing in a pile of shit."

On the boat over, Manuel slept below deck in a cramped space where the moneyless men were hoarded. Although he had lived his entire life on an island, he had never been on a boat before. At night the hum and clank of the engine and the creaking of the hull were so different from the living night sounds of his home.

In São Paulo, he stayed in a cheap boarding house. Most of the men staying there were Portuguese, but in the streets he saw blacks and mulattos and Indians! He had enough money to last him a few weeks if he was careful but he wanted to find work before it was all gone. He hoped to stay in the city but he wasn't able to find a position: when it came out that he had always only done farm work, he was told that's what he should be looking for. He didn't want to work on a farm—that's not why he had come thousands of miles— but finally when he heard the foreman of a farm 100 kilometres inland was looking for help he decided to take it and save money until he found something in the city.

Manuel was pleasantly surprised when the foreman offered him three times the amount he made back home. It was a good start. The farm was a strange place: he saw no sign of an owner, just the foreman and a teenage boy, who worked with the hired help but took his meals and slept in the farmhouse. The only other people he noticed in the farmhouse were a fair-haired middle-aged woman and a young girl with long black hair billowing about her like waves. She wore a man's white shirt over a black skirt. Manuel couldn't help looking at her, not only because she was pretty, but because she looked nothing like the women in his home village. He often found himself looking for the young woman, especially after he learned from the other workers that she was the owner of the farm. That was Marina.

She noticed him as he noticed her. First, it wasn't as if new people came to the farm all that often. Then, of course, he was exceedingly handsome—fair and almost pretty like a woman.

One day she was wandering by when he was speaking with the foreman and she stopped to listen to his strange accent.

"Where are you from?" she asked. Maybe that was too bold but she knew no better growing up around here.

"From the Azores, Menina. The island of São Miguel.

"You don't say! The poet Antero de Quental was born there. My father loved his poetry. He met him once."

He could read and write but he had no idea who this Antero de Quental was and he had never read poetry.

"What is your island like? Is it like here?"

"No, Menina. It's a small place. In my village you can see the sea from almost everywhere."

"Is that so? Antero wrote about the sea. Maybe someday I'll visit your island and then I'll understand his poetry better than I do now. My father was Portuguese, from Porto; I would like to see his birthplace. If my grandparents were still alive I would go there."

He had been told that her father was mad and had been murdered.

His lips opened in a thin smile but he continued to gaze at her with an almost insolent, stare. Did she believe that even with money a woman could travel by herself? It wasn't just São Miguel that she didn't know anything about, she didn't know the world.

"Is that young man Menina's brother?" he asked, curious to know what the relationship between her and Armando was.

"No," she laughed in a voice that bubbled like sweet water. "Armando's not my brother, although I think of him like one. He and his mother, Dona Nanette, have lived with my family all my life. They are my family."

Manuel nodded but his nostrils flared as if he already knew that he yielded some power over her.

She found herself looking for him. It was easy to spot him: the cocky self-confidence in the way he moved and held himself. When he walked, his hips swayed slightly, as if carried by a breeze, but there was strength in his step as well. The sight of him excited her. At night she lay in bed imagining him before her and she was as joyful as when she was a little girl and couldn't wait to see her father the next day. Papai always had the most wonderful ideas and she couldn't wait to hear what he had to say or find out what book he had chosen for her to read. Even when he was sick her father had filled her heart with excitement about the world. Papai had loved her completely. Marina missed him so. She was fond of Nanette but had always felt a little distant from her. Nanette's great love was Armando, whom she protected like a mother bear with her cub, keeping him close and everyone else at a distance. Even Marina. As if Marina would ever hurt Armando! After Papai, Marina loved him most. She had known him her whole life, and except for the one episode, she had always felt safe and protected by him. She didn't like to think about that episode because it was jumbled with Papai's death, a time of dark memories.

Marina liked to walk the fields around the farmhouse in the evenings, when the nights were alive with the sounds of nocturnal creatures and the men were at the café in town; Nanette sat with Armando going over the day's work. It was Nanette's time to claim her son. Marina understood this and often stayed out late until she knew they had gone to bed. One night she was on her way back to the farmhouse when she heard light steps coming towards her on the dirt road. Her heart fluttered like a moth exposed to light and she held herself still as the steps drew near, anxious to see Manuel, for she knew it must be him. No one else walked as if he so owned the ground beneath his feet.

He was startled to see her.

"*Boa noite*, Menina. Has something happened?"

"*Boa noite*, Manuel. Everything's fine. I'm just taking my nightly walk. Would you like to join me?" She hid her delight in the darkness.

"Shouldn't a young girl be at home at this late hour?"

"I'm always out and about at night. What could happen to me around here?"

Manuel blew his cigarette smoke into miniature clouds around them.

The smoke tickled her nostrils.

"Can I have a drag of your cigarette?"

"Menina smokes?" His voice was sharp.

"No. But I want to try it," she laughed.

He handed her the cigarette, pointing the lit end towards his face and revealing a look of disapproval.

She sucked in and blew out a hot little puff of smoke as they wandered into the long grass. She felt a child's excitement. She handed him back the cigarette still lit, but he stamped it out with his foot. Manuel's hand on her wrist felt tight and sharp but she gave herself to his force and fell into a hollow of dry grass. She didn't know what was going to happen, only that he was in control of her body, and she welcomed the pressure and warmth of his hands and fingers and the new, unknown pleasure. He kissed her on the lips and then deep into her mouth and he tasted like sweet, soft, smoky fruit. He pulled up her skirt and she could feel the cool night air on her bare legs. He moved quickly and forcefully. Suddenly she felt his heavy penis rubbing her softest flesh and then rubbing against her moist insides while she moaned with delight like one of the small farm cats. Soon he was pulsing inside her.

He slipped off her and rolled over onto the grass, their shoulders not touching. They lay still, staring up at the star-bedecked sky. After a while he leaned over and started to kiss her again. This time she returned his kiss, her tongue flicking inside his mouth, her fingers digging deep into his back as he stroked her belly. She opened her legs and swung them around his buttocks, steadying him. He responded with firm caressing. When she began to moan he thrust himself deep and hard inside her. She moaned longer and longer and her fingers scraped the bones of his spine. Then he came again. This time he rolled off her but not before she had kissed him on the cheek. He stood up and walked a few feet away from where she lay, as if he were embarrassed by her nakedness, as if they were no more than strangers.

Four months later Marina told Nanette she was pregnant. Then she told Manuel.

"Are you sure, Menina?"

"Oh yes," blushed Marina, not understanding the doubt in his question. "I'm three months along already. Nanette and I have discussed it and it might be best for you to move into the farmhouse with us."

They were married in a small ceremony and afterwards Nanette had a lunch reception at the farm with about fifty guests including the hired men and their families. Manuel was now included by Armando and the foreman in the planning and decision-making of the farm.

Marina was giddy in love. She waited for Manuel every night, for he continued to go to the village after work, and she was never tired when he came home and joined her in bed. She loved his hardness in her hand and inside her. She would reach for him under the covers, stroking his smooth, moist skin, pressing deeply and tenderly, as she clung to him like to the rope of a swing about to soar. Her lips brushed him as they slid and tumbled about each other's bodies. At dawn she would fall asleep after he got up to go to work.

Nanette looked on with concern.

"Why don't you and Manuel go for a picnic on Sunday?" she suggested.

"I'd like that, but Manuel always goes to town on Sunday. He knows men from his island there and I think he's still a little homesick. Besides," she added, "he's very traditional. He doesn't think women and men should mix."

After a pause she said, "Manuel doesn't say much but I know he'll be a good father."

"I wouldn't want you to have to raise this child by yourself."

"How could I ever be by myself? I'll always have you and Armando."

She had the two of them there when she went into labour. Nanette covered the bed with clean, old sheets for Marina to lie on and bathed her face with wet cloths and stroked her back when she gasped with the pain of each contraction. Armando went to town to get the midwife. He looked for Manuel at the cafes but couldn't find him.

Marina's insides tightened in pain.

"Breathe deep," Nanette urged her.

Marina gazed at the photograph of her mother on the wall facing her. She looked into her mother's kind face and begged to be saved.

"Don't be afraid," her mother whispered in a warm voice.

Marina closed her eyes and cried.

"Mamma!" A force so immense it knocked her into unconsciousness for a few moments. She opened her eyes to numbness.

"Marina, the baby's here: it's a boy!" Nanette announced.

Marina's eyes searched for her mother but the image had been stilled.

She felt the warmth of wool blankets on her arms and looked down at a tiny red face whose eyelids were still sealed with wax.

"I saw your grandmother. She came and helped me." She cooed her secret into the tiny ear.

Marina would not sleep until Manuel came home. She clutched the baby close to her waiting to present him to his father.

"We have a son," she sang when Manuel walked into the bedroom late in the night.

He couldn't hide his male pride.

"We'll call him Gabriel, after my father."

She let herself drift off into sleep.

Marina saw to it that Gabriel's childhood was happy, full of play, laughter, and sunshine. Marina devoted herself to him while the others ran the farm.

"You should pay attention to what we're saying, Marina," Manuel warned her when he, Armando and Nanette sat down and talked about the farm in the evening after the work was finished. He and Armando managed the business and Nanette looked after the books. They no longer needed a foreman.

"I could use some help with the books," added Nanette.

"You know I'm not good with figures and you do such a good job. All of you. I'm grateful to have such a wonderful family. Gabriel needs me more than the farm does. There's still daylight outside. I'm going to take him to the swing." And she would take the little boy's hand in hers and prance outdoors.

She had been so happy watching Gabriel grow that the rest of the world slipped out of her sight. Underneath the shade of the apple trees Marina would sit on a blanket admiring the little boy waddle his first steps and tumble down on the grass; in time she would read, occasionally looking up from her book to catch sight of him running around the yard.

"Mamma, watch!" he would shriek, just as his little foot kicked a ball.

At the dinner table she delighted in entertaining them with Gabriel's small feats.

"He kicked the ball as far as the fence!"

"He's an athlete alright," Armando laughed. "Maybe we can have a game after dinner?"

"That would be wonderful," chirped Marina. "What do you think, Manuel?"

"I'm going to town."

"Well then, maybe tomorrow."

From the window Nanette would watch the three of them run around the yard kicking the ball, the two grown-ups shortening their steps to match those of the little boy, letting him get the ball and cheering him on.

"Marina, don't you think it's time for Gabriel to be in bed?" Nanette would ask.

"He'll sleep better if he tires himself out."

"He should be in bed. You're spoiling him."

By the time they came into the house Nanette was already in her room. Marina would wash Gabriel, put him into bed and read to him. Sometimes she fell asleep with him and spent the night in her son's bed. If she was awake when Gabriel nodded off to sleep, she would get up and go into her bedroom and the bed she shared with

Manuel. He was never there. Marina was asleep when he came to bed. In the morning they made love, most days, like the first time without saying anything to each other. Marina had come to accept Manuel's way and besides, she was enraptured with her son.

She sat with him in the sun on nice warm days.

"Feel that!" she would say. "As long as you live you'll never get tired of the bright warm sun on your face!"

When Gabriel was asleep in bed she sat and talked to Nanette and Armando.

"Do you think Gabriel should go to school or stay home and I can teach him? He already knows the alphabet and can count up to fifty."

"He should go to school. He needs to make friends and you need to get involved in the farm." Nanette was resolute.

"It will take half an hour to drive him to town. It doesn't seem worth it when he's still so young."

"His father can take him. He goes to town every night and doesn't seem to mind."

"I can take Gabriel sometimes," volunteered Armando.

"It's for the boy's own good," declared Nanette. "He's growing up. He needs to get out." Then after a pause, "You need to do other things besides look after Gabriel."

Marina was unconvinced.

"I'll think about it."

It was plain to see that Manuel was discontented, although it was not clear exactly why. Here he was *patrão* of a farm much bigger than the one where he had only been a day labourer on his island. The villages around were expanding, eager to buy crops; there were enough workers that they could hire only good ones. If Manuel's ambition had been to make money he couldn't have asked for a better opportunity. Yet he never had anything good to say about the farm. Not that he neglected his duties or was anything but a good *patrão*. Nor did he scorn or mistreat his wife or their child, although the lavish way she loved little Gabriel had the effect of making him even more distant and withdrawn. At times he seemed genuinely proud of his son, when the boy showed an inkling of future courage and strength of character, not crying when he was hurt or climbing so high in the trees that his mother became anxious. Marina often still found Manuel to be a somewhat avid and satisfying lover, although she knew people said that he was always so late in town because he visited whores. She didn't want to believe that, but after all he was a man and he had his needs. Marina loved him, was always trying to please him, never complained about him neglecting her, although it was clear to her and everybody else that she had transferred her deepest allegiance to her son.

"You have the soul of a mother," Manuel told her. "My mother was just like that with me. Someday you'll have to let the boy go."

"Let Gabriel go?!" she laughed playfully, taking the child up in her arms: "Never! He's my prisoner!"

The little boy giggled as she tickled him.

She had no sense that this morning would be different from any other. Manuel had come in late and they had made love as usual. In the night he had arisen, but when she asked if anything was the matter he had said no, he was just restless and she should go back to sleep. Sometime later she came out of sleep, but not for more than a moment, when she heard the dogs barking. When she awoke in the morning the bed was empty next to her. Manuel must have arisen before her and would be out in the fields already. Still groggy with sleep, she drifted into the hall and then into Gabriel's room, as was her habit. At a glance she didn't see him in his bed, just the rumpled sheets hanging down to the floor. The room was cold, without the warmth of a child's sleeping breath.

"That's odd: Gabriel always comes into my bed when he wakes up first," she said to herself. "Where could he be? I wonder if Manuel took him out to the fields?"

She skipped down the hall, through the front door, and onto the front veranda. The air was moist with dew. She looked out, in every direction, for a sign of Gabriel and Manuel, but there was no one around. The men's cabin stood empty and silent.

She went back inside the house. Nanette was coming down the stairs, her greying hair braided down her back.

"Have you seen Gabriel? I can't find him."

"No."

"He isn't in bed. I can't find him."

"He must be with Manuel."

"Do you think so?"

"Of course. You know how anxious he is to teach him to ride a horse now that he's four and a grown-up boy. It's the sort of thing Manuel would like to do. Make a man out of his son."

"I'm afraid he might have wandered off on his own," said Marina. "But you must be right. Manuel must have taken him because he took off his night clothes and Gabriel wouldn't do that on his own."

"If you're worried, let me ask Armando to look for them. He's still upstairs."

"Yes, please, and I'll start breakfast while we wait for them."

"Good idea," said Nanette going back upstairs to talk to Armando.

In the kitchen Marina brewed coffee, warmed milk and decided to make cornbread muffins for breakfast. Gabriel loved muffins warm from the oven. He would be famished when he finally got home.

She mixed the batter in slow, tight movements, her eyes darting back and forth to the kitchen window to catch a glimpse of Gabriel. The whole house was dead quiet without him. She waited for him with a hungry heart and imagined his delight when he smelled the warm muffins. They would spread the muffins with quince jam, his favourite, and she would watch him eat while she drank her coffee. In the afternoon she would take him to town, as a treat, and buy him a spinning top. Everything seemed to happen without her—the muffins were already baking. When they were done, that would be the moment, she believed, when Gabriel would walk back into the house, just in time to enjoy his breakfast.

She had no idea how long she kept the muffins in the oven, to keep them warm. When the oven no longer felt warm she called Nanette.

"The muffins will get cold!" she cried. "Gabriel likes them warm."

"Don't worry about that! When he comes back he'll eat them even if they're cold. He'll be hungry. It's lunch time and wherever Manuel has taken him I'm sure he won't think of giving the boy food."

"But where could Manuel have taken him? He didn't say anything to me."

"Who knows? They could have gone to São Paulo for all we know. You're going to have to tell Manuel that he just can't take off like this without telling you anything. It's one thing for him to go to town and come back whenever he pleases, but he can't take little Gabriel without telling you."

At the sound of horse's hoofs they both rushed to the window.

"It's Armando, but he's alone. I don't understand." Marina's voice was very tight.

"Armando, why didn't you bring Gabriel back?" Nanette asked.

Armando kept his eyes lowered and said nothing as if he had not heard the question.

"Where's my Gabriel?" Marina asked.

Armando raised his eyes to her face and stretched out his arms to hold her by the shoulders.

"What is it?" Marina pulled away.

"They're gone."

"Where? When are they coming back?"

"Sit down, Marina. I'll tell you what I know." He weighed his hands on her shoulders and gently, but forcefully, pressed her down on a chair.

"When I couldn't find Manuel in the fields and the men said they hadn't seen him this morning, I went into town. I asked around, but no one had seen them. I'd almost given up when the railroad clerk came up to me and told me that Manuel had been with Gabriel and had bought tickets and left for São Paulo."

"That's what I said," said Nanette in a huff. "That man is so inconsiderate! You've got to teach him a lesson, Marina. If you don't, I'll do it. Worrying us half to death. They probably won't be back until late tonight. The little boy needs his routine. He can't go gallivanting about."

"I don't think they're coming back, mother."

Marina cocked her head.

"Of course they're coming back," insisted Nanette. "Why would he want to take Gabriel away? It doesn't make sense."

"But the tickets Manuel bought were one-way."

They searched Gabriel's room and found that many of his clothes and a suitcase were missing. Another bag was also missing, as were Manuel's clothes. He had taken a small amount of money from the strongbox.

Marina looked to Armando, but he could only look away from her.

She stood up to go into town to follow her son, but they restrained her. Nanette was the stronger on. After struggling with all her might, Marina collapsed onto the floor. Nanette cradled her and sent Armando for the doctor.

Crossing the Atlantic, near the Azores, 1919

Marina awoke with a start. Julio was heavy in her arms, but she would not release him for fear that he too would be taken away from her. One more day on the sea and they would land on the island of São Miguel and she could claim her lost son. But she was full of terror and anger at having to face her estranged husband. He who had snatched her son from her in the middle of the night when she was sleeping.

Chapter Seven

Dearest Father and Mother,

So your son is now a married man with his own business! Can you believe it? I hardly can myself. I was so afraid that good things would never come my way and I would never seize hold of life, but now I'm sure I've caught the very thing in my arms. I wish you could be here to see me so happy.

For mother's sake, let me start by telling you about the wedding. During the preparations, which kept us all very busy, especially Imaculada, who took charge of the arrangements like a general (a very beautiful general), and which finally took us away from the long mourning for Julio that had consumed us all, I turned my mind to my future. The coffee plantation was never to my liking, so I went back to finish up and give my notice. De Figueiredo was quite disconcerted at my leaving. He planned, I think, to get himself a son-in-law and accountant all in one. Padre Jesus, who had filled in for me while I was away, left the bookkeeping in a mess. It took me a week to fix things. Dour little Beatriz I saw repeatedly moping near my quarters. I spent the free time of my final weeks there in my room reading and writing in my journal and avoiding everybody.

Back in Rio everything felt so much happier. It rained the morning of the wedding and the sky was a sheet of grey clouds. There was the off chance that it would clear up but we made the decision to order extra carriages and to keep the entire ceremony indoors. This turned out to be wise because as it turned out it never stop raining. I didn't see Imaculada until she walked down the church aisle. She was the most beautiful thing in the world.

The homily and the whole church business were long and boring. Imaculada wanted to marry in a Catholic church. I don't care. I'd convert to Islam, Zoroastrianism, or Voodoo if she wanted me to. Sorry, mama, I know you don't like to hear me talk like this, but rest assured that even an atheist can love his parents. The church felt like a hothouse with the humidity and the rain. The air was thick with the fragrance of roses and carnations. When mass was over and we had signed the marriage documents, we rushed into the carriages because at that moment there was heavy rain and we drove to the reception, which was now on the second floor of the house and not in the garden as Imaculada had planned. This part was enjoyable—I could at least loosen my tie and take off my jacket, but I have no idea what we ate. I'm sure all the guests enjoyed Imaculada's hard work and planning, but I can't remember a thing. I am told, however, that it was a great success. I realize I haven't got as much to tell you about the wedding as you might have hoped. Forgive me. I'll ask Imaculada to write to you with more details—especially about her fantastical gown.

Married life has been sheer bliss. But what was I to do with myself? I felt that my life was on the verge of completion, but what good would it do to have the perfect wife if I had nothing to do, nothing to repay her with? Xixto offered to take me on, but I can't help but feel that would be somewhat shameful and humiliating. I have a deep need to make my own way. The talk here is all of rubber barons, so Xixto introduced me to a man named Cruz who has experience in that business. I told him

I had the money you had given me and a similar amount from Xisto.

"That's not so much. You need money to buy the land and you'll have to pay to send men to scout it and set out trails. That's before you start any work. Then you'll have to hire the workers and buy their equipment. And, of course, if you want to hire me, I'm expensive and I'd want a percentage of the profit."

I asked him if that was the usual procedure. He said it is when the owner has no experience. You can have all the money in the world but it won't do you any good unless you know about the rubber business or are willing to spend all your time in the jungle and see to everything. He was certain I wasn't the kind of man who wants to work twenty-four hours a day. "It wouldn't be much of a life for your wife if you're never there. Besides even if you want to do all the work you'll lose money at the beginning because of what you don't know. And you don't have that much money to lose." The insolent way he spoke made me feel as if he were doing me a favour to take on the job.

I asked him how much of a percentage he expected.

"Ten. Off the top."

It struck me that his price was high, but I was in no position to barter with him. I need him more than he needs me.

I have been reading all that I can about rubber. It seems to me that rubber is the great opportunity of the next century, a great future to be exploited. And the world's greatest supply is the wild trees of the Amazon Basin. Already great tracks of river land have been bought up, but there is still land to be had, farther into the jungle, if one has the necessary capital.

I asked Cruz if he had heard of an Englishman called Wickham who has set up plantations in Ceylon. I wanted him to realize that I'm at least well-informed, if not experienced, about rubber. I asked him if it wouldn't be a good idea to start a plantation in Brazil and cultivate the trees so you wouldn't have to run off into the jungle.

He mocked that idea. "If you can afford to wait twenty years for the trees to grow. I assumed you wanted a faster return than that."

I told him of course I wanted to profit now, but wasn't it worth considering?

He dismissed the idea categorically. The trees grow better in the wild. The quality of this English rubber, if it ever comes in at all, will be poor, very poor indeed.

"How do you know that?"

"Everybody in the business knows that."

I don't like Cruz. In the same way I didn't like Pereira and de Figueiredo. They use their confidence and experience to sneer at the rest of the world and are absolutely averse to thinking in a new way. As long as they're successful they'll have no reason to reconsider their approach. Maybe that's the right type of personality for business. But then there's you, Father, and Xixto, who have kept an openness and respect for new viewpoints and choices.

So I am in the rubber business now. Cruz is deep in the jungle setting things up and I am waiting for his news and preparing to depart for Manaus and to miss my wife. That is the one sad note I must pass on to you. But our separation is necessary and temporary and soon we will be together again on new footing. Missing you and loving you, I remain

Your intrepid son,

Edmundo

August 20, 1892

Querida Imaculada,

The last few months have been the deepest and richest of my life. I have never felt so whole as when we are together, doing the simplest of things, walking in the park, drinking tea in mid-afternoon, or caught in a mutual paroxysm of physical intimacy I never thought possible. You must think that I'm mad to leave you, but I beg you to trust and believe in me. I'll make you proud and we'll have a good and long life together. As hard as it is for me to leave, I know it is harder for you because you're the one staying behind and I'm the one who believes in this whole venture. I know we don't require more money and that your father has made enough of a fortune for both of us to be always more than comfortable. I simply need to do this to prove myself worthy of your love, even if it means nothing to you. I promise you that we won't be apart longer than a year. It will go by quickly. We'll have our entire lives to be together once I establish this business.

I cannot think about our wedding night without becoming flustered and turning red. Do you carry it with you all the time the way that I do? When the hotel porter finally closed the door and left us to ourselves, I was so nervous I didn't know how to start. All this time I had been dreaming about being with you like this yet when the moment finally came, I was mortified. To my everlasting shame, I wasn't aroused! But you kissed me and brushed against me and I jumped right up like a little soldier at attention, as you say. We were still in our wedding clothes and it took a long time to take them off. Your gown was practically impenetrable, so stiff with layers of fabric and wires that it actually stood on its own, as I remember. I believe it even walked itself to the closet, in a huff at being left out of further festivities. Your skin was so soft, especially around your belly as I caressed you with my hands sticky from the day's and my own heat. It was a wonderful sensation to feel the firm heft of your breasts. I felt your fingers on my penis, and that was almost it for me right there. You cupped me in your hands and guided us together. I broke inside you so hard that I couldn't breathe. I remember throughout the night and into late afternoon of the next day how we continued to press and writhe together. In the bed. In the bath as we sponged each other. I will never be able to get enough of you. I had never imagined such pleasure! It was worth sitting through the insufferable church service (don't hate me for saying this), even the pompous and priggish homily—it would have been worth sitting through ten thousand such homilies—to know you in this way for even a moment.

I watched you sleeping, your loose dark hair like a flood of ink on the white sheets. We continued to make love day and night. We didn't leave our room. The porter left trays of food at our door and if we were hungry we'd take them in, but mostly we didn't bother. The ecstasy! I hope and believe these are not just my feelings and that you've been just as happy. Of course, your body is so beautiful and mine is so unimpressive.

I must say I enjoy writing to you in this style. I fancy myself a bit of a Cleland or Laclos.

But more, so much more, than erotic pleasure, I cherish the love that I never expected you could feel for me. If I had any doubts about your feelings they were put to rest at the moment I told you about my plans and my departure, which I avoided doing as long as possible. It was almost as difficult as the first declaration of love. I came close to deciding against this whole business when I was buying my ticket to Belem. I said to myself, "Why don't you just call Cruz, tell him to sell the land, if he's bought some already and you don't even know that he has, and stay in Rio and work with your father-in-law like everyone wants you to? I went for a coffee and sat thinking for an hour about what to do. In my head I had a conversation with Julio and I imagined what he would have advised me. He never hesitated. So I too must stick by my cause. Just as the clerk was pulling the blind on the booth I bought a ticket. There has always been something inside that cripples me from action. My whole life! Sometimes I wonder how I managed to get myself to Brazil. It's the same thing every time: I churn things over and over in my soul until I'm exhausted.

But I had no idea that I could hurt you so deeply. I am so touched by your feelings for me. I know how unhappy this decision has made you, and I am so sorry to hurt you after all that has happened, but I am proud of the way you've accepted it. I hope I have helped you understand why I must do this.

My boat is sailing along the coast towards Belem.

Always completely yours,

Edmundo

August 25, 1892

Querido Edmundo,

I miss you terribly. At night, before I fall asleep I imagine that you're lying beside me and stroking my face. I can almost feel the touch of your fingertips gently on my skin.

We are all well. Baby Armando is beautiful. But something remarkable has happened. Papai has proposed to Nanette, even though we can all see that Armando cannot possibly be his son—he's mulatto like me—and she has refused his offer! Can you imagine? It would be the best thing for everybody if they were married, especially for Papai, who's still so overcome with grief for Julio. He has been so kind as to secure Carlos a new position elsewhere. I asked Ida to try to convince Nanette to marry Papai, which would only help her and the baby. On a few occasions I've tried to reassure Nanette that I love and respect her and nothing could make me happier than to welcome her into the family and that I'm quite uncomfortable having her as a maid. I simply don't understand. I wish you were here. I'm sure you could convince her to do the right thing and marry Papai. Even if she doesn't love Papai in a romantic way, it would still be the right thing to do for herself and little Armando. Ida tells me not to interfere—but how is it interfering to take an interest in the welfare of those I love?

Every night I look at the map and imagine where you are at that moment. Soon you'll be in Belem where this letter will await you. Of course, querido, you know in my heart we are always together.

My love,

Imaculada

September 14, 1892

Querida Imaculada,

The first thing I did when we landed in Belem was to head for the post office and ask for letters. I washed and ate a light dinner and spent the rest of the evening in my hotel room feasting on your words. I long for you, querida! In the morning I walked through the market—they call it "Ver-O-Peso" because you can't trust the merchants to give you as much as you've paid for. They were selling such strange things—leopard tails, the heads of boa constrictors, crocodile teeth. One can dine on alligator tail or monkey meat, which is supposed to be an aphrodisiac. Having no such need, I ate prawns before departing.

I advise you again not to put too much hope in Nanette and the baby changing your father's state of mind. We cannot know how he really feels about the boy. Nor can we really know the true nature of his relationship with Nanette. Whatever keeps her from accepting his proposal must be respected and not dismissed. I wonder if your feelings for the boy affect your perception. You seem to care for him even more than his mother does. You tell me he is good natured, kind, and sweet. I don't know much about babies. Maybe it is too early to tell how this one will turn out. I'm sounding a bit jealous, I realize.

I'm back on board ship. This time I'm sailing on the Maranhão, a Lloyd Steamer. We're destined to reach Manaus in two weeks. The desk in my cabin is covered with business papers and books and all the magic of our honeymoon seems so far away. Shortly after we left Belem we sighted the Island of Marajo. The captain told me this is where a German archaeologist claims to have found the grave mounds of Amazon women. But I can believe in the existence of such women no more than I can in the other mythical creatures I hear talk of—the mapinguari, a giant with red hair who can only be killed by a wound through the navel; the anhanga, a white deer whose fiery eyes induce fever and madness; the curupira, a little man with green teeth and feet pointing backwards to befuddle those he pursues; the fool who leaves an amazing wife in search of rubber.

The Amazon is so wide at certain places that I see land only at the crest of swells. There's so much to observe I find I'm not doing as much reading as I'm used to. I see dolphins gliding by the boat and the next moment it's a multitude of shacks built along the river on rickety stilts.

I am told some Indians have blow guns eight feet long that shoot poison darts; others will scoop out your brains and dry your head in smoke as a trophy. Sometimes I wish you were here to see the strange things I'm encountering: water lilies the size of carpets, tides that cover the tree tops, underbrush so dense that two steps from shore it's always as dark as midnight. Now we're sailing up the Rio Negro. The water is saturated with dead vegetation and it runs black and thick as soup. This afternoon, when I was strolling around the deck, the far horizon suddenly turned purple as wine and a momentous noise came from up river as the thunder rolled toward us. Under sheets of lightning the jungle whitened to an iridescent glow. First there was a dead calm that immersed everything in its rank damp odour and then the whole river danced under blasts of wind that lowered the temperature many degrees in seconds. As the waves rolled in and the rain beat down, I started to make for my cabin, but suddenly the storm was over and the sun was already breaking through a blue sky and the black water was quiet again.

I've tried to write a poem about it all, but it just won't come together. I am proud of a few lines, however:

Rain and ova, indifferent profusion,
Eyes close in heart-felt confusion.

Alas, two lines don't make a poem.

We should arrive in Manaus tomorrow and the first thing I'll do is dash to the post office to claim my letters.

Of course, I'm missing you desperately.

All my love,

Edmundo.

September 14, 1892

Querido Edmundo,

Wonderful news! I'm pregnant. We're going to be parents in May!

Promise me that you'll be back by then. I know how important it is for you to succeed in this business, but you must always remember that it's you who make me happy, who saved me. And soon we'll have our own child. The doctor assures me that we'll have a beautiful, healthy baby. A playmate for little Armando. Perhaps this child will give us back some of the joy that we lost when Julio died.

Ida and I go for a walk every day. It's not the Brazilian way, but she's a firm believer in exercise and fresh air and I know better than to question her. Besides she's absolutely right, I feel very healthy and strong. We take little Armando with us and he's the sweetest child. Nanette has gone back to her duties as a maid for the house and nothing more has been said about marriage. I think Nanette is very proud and she won't marry Papai because he's not passionate about her. We all know that Mama was the love of his life—that's a great comfort to me, the deep affection my parents had for each other—but it's not right for Papai and Nanette to stay apart. Armando needs a family and I'll continue to scheme and connive to bring the marriage about. Ida advises me to stay out of the whole business and reassures me that things will work out the way they were meant to. As much as I love and respect Ida, this is one area where she'll never convince me that she's right.

Ida and I went to see La dame aux Camélias. You would think nothing else was happening in Brazil, in the world, the way the newspapers are filled with stories about the great Bernhardt. No detail is spared. We know that she travels with 45 crates of costumes and 75 trunks for off-stage apparel, including 250 pairs of shoes. Imagine! I wonder if she has more feet than the average woman. I find it all a bit ridiculous, but I must be in the minority because the papers are enjoying record circulation. She gave a brilliant performance and she made me cry, but that was partly because I kept thinking about Julio and how he would have loved to have seen her.

During the intermission I caught sight of Marco de Bettencourt with his wife in the lobby but they returned to their seats to avoid meeting us, I mean me, for they had no reason to avoid Ida. Poor Edmundo, I

*realize I'm overwhelming you with things in this letter! But believe me,
querido, that I felt nothing when I saw him. Just the meaninglessness of
my brother's death. I can hardly remember how I was once in love with
him. I do not hate him for Julio's death—he only pulled the trigger as
Julio wanted him to. The three of us, Marco, Julio and I, played with such
disregard for convention. Marco and I started it with our infatuation,
which could never be accepted by the society that celebrates him and
tolerates me. To his credit Marco was the first one to pull back and accept
the role that had been assigned him, while I continued to indulge in
folly and fantasy. As for my beloved Julio, even though he realized that
he could not change the way our world works, he refused to accept its
conventions. It was, I believe, youthful arrogance that led him to sacrifice
his life. If he had been a few years older, I'm convinced that he would
have lived and worked for the slow changes that someday will make a
difference. Progress and Order, says our nation's motto. But nothing
absolves me of having started down the road that led to my brother's
death. How empty and futile it now feels when I have no feelings for
Marco and Julio is gone. He would have been so happy to know I was
expecting a child, that it was your child. Papai doesn't say much, and
I fear he feels less. Promise me, Edmundo, that you will love our child.*

*What you wrote about our honeymoon made me tingle. If I had a
little soldier myself, I'm sure he would have jumped to attention. If all
else fails (though I'm sure you'll be a great success), you can make a
living writing for the boudoir. You have no reason to doubt, my darling,
that you are the love of my life. I don't even know the girl I used to
be, so foolish, melodramatic and self-centred. Julio's death changed
everything, rearranged everything, wiped the slate clean. For a while I
was lost. When you told me you loved me and would marry me if ever I
could accept you, at first I didn't know what to make of it. It was as if a
too bright light had suddenly gone on in a very dark room. I don't think
you know, but I remember exactly every word you said.*

*"Imaculada, I love you," you said. "From the moment I met you I
have been in love with you. Everything that has happened has only*

made my affections stronger. I know your feelings and I don't expect that you can love me. I want you to know that I will do whatever I can to help you. If there ever comes a time when you might want to marry, think of me. I will have you on any terms. I don't expect you to say anything. I don't want any answer now. I just want you to know that I have dedicated my life to you."

It took some time but now you must realize I am all and only yours. I love you in every possible way. You brought me back to life. You allowed me once again to love everyday things. But you must also know that my passion and desire for you are greater than any I have ever known. I have grown to love you and I have grown in loving you. On top of everything else, you have my eternal gratitude. Edmundo, you get the sadder and wiser me, but I think that's the better me.

Your Imaculada.

P.S.: You can be bored by masses and homilies all you like. I forgive you. My wedding dress forgives you too.

October 1, 1892

Querida Imaculada,

A child! My heart bursts and I don't know what to think or say. I long all the more to be with you and yet need more than ever to make a success of myself. There's nothing that I would like better than to be with you in Rio in May, but it's such a long voyage from here to there that I can't promise anything although if it's at all possible I'll be there.

My heart bursts.

Edmundo.

October 8, 1892

Dearest Love,

I must tell you all about Manaus. They call it 'The White City' *because everyone wears white: white jackets, white Panama hats, white suede shoes, white gloves. I've been here only a short time, most of which I've spent resting in the pension where I'll be staying, but I can see that although it is in the middle of nowhere, this is a very modern city, more European than Europe itself, with every convenience and amenity known to civilization. The avenues are broad and lined with stones imported from Portugal. I've never seen so many azulejos as adorn my pension, which is fairly modest in comparison to others. The driver who brought me here boasted about the 15 miles of electric streetcars and the plans to build an opera house.*

"Rio has nothing that you can't get here," he assured me in a distinct Azorean accent. "Champagne from Paris, tuxedos from London, silk wallpaper from Italy, and soon we'll have electric lights. You won't want to go back to Rio after you've become accustomed to the luxuries of Manaus."

I smiled and nodded in politeness, but told him I was only here for the rubber.

Manaus may look civilized, but I'm beginning to think that it really isn't. It is extravagance without limits. I never thought I would appreciate the restrictions and repressions imposed by religion and conservatism, but I'm beginning to think that there's a need for them here in Manaus. In the evenings I go for a drink at the Phoenix café, to see if I can make any contacts and to get away from the pension, and the sort of things I hear appal me profoundly. Last night a patrão sitting at a table near mine bragged about having his French mistress shower in champagne for the entertainment of his friends. I'm no prude (as you know) but it was all so sleazy and vile. One of them owns paintings by Titian and Tintoretto but is proud to say that he signs his name with an X. It's worst to hear them talk about their business practices. Brazil is a free country, slavery has ended, and enforced labour is illegal, but they say it is quite alright to force the Indians to tap the trees. One bragged loudly of the regime he has in place for punishing workers who don't meet their quota: first time they're beaten; second they lose an ear; third they lose the other; fourth time they die. What iniquity have I gotten myself involved in?

I took quinine this morning. Drank it with my coffee. I am advised to take it regularly as prevention for malaria. There are mosquitoes everywhere and people are terrified of becoming ill since many don't recover from it.

All my love,
Edmundo

October 17, 1892

Dearest Father-in -Law,

I received another letter from Cruz this morning. He purchased land on the Moaco River, a tributary of the Pavini that in turn is a tributary of the Purus that flows into the Amazon 160 kilometres west of the Rio Negro. My tract of land is 1,126 kilometres south-west of Manaus. Now he writes to say there are not as many trees as he expected and what trees there are, are spread out. He's sent out men up river to scout for trees and set out paths. He also sent men into Ceará to recruit workers, but they've not been able to hire many since this year's rain means people are not starving and desperate for money. The money, he warns me, is fast disappearing with his having to pay the men and purchase supplies and boats. At first the rubber will only be coming in very small amounts, and in comparison to the expenses, the profit will be negligible. Cruz tells me to pray for a drought in Ceará because that would mean he could get the workers that he needs.

I know you were surprised that I chose to get into rubber and disappointed that I didn't take up your offer of a junior partnership in your business. You have respected my decision, but I know you were disappointed. The last thing I want to do is hurt you or your family. I will always thank you for introducing me to Cruz, but I have to admit I don't like the man, although I can't let my personal feelings get in the way. He's never shown anything but scorn for me and my money.

But none of this makes a bit of difference when it comes to business. Cruz knows what he's talking about. I don't have to like him, just trust him to do a good job. But his letter unsettles me. What he's saying is that he needs more money, but there's no way I can raise more money without compromising my honour. My parents are in no position to give me any more and I'm loath to ask you after all you've done. Besides it's so much of a risk. How do I know it won't be swallowed up and produce no return? Here I am in a business that I know nothing about, dependent on someone whom I don't completely trust. Of course it's to Cruz's benefit to make a success of this. I spent a couple of hours writing various responses to Cruz and scrapping them all. Maybe the best thing is to do nothing. Wait and see.

Forgive me for burdening you with my worries. I wish you were here so that I could talk to you. That would comfort me, just to have you by my side. I wouldn't feel so alone and helpless. I must be strong.

You have been the kindest of men. I know you have a sadness that will never go away. But take comfort from the love and respect of those who care about you.

Edmundo

November 2, 1892

Querido Edmundo,

Will you be coming home for Christmas? It would be wonderful if you did and stayed for a month. Imagine all those hours we could spend together? Please, please will you consider it? I promise not to come near you during the day so that you can work. Only at mealtimes and all through the night will I claim you.

The garden is overgrown with flowers. Every morning I cut roses, mimosas, carnations, and gladioli and scatter them around the house so that it smells of sweet fragrances. I take lunch with Papai in his office. He wouldn't come up to eat so I started taking a tray down to him and staying with him while he dines. He never says much, but doesn't seem to mind if I do. I tell him about my day and he smiles in that quiet way of his. Now he's always waiting for me when I enter his office and he's already made room on his desk for the dishes and cups. For the last week I've discussed preparations for Christmas: we'll host a number of dinners, one for some of the families at church, one for the entire household, and Christmas Eve it will be just us. Of course, I continue hoping that Papai and Nanette will marry. It's strange, but that's one thing I can't manage to talk to him about. I love little Armando. He cuddles against me as if it were the most natural thing, as if I were his mother. I'm delirious with joy when I think of having our baby. Oh my querido, forgive me but I want you home with me for Christmas and afterwards too as we await the birth of our child. O Edmundo, I pray that everything will be settled and you'll be home for good and forever.

As always, I pledge you my everlasting affection,

Imaculada

November 15, 1892

Querida Imaculada,

I must tell you now and not prolong your disappointment. Our disappointment, for nothing would please me better than to be with you always. I will not be able to be home for Christmas. You must be strong, querida. Not only would the trip be an extravagance, with the way my finances are going, but I can't lose the time going to and from Rio. Cruz writes me every other day and there are always decisions to make, money to send. The rubber is coming in, but in small amounts, and the supplies are outrageously expensive. But how can I complain? I'm selling the supplies to the workers at a 200% mark up. It's robbery and I initially refused to do it, but Cruz threatened to quit. Everybody does it, he says. That doesn't make it right, but I lose everything—money that doesn't even really belong to me—if he quits. If the workers don't produce enough rubber, everybody loses. Forgive me, my querida, for burdening you with these problems which I've brought upon myself by choosing to

start this business, and forgive me for not being with you for Christmas.
Yours,
Edmundo.

December 1, 1892

Querido Edmundo,

You mustn't worry about us not being together this Christmas. There will be next Christmas and it will be all the sweeter for then there will be the three of us and all the rest of the family. Of course, I understand that you need to be there now. After all, my father too is a businessman and there were many, many times when he was away from us. Promise me we won't talk about this anymore.

I've sent you a box of dried figs which are so heavenly and sweet with the Porto that your father has sent us. We'll be drinking the same vintage here at home. The chocolates are another treat. I bought them at a store that sells nothing but chocolates imported from France. I love them so and treat myself to one every night. So must you, Edmundo. You can probably buy finer things in Manaus, but these will be special because they will taste like me.

Please don't worry about the business. You're clever and you have worked very hard. I'm sure things will improve. As for money, that's not a problem. Papai has had a successful year and he's given us a little something for Christmas which I'll send to you next week. So you see, my querido, you mustn't worry. We'll be together very soon.

All my affection,
Imaculada.

December 20, 1892

Querida Imaculada,

Please thank your father for the money. I can never express my gratitude to him. I haven't wanted to worry you, but capital has been very tight, so your father's loan—I can only accept it in those terms—was like a godsend. Unexpected and, I humbly admit, undeserved.

Every night, usually it's about eleven, I treat myself to a glass of Porto with figs and chocolates. I close my eyes and pretend you're with me. If, my querida, you're still awake at that time, think of me thinking of you. The Porto reminds me of so much, of you and the way you taste, but also of my family back home. Here if they knew how much pleasure I took in it, they would mock me. Here it's only champagne for anyone who thinks highly of himself. I am so lonely for you.

I want to believe you're right about the business, that success is around the corner, but there are always the setbacks that were never imagined, let alone prepared for in the dozens of contingency plans that I painstakingly develop. Just this morning another disaster! A boat full of supplies sank up river. Thank God, or whatever, no men drowned. That would have been unbearable. I would have called the whole thing off, sold the land, and taken the next boat back to you. How divided I am, my querida. Part of me would be relieved to go back and forget about rubber, spend the rest of my days with you, reading and watching the world turn around me and without me. Edmundo the witness, never the achiever. If I'd had the talent I would have been a poet. Yet the other part of me, and maybe it's no more than a small fraction of my soul, can't let go of this ambition to succeed. I won't be able to grow old and contented unless I prove myself. I will not give up until the loss is unsustainable.

I didn't want to admit it, especially to myself, but I had been hoping to surprise you and be home for Christmas. I need to be with you, where I can hold you and feel your joy and reassurance, not half a continent away.

Always yours,
Edmundo

December 25, 1892,

Querido Edmundo,
Feliz Natal! It's late morning and the house is still quiet with sleep. I'm

in bed with my pillows, luxuriating like one of your great demoiselles of Manaus, as I write you this letter. I'm facing the window and, whenever I gaze up from the paper, I can see the soft blue sky done up with tufts of white clouds. So peaceful and quiet. I can hear soft snoring from the other rooms. Morning is my favourite part of Christmas, warm croissants and marmalade with oranges and little sips of strong coffee, after all the rush and excitement of the festivities. It's heavenly to reach that moment when there is nothing left to do.

I will not tell you what, or rather who, we missed this very special Christmas. You well know. Christmas Eve the family went to midnight Mass. The church was beautiful and sacred with the organ music and the lovely voices of the choir. I held Papai's arm the whole service like I used to when I was small. It made me feel so happy to show him my deep affection. The priest spoke of the promise of joy and new life and I believed him—imagining little Armando's smiling face and feeling the baby inside of me. It was easy to trust in the renewal of life. We walked home and you would never have known that it was the middle of the night, the sky was lit with stars and there were so many people walking about, going home from church or visiting family. There was a fine feast when we came home from church: chicken rice soup, glazed turkey with almond stuffing, cod and potato casserole, beans, sweet squash, and salad with orange pieces and nuts. Hard to imagine that we had room for the desserts, but of course we did, especially me. There was chocolate mousse with berries, English trifle so very, very light, and a German coffee cake that's Ida's favourite and a tradition with us. We could hardly move after so much eating. We drank our tea and gazed at the pretty candles on the tree. I don't remember going to bed, but it couldn't have been before four. Ida must have helped me up the stairs. I hope, my querido, that you are able to enjoy a Christmas full of good food and hours of sweet abandon.

You know how much I miss you,
Imaculada.

December 25, 1892

Querida Imaculada,

Feliz Natal! A beautiful day, full of light and colour. I've never felt so lonely. I should be with you. Yesterday, when things started to close down, I almost booked passage out of here, without thinking that it would take me weeks to get to Rio. My heart is aching with love for you.

Manaus is quiet. No one was out on the streets when I strolled around the centre early this morning. Everyone is home celebrating with their families. The pension is hosting a Christmas dinner for the guests who are in today, but I'd rather eat in my room. More comfortable to sit sadly by myself than make small talk with strangers. Next year I will be with you and our baby. I promise you.

I'm sipping a glass of the Porto that you sent, tasting you and yearning so desperately to hold you in my arms.

Feliz Natal, my querida.

January 9, 1893

Querida Imaculada,

Manaus is back on track. Everyone's forgotten about Christmas and peace on earth, goodwill to men. It's grab what you can in the day and drink as much as you can at night. I shouldn't judge. If I were any better, I would have nothing to do with this whole business. I have enough to enjoy a comfortable life and I choose to want more. Cruz says that there are more workers for hire because of the drought in Ceará, but I'm short of cash to outfit them. So Cruz has come up with a plan: sell the debts of some of my workers to another patrão, so that the workers will then work for me to pay off the debt they owe to someone else. Still I don't like it. I'm treating my workers like slaves, as if they're no more than a commodity. I don't like it but it looks like I've no other choice if I want to stay afloat. I suppose I should even consider myself lucky. At least my workers are not dying from the many diseases you can get up here. Cruz says one patrão has lost as many as fifty men. And I myself have experienced no personal suffering. Just a great deal of work and loneliness from being away from you.

How are you feeling? I'm so glad you have Ida to look after you.

All my love,

Edmundo

January 28, 1893

Querida Imaculada,

Now it's raining in the Ceará. Cruz says it might not be possible to get through till the next dry season. When I started this business I never imagined anything but success—I had some capital, all the forecasts indicated that rubber is the new money-maker, plus I've devoted most of my waking hours to studying the business, and I have one of the best, if most unlikeable, managers working for me, but it hasn't guaranteed me success. Certainly not the kind of success I anticipated. And now it's no longer about success, it's about failure. I feel shrivelled inside.

Slept in the afternoon and when I woke up it was already dark outside. I didn't bother getting up. Stayed in bed and slept right through until late this morning.

It must be me that's at fault in all this. It has to be. I'm not a businessman. I want to live like a poet but I don't have a poet's talent. I knew that much when I came to Brazil. I came to this country in search of, if not a vocation, work. My marriage to you has made all these things clearer to me. I used to believe that it was my lack of focus that was keeping me static, not able to choose something and try my hand at it, but now I suspect that what I lack is some basic element of character. I fear too much. Shut up in my small pension room, most of my waking hours facing ledgers and business documents, I feel like I'm going to suffocate. Last night I couldn't face it anymore. But I managed to survive that crisis and today I'm still at it and I'm going to see this venture to the end. It's not just my life now, my workers are dependent on me. This business of selling them bothers me. It's no different from slavery. It's the way the whole business operates. The ones at the bottom, the seringueiros, are pawns to be traded back and forth. The only way I can help my workers is to be successful and to give them a good wage for their work. Strength, strength, I pray for strength.

Edmundo

May 24, 1893

Querido Edmundo,

We have a daughter! Marina! Like the sea. I hope you like the name. I wanted her to have her own name and not be named after anyone in our families. Not that I mean any disrespect to our families but our child will belong to the 20th century and she'll be modern, different from her ancestors, different from us. For a moment I thought I might name her Order and Progress! God seems to agree with me because Marina doesn't look like either of us. Her skin is ivory, our colours mixed together. Of course, she's beautiful, even Ida says so. Our child is very calm, Edmundo. I know she'll be a comfort to us both, especially you. Let's pledge to give her the freedom to be what she wants and the opportunities to do what she aspires to. She's turned me inside out and my feelings are right there on my skin. I can touch them. I'm so full of energy and happiness I want to get out of bed and dance with our baby. Of course, Ida won't let me do that. She keeps me bundled down and gives me tea that is supposed to let me rest. It's so hard to sleep when you're bursting with happiness. I wish you were here to hold her and to feel what a precious gift we've been given. If I die tonight, it won't matter because I've experienced the greatest of happiness and purpose. Ida says I must stop writing and rest and so I bid you goodbye, dearest love.

December 27, 1893

Querida Imaculada,

I could smell the figs and the chocolate through the brown paper before

I even opened the package. The jacket fits me perfectly. Thank you for the gifts and forgive me for not being with you. Our second Christmas apart.

This holiday was more pleasant than last because I was invited to a number of the homes of other rubber patrões with whom I sometimes socialize in the evenings. I talked and listened to their little ones and tried to imagine my own child in their faces and voices. Fortuitously, my enthusiastic and sincere interest in their children made me popular with my hosts, who are showering me with further invitations. I'm not unhappy to be received in these homes, for I've come to realize that I enjoy being with people, even people with whom I have little deeply in common. Imagine, my querida, how much I yearn for your company. You with whom I share my deepest feelings!

I've learned much about business. What I need, what I had not counted on the importance of, is perseverance. It might take me five years, or even longer, but eventually I'll make a profit on rubber. That's the real test, not the outlay of capital (although I'm not underestimating the value of that); it's putting my life on hold and doing nothing but work. I'm quite sure your father would understand that. I'm sure that's what he did himself. Thank goodness we are both young. If I'm lucky, I will return to Rio and my family a wealthy man, still young, and completely committed to you and our child. The sacrifice of having been apart all this time cannot have been for nothing. The profits from the rubber are coming in more regularly and I'm confident that I'll be able to visit you in June. Marina will be a year old then. Be patient, querida, we'll be together soon.

Always my eternal love,
Edmundo

January 3, 1894
PAPAI DIED IN HIS SLEEP STOP HEART ATTACK STOP
PLEASE COME HOME

February 20, 1894

Dearest Father and Mother,

I write to you with unhappy news. Poor Xisto has died of a heart attack. This has necessitated my return to Rio, from where I am writing you. I feel very sad about the old man. He deserved more happiness than the small taste he was teased with. A wife, and then a son, dying young. Most of all I remember his kindness and humility. The man had made a fortune, but you would never know it from the way he acted. The money made no difference to him, other than for the pleasure it gave his children. The only good thing in this present situation is that it has allowed me to see my wife again after an absence of a year and a half and to become acquainted with my beautiful daughter

I have found Imaculada in a mixed state of anguished euphoria, devastated by her father's death, but also besotted with joy for our child and, I must say, not discontented to see me again. Marina! Chocolate curls and dark, hooded eyes. She was very quiet and still when I embraced her for the first time. I could feel her breath soft and warm on my face.

"Kiss Papai, Marina."

She seemed to look at me in awe. I have never before felt like such an imposing character. It immediately struck me that being a father is the most serious of matters, one at which it is imperative not to fail. My heart is gripped with love and devotion for this child. At that moment I recalled the pain in Xisto's face when he learned of his son's death and truly understood it for the first time. Suffice it to say the company of my wife after so long is pure bliss.

I miss Xisto, who would have been precisely the best person to advise me on administering his estate. By the time I arrived he had already been buried. There was a quiet power and comfort in his presence and I, like everyone else here, feel his absence. I'm sorry that I never expressed my gratitude to him to the extent that he deserved, for he made my new life possible, starting when he welcomed me into his home. He's the one who set me up in rubber, kept me going in the hard times, and now has put me on solid ground.

There have been many decisions that I have had to make here at home.

Imaculada and I have talked about what to do with the business, the house and, depending on what we decided about those two, the servants. This has been an anxious time for everyone: Gilberto and his family, Nanette. Ida, of course, will stay with us, whatever happens. Imaculada defers to me and that makes me more cautious about my decisions. As for my own business, I can't give that up at this point. I feel like Macbeth, so far into the river it only makes sense to keep crossing to the other side. But I have confidence it will only be a few years before I will be able to set this intense work aside and settle down with Imaculada and devote myself to my family. What is to be done with Xisto's business? From the beginning I was never drawn to the coffee trade, but I have been of course hesitant about giving up something that's profitable and stable. There's no way I could keep the two things going. It is a very successful business but one that couldn't possibly be run from Manaus. Even with Luis running things, it would be too much of a risk. Luis is too crafty to be trusted. Xisto spoke well of his skills, but he never let him out of his sight and he never relinquished control. If Ida were a man, I wouldn't hesitate to leave her in charge. I trust her and she has sound judgement. She sees things pretty much the way I do only more clearly.

Ida says exactly what I think about Luis:

"He's malicious and would humiliate the family if he had the chance." I asked her what the family business means to Imaculada.

"She's very young, Senhor Edmundo. It's been her whole life. I think she sees it as a blessing and curse at the same time. Imaculada understands that her lifestyle and pleasures come from the business, but without her father there's no emotional connection for her. She was closest to him. Now that he's gone, I think it would be good for her to start a new life. With you and the child."

"And you." I added.

"I'll always be here for the family, if you want me."

"Yes, of course we do." I realized at that moment that Ida might have

been thinking that I was about to give her notice. "Especially with me in Manaus, we need you more than ever. We'll always need you, Ida. To help us raise Marina. You don't have other plans, do you?"

"No, Senhor Edmundo. My home is with Imaculada."

So I have sold the coffee business. To Luis! I was surprised that he has so much money, but he does, and in the end it was the most efficient way to go. I have also settled with Gilberto and his family. Xisto left them each, including Carlos, money for their years of service. Gilberto and Graça have enough money that they can live comfortably without having to work anymore.

I wasn't sure about Nanette. Xisto had also left her some money and I was ready to give her good references. But she has asked to stay on with the family.

"If that's what you want, Nanette, Dona Imaculada and I would be happy to have you with us. We're not sure where we'll be living, but we'd be pleased to have you. I see your son takes care of little Marina."

"Oh yes! He is her guardian angel."

Imaculada is delighted that Nanette is staying, even more so that Armando is staying.

"I can't imagine having to tell Marina that Armando wasn't staying with us. He's like her big brother and she needs him."

So things are moving along nicely. I just have to finish the paperwork and then I can start back to Manaus. With Ida's help Imaculada will find a house for everybody and I'll be at ease knowing that she's with good people.

I hope you are all well. I send you my love and deepest respect.

Your son,

Edmundo

May 17, 1894

Dearest Father and Mother,

Things have not quite gone as planned—at least not as I indicated *they would in my last letter. Imaculada would not hear of me going back to Manaus without her. "We did not marry to live apart," she declares.*

I assured her it would not be forever and that she would not like Manaus. She tells me she has thought long and hard about this and was planning to join me even before her father died and had discussed it with him. Ida too has been in on the deliberations and agrees with her. She wasn't to be dissuaded, so I have packed up the household and taken them with me. I'm to be in charge of all this! The patrão! I can scarcely believe it.

Everyone is exhausted from the trip up the river. Both of the children were ill on the voyage. Marina was sick first. She had a fever and her temperature was up to 40 degrees. Imaculada was beside herself with worry. She refused to let anyone else look after the child and didn't sleep for days when the fever was at its peak. There was a doctor on board, but there wasn't much he could do other than advise us to give her plenty of fluid and keep her comfortable. Privately, he warned me that it could go either way.

"Children her age have died with less severe symptoms."

Ida and Nanette stayed with Imaculada to help her and I stayed in the little cabin and kept watch over Armando. I couldn't focus on anything so I spent the time playing word games with the little boy. He's quite sharp.

I read to him to keep our minds off our worries. Armando listens quietly, although I don't think he understands much. When Marina's fever broke, we were all so relieved, but a day later little Armando took to bed with a fever. He was not as sick as Marina, but his illness lasted longer and he still hasn't fully recovered his appetite.

In Manaus we have found a big house with three storeys. I'm working in a room on the third floor, away from the activity and noise, as the women set up the household and the children run around playing. Marina is getting used to me. She likes me to carry her on my shoulders when I go downstairs. Armando follows behind. Sometimes I offer to carry him on my shoulders and he's delighted.

There is another drought so I have no worries about finding workers. Cruz has come down to Manaus and he's rounding them up to take back with him. They are desperate to find work. They'll take anything.

Cruz says that now that things have settled into a nice rhythm I should go up river and see for myself how things are done. He's right, I know, but Imaculada will be displeased. It wouldn't be long, just a brief interruption in our new life together as a family.

We all send you our love,

Edmundo

July 9, 1894

Dearest Imaculada,

There have been major and unexpected developments that have opened my eyes. I expect to start home to you shortly, sooner than expected. I will, most likely, never want to leave you again.

The trip up river was unsettling and a prelude to what has happened since. One day we saw an anaconda squeezing the life out of a monkey, who squealed in despair. A school of piranhas thrashed the water into foam when one of the crew threw a panther carcass overboard. On the bank I saw new shoots already growing from the remains of something unrecognizable. Cruz was fascinated, even delighted by it all. He has a deep streak of cruelty.

In the darkness of my room, I dreamed of the civilized life I'd left behind.

We arrived at my land after a month on the boat. Nothing was as I had imagined. The air is filled with smoke and the smell of burning rubber. My company store is made of rotting planks and smells of bad food and mould. I could hardly stand to go inside when Cruz introduced me to the manager.

"Everything is fine, Senhor Cruz," he assured us. "There's only one man locked up in the brig."

I asked why we had locked someone in the brig.

The manager looked at me as if he did not understand my question.

"He tried to run away, Senhor Patrão, but don't worry because he got a good whipping. He won't do that again."

I demanded to see the man.

"Senhor Patrão, I told you he got a good whipping."

"I heard you. I want to see him."

The man imprisoned was a mestizo. When they brought him to me, he could hardly walk. He was completely emaciated. I tried to look him in the eyes, but he kept them on the ground and was clearly afraid that he was going to get another beating. I introduced myself, but he remained silent. I looked at him more closely and saw how weak and sick he was. I think he has scurvy.

I asked to be shown where he had been locked up and they took me to a shack made of green wood and leaves that smelled of garbage and excrement. I slipped and almost fell on the wet floor.

"What have they given you to eat?" I asked, sucking my breath in so that I wouldn't retch from the stench.

I was shown a piece of bread covered with blue mould and beans full of maggots.

"Why have you done this to him?" I demanded.

"He owes you 200 milreis."

"Doesn't he work? Doesn't he bring in rubber?"

"Yes."

"Then why does he owe us money?"

"Things are expensive. He's been sick."

"Then he needs medical attention."

"He's in the wrong place for that, Patrão. They all get dysentery sooner or later."

"Why wasn't something done for them?" I had no sooner spoken than I realized that I was as much to blame as anybody.

"There's hardly been enough money to cover business costs, Patrão. You know that better than anyone else."

I demanded to be shown everything that was going on. I saw nothing but human misery and abject squalor. No one should live this way. There were unmarked graves and deaths I have never been told about. Hardly any of the workers are free of debt to me. All their work has only made them worse off. The money they owe means we force them—I force them—to stay here like men in prison, or worse, animals in a cage.

At night I couldn't sleep. For the last two years I've been obsessed with making money while the workers suffered from barbarous neglect. Cruz never told me, but I didn't want to know. I kept myself free of it in Manaus and paid Cruz to do the dirty work. I who congratulated myself on my moral superiority am, in the end, responsible for this deplorable exploitation. Eventually, after several sleepless nights, I realized that there was only one decent thing for me to do: give the workers a choice whether to stay on or to leave. Those who want to leave could go back to Manaus and those who chose to stay would have their debts waived and from now on would pay less extortionate amounts for supplies. So I gathered them and gave them the choice. Most of them have chosen to leave. They don't trust me, and I can hardly blame them. So now I have only a handful of workers left. Cruz is furious. He says I have ruined a business I know nothing about and don't have the stomach for. He has tendered his resignation. I'm not surprised.

I could try to find a new manager and more workers from Ceará, but why? I've made a terrible mistake! I've wasted these last two years away from you. Yes I wanted to succeed at something, but this was absolutely the wrong choice. In the end the whole business will be easy to dissolve. All that remains is to sell the tract of land. I should be able to do that in Manaus. The only question is what I'll get for it. I'll never recoup all the losses, but there's still enough money for us to live in comfort. Let someone else get stinking rich this way.

For the first time in two years I feel free. A few days and I'll be on my way home.

Love and shame,
Edmundo

August 30, 1894

Dearest Father and Mother,

I am sorry that I must inform you that my dear Imaculada has died. She has been overcome by malaria. I can hardly bear to take up a pen to write this, but I am certain that in your love for me you will be shocked and distraught, so I will force myself to write a brief account for your sake. I miss you both so terribly now.

First, you will no doubt be surprised to hear that I have abandoned the rubber business. I will provide the details soon in another letter. Suffice it to say that it was a cruel and immoral venture I have entered into. My time in it has been, as the philosopher Hobbes would put it, nasty, brutish and short.

I arrived back in Manaus from my first and last trip up river to find my dear wife very sick. I had never seen her ill before, she has always been the picture of health, as she was when I had left her. I found her drawn and with her eyes closed, although she was not asleep. There were beads of perspiration over her face and her nightgown was so wet it clung to her. I took her hand and she had no fever. She opened her eyes and smiled at me.

I was very distressed by her appearance, and I found it extremely hard not to show my reaction to her.

She told me she was so happy I had returned, that she had been so worried about me. Worried about me!

I told her I had settled all my affairs and that soon we would be moving back to our beloved Rio—as soon as she was well enough to travel. I expected her eyes to light up with that lustre that I love so well, that always shows me how to seize the joy in the world, but her eyes were still and dull.

She said we had to talk about Marina. She was quite forceful, but I insisted that she rest some more, while I settled back in. I told her I would be back in a short while.

I crept away from her bedside, softly closed the door, and rushed down the stairs to confer with and seek assurances from Ida. I found her sitting in the living room, gazing absent-mindedly out the window. She rose eagerly and took me by the hand. I asked how long Imaculada had been ill and she told me it had begun a week before with a headache. She had been working too hard, looking after Marina and rushing around getting things done to the house. She rested for a couple of days, but she continued to feel sore and then she started having chills. I said I was alarmed at her appearance but was reassured that she didn't have a fever. Ida told me that the fever came and went and that according to the doctor this was the normal course of the illness. And so, the next day Imaculada was racked with chills. She shook so badly that the bed shook too. The doctor came, but he only said there was nothing to be done except give her more quinine. A little later she was feverish. I kept bathing her face and arms in desperation.

The next day her fever abated. Ida saw the improvement too. I madly hoped that another couple of days and we would be in the clear. But the fever returned and then the chills. She started passing blood in her urine. The doctor said that it was black water fever.

The next morning she was very weak but lucid. I didn't want her to talk but she insisted.

"Edmundinho," she said to me, "you must take care of Marina, as my father took care of Julio and me."

I insisted that we would take care of Marina together. That we would live in Rio and have more children. That's when she told me that she was pregnant. I felt such joy and fear together. Then she said that she thought the baby had already died inside her. She hadn't felt it move for three days.

I wanted so much to control myself, but I couldn't bear the thought of losing her. I started to sob uncontrollably. She took my hand and gestured for me to lie beside her. I cried for a long time while she held me and stroked my hair. Eventually I dozed off for a while and I woke up to feel her body burning up beside me. I bathed her, but it was no use, she grew hotter and hotter.

That night Ida kept vigil with me. She asked me if she could call a *priest. Imaculada would want it.*

Anything! I didn't care. Whatever might help!

The priest arrived around four o'clock in the morning. He anointed her as he prayed over her in Latin. A short while after he left, dawn crept into the room and streaked the bed with a ray of light.

So very recently I believed that I had finally found my way in the world, but now I am utterly lost.

Chapter Eight

São Miguel, Azores, 1919

Old Gabriel could hear that Manuel kept stirring and rising and could not sleep the night after he ordered him to write to his wife. Gabriel could tell by looking at his son and grandson that they had led a hard life, perhaps harder than his own. He knew that his son was a proud man and it could not be easy for him to come home with nothing after all these years. People in the village would mock him and talk behind his back. Once he was handsome and young and sure of himself, but that was all gone now. In the morning when Manuel came out he had a headache and his eyes were puffy and red from lack of sleep.

"Here, drink some coffee and eat some bread," his father said.

After his son had taken some nourishment, Gabriel began to ask him questions.

"Tell me, where have you been and what work did you do?"

"Many places and many kinds of work. California, Kansas, Massachusetts, farms, factories, mills. I picked grapes in California and hammered tacks in a shoe factory in Boston. Nothing suited me.

165

I was always needing to move on."

Gabriel could not understand that.

"Did you make much money?"

"Never enough to save. I have nothing."

"People will expect you to have come home with your pockets full of money like a *patrão*, not like you are with nothing."

"Hmm. Let them talk. I don't care."

Gabriel cocked his head and screwed up his face to show his scepticism.

"My son, I know how proud you are! Your wife has money, you say."

"Yes."

"Enough to buy land of your own and build a house."

"Certainly, there's that much."

"So that you could have hired men of your own."

"Hmm."

"It's a hard life working the fields for another man, you know that."

"Yes."

"And you raised the boy on your own?"

"Yes."

"That must have been hard. He's handsome but he doesn't look like you. He looks like his mother?"

"I suppose so. But I've made him strong like me."

"Was she a good mother?"

"She was soft. She made him soft."

"Softness is not a bad thing in a woman. Listen, Manuel, you are no longer young. You have no money. You have no wife and family. You have no plan for your life. I want you to think about this. I know how proud you are. I know you are ashamed to ask her. But it would be much better if she came here. Much better for you. And it is the right thing to do. God would bless you. God would save you."

They took the boy into Ponta Delgada, the city, and had a photograph taken of him to send to his mother. In the photograph young Gabriel was wearing a dark blue suit with long pants. He was standing in front of a backdrop on which an ornate column covered with vines had been painted. He rested his right hand on a prop, a railing, with his left foot forward showing a white shoe. The photographer had tried to make him smile but he wouldn't soften his scowl.

Near São Paulo, Brazil, 1913

For a long time after her husband and child disappeared, Marina was fixated and inconsolable. Over and over she asked herself the same questions. What had Manuel told him? That they were going on a little trip? Maybe that's all it was, a little train ride. Maybe they would come back. That they were going away forever? Gabriel would never have wanted to leave his mommy. He would be so alone and frightened without her. Manuel didn't like him to cry. Did Manuel promise that Marina would come to them? Gabriel would be so disappointed and hurt when she didn't. Would he grow to resent her? Maybe Manuel would send for her. But why had he kept everything secret? No, he had stolen away and they were gone from her forever! Why had he done this? If he had to go, why take her son? Why take everything from her? Did he hate her so much? Gabriel wasn't strong enough for this. He wouldn't know what to feel. What could she do to help him? Nothing! What would she do without him?

She stayed in bed for several weeks, too medicated to go searching for Gabriel. Nanette spent most of the day by her bedside, doing the bookkeeping and sewing. There was not a sound except for the ticking of the clock marking the end of each empty moment. Nanette prepared a light dinner, usually soup with bread and cheese, and she and Armando ate in Marina's bedroom. Marina was at her most alert at that time and she would sit up in bed and take her soup. Nanette was anxious that Marina eat so that she would get some strength and also so that she would stay sedated, for Nanette put the doctor's medication in the hot soup. At the beginning at least, neither Nanette nor Armando could think of any other way of keeping Marina calm. The doctor agreed. After two weeks they could start to reduce the medication, a little bit at a time, if by then Marina showed she might be able to cope with her son's disappearance.

Usually they spoke little during their evening meal. One evening, after they had finished dinner, Marina spoke.

"I miss Papai," she said. "He's been gone nine years already."

"Almost ten."

"I loved it when he used to read to me. I remember his voice."

"Would you like me to read to you?" asked Armando.

She nodded. He picked a book of short stories by Eça de Queiroz from her shelf, opened it to the beginning, and started reading. Marina didn't say anything else that night, but she listened to the story, and the next evening, without her asking, he read another story. By the time he had finished the stories Nanette was adding nothing to Marina's soup and she was able to get out of bed.

"There's darning to do," Nanette suggested, and the two of them threaded their needles and set to work.

Nanette kept Marina busy during the day and in the evening Armando read to her. He started *Os Maias*. They sat in the living room, Marina huddled inside her shawl as she listened to the comforting words of imagined lives. It made her feel safe and reminded her of her father, the lost one it helped for her to remember, when the other was still inconceivably painful to think about.

When Armando came in from the fields, the scorching sun making work unbearable, Nanette would be working on the farm books at the kitchen table, running down columns of numbers with a pencil, making sure everything added up. He would plant a kiss on the top of his mother's head and pour himself a glass of wine. He answered his mother's questions about work, while Marina, resting, watched and listened.

Marina began to help Nanette with running the house and even with the business. She spent her spare time reading in her bedroom. In the evening she and Armando read together: they were almost finished with Eça de Queiroz and talked about which author they would read next. Sometimes Armando persuaded her to go for a walk, but seldom, for she felt secure only inside the house and inside books.

Five months after her husband and son had disappeared, Marina received a letter from California in the United States.

Dear Marina,

Wishing that you are well, I write to tell you that Gabriel and I are fine. I have decided to live in the United States and at the moment we are in California. What a rich country this is! I want to see it all. It will be good for the boy. Already he has learned to speak a little English. Imagine the future he can have. I didn't say anything about taking him because I knew you wouldn't agree with me. I don't want you to worry about him. I promise I'll take good care of him. You are young and should start a new life for yourself.

I thought it would be best to let you know that Gabriel is fine.
Manuel

That day Marina stayed in her room, dwelling on the news the letter had brought her. She savoured the few details as if they were a great feast: he was well, he was in California, he was learning to speak English. Her heart was filling with love and hope. But there was certainty and finality as well: they were gone and they weren't coming back. There was no fooling her heart about that.

The letter brought Marina more fully back to life. She waited for another and in the meantime she began to step into the world again. In the mornings, before she and Nanette started working, she often went into the fields by herself when everything was still, without the noise of the men working, and when the sky appeared full of promise, with no inkling yet as to how the day would unfold. At night the dark made her pray that Gabriel was safe and warm somewhere. In the evening Armando didn't have to coerce her to take walks; she joined him freely. He was very relaxed around her, now that Manuel was gone. He often brought her fresh flowers for the house.

Armando had been seeing a young woman in the village, and Marina had heard that this young woman was fond of him and wanted to marry him. Armando was a man of infinite patience, but Marina knew how much he wanted her—he had loved her his entire life, although for her he was more like a brother. She also knew that if anything were to happen it would have to be at her instigation. So one night she asked him to come to her bed.

He was a very gentle lover.

The next morning they could hear Nanette walking in the hallway outside Marina's closed door.

Marina and Armando did not say anything about their relationship but in front of Nanette Marina stroked his hand in an intimate and familiar manner when they were near to each other. Nanette appeared to be pleased but somewhat anxious. A few months later Marina confided that she was pregnant.

"I'm going to have a child," she told Nanette.

Marina gave birth to another son.

When Armando saw Marina with his new-born child he wept and exclaimed that he was the happiest man in the world.

Avó Nanette suggested they call him Julio, after his great-uncle.

"Everyone loved Julio," she said. "And everyone will love this baby as well!"

1919

Marina had awoken early. She stole out of bed as quietly as she could, not to disturb Armando sleeping. She closed their bedroom door with a gentle pull and tiptoed across the hall to Julio's room. He was sleeping on his back, without any covers, his little mouth chewing the air. She breathed a prayer and scurried to the kitchen to start her day. She made plenty of coffee, for Armando and Nanette, when they got up, and started drinking hers as she made a mental list of things to do: go to town, pay bills, order supplies, hire someone to paint the farmhouse. If she left early she could get back in time for lunch with Julio. He would be disappointed at not going into town with her, but there was no way she could do everything with him: he would want to go to the square, then he would want her to buy a treat, and everything would take twice as long.

Marina prepared the carriage and climbed into the seat. She tapped the horse lightly and was off, leaving the farmhouse sound asleep. The trees and shrubs were wet with dew. Marina liked to be outdoors by herself this early in the morning. She could talk her dreams out aloud and they sounded real. In the quiet of the woods she imagined her son, tall and smiling, coming toward her with an open embrace. It only lasted for a few moments, until the activity and movement of the town rustled her out of her fantasy.

She stopped at the post office first because it was the first place en route. There were letters in sturdy, brown envelopes, the usual business correspondence from Rio, and between two of these was a straw-coloured, flimsy envelope. Her throat went dry and her fingers shook as she tore it open and pulled out a photograph. She recognized the cinnamon-coloured wavy hair and the dark eyes, but there was no beautiful smile. He looked so stern, so unlike the face in her dreams.

She looked at the photograph for a long time before she turned to the letter. She knew that she would not be able to do any of her chores that day as she folded the letter over the photograph and slipped it into the darkness of her purse.

She walked around the village aimlessly, her face turned to the ground, for she was afraid it would give her secret away. She stole into the safety of the square and sat on a bench, her mind filled with confusion. A son and husband she had lost long ago, as if they had risen from the ashes, were beckoning to her.

She stayed in the square, dazed, for hours.

She told herself that she would not decide right away, that she would give herself time to think things over, but right away she knew.

The only other letter had been written long ago, before Armando, before Julio, and if it had given her an address she would have followed it, no matter how far, for it would have been only her sacrifice, not Armando's nor Julio's. Life had been unformed back then; it would have been easy for them to do without her, without what they had come to claim as theirs. Gabriel, with that sad, stubborn face, would still have known her and she would have mended the separation with love and devotion, but now, after so much time, she didn't know how she would reclaim his love. Yet she would risk everything for the chance. She would go to them and do as Manuel had asked and she would take Julio with her. Never would she abandon her younger son, even if she had no choice but to leave Armando, his sleeping breath so close to her.

The next days she felt like a thief, while she made plans to do what the letter was compelling her to do. The hardest was lying next to Armando at night, for she could not sleep, knowing how he had always loved and protected her, his warm body curling towards her with innocent trust. She was going to betray him, even though she loved him back and could be as happy with him as she could be with anyone, if it had not been for her lost son. It was he who had the claim on her soul; the sad, stubborn face in the photograph, which she did not recognize but which possessed her, seemed to say, "You must come, although it will do no good."

She made the arrangements to leave Brazil. She sold the farm, with the condition that the buyer keep Armando and Nanette as manager and bookkeeper, if they wanted to stay on. She set aside a third of the money from the sale and left it with the town lawyer with instructions to give it to Armando and Nanette after she had left the country. The arrangements were made with surprising expediency. She had half hoped that they would drag on for a few months, but less than a month after she had received the letter from Manuel, all the papers had been prepared and signed.

Armando was already working in the fields on the morning she left. She dressed herself and Julio and packed a small bag. She made sure Nanette was out of sight, in the kitchen, when she put the bag underneath the carriage seat. She told Nanette she had to pick up heavy supplies in town and would ask one of the farm hands to drive her and Julio.

"Leave Julio here. He'll just get in the way," advised Nanette from the kitchen, where she was shelling beans.

"I promised him he could go," Marina explained in a loud voice from the porch. She did not want to see Nanette's face. She felt she was a little girl again, about to be caught lying.

"You spoil my grandson too much," said Nanette.

"Goodbye," Marina said it in a soft voice, as a substitute for the kiss that she wanted to give but could not without raising Nanette's suspicion.

"Kiss your grandmother goodbye," she urged Julio who did as he was told but ran back quickly so that he would not be left behind.

When they arrived in the village Marina told the farm hand to drive to the railway station. He said nothing and did as he was told. At the station she bought two tickets and told the driver to return to the farm and gave him a letter to give to Armando.

Julio was excited. He had never ridden in a train before; he spread his little hands across the leather seats.

"Mamma, are we going somewhere?"

"Yes. Far away, my *lindo*."

"Why aren't papa and *avó* coming with us?"

She took the photograph from her handbag and showed it to him. "This is your brother, Julinho."

"I have a brother," he jumped on his seat.

"Yes, and we're going to go and live with him on a beautiful island." She paused before adding, "And you're going to have a new father."

That evening Armando returned from the fields to find Marina and Julio had not returned from the village. The hand who had driven them couldn't say anything, just that she had given him a letter to deliver to Senhor Armando.

Dearest Armando,

Forgive me! I have taken Julio and we're going to the island of São Miguel to live with Gabriel and Manuel. Believe me that I love you and will miss you, but I could not abandon my son. Either of my sons, and that is why I have taken Julio away from you.

I sold the farm and left a third of the money for you and you mother with the lawyer in town. The new owner has agreed and would be pleased to have you stay on as manager and your mother to do the bookkeeping as she has always done. I don't know what you'll want to do, but it makes me feel a little less guilty to know that you have that choice. I know your kind heart will forgive me, even worry about me, and you must help your mother. You must start a new life and have a family. Julio and I will always belong to you, if only in your heart. I don't think I'll ever see you again, but you will always be with me.

I kiss you adeus,

Marina

São Miguel, Azores, 1919

The evening before Marina was to arrive, old Gabriel and Manuel sat together outside the house. Old Gabriel insisted they each have a glass of wine, though they rarely drank.

"Everything will be well now," the father said. "I was so uncertain but now I know. When you came home you had almost ruined everything, but now it has been made right. She will bring money with her. That is good. We have been poor and life has been too hard. God is showing us some mercy because we have repented. I am happy."

The dusk came on and they sipped the strong red wine in silence.

"I must tell you what I know," the old man said at last. "I have tried to keep it to myself but it is too much. And now you have made things right. But once I have told you we must never speak of this again. It cannot be changed. No good can come of it. But then you'll know why we need this fresh start.

"Before you came home there were many deaths. First there was your mother. And without ever seeing you again. Then there was the influenza and it took João's Maria de Conceição. He was no good to her. She deserved better. Your brother has brought me nothing but heartache. I tried beating him but nothing has done any good. After Maria de Conceição died I worried about Maria de Deus, that he would mistreat her too. I hoped maybe someone would marry her and take her away. But João is an animal. I didn't realize how much. He can control nothing. I knew people were talking but I didn't know what they were saying. Maria de Deus was always small and scrawny. Like a mouse. She never went out, especially after her mother died. I visited to make sure there were no bruises. I couldn't see any. But small as she was, even I noticed she was getting bigger. I couldn't believe he would do that. I didn't know what to do. Who would want her after that? How could any of us look people in the eyes? I wanted to beat him but what good would it do?

"I knew her time was approaching. She had no food, so I brought her some, salt cod and a sack of flour. Her father would have let her starve. I didn't know what we would do. Then I was sick for a week. When I went to visit she was small again. João looked at me with fear but with insolence, daring me to ask. I couldn't speak. I noticed the flour was gone, the whole big sack. I asked where it was and he said they had used it all up. No way they could have done that. I know what he did with the sack. I never thought he could be such an animal. He is lost to me. So it is up to you and me to do things right. We have to mend our ways or we will be lost just like him. We have to be good. God wants us to prosper. Our Lady wants it. Your mother wants it. Do you understand?

"We must never talk of this again."

Manuel lit another cigarette and looked to the dark waters for a sign of the ship. He and young Gabriel were waiting for Marina. He had already grown familiar with everything around the dock: the grey stone benches, cold and hard underneath his pants whenever he sat down to rest; the two small boats tied to the wharf and bobbing up and down with the waves; the dark slimy moss growing on the wall up from the water.

There were other people waiting for the ship. An old woman, covered in a black shawl, had spent most of the time crying and calling out to God. Her husband had died recently and she was waiting for the return of her son from America. Gabriel sneered at the old woman's loud lament and Manuel smiled down at him, shaking his head in shared disapproval, but after a while he grew weary of responding to the boy and he remained silent, his head heavy with thoughts. Then Gabriel had nothing left to do but throw pebbles into the dark waters.

Manuel could not believe that she was coming. It had been almost seven years since they had seen each other. He wondered what she looked like. He knew he looked older: a tuft of grey hair had sprouted on the left side of his forehead and his eyes were puckered with wrinkles. She was still in her twenties and her life, unlike his, had been settled and comfortable. In America he had lost his desire for pleasure; it had been many years since he had been with a woman— it cost too much, like so many other things, good clothes, good food. He wore poorly fitting, second-hand clothes that made him look middle-aged; his teeth were yellow, and a couple on the side had been extracted. Young women had stopped noticing him.

It would be hard to look her in the face, after what he had done to her, and looking defeated and worn as he did. Maybe it would be best if the ship never came but was lost to the sea forever. Why should his life be so dependent on someone he had cared so little for? And then he saw a small light on the ocean.

Manuel turned to his son. "That's your mother's ship."

Gabriel threw another stone.

It was a long while before the passengers stepped across the plank onto the darkness of the dock. Manuel pulled Gabriel under his arm, like a present, and awaited his moment of retribution. He had stolen a child from his mother and now he would have to look head on at the pain he had caused. She stepped out on the plank, and the first thing he noticed, as always, was a cloud of dark, curly hair. She hastened towards them. There was not a trace of anger in her face that Manuel could see. He breathed a sigh of relief and almost smiled, but then noticed for the first time the young boy she was holding before her.

Her eyes bright with tears Marina knelt down and scooped Gabriel in her arms. She cradled and caressed his face with her hands. He stood tall and stiff and looked far into the night past her loving gaze.

"I am your mother," she sobbed. "This is your brother, Julio." She raised her eyes to Manuel. "He was inside me when you left."

Manuel was silent.

"Julio, ask your father for his blessing," she tenderly nudged her younger son toward him.

Manuel hid his disgust in the dark. How dare she dishonour him!

He opened his mouth to put an end to her mockery but couldn't find the words.

"God bless you," he answered in a dry, empty voice.

They were, all of them, confused and exhausted, not knowing what to do next.

"Mamma, I want to go to sleep," cried Julio.

"Yes, of course. We're all tired and need to sleep. Will you take us home?"

Manuel had hired a two-seat horse carriage; Marina sat beside him, holding Julio, who was soon fast asleep, in her arms; Gabriel sat on top of the trunks in a box behind the carriage seat, his back turned away from his parents, his arms defiantly crossed at his chest, refusing to hold on to anything as they drove the bumpy narrow road along the coast. The only light was the kerosene lamp hanging from the side of the carriage. The city they left behind and the villages they passed were deep in darkness. Manuel drove the carriage in turmoil. The boy was not his. She had betrayed him and had the nerve to bring her bastard son and expect him to believe her lie. Did she think he had no honour? What sort of man did she take him for? He was so angry he felt like throwing her and her bastard into the ocean. Suddenly he thought of what his brother João had done. He gripped the reins tight, as if he were keeping them all from plunging down the cliff into the dark waters.

Marina squeezed Julio's warm sleeping body tight against hers and listened to the waves on the rocks below them. She remembered her father explaining to her how her name meant water; she could feel the salty moisture coat her like a layer of skin. Her father had told her stories about how the ocean had given him a new birth when he had crossed it to Brazil; now she was starting a new life, retracing her father's voyage in the opposite direction, not quite reaching his starting point, but closer to it. Her father had gone to Brazil looking for a new life, but she had come to this island to reclaim her lost one; to hold it to her heart once more; to have her children together. The family she had always yearned for. Without Gabriel it could never have been, no matter how faithful and generous Armando's love. She would warm her son's cold heart. It did not matter that it was his father who had taken him away; he felt abandoned by her and blamed her, she knew. No matter how long it took, Marina would fill the emptiness that separated them and someday Gabriel would be as close to her as the boy in her arms he had once been.

She felt no such longing for Manuel's love. He smelled of rotten onions and damp earth and that made her want to retch after days at sea. He had not changed so much, only grown older and harder from working the earth. Perhaps he had never been as graceful as she had imagined. She had been a young girl, her head full of poetry and romance; she had not seen him as he had been; now in the blindness of the dark night, riding along the edge of this small island, she saw him as he really was. She had memories of desire for Manuel, packed away deep inside her, like dried flowers that had lost their odour. Perhaps, the desire might come again? Would that not make them a family? She saw them all clearly: how she was at the centre of their lives, and how they depended on her love, strength, and money to make something of themselves. It didn't matter that she was tired, uncomfortable, and disoriented in a strange place, Marina was full of purpose: her family was reunited and now she would devote her life to keeping them together.

No one in *Agua d'Alto* believed that Julio was Manuel's son. They talked about how much darker he was than Manuel, how the two brothers did not look alike, but no one said anything openly to the family. It was all polite smiles and greetings, especially after Marina and Manuel bought land, on top of a hill looking out to sea, and started to build a house. It had been years since anyone had built a new house in the village. And such a fine house at that.

Chapter Nine

Near São Paulo, Brazil, 1904

A rmando pulled the wooden seat of the swing with both hands and then heaved it high into the air, away from him. Marina gasped, then laughed, as she pushed the air with her legs like the handle of a pump. She loved the exhilaration of being high in the air, her skirt inflated like a balloon, flying towards the sky, then falling precipitously backwards.

"Higher, Armando!" Marina shouted, as she swung out of his reach. "Use all your might!" She knew she could count on Armando to push her for as long as she asked.

"Ow!" Armando cried out suddenly, moving away from his position at the back of her pendulum.

"What is it?" she asked, turning to look at him. He was holding his upper arm. She heard a harsh laugh and turned to see Rui, who lived down the road, coming towards them. He had hit Armando with a stone.

"What are you two kiddies playing?" asked Rui with a sneer.

"We have to go inside pretty soon to help my mother with dinner," said Armando with a combination of firmness and fear.

"Only sissies help their mothers. Where's your father, bastard?" Rui spit onto the ground and dug his heel where the gob had hit.

Marina had brought the swing to a stop gradually through three of its arcs and got off to watch what would happen between the two boys. Rui was always saying things to upset Armando. But Armando was so sensitive. He had never known his father just like she could not remember her mother. That was just the way things were. She felt strong loyalty to Armando, kind and very attentive, but wished he could be stronger, like Rui. She kept herself back a bit and started to pick daisies to take to her father.

"Hey Marina, don't bother with those stupid flowers. If you want some real beauties, I can show you some up the hill."

"Where? What kind?"

"You'd better not go, Marina. You know what my mother said. We should be going in to help her." Marina knew Armando was looking to make eye contact, to beseech her that way, but she avoided looking at him.

Marina liked the idea of finding her father beautiful flowers, especially since he had been sick for the last while, and she disliked helping Nanette with cooking. If she did not get back in time to help she knew her father would not let Nanette punish her once he saw the flowers she had brought him. Besides, she liked the idea of going with Rui.

"Why don't you come too, Armando? You can get some flowers for your mother."

"No. Marina. We should go home now. It's time."

Marina hesitated, not sure what to do. Just when she had almost decided to go home with Armando, Rui grabbed her by the arm and pulled her in the opposite direction, and she let herself be led away towards the hill.

"Armando, come on!" she shouted as she started to run with Rui, excited at the prospect of adventure.

But he stood behind, resolutely resisting her, and then turned and started walking firmly home to the farmhouse.

Rui sang a little song as Armando hurried away:

The white man drinks champagne,
The caboclo Port wine,
The mulatto drinks rum,
And the negro pig piss.

Rui was always doing things to put Armando—and Marina too—in place. They were both mulattos, not quite at the bottom but one rung up, while Rui, like her father and Armando's mother, was white. Nonetheless, Marina new that Rui liked her.

"Your friend's a faggot," Rui declared harshly.

"No he isn't," Marina answered, though she didn't know what a faggot was.

"No? Does he do it to you then? Does he show you his dick?"

"Of course not."

"I bet you'd like to see a dick."

"No I wouldn't."

He led her up the hill and a bit off the path to where great mounds of bougainvillea lay over the other plants.

"Oh, they're so beautiful!" she exclaimed, and reached out to take some.

"Watch the thorns, dummy," said Rui. "Here, let me get some for you."

When Marina came home, her arms bearing magenta-coloured bougainvillaea, her father was sitting on the porch with a far off look in his eyes.

"Pai! These are for you! Aren't they beautiful?"

"For me!" exclaimed her father, smiling and reanimated by her. "Yes, they're very beautiful! But we have to go in and eat. We've been bad."

When they came into the kitchen, Armando was slicing the thick heavy bread for supper.

"Look what I've brought pai for the table!" Marina exclaimed.

"You should have been back long ago to help with supper," said Nanette sternly.

"But Nanette," pleaded Edmundo, "Look at how beautiful the flowers are!"

They sat down at the table without another word and started eating. Her father was lost again in his own world, Armando was sulking, and Nanette wanted to go on about Marina's transgression but thought it best not to. Marina, who was aching to have her flowers praised, remained quiet nevertheless, not wanting to attract attention to how she had run off to pick them.

Edmundo was the first to leave the table; without saying anything he just stood up and left. Marina wanted to follow him and sit on the porch with her father, but Nanette stopped her.

"Since you were too busy to help with dinner, you can clean up," she told Marina before she went upstairs where she spent the evenings with her needlework.

Armando waited around the kitchen watching her wash the dishes. He wouldn't help her, but he wanted to be near her.

"Are you mad at me?" she asked.

"No."

"You are."

"You knew I wanted you to come with me."

"Yes, I know. You should have made me, Armando."

After Imaculada died, Edmundo had sold his land up river and with the greatly diminished capital purchased a small farm fifty miles from São Paulo. He took Marina with him and Ida and Nanette and Armando. He would have liked to live the life of a hermit, somewhere deep in the Amazon jungle, but he had a child to raise. For a year he went to bed with the light on. Every morning he awoke to the awful realization that the love of his life was dead. Slowly the days began to acquire a numbness, benign and welcome and all he could hope for.

When Marina was five, Ida who had raised her in her mother's stead, died of a heart attack, leaving the little girl desolate and in the care of Nanette who had never shown her much affection. After Ida's death Edmundo withdrew even more. He spent the summer months and most of the fall in bed. In Ida he had someone to share his love for Imaculada, the short time he had enjoyed with the Xistos, and with her death there was no one who could feel the depth of his sorrow. He recovered slowly, fitfully, and incompletely, with brittleness and hands that shook nervously. His parents wrote begging him to come back to Portugal so that they could know their grandchild, but he could not abandon Imaculada's land.

'Someday I will be under the same earth as her,' he promised himself sorrowfully.

His mood improved and he started to take an interest in his daughter who was by then seven. She was a flighty, active girl, but not at all stupid, not at all unattractive. He bought her books which she read avidly—Ida had taught both her and Armando to read and write—and then he would talk to her about them and make a point not to condescend to her. Being with her and seeing her deep affection for him was the only pleasure of his sad existence. It was different than any feelings he had ever known. There was the instinctive attachment to his flesh and blood, although she did not look like him. She resembled more her mother, for which he was both grateful and anguished. The fainter Imaculada's image in his mind, the easier it was to bear.

Sometimes he read poetry to her or quoted passages by heart. Certain lines he often repeated. Sometimes he managed to remember something positive and uplifting:

Rise up, soldier of the future,
From the rays of pure dream
Make yourself a sword for the struggle

or

> *Listen! It is the great voice of the people!*
> *Sometimes the positive had a bit of a melancholy edge to it:*
> *There comes sometimes to sit at my feet*
> *When night falls over the roses*
> *There comes to me in the hours of my doubt*
> *A vision with wings of satin.*

Or worse:

> *Wake up! It is time. The risen sun*
> *Has chased the worms from the sepulchers.*

Such lines would lead to others:

> *What anxious wish tortures you?*
> *A howl, a groan, and nothing more.*

And then he couldn't help himself:

> *Why is your life so lonely and low?*
> *In the dusk there are painful whispers.*

Marina was being raised a Catholic. It was what Imaculada would have wanted and he honoured his dead darling's wishes. His daughter was impressionable by nature and Edmundo saw how Nanette used religion to make her submit to authority. He compensated by never disciplining her, even when she disobeyed. Edmundo had nothing but uncertainty about God.

He said to himself, 'What if there is a God? What if I have denied him for nothing? Lived without solace for nothing? Suffered without hope for nothing?' And yet he couldn't believe, and so he had to go on as always, only more filled with anxiety and frustration, with no certainty at all in his own choices. But there was nothing to be done.

The next year he was depressed again. Often he wanted to die. The worst moment was when he awoke each morning, too well rested to sleep, and had to face the long day till merciful night came again. Marina would come into his room and sit beside him and ask him why he didn't get up, why he didn't smile. He couldn't, and seeing how this hurt her only made him weep all the more with anguish.

He was slow to get better, but by her tenth birthday he felt well enough to go into town with her and buy her a new dress. When he looked back on the dark months he had passed through it was awful for him to think that someday he would feel that way again. The fear cut into his sense of relief.

He thought how pointless his life had become. He was intelligent, but something was missing in him: intelligent enough to want to accomplish great things but incapable of doing anything great, and now of doing anything at all. He had always been the same: there was in him a fearfulness masquerading as disinterest, or a disinterest masquerading as fearfulness, which had kept him away from life. The tragedy was that Imaculada had been his chance to make himself complete, but he hadn't completely recognized it until she was gone. In her spirit she had what was missing in him. He had wasted all that time in Manaus running away from what he needed, trying to make the fortune she had never asked for. His ambition had led to her death—though his natural inclination was to feel sorry for himself rather than guilty over what had happened to her. He felt that he had always been carried along by existence, not mastered it, or molded it, as great men do, as he had wanted to do. No history books would note his name, no societies would be different because he had lived. Sometimes he felt that he almost hadn't lived, that life had been a shadow for him. There had been so much time, when he looked back, and it had all slipped away ungrasped. "What if I had been given the lifespan of a firefly?" he wondered. "Would I have accomplished any less than I have as it is? Why have all these years been wasted as if they had been no more than a few seconds?" He had wanted to experience the world, as much of it as possible, to swallow it whole, its feelings, emotions, and sensations, its tastes, its smells and colours, its invigoration, its flora and fauna, its loves. He had wanted to dip his hand into every cold, clear stream. And when death came he would hardly have begun. But now he did nothing but think about it. Even now that he felt recovered, it seemed to him still that real life was happening elsewhere, in other hearts. He longed for it, but he lacked the strength, the resolve, the direction to do anything about it. He hated the isolation of his farm, but he never wanted to leave it. It was already too late.

But then sometimes he began to think that life wasn't quite over yet, that maybe once more before he got old, life would start up for him again, and if even for a brief time, things would happen, that there was some adventure awaiting him. There was still time. "Maybe there's life in these bones yet," he would say to himself, hardly daring to believe it. And so he languished and waited.

The tenth anniversary of Imaculada's death came and went. Had it been that long? He tried to remember her, but it was almost as if she had been part of another, imaginary life. Her death almost didn't matter to him anymore; what frightened him was the passing of another decade.

"Is there nothing to look forward to?" He would go on this way until death came, with nothing happening, nothing to give importance to his existence. The drama of his life, what little drama there had been, was long past. He would never be young again.

"Is that a bald spot?" Nanette asked him one day. "Let me see! Why yes it is!" And when he held a mirror up behind him, there it was.

Along with his great unhappiness, Edmundo had health problems, first chronic aches and pains, then numbness along his left side that triggered an abiding clumsiness. Finally he began to have soft tumours appear under the skin on his belly and his back; one grew to the size of a plum. For a long time he did nothing, but at last he went to see a doctor in São Paulo.

The doctor listened to Edmundo's account of his symptoms and looked at his belly and his back. He knit his brows.

"So, what do you think?" Edmundo asked.

"It's impossible to be sure—there's no test for this—but my suspicion is that you are suffering from syphilis and that it has reached the tertiary stage."

The doctor explained that sometime in the past he had contracted the disease, that it had lain dormant for years, but that it had now begun to attack the nervous system.

"And what can be done?"

"I'm afraid there is no cure."

"And what is the prognosis?"

"It will get worse. I suspect it will attack the heart or the brain. Eventually it will kill you."

When he left the doctor, Edmundo wandered the busy streets contemplating what he had just been told, oblivious enough that several times he bumped into strangers hurrying by.

Not completely trusting a Brazilian doctor, Edmundo sent away for medical textbooks, in English, which he hoped would give him better news. Unfortunately, they confirmed the prognosis. There he read about general paresis of the insane, when syphilis reaches the brain and causes depression and dementia. There was a piece of doggerel used by medical students to help them remember the stages of syphilitic development. This was the last verse:

He's been treated in every known way
But his spirochetes grow day by day
He's developed paresis
Has long talks with Jesus
And thinks he's the Queen of the May.

Edmundo felt as if merciless fate, which had long toyed with him and abused him, was coming in for the final blows.

About this time Nanette, Armando and Marina began to notice Edmundo doing certain strange things, stranger than usual. When they went into town on market day he began to buy things, useless things that struck his fancy, things he had never shown any interest in before. He would put them up on the mantle or on the table and look at them and declare them "Magnificent!" After a few days he would forget about them and next time would buy something new. Edmundo was also becoming forgetful. He forgot where he had put things, or forgot to do things, or sometimes that he had already done them. If anyone pointed this out to him, he would lose his temper. Sometimes he became frustrated when he couldn't remember lines of poetry. His forgetfulness was worrisome because the farm had not been particularly well managed and there was no longer the money that there once had been. When Edmundo was well he ran the farm with the help of a manager, but when he was ill the manager was on his own, and there had been a series of managers, none of whom showed commitment. In fact, the manager usually took the hired workers with him when he left. A few times they were left without a manager and workers when Edmundo was confined to his bed. Recently Nanette had taken the initiative and chosen a manager herself.

One day Armando and Marina found a letter in Edmundo's handwriting which had been left lying about. It was not addressed to anyone so they gave it to Nanette and asked what should be done with it. It was a very odd letter, convoluted and falling over itself:

Why have you abandoned me? From the first moment I saw you my life was yours. Tell me, is this my reward for loving you so much? I am resolved to adore you as long as I live, and never to see anyone else. Never, never will you find so much love—all the rest is nothing!

They couldn't imagine who it could be addressed to. There was no one in the village that Edmundo could have had the slightest intimacy with. Maybe it was addressed to his dead wife. Nanette told the children to put the letter back where they had found it. It lay there, unnoticed, unclaimed, for a week, and then one day it was gone.

On market days Edmundo began to stop and buy oranges from a particular stall, the stall of a peasant and his wife from a nearby village. The peasant had a daughter, a girl of fourteen, who was shy and quite pretty. Edmundo would always ask her to pick out the best oranges for him, and a special one for him to eat right there. He would peel the orange with his fingers, take a slow, savouring taste, and then exclaim that it was absolutely magnificent. The girl would blush uneasily. She was supposed to be friendly with customers, but Edmundo's behaviour made her uncomfortable. When he was leaving Edmundo would take off his hat and bow to her extravagantly as students used to do in the Coimbra of his youth. The peasant and his wife watched this with a certain amount of suspicion. One market day when Edmundo was sick he insisted that Marina go purchase the oranges on his behalf.

Edmundo started to take long walks that would take him to the peasant girl's village. Sometimes he would take Marina and Armando with him. Somehow he had found out where the girl and her family lived, and as they passed by their shack, he would grow quiet and alert. He never stopped, or sought her out, but sometimes she would be there, in the distance, out in the fields, or near the shack. Edmundo would catch her with a quick glance and then turn away and go on as if she were of no concern to him. She must have told her parents that he had begun to walk by, for whenever she saw him she would hurry inside and her father or mother would come out and glare at Edmundo as he hurried past.

They began to be almost uncivil to him when he came by their stall to buy oranges. Edmundo tried to ignore this and he became in response more desperately charming. At home he was silent, pensive, and if anyone tried to break in on his concentration he became angry.

One Saturday he went to their stall and the girl was not there. Her father told Edmundo that his daughter was sick, but Edmundo didn't believe him. During the week he walked through the village and asked about her, but everybody confirmed what the peasant had said: she had taken to bed with a fever. Edmundo accused one man of lying.

The next Saturday the girl was again absent. Edmundo, trying to control his outrage, asked the peasant why she no longer came to town. The peasant, who was very worried about his daughter, resented Edmundo more than ever and told him that it was none of his business and to leave his daughter alone. Edmundo yelled at him and threatened to beat him with his cane. Several landowners who knew him intervened and quietly, but firmly, led him away.

Edmundo then went every day by the peasant's shack, waiting for the girl to appear. She never did. On the next Saturday he stood across the road from the peasant's stall and glared at him for half an hour. The peasant was beside himself with rage, for his daughter was dying.

That week she died. Edmundo stood on the pathway near their house and watched the villagers come to pay their respects. He watched the procession to the church and then to the graveyard and he followed and watched the funeral from a distance. Several men came to chase him away. He had no place here, they said gruffly, he was making it worse for the girl's mother. They nudged him and tried to lead him away by the arm, but he resisted them. Someone knocked him down and then they kicked him. They left him lying on the ground. Later someone saw him walking home, defiant and stiff.

There was no sight of him near the orange stall for several Saturdays. Then one morning someone discovered that the girl's grave had been dug up overnight, and her body was gone.

Armando and Marina were used to the undisciplined rural life that they were allowed to lead. They wandered wherever they wanted and workers on the farm showed them little deference. They were used to seeing what bulls do when they were made to mount the cows, or the dogs when the bitches were in heat. They were used to overhearing the crude talk of the farm hands.

Armando began to have sparse whiskers appear on his upper lip, his chin, and where his sideburns would someday be. People noticed and told him he was becoming a man.

"You know what this is for?" asked one man grabbing his crotch.

"Are you joking?" exclaimed another. "I bet he's whacking it all the time."

"Save yourself for a woman."

"Someone should take him to a whore."

The first time Armando masturbated he was lying in his bed on his stomach and became aroused when he changed position and his penis rubbed across the mattress. He rubbed it again, and again, and began thinking of Marina. He was enjoying the sensation immensely when suddenly it changed and his penis began shuddering and spurting onto the mattress. He looked and at first thought it was some kind of puss and that he had injured himself somehow. But on reflection he realized what had happened to him.

It was a strange and overpowering sensation and he did it again and again, always thinking of Marina. Recently her body had begun to change. He noticed her new breasts, which embarrassed her so that she wore a sweater even when it was hot, and the new look to her hips, round and fleshy. He wanted to rub himself against her, but she had become more aloof, and there seemed to have arisen an unspoken law that they were never to touch under any circumstances. It seemed too much even if he were to hand her something at the table or sit beside her in the carriage. Sometimes he stared furtively at her clothes drying outside in the wind, and that made him need to go to his room and rub himself against the mattress or out into the fields where the hot sunlight would fall on his penis as he pressed it in his hand. He thought he would die of shame and embarrassment if he ever did this with a woman.

For a long time he thought about Marina in this way. The very idea that such a thing could possibly take place led him over and over again to his mattress. But this was dissatisfying. He wanted her as much as he feared desiring her. Men began to nudge him and ask if he had done anything with her. He smiled uneasily and said nothing. He was so frightened and confused.

At last he began to force himself into a plan of action. He would accomplish something by the end of the summer. In December he began to make small gestures of boldness, small liberties, which were to be the first steps. These made him feel he was progressing. But then it was January and nothing more had happened. February had lay ahead, but now February was almost over. So he had set his sights on this week, and now it had come down to today.

It wasn't often they took walks alone together anymore. People their age needed a chaperone. But this day Armando, in the morning, before the day grew unbearably hot, asked Marina to go with him to take milk to a farmer whose cow had died.

He knew she was worried about her father, but she didn't like to talk about it, even think about it, so they walked along in silence. They got to the farmer's place and delivered the milk.

"How is your father? I hear he's not been well," the farmer asked.

"He's feeling a bit better today," Marina answered because that was what she wanted to believe.

On the way back Armando thought about touching Marina somewhere. The thought gave him an erection and made him very excited. He felt like he was going to explode.

"Marina, stop!"

"What is it?"

His hand moved towards her chest and suddenly his fingers were touching her breasts.

"Armando, what are you doing?" She pulled back.

He hesitated, then seized her and kissed her on the mouth. He felt her body warm and soft against his. His penis was hard and he pressed tightly against her when suddenly he felt it shoot into his pants. Immediately a sense of remorse and emptiness came over him and he pulled back from her.

"Marina, forgive me, forgive me." He was completely flustered.

Seeing him repentant and weak again, her strength came back to her, and she pulled away from him.

"Armando, how dare you! What if Papai knew what you did? What if your mother knew?"

"Forgive me!" He was so ashamed of himself.

"This is not like you! I thought you were a good person."

"I am a pig. I will never do it again."

"You've disappointed me."

She told him to pick up the empty milk can and they walked back: she ten feet in front of him, he cowering behind.

"I can never walk like that with you again, Armando," she said when they were close to home.

"Are you going to tell anyone?"

"No. Because I know you have learned your lesson."

"Yes, I have."

When they arrived home there was a commotion before the house. There was a small crowd of strangers with strained faces. Women were crying. Marina wanted to see her father. Where was he? She came into the crowd to look for him.

"That's his daughter!" Someone had recognized her.

She felt their eyes all shoot towards her.

The farm manager rushed to her.

"Come away, Menina Marina!"

It was too late. She saw her father lying on the veranda with Nanette kneeling beside him. Her father's red wound ran from his shoulder all the way down across his chest. Nanette was frantically trying to stop the bleeding with white sheets which she had torn into strips. Suddenly she stopped and her arms and shoulders collapsed to her sides.

"He's dead," she said in surrender, then saw Marina staring at them with her wild eyes.

A man tried to come forward but he was being restrained by others. It was the peasant girl's father. His face was full of anguish.

"I'm sorry," he cried. "But he took my daughter's body and he wouldn't give it back. He said she was his wife. He was crazy!"

As the years passed, events took place in the world that Marina wished her father could be there to share with her. After the English successfully cultivated rubber in Ceylon, the Brazilian rubber business collapsed, the barons sold pencils on the streets of Manaus, and their mistresses went back to whoring. On February 1, 1908, Carlos I, King of Portugal, his wife Amelia, his heir, Luis Filipe, and his younger son Manuel, left their palace at Vila Viçosa and took a train towards Lisbon. The station was across the Tagus River from the city, so they boarded a launch and arrived at the foot of the Praça do Comércio. There had been unrest and the King had been forced to take certain repressive measures. Now he was concerned for his safety, but his Prime Minister, who was there to meet him, assured him that all would be well. The royal family entered their landau and started out of the Praça.

Just as they turned into the Rua do Arsenal, two men in the crowd ran forward with revolvers and began firing into the carriage. The King was hit in the throat and then in the shoulder. The Crown Prince was shot twice while he was drawing his revolver to shoot back. Manuel was shot in the arm. The Queen tried to beat off the assassins with a bouquet of flowers. Meanwhile those in the King's entourage who were following behind in an automobile began to fire at the assassins, but they only succeeded in killing an innocent bystander, Subino da Costa: he was twenty-two and from Madeira.

The assassins ran for their lives, but the police soon caught up with them. They killed one, and the other, with a sword through his side, finished himself with his own revolver. One of the assassins was a professor and everyone who had known him was shocked. The other was a former student and journalist who was at the time working as a clerk. The professor left a wife and children, and a note:

My children will be left in the poorest circumstances; I have nothing to leave them besides my name, my respect and pity for those who suffer. I beg that they may be educated in the principles of liberty, equality, and fraternity, principles which I uphold and in the cause of which they are soon likely to become orphans.

The King and his heir could not be saved. And so Manuel became king. But he was just a boy, and he was not strong enough to uphold the old traditions. On October 4, 1910, he was deposed and fled to France. The first Portuguese Republic was declared.

Marina was sorry that Edmundo had not lived to see it.

At any rate, it didn't last.

PART TWO

Chapter One

Lisbon, 1999

I was born in a fascist dictatorship and colonial empire, in a place where flags flew at half-mast when Hitler died. The first dictator was Salazar, the mild-mannered peasant professor, then later, for a much shorter time, Caetano. I grew up with the secret police, with informers everywhere, in the schools and in the town square. Many priests were informers and breached the secrets of the confessional with a clear conscience. Others, I know from experience, were good men. You learned to watch what you said. I kept my thoughts to myself. Many didn't have thoughts they needed to be guarded about. The Portuguese, said Salazar, are not a very intelligent people. Of course, the truth is more complex than that. Politically, things are, of course, better now, and freedom reigns, but the happiest days of my life were in those days of oppression and secrecy, although politics had nothing directly to do with that.

Isabel and Judite have gone out for the afternoon to visit Maria de Deus in the convent. She's ninety-five and doesn't know where she is anymore. They've always compared me to her, ever since I was young—Judite did it again just yesterday—because they saw us both as quiet and shy, conformist and deeply lacking in rebelliousness. A bit shell shocked she was too. She had a way of cowering through life, as if waiting for the next blow. For the first time in many years, Isabel is visiting from the island. Although Judite has set up a very nice room for her, she refuses to stay more than a few days—partly because of her health but mainly because she can't stand to be away from her routines for any substantial length of time. Over the last few days I have been spending most of my waking hours with them—sitting and chatting over coffee, driving to visit a few landmarks (mostly those that commemorate the imperial glories of the Golden Age), listening to them rake over the embers of the past. Sisters, in conversation they like to pick at old wounds, and I find myself (despite myself?) seduced by them into that compulsive and bittersweet activity. Normally I live a life in which I can let yesteryear sleep, but having my two older cousins together like this (probably for the last time) has nudged me to turn my head and look behind for a while at what used to be. Tomorrow I must stop. I will have to fashion myself a cone, the kind one puts around a cat's head to keep it from licking its stitches.

This afternoon I'm taking advantage of their absence to listen to music, sweet lovely music, and enjoy a respite from their company. They'll be here for supper along with everyone else and I'll be refreshed for them, but for now there is no one here to listen to. Only the quiet but insistent music that fills the room and the hours. I remember when we lived in Angola all we had were phonograph records that we played at parties where there was always dancing, many, many records—*fado, bossa nova*, American jazz—which we had to leave behind when we fled the country. They would be old now, if they still exist. When records were worn out they skipped: they would either play the same thing over and over, not letting it go, or there would be some moment they couldn't play at all or ever again. Even records that were alright had scratches and marks you could hear as they sang. They resembled, obviously, people in those regards. Now we have CDs. CDs are more resilient than we are. I know sometimes if they are smudged they can go crazy like manic wind-up toys, but if you just wipe them clean with something soft all is forgiven. But I've heard that eventually they react badly to the air. I'm not sure what that does to them, whether they turn into noise or silence, whether they end in chaos or in nothingness. What is to be their fate? Being Portuguese, I am deeply attached to the idea of fate. What would I sing in my own personal *fado*? I think my fate has been, in large part, to live long, to observe, to feel, and to come to know. Eyes, ears, heart, understanding. There are many things I have learned that I never speak. One thing I know, for instance, is that if you live long enough, it will come to pass, sometimes very slowly, sometimes suddenly and harshly all at once, sometimes in a series of shocks like earthquakes of varying magnitude, that your deepest connections are no longer with the living but with the dead.

Gone are the artefacts of my youth, the wooden things, the cloth and clay. For my children and my grandchildren, even for Jorge because he is an engineer and they are the tools of his work, it is the computer, the cell phone, the digital products. I have learned to use all of these out of convenience, but I have no attachment to them. Not the way I was attached to those old records.

I was born on a small island in the middle of the ocean almost 60 years ago, although not the island on which I was raised. My father had moved to Terceira to work on the American air force base. Some of us have wandering in the blood. My earliest memory is of my father buying me a Coca Cola and a hotdog—exotic and extravagant fare indeed. He met my mother there. I like to think that he was happy and they were in love with each other and happy to have me. I like to think the three of us would have stayed together if fate, my *fado*, had not interfered. She was an orphan and had no family. People usually have many families—one from their mother, one from their father, one or more they marry into. I have always had only the one.

What do I remember from my earliest days? The blue and white tiles, of course, the *azulejos*, that are still everywhere, and the ocean. And things that are less a part of life now, especially a life like mine: women embroidering table cloths; feeding the pigs sweet potatoes, which I loved to do, to fatten them up in the fall for slaughter, which is not why I liked to do it. I remember earthquakes, cornbread hot from the coal fire, Masses, endless Masses, *festas*, processions and marching bands, the streets decorated in sawdust and flower petals, rhododendrons, carnations (which later came to stand for revolution), grapes, sticky figs, oranges and bananas from our *quinta*, almonds, olives, being meek, silent, watching. I remember a man everybody nicknamed Julia Florista, who became a tailor, it was claimed, so that he could measure men in their pants. I had no idea why that would be an interesting thing to do. I remember many things, some that others—my cousins, for instance—have chosen to forget.

When my grandmother died I inherited the family records— letters, legal documents, photographs, notebooks, and diaries, that go back to Brazil, a place I have never been. I have looked over these records, partly out a sense of loyalty to my grandmother, and they are not in themselves uninteresting; they have told me things no one else still alive knows; but I have always been a rather insular person, I do not have an expansive heart, and I can have a deep concern only for those I have known and who have been close to me. I can't apologize for that. Those concerns have kept me busy enough. I have suffered the so-called Chinese curse of living in interesting times. For the most part, my reaction has been to withdraw and turn inward, into the home, into the safety of books, into myself.

I remember what happened to the Baptist church. They were foreign missionaries trying to convert us, we all thought, were all told, from the true Catholic faith. People said they would take pictures of all the people on the beach on a summer Sunday and send them back to England or wherever and claim they had converted us all. When we little ones saw them with their cameras we would try to hide. Later, in Angola, I would sometimes see black children act the same way. The Baptist church was near our little village and on Sunday they came by bus from all over. One Sunday our men came from the bar, filled with drink and religion, and xenophobia, or something more insular and small minded, and began to throw stones at them. They fled and our men broke in and wrecked the place. Next day they finished the job, tearing down the outside walls. The police were called in and there was an investigation and a trial. Everyone lied: no one saw anything; no one was there. We were a tight-knit community. A few men spent a brief time in jail. Some were fined. My uncle Gabriel was fined 50 escudos for ripping apart a pair of children's shoes he found inside the church. They were much like the shoes I myself wore. Later, in Africa, the children wore no shoes. The Baptists, showing more prudence than zeal, relocated elsewhere.

By then we were living with my grandmother in *Agua d'Alto*. We moved there when my mother became sick and my father wasn't up to taking care of us. My Avó was one of the great loves of my life. I've felt closer to her than I ever have to anyone, more like her. She loved to cook for her family. I have been busy cooking for the last two days: *bacalhau à Gomes de Sá*, turkey stuffed with chestnuts; they're keeping warm in the oven. I made *caldo verde* yesterday. Isabel loves it with little pieces of *chouriço*. My sons and their wives and their children are coming too. They won't eat the soup. It's one of the foods of the past. My grandchildren only like chicken rice soup which I make for them when they stay overnight. The *pão de milho* is still warm, so I'll slice that when we're at the table. That's another treat for Isabel. There's a bakery nearby run by a man from São Miguel, and his is just like she loves it, heavy and moist with a thick crust. There are cheeses too: a sharp *São Jorge* and a ripe, runny French one. There are mild ones for my grandchildren. I don't usually eat much at these meals. Afterwards, when everyone has gone, I collapse on the couch and eat from a plate that Jorge makes for me. He'll clean up the table, put away the food, and put the dishes in the dishwasher while we chat. He doesn't especially enjoy these family meals—after all they're not his family and he doesn't even bother to stay in touch with his own, but he knows that these meals are important to me. His favourite part is when everyone has gone and he has me to himself. That and all the delicious food. Jorge loves my food. I hope I've made enough. At the end of the meal everybody will complain about being stuffed. That is as it should be.

Jorge went to the office but promised to be here early, before everyone else arrives, so that he can greet them while I dedicate myself to serving the food. The kitchen smells warm and sweet. I have taken the *bolo de ló* out of the oven. It's the only cake that doesn't upset Isabel's stomach because there's no butter, just eggs, flour and sugar. I've made so many desserts that I've had to distribute them throughout the cupboards—*pudim flan*, orange almond cake, and dark chocolate mousse. My sons are like little boys when they eat my chocolate mousse. They chortle with pleasure. I didn't learn to make chocolate mousse from my Avó. Her recipes were much simpler. Avó taught me to make *massa sovada*. I remember the smell of yeast mixed with sugar in warm water. I thought about making it for today, but it takes so long and I never know when to knead the second time—it's always in the middle of the night. So I bought a loaf at SolMar. Avó would be surprised at how easy it is to get it now. In her day it was only on special *festas*—Christmas, Easter, First Communion, Confirmation. My sons and daughters-in-laws and my grandchildren don't care for it, but my cousins won't think the meal is complete without it. It was the height of their feasts of yesteryear. Jorge and I like to eat it once in a while, especially when it's rainy and damp. I toast a couple of slices, spread them with sweet butter, and we eat them with tea.

Now that everything is more or less ready, I'm going to pour myself a glass of wine. I like the way it makes me relax just a little, so I can enjoy the company of my family, which is not always the easiest thing to do. Even when they are broken, there is nothing more important than families. I know that my family has lived through much unhappiness, and I also know that we were occasionally deeply contented. When my sons were little, I so desperately wanted to make a happy family for them. That longing and striving made me happy, if not my sons. It has been a long time since they were mine in that way; so much longer since I belonged to my Avó and my father.

It was not unusual in *Agua d'Alto* for generations to live together like we did. My grandmother's house was big and perched high on top of a hill at the north end of the village, with a goshawk's view of the ocean in every direction. Brown earth, blue sky, green fields and hills, and the smell of the salty sea. My Avô Manuel lived in the house too, but I don't remember him. I know now that he died of cancer, and Judite, who was old enough to remember, once told me that Avó nursed him through an ugly death. My mother died too. I remember the way she smelled of talcum powder when I crawled into bed with her and put my head against her breast. No one uses talcum powder today, but even when it was popular, when I was growing up, I never used it and I didn't like to smell it on anyone else. It made me feel empty inside.

"Can I sleep with mama?"

"No, *querida*. Kiss her goodnight. She needs to rest."

Resistant, I crawled in beside my mother and wrapped myself against her powdered body. I sank deep into my mother's bosom and then I was airborne, in Avó's arms, and she carried me upstairs to a bedroom on the second floor.

Every night I would ask to sleep with my mother and every night Avó would carry me upstairs.

"Margarida, your cousins Isabel and Judite are coming to get you. You're going to sleep with them for a few nights."

"I want to kiss mama goodnight."

"Not tonight, *querida*. She has a fever."

Avó went upstairs to collect my things. My father was not at home.

He drank sometimes. I wanted to kiss my mother before I left for my cousins' house. The door to her bedroom was closed. I tiptoed across the hall and stood motionless at the door for what felt like a long time before I took the cold brass doorknob into my hand. Softly, without daring to breathe, I turned it until the door opened, stepped inside the room, and walked to my mother's bed. The shutters were closed and everything was dark, except the crocheted counterpane on my mother's bed and the shine of the hardwood floor. My mother was sleeping. Her face was still. I stretched across the bed and kissed my mother's dry lips. She felt cold. I wanted to hug her, but didn't because it might wake her up. Instead I turned around and tiptoed out of the room, closed the door softly, and left my mother to her sleep.

When Avó came down the stairs with my bag of clothes, I was relieved that the hall was dark and she wouldn't be able to see my face. My cheeks burned hot. I had done something I shouldn't have and I was afraid that Avó was going to find out.

Isabel and Judite ran down the hill swinging me between them by the arms.

"You have to get better marks if you want to be a teacher," Isabel said.

"I knew the answers but I got nervous when Profesora Dona Eugénia asked me the questions," answered Judite.

"If you knew the answers, you wouldn't be nervous."

I craned my neck to see Judite's face, but I couldn't see through her black hair falling over her shoulders like a shawl. I curled my fingers softly around her big hand and inched my body closer to hers to let her know that I was her friend.

"I'll pass the exam next time. I'll be a teacher."

"Can I live with you if you live in the city?" I asked Judite.

"Of course, you can. You'll be in the college then and you'll need to live in the city."

"I can visit my mother and Avó on the weekend."

The ground below us was hard and cracked and I kept losing my footing. My cousins scooped me back up, until I went down again, and again they would lift me up. It was a like a game for me, and by the time we arrived at their house I had forgotten about my mother.

I loved spending the night at my cousins' house. They were our closest neighbours, on a hill that rose from the fields behind Avó's house. She had bought the land, years ago, for her family, my father and tio Gabriel. Tio Gabriel had built a house for his family, but my father had never built a house of his own, even after he had married my mother and I had been born. Avó's house was quiet, with adults shut up in their bedrooms—my mother in her room downstairs and my father often depressed and curled up in bed. It felt so different walking into my cousins' house, full of children like me. I thought of it as my cousins' house. I didn't particularly like my aunt and uncle. My aunt's maiden name was Teresa Coelho. She was very traditional but not really so strict. Her two younger brothers had gone off with the *Legião Portuguesa* to fight with Franco in Spain. Their rallying cry was "*Viva Muerte!*"—"Long Live Death!" They were both killed. Aunt Teresa kept their pictures and medals on display in the sitting room. My uncle was frightening to a young girl like me—stern, intense, judgmental. His drinking and his unhappiness were the only things he had in common with my father. On this evening I smelled *chouriço* and green onions sizzling on the fire at the back of the kitchen. The kitchen was heavy with shadows, the only light coming from the fire and the kerosene lamp set in the middle of the table. Tio Gabriel was sitting in a corner in darkness.

"Poor thing," moaned tia Teresa from near the kitchen fire where she stirred a pot of soup.

"What kind of soup is it, tia Teresa?" I wanted to know.

"Red bean soup," answered Isabel who had started slicing a loaf of corn bread.

There were so many of them, and I was used to eating alone with my Avó and, sometimes, with my father. Being the youngest I was pampered.

The softest bread.

The first one to be served after tio Gabriel.

"Tomorrow you and Judite must help your Avó. Clean the house and get everything ready."

"What's the little one going to do?"

I knew the "little one" was me and it made me feel good to be part of the conversation. I swung my legs under the table.

"She can stay with me. I'm baking bread. She can help me."

"I think it might be too much for Avó." I did not understand what would be "too much for Avó."

"We could offer—"

"No!" Tio Gabriel's voice was very harsh. "We have enough as it is. And not *his* child."

"Say, Margarida, would you like to go swimming with me tomorrow?" my cousin David asked. He was closest to me in age.

Everybody stopped eating except David and I.

"David, what can you be thinking!" gasped tia Teresa. "What would people say?"

"She's five years old!" argued David.

"And you're old enough to know better." Tio Gabriel's voice ended the conversation.

For a few moments I could hear the sound of my breathing. Then someone, maybe tio Gabriel, started eating again and everything was like it was before. When we finished, my uncle and David left the house. Tia Teresa, Isabel and Judite started cleaning up, scraping the plates clean and shaking the crumbs from the tablecloth into a pail of leftover food that would be fed to the pig. I curled up in my chair, determined not to fall asleep, for the best part was when we climbed the stairs to the bedroom and I sat up in bed with Isabel and Judite.

"Want to help me feed the pig?" Judite asked.

I jumped up and together we walked to the backyard, which was black with the night and full of animal sounds—crickets, chickens, dogs, and the pig. I stood close to Judite as she heaved the leftover food into the sty. Then we ran back into the house and up the stairs to the bedroom where Isabel was turning down the sheets. The three of us undressed by the light of the candle on the table by the bed. My long flannel nightgown smelled of soap.

I was the first one in the bed, in the middle, but before we went to sleep we had to brush each other's hair. The three of us had the same hair, thick and curly. The best way to comb it was with your fingers. Avó Marina had taught us how to do it. Only when we washed our hair did we use a comb, but, when it was dry, fingers worked best and left the hair fluffy. We worked on Isabel's hair first, crackling with electricity, before we braided it tight so that in the morning it would fall in even, smooth waves. My hair was finer, and as gentle as my cousins tried to be, I could feel the pulling at the roots. It was a sweet pain. I was disappointed when they were finished.

We snuggled under the sheets and Isabel blew out the candle.

The sheets were cool and crisp.

"Why can't I go to the beach with David?"

"In a small village everybody talks about everybody else. Even little girls. That's why I want to live in the city." Judite whispered her explanation.

I didn't understand what she meant, but she made me feel better.

"Little girls need to behave. It doesn't matter whether you live in a village or the city. Everyone has to learn how to behave." Isabel's voice was clear and strong. I understood from her tone and her words that it was wrong for me to go to the beach with David, but she didn't explain why it was wrong.

I fell asleep, imagining myself sinking into the cracks in the ground and being lifted up by my cousins.

The next day I spent with tia Teresa while my cousins were at school. Usually I went back to Avó's house the next morning, but this time I stayed longer and when I did go back it was to find my mother gone. Her bedroom door was open and I could see her bed neatly made. The floors shone with wax like they did for Christmas and Easter, but there were no fresh-cut flowers in vases. The living room door was shut. Avó took me to the kitchen where my father was sitting at the table.

"Margarida, I've made you *arroz doce* with cinnamon." Avó put a bowl that was still warm before me and I forgot about my mother for a few moments. It was my favourite dessert, and especially delicious when it was still warm.

"Margarida, we have something to tell you," Avó continued.

My father was slumped over the table, his face hidden in his hands.

I was five years old, but I knew that my mother was gone. Otherwise, she would be lying in bed, just as I remembered her doing most of my life. Suddenly, I felt cold. I loved Avó and my father, but it was my mother's body that I craved. Her sweet-smelling warmth.

"Your mother died, *querida*. She loved you very much and she'll always be with you, but you won't be able to see her anymore. You must be brave, *querida*."

Avó covered me with her arms, but it was as if she wasn't there. As if nobody was there with me. As if I were all alone.

I remember nothing of my mother's funeral. Later, I watched and learned the rituals when someone died in Agua d'Alto. The body was laid out in the home for a day or so before being placed in a coffin that would be carried by a horse and carriage with a procession of people following behind. The church bells always rang when someone died: first, to announce the death and then later to announce the funeral Mass. All this must have happened when my mother died. I'm sure I walked behind her coffin with my Avó and father beside me and tio Gabriel and tia Teresa and my cousins behind us. All this must have happened, but I remember none of it.

I don't remember wearing black. My father wore black for a year, but I don't remember. I don't remember the big vat of black dye in the yard, but there must have been one. There always was. If there was a widow, she might as well throw everything in, because she would never wear colour again. That would be even my Avó when my grandfather died, although she was strong and had a mind of her own.

Here is a story I remember hearing. A woman's husband dies and she dyes all her clothes black. She's in mourning so she's not supposed to want earthly pleasures such as food. But when she's alone she cooks herself pieces of meat. One evening while she's cooking, guests come to pay their condolences. Not wanting to be the object of gossip and condemnation, she hides the meat behind the stove. As she talks with the guests, she notices a farm cat—very much a fend-for-itself cat—come and take away a piece of meat. Then another, then another. Finally the woman cries out.

"Santa Maria, he's taking them one by one!"

"O Senhora," says a guest, misunderstanding, "you must be patient. It is God's way!"

Such stories are very basic in their insights: people care about appearances and cats eat whatever they can pilfer.

I liked to play outdoors with my dolls, where there was space in the garden for me to sit, the earth my cushion and the flowers the walls of my playground. There were always cats curled up sleeping under the shade of flowers and shrubs. I saw less of my cousins. Isabel was teaching in a village on the north coast of the island and boarding with a family there. Judite was studying in Ponta Delgada, also boarding with a family, and coming home about once a month. David was still at home, and sometimes if Avó needed him to buy supplies in town she would send me with him.

"It's good for you to go out, *querida*," she would say.

I loved walking with David. He would start the walk by holding my hand as we descended the hill, but by the time we reached other houses he would let go of me to stop and talk with other boys. I loved it that he had so many friends. Often, we wouldn't be back home until suppertime and he wouldn't have any change for Avó.

"What took you so long?" Avó asked. "I was beginning to worry."

"I like to stop and chat with people. It's better for Margarida. She gets to rest."

"Of all my grandchildren, you're the friendly one. It's a good way to be, *querido*. As long as you don't forget about Margarida."

"How could I forget this beautiful head of curls?" he laughed, mussing my hair.

Avó looked at us and said, "I'm glad you get along. All my grandchildren like each other. That makes me happy."

She took us both in her arms for a hug.

"I couldn't pay for everything at the pharmacy," admitted David. "There's no problem though. I can pay it next time. They said not to worry. They know our family can be trusted."

"But, David, I gave you enough money."

"Yes, but my friend José Lourenço came along and you know how poor they are, so I bought some treats. I knew you wouldn't mind."

She didn't get angry at David, but once in a while she would make the trip with me to pay the bills at the pharmacy or the store.

"Don't let my grandson buy anything on credit," she warned the pharmacist and the store owner. "He's young, after all, and you should know better. Please don't take advantage of him next time."

I was clever and eager to learn from a very early age, unstimulated at home but too young, officially, to go to school. Avó intervened with Padre António, who was her friend and visited her everyday. He would sit in the kitchen and eat butter cookies and drink tea. In church he was all costume and pomp, a bit stiff and intimidating, but at home in his plain dusty black cassock he was relaxed and almost part of the family. My grandmother, I could tell, loved the company.

"This little girl needs to be in school around girls her own age. Up here she has no one to play with."

"She's only five. The inspector wouldn't hear of it."

"My dear António, Inspector Martins would do whatever you told him to do. Why keep a child back from school if she can keep up? Margarida already knows her alphabet and she can read."

"Let's see what Margarida has to say."

"I want to go to school."

No hesitation there.

A few months later, when I had not yet turned six, I was given special permission by the school inspector to enroll in school. My grandmother bought meters of stiff white cotton fabric and hired a dressmaker to make pinafores for me to wear over my clothes. The school was in Vila Franca de Campo, once the capital of the island before an earthquake leveled its buildings and harbour. The statue of Prince Henry the Navigator looking out to sea was the only nod to the town's past glory. It was a forty-five minute walk to Vila Franca from our house. I would go with my cousin David who was also studying in Vila Franca.

School started in October when the land smelled of grapes. Men, women, and children stooped and plucked them by the bunch. Fingers and tongues were stained purple. Avó and I leaned over the balcony on the second floor, waiting for David to come for me. I was all white and starched in my school uniform, my hair pulled straight back in a ponytail, my face scrubbed and shiny.

"Little cousin, are you ready for school?" David called from below.

I clutched my satchel and ran down the stairs to meet him.

"I'll see you this afternoon, *querida*. I'll make *fatias douradas* for dinner," promised Avó. "I'll make lots so that you can take some home, David."

We walked down the hill from Avó's house, passing one or two houses and then more as we approached the heart of the village, with the road bending and dropping closer to the ocean. When we reached the foot of the village the sea spread out before us wide and blue. We followed the road to Vila Franca. The road was lined with plantain trees covered with dappled bark. The children walked to school in pairs and groups, the girls with arms linked together, the boys jostling each other. David chatted with his many friends and forgot about me. I tried to stay close to him, but he was weaving about like a football player trying to break ahead with the ball. I gave up and walked at my own pace, surrounded by children I didn't know. Everybody was talking: the girls in hushed secrets, the boys in loud jokes. I was quiet. There was so much to take in and before I knew it I was at the school. David, who was way ahead of me, stopped and waited for me to catch up.

He was standing by the iron gates, surrounded by a group of girls.

"Here you are! Girls, this is my cousin, Margarida. It's her first day of school, so keep an eye on her."

The girls answered with a chorus of laughter.

"You're all set. These girls have given me their word that they'll look after you. Just the first couple of days, she's independent and will be fine in no time."

He had their attention because he was older and he was a boy and because he always had a way about him.

"I'll pick you up after school. Right here, outside the gates. See you later." And he was off with his friends.

I was on display, in the middle of a circle of white pinafores, watched by a dozen eyes. What should I do? I felt my heart flutter. I wanted to run back home and forget all about school. I wanted to be sitting in the garden playing with my dolls.

A girl with black hair and bangs stepped up to me and took my hand.

"I'm Inês. I'm in grade one with Dona Eduarda. She's nice. My older sisters had her as a teacher. I'll sit with you." And with that Inês took my hand and led me through the steel gates, across the garden of hydrangea and azalea bushes, and into the classroom.

The classroom was full of light. The long walls had large windows that curved into half-moons at the top; on one side they showed the sea, endless and blue; on the other side they showed the garden in full flower. The desks were built in twos and the girls sat themselves in pairs. I followed Inês to a desk close to the front.

At the front of the classroom stood a small, stocky woman, Dona Eduarda, with black hair pulled back in a chignon and black glasses that flared at the top of the frames. She was as still as a statue in her white uniform. She held a booklet in her hand. She went to the first girl in the first desk, handed her the booklet, and told her to read from the first page. She couldn't. She asked the second girl, who mumbled a few words.

"Louder. We can't hear you." She said it very nicely, but the girl was still mightily intimidated.

For some of the girls, she said, "Good."

Inês's voice shook when it was her turn to read. She was almost finished, but got stuck near the end of her passage.

Dona Eduarda helped her finish.

Now it was my turn.

Dona Eduarda handed me the booklet.

It went very quickly. A paragraph about a quinta of orange trees. I read the last word and looked up to the teacher.

"Good," said Dona Eduarda, before she nodded her head gently.

I wanted to hug her, but instead I just sat quietly listening to the other girls reading, my eyes fixed on the solid, kind, all-knowing face of Dona Eduarda.

At the end of the day David was not at the gates waiting for me.

"See you tomorrow," said the girls as they walked away. I noticed that Inês' uniform, unlike my own, was frayed around the cuffs. She wasn't the first to have worn it. "I'll see you tomorrow," said Inês. "You read very well, Margarida."

I was proud of myself. I knew I had read well, even though I was younger than the others.

The street was full of children but I couldn't see my cousin. Then he embraced me from behind. I turned and buried my head in his chest.

"Hey, how was it? Do you like your teacher?"

"Dona Eduarda is nice and I like the way she talks. I like school. I'm going to be the best student and I'm going to make friends. But I want to go home, David." I clutched his hand all the way back to

Agua d'Alto.

David had a group of boyfriends who walked home with him. He amused them with stories and jokes. I felt safe and protected holding David's hand as they chatted and laughed, skimming along the coast.

At the end of the day, when the girls pushed back their chairs, I was always the last one to get up, my fingers still clinging to the chalk.

After school I dawdled in the garden with the other girls. At first I talked only to Inês, but before long I was friendly with others.

"Where do you live?"

"Do you have any sisters?"

"Is your house far away?"

Most of the other girls came from large families, crowded into small houses with earth floors. Often the other girls would have to go before David came by for me. I would sit on the bench beside the azalea bush and repeat to myself the conversations I had been part of and imagine what I might say to my friends the next day. I didn't have to rush home to help prepare dinner or look after younger brothers and sisters. Avó always had a small dinner ready for the two of us. Sometimes Padre António would join us, and after dinner we would read: Eça de Queiros, Aquilino Ribeiro, Miguel Torga. Avó had books that she had brought from Brazil, and Padre António regularly had new books shipped from Lisbon. I remember reading Fernando Pessoa's *Mensagem* with them—*"Deus quer, o homen sonha, a obra nasce."* God wants, man dreams, the work is born." I have not forgotten the words, but I understand them differently now. Yet when I told Avó and Padre António what I thought Pessoa meant, they listened, and let me keep my child-like understanding.

Saturday afternoons and Sundays were free. David marched on Saturday with the *Mocidade Portuguesa*, Salazar's youth movement. All the boys did, making the fascist salute and shouting out answers to the officer's questions.

"Portuguese, who lives?"

"Portugal! Portugal! Portugal!"

"Portuguese, who leads?"

"Salazar! Salazar! Salazar!"

David looked so handsome in his green shirt and beret. He stood straight and proud and confident as if he were positioned at the centre of everything.

Often David and his friends played football on the road. One day he planted me on top of a hill where I could pick little flowers to stroke my face with. The afternoon sun gilded the sky and sea. When I closed my eyelids, everything was sun; it was in the sound of the ball and the cheers of the boys.

"It's so hot! I'm going for a swim."

David was running down the path to the beach. The other boys followed behind. I brought up the rear.

I slipped down the steep, stony path, my feet twisting from side to side. By the time I landed on the black sand, David was already in the water, his arms churning up foam. I sat on the black, jagged rocks at the edge of the beach where the waves sprayed. I took off my shoes, threw them as far as I could towards where the sand was dry, and slid down the side of the rock to a pool of warm water that covered my feet.

I heard the boys yelling in some commotion. From where I was I couldn't see what was happening. They seemed to be looking at something floating in the water, something they were wary to get too close to.

After a while one boy turned toward the shore and yelled out, "David has found a dead body!"

One of the boys went up to the church to tell Padre António. He came down to the beach with three other men. They wrapped the body in sheets and carried it up the steep path to the village.

It was no one we knew. The body had been in the water so long it was hard to tell much of anything. During the war there were German sailors who washed up occasionally and some people said this was one of them. Whoever it was, some people said the discovery meant

David was jinxed. Teresa Coelho dismissed the idea, but everyone could see she was worried and she had David bless himself with holy water every day for a long while.

While studying in the city, Judite met an upright young man named Valentim Lima. Young but a number of years older than she. Judite brought him to our village to meet the family. He was from the mainland. Very proper. It was all rather unclear what he did for a living, but he said vaguely that he had an administrative position with the government. We heard rumours that he was stationed on the island with P.I.D.E., the *Policia Internacional e de Defesa do Estado,* the state police.

Everyone, of course, tried to avoid running afoul of P.I.D.E. The local recruits were illiterate thugs and sadists, ne'er-do-wells who relished the chance to exercise a little brute force. They were originally trained by the gestapo but now by much more educated men from the mainland. The agents were connected to a network of informers who kept an ever-watchful eye on what people did and said. That Judite's friend could be part of such a network was, for better and for worse, a thing of note. Nobody dared ask him directly, though, and he volunteered little information.

He'd met Judite at *Igreja da Matriz*, the big church in Ponta Delgada, where he was friends with the priests. He said he'd thought about being a priest himself once upon a time. He was very polite to my aunt and uncle. I was sent as chaperone when he went for walks with Judite, although my presence was completely unnecessary—he was too proper to take any liberties. Judite was obviously elated and proud of him but also anxious that something might go wrong.

When he sat with the family he talked about the importance of religion and family and admired the pictures of Teresa Coelho's brothers and their medals. He said they were brave boys who died in a righteous cause. Gabriel was stiff and wary around Lima, but Aunt Teresa kept him from drinking when Judite's friend was scheduled for a visit. After a proper amount of time, Lima asked tio Gabriel for permission to marry his daughter.

Judite was pretty with an engaging smile and kind eyes, outgoing but never inappropriate, not so different from the way she is still. No one was surprised that she was engaged before Isabel, who was older. People wondered if Isabel would ever find a suitable husband. She seldom smiled. Some thought she'd make a good nun. Instead she dedicated herself to teaching. She was very strict, but she could also be inspiring. There are generations of students now who treasure what she taught them. Once I asked her if she regretted not marrying.

"I couldn't suffer any man."

'Nor they you,' I thought to myself.

When Lima wasn't around, my uncle spent more and more time drinking in *adegas*—wine cellars where men congregated after dinner. He had a reputation as a tough guy, more than capable of picking a fight, winning most of them, and refusing to flinch or surrender when he lost. When drunk he became loud and obnoxious. He had many topics for his ire, but I don't think it mattered really. He was driven by hatred and anger more than convictions.

Everybody in town knew that one of our local informers was Freitas, a poor farmer who hung out most evenings in *adegas* snooping for dissent. Informing kept him in drinking money. He smoked tobacco wrapped in corn husks. One evening Gabriel was drinking in the *adega* and trying to stir up trouble. Everyone was ignoring him; his usual tirades were not getting a rise out of anyone. So my uncle turned his attention to Freitas.

"Hola, informer! Judas! How can you look yourself in the mirror? How can you sleep at night? You're no better than a cockroach! A piece of shit!"

My uncle didn't have many friends, but people in the *adega* tried to get him to shut up for his own good.

"Go tell your friend Salazar you're a queer. Julia Florista. Tell Salazar he's a queer too. He's worse than the communists."

Freitas never looked up. He just stared down at his glass. Sometimes there was a little sneer. When people tried to get my uncle to stop, he just became more incensed. Eventually he stormed out clumsily and went home to sleep it off.

Word got around. Everyone wondered what would come of this. Uncle Gabriel was unusually sober and stayed at home. Even he was worried.

One day Gabriel was not to be found and he didn't come home that night. The next day Teresa sent for Judite and asked her to talk to Valentim to see if he could find out anything. Lima protested that he was only a lowly functionary but he promised to find out whatever he could. A few anxious days later, he reported that Gabriel had indeed been picked up by P.I.D.E. for "questioning." He had been taken to the Fortress of São João Baptista at Angra do Heroismo on the island of Terceira. Lima explained that the police were allowed to detain people for three months without laying charges and then for two forty-five day extensions after that. He said we shouldn't worry and he would do what he could.

P.I.D.E. used various standard modes of torture. Beating was the most common. Also sleep deprivation. There was something called "the statue," whereby the prisoner was made to lean against a wall by the fingertips for days on end. Above all, you didn't want to be sent to the concentration camp on Tarrafal in the Cape Verde Islands.

There was little news for a month. Valentim was very comforting and a rock of support. He found out that my uncle was still alive and in the fortress. Tia Teresa was torn between the need to wail and lament and the prudence of keeping her mouth shut. She kept reminding Lima that her brothers had died for Franco. He assured her that he had passed on that information.

My grandmother said nothing the whole time and tried to be helpful, but I could tell how worried she was.

After six weeks Gabriel was released. He had all of the fight kicked out of him. He went into his room for a week and only came out for Mass on Sunday. We were all very grateful to Valentim for his safe return.

Gabriel didn't speak about what had been done to him. As far as I know, he never did. All he stated was that while in jail he had prayed and promised that if he got out alive he would walk on his knees on the great feast of *Senhor Santo Cristo dos Milagres*.

So when the feast day came around, the family accompanied him to Ponta Delgada. It was a glorious late spring day: blue sky and white clouds bright in the sun. The streets were covered in patterns of flower petals. I was wearing a white dress with tiny pleats in the skirt. There were bags of fava beans for snacking and a basket of food for lunch. My uncle was wearing his best suit. He was one of several who would walk on their knees in the procession behind the statue.

The statue of Santo Cristo stands on golden flowers wearing a crown of thorns made out of diamonds that once belonged to a countess. His face is sad; rivulets of blood run from his forehead. It is carried under a satin canopy surrounded by priests who bless the onlookers with incense and holy water. The penitents follow through the streets. Soon the knees of their trousers give out, and eventually there is blood and pulp. They cry out in pain and ecstasy. Their wives, children, and mothers are proud and distraught.

Tio Gabriel had to be taken home in Lima's car. At home he was laid on his bed and my aunt and my cousins and my grandmother nursed his wounds.

After they had bandaged him, my grandmother broke down and began to cry.

"My poor little Gabriel, you're in so much pain, so much pain!"

He looked at her for a long time and finally said, "*Puta.*"

When we got back to our house, my grandmother was quiet and very sad and didn't want to come out of her room. It took much coaxing and solicitation from Padre António to bring her out of it.

From then on, for as long as he lived, my uncle was a model citizen. He walked with a cane.

Judite and Lima were married at the end of the summer. Nature and the family spared no expense. The sun shone in the blue heavens over the lilies, hibiscus, carnations, gladioli, roses, bougainvillea, and azaleas. Judite's dress had been made in town and was as elegant and stylish as *Agua d'Alto* had ever seen. Judite wore lipstick because she was a city girl now, but none of the women from the village did. Teresa Coelho said, "She's a teacher and people respect teachers no matter what they do because they're educated." I was the flower girl. Isabel, in a wide-brimmed white hat that covered her face, was the maid-of-honour.

There was a long procession to the church. The women who lived along the hill craned their necks to admire Judite's gown and the boys, some barefoot, ran behind the wedding party, whistling and skimming pebbles into the hydrangea bushes along the edges of the road. Behind the wedding party and the family followed friends, Judite's and Valentim's, teachers and men who had government jobs. The women teachers were all single and had paired themselves up, arms linked through each other's. The men who worked for the government, married and accompanied by their wives, walked stiffly, as if they were uncomfortable walking on the village road, when they were only used to driving on city streets.

There was a Mass in Latin—Padre António, his arms raised in crescent moons towards the roof of the church, sounded so different in that language of ritual than he did sitting at my grandmother's table. When Judite and Lima exchanged their vows, everyone hushed to hear them. Valentim sounded formal and sure of himself, but Judite's voice quivered and she couldn't keep the sobs out of it.

A picture was taken of the wedding party in front of the church. Everybody is smiling. Many of the men look intent, as if waiting for the camera to click. Some of them have just flicked their cigarettes into the hydrangea bushes. I am standing beside my cousin David. I still have that photo. There have been thousands of weddings at that church, *Igreja de São Lazaro*, all of them following the same rituals, even today, and captured in similar photographs. Although the photo is very staged, it has a documentary air to it, as if it belongs in an anthropology textbook or a history book. There are a number of pictures of me as a child. Most were taken in a studio, to mark my first communion or to send to my father. In each I am wearing a white dress and looking quite stiff. I think it is in Judite's wedding picture that I look most at ease. Surrounded by a family that loves me.

The church bell rang out in celebration. We all walked back to my aunt's house. The women took off their gloves, and the men loosened their ties and unbuttoned their jackets. David kept falling behind to chat with onlookers. My father was nowhere to be found. I walked with Avó.

The furniture had been taken away and the living and dining rooms were set out with tables as in a cafe. More tables had been set up outside, under a canopy of bougainvillaea, for the overflow of guests. A woman from Furnas had been hired to cook the food and she had been at it for days. There was a great deal to eat—it would be embarrassing for the family if there wasn't. People gave presents and money, which my aunt and uncle tallied and stored away in their heads, so they would know who deserved more and who deserved less when the proper occasion arose. Most people drank little, but a few drank more. My father was one of them.

There was guitar playing and communal singing of songs everyone knew. A man whom I didn't know—he must have been one of Valentim's government friends from Ponta Delgada—stood up and sang *fado*, his hands rising and falling with his voice. By the time dessert was finished, some were dancing outside. I remember dancing with Avó. I remember dancing with a man, one of Valentim's friends. It was the closest I had been with a man who was not family and it made me feel funny in my stomach.

Later in the evening there was a sudden commotion. A scuffle broke out. My father was at the centre of it: he was drunk and had touched a woman's bum. Her husband pushed him and knocked him down. My father banged his head against a table and knocked

224 · Graziela Pimentel & Mark Fortier

over a china vase, which fell and broke. Padre António intervened to hold back the husband. My grandmother rushed to kneel beside my father.

"That bastard is disgracing my daughter's wedding!" said my uncle Gabriel.

"Julio, are you alright?" asked my grandmother.

"No, I'm not alright! I have nothing! I have no one! I am so unhappy! Why did you ever bring me to this island? And I was only five!" And my father began to cry.

It is not a good thing for a Portuguese man to cry in defeat: although it happens, it will be the object of scorn and ridicule. Many years later we were vacationing in the Algarve in the village of Albufeira and one night we went to a film. I was one of few women in attendance. It was an American film, *Cool Hand Luke*. Near the end of the film, Luke, a convict who has shown incredible strength of defiance, after relentless brutalizing breaks down in submission and weeps. The theatre was rocked by an explosion of derisive laughter: no man there would have done such a thing, no man there—they were each asserting—would have acted so much like a woman.

My uncle was very angry. Men snickered and made jokes. The husband of the woman with the bum said next time he saw my father he would punch him in the face. Teresa Coelho tried to maintain a sense of merriment. Judite looked somewhat aghast and Lima observed. My grandmother took my father back to our house. It was clear that his days in our village were numbered.

Just before midnight there was an even bigger commotion: sudden rumbling and the earth and house began to shake. Glasses and cutlery rattled on the tables. Guitar playing stopped and women cried out to Jesus and Santa Maria.

Then the rumbling subsided.

Like finding a dead body, an earthquake on your wedding day is not a good omen.

That night I had a bad dream—something heavy and black had

fallen and was smothering me. When I started awake, I made my way through the dark house and knocked on Avó's door. Avó's white nightgown was the only light I could see as she took me in her arms and embraced me. I wanted to crawl into her bed where she would keep me safe. Instead she walked me back to my room and sat with me until I was asleep again. It was not for many years that I understood what I had witnessed in the dark in Avó's bedroom and why I couldn't sleep with her that night. How strange life is! What disappointed and confused me that night is what has since given me so much comfort.

Chapter Two

I hear Jorge coming in. After he hangs up his jacket near the door he enters and kisses me on top of the head.

"Hello, my dear," he says.

I turn my pursed lips upward and he kisses me there, holding his tie out of my face.

"And where are the weird sisters?"

"Not back yet. Visiting the saint."

"Hmm. What are you drinking?"

"The *vinho verde*. Have some."

"No, thanks, a martini for me."

"Bond, James Bond."

And he's off to get the gin. Our talk, except in times of misfortune and disruption, has become minimal, intimate, and comfortable, like Pierre and Natasha's at the end of *War and Peace*. Ours is the bond that comes at the end of a long story.

I hear him pouring and clinking in the kitchen. After a few minutes he comes back with a drink in his hand.

"Shaken, not stirred," he says in English.

He sits down in his favourite chair and puts his drink on the table beside him in the same way that he always does. He begins to tell me the small, unimportant details of his working day.

Then we hear Isabel and Judite at the door. They are bickering as they used to, as sisters do, something about the elevator door to my floor. Jorge cringes in mock horror and retreats into the kitchen.

"Chicken," I mouth to his retreating back and answer the door myself.

Before this visit, it had been many years since I'd seen Isabel. This is her second time to Lisbon. The first was years ago when she came for radiation treatment for breast cancer. She beat the cancer, but she won't beat old age. How small she has become! Her thick wavy hair is all grey now. She stands erect but her right hand is resting on a cane.

"Hello, Margarida, still lovely." Her voice is the same as always. Strong, confident, clear, staccato, cold. "Judite and I were having a disagreement about your elevator. There was not that latticed door when I was here before."

"How can you possibly be sure about something like that from one visit here years ago?" Judite objects.

"I'm positive. Especially because I've only been here once before. It stayed with me. That's the way memory works. We remember the unique experience, not the daily one."

Isabel is wrong about the door but I don't need or bother to say anything.

"And how is Maria de Deus?" I ask.

"She's a saint," declares Judite in a voice that still rings with verve. There's only five years' difference between her and Isabel but she looks much younger. She colours her hair dark brown and her lips are carnation red. She's wearing a white silk blouse and black slacks with flat shoes.

"Saint? Who's a saint?" Jorge laughs as he emerges from the kitchen and embraces first Judite, then Isabel.

"Cousin Maria de Deus. She sits in her wheelchair and says the rosary over and over again. She never complains. She just prays."

"Now, there wouldn't be much progress if everybody sat around and did nothing but pray."

"You're right, Jorge," says Isabel. "Work keeps us alive. The saddest day in my life was when I stopped teaching."

"Did Maria de Deus recognize you?" I ask Isabel.

"She did. It took her a few moments, but she finally said my name. She thinks she's back in *Agua d'Alto* and that I'm still teaching. She asked me about my students. It's good that she became a nun. The sisters gave her a place in the world and now they're looking after her."

"And she's a saint. If Maria de Deus doesn't go to heaven, nobody will," says Judite.

We go into the living room and I offer everybody a drink.

"What are you having?" Judite asks.

"I'm having wine and Jorge's having a martini."

"Ooh! I'll have a martini too!"

"Water will do," declares Isabel.

Over Jorge's objections, I insist on making Judite's martini. When I return a few minutes later, Isabel and Judite are bent over a photo album. Jorge is standing behind them letting them explain things to him as if he's never seen these pictures before.

"Here's a picture of Maria de Deus at your wedding, Judite," Isabel points out. I know the picture she is looking at. Maria de Deus looks, as always, so small and frightened.

"We all look so young!" says Judite, with surprise and sadness. I know how she feels: she hasn't seen these pictures in a long time and now suddenly they are old, so old now that we are only partly the people in them and those people are only partly us. They look back at us the way people from the old country look at those who have moved away.

"You have so many photographs," said Isabel, scanning the albums stacked on the book shelves. "You're quite a collector."

"Not really, I think. I've gotten rid of so many." I remember the purges in Angola. "Most of these are from Avó. I also have her letters."

"Whom did Avó write to?" asked Judite.

"My father after he emigrated. Armando. She wrote to him right up to his death and after that his widow sent Avó's letters back to her. I have the ones he wrote to her as well."

My cousins say nothing. They don't want to hear about my grandfather, who wasn't theirs. Even now, as old women, this truth hurts them because it stains the family honour—

our grandmother had a son by a man who wasn't her husband. They want to deny it and forget. It surprises us all that I have transgressed by mentioning this. Sometimes even I must disturb the peace.

Isabel and Judite say nothing and continue to look at the old photographs, oohing and aahing over the faces of those that have long since died. They come to a picture of my father—tall and skinny, his hair high on top. The image is too small, the photograph too old and worn, to see whether he's smiling. But I doubt that he was.

On the next page is a photograph of him in Canada. A number of men are sitting at a table somewhere—a bar, a party, I'm not sure— and in front of them the table is completely covered with empty beer bottles (which they, it turns out, had assiduously collected from other tables). They are all smiling at the camera, crowding into the picture. Even my father smiles, though it looks very fake and unnatural on him. When this picture was sent back home it impressed and amazed us. "Look at all the bottles!" people said. "The money that must cost!" The men looked so unfettered. It was a picture much less stiff and formal than the ones we were used to, but probably no less staged.

After Judite's wedding the writing was on the wall for my father.

"He has no future here," Padre António advised my grandmother.

"But how is he going to manage by himself? Without anyone to help him?"

"I'm afraid all your help hasn't made much difference for him."

It is not easy to be the child of a deeply unhappy parent. Nor was my father always a particularly sweet man. I remember one look of his in particular: it seemed to say, "I have no idea what you're trying to say, but if I did, I'm sure it would be the most absurd thing I've ever heard."

Azoreans didn't go much to the mainland for work since the pay was poor and they were treated as hicks. Canada was sponsoring immigrants to work on farms and the railroad. We all knew about Canada because of generations fishing for cod on the Grand Banks. Padre António helped my father with the paperwork and he knew government clerks in Ponta Delgada who processed and approved his application even though he was older than most.

On the day of his departure, Avó, Padre António and I drove my father to the recently built airport, past Ponta Delgada, on a grassy field with an edge that dropped down to the sea. He was flying to Santa Maria where a larger plane would take him and a dozen or so men across the ocean. The emigrants were dressed in suits and wore fedora hats. I wore a pink and blue plaid box-pleat skirt and jacket and a wool pink cap.

"I'll send for you once I get my own place," my father promised when he kissed me goodbye. He was going to a farm outside Toronto, in a place called Holland Marsh, where the soil was black and fertile. With two other men he would live in a trailer parked near the barn, away from the farmer's brick house.

I cried, but I didn't say that I wanted to go with him, and we both knew that he would never send for me.

Avó clasped him close to her for a long time. Neither of them spoke or cried.

Agua d'Alto had a lot to say about the emigrants.

"They won't stay there. Canada is cold."

"They don't make wine in Canada. It's too cold to grow good grapes."

"The first winter will kill them. They'll come back in a few months with their tails between their legs."

"They'll have to find jobs when they come back. They'll be the laughingstock."

The letters from Canada spoke of confusion and loneliness.

"I don't understand what the boss wants me to do. I can't speak to anyone."

"I don't know how to drive a car and it's too far to walk to town."

"It's very cold here. My hands are raw and cut. It's hard to work with gloves and besides they don't help much."

"Canada is so big, you can't even see the ocean where we live."

"I dream of eating stew. All we eat is boiled potatoes and tuna fish from a can."

"I miss *caldo verde*."

My father wrote rarely. And said very little.

Some came back and took their comeuppance, but most stayed on. Some had accidents because they didn't know how to work the tractors and the other farm equipment, or because their attention was distracted by the sight of what were, by Portuguese standards, scantily dressed young women. Years later that was how my father ran his Chevrolet into the back of a streetcar. He didn't tell anyone that's what happened, but word gets around.

Two years after he went to the farm, my father moved to Toronto, to work in a factory.

By then *Agua d'Alto* didn't say as much about the emigrants. More and more men were going to Canada. The first group had started to send money back home, complained less in their letters about the cold, and swore summer was just as hot as in São Miguel, if not hotter. In a few years some of the men started to send for their families. They had saved enough to buy a house and they wanted to see their wives and children, or have children if they had left none behind. They wanted someone around to cook Portuguese food. My father did not send for me. His letters repeated the same platitudes of being healthy and hoping we enjoyed good health. His photos were always the same. Him smiling uncomfortably with a group of men, and later women, and always with a bottle of beer in his hand.

For me those were the years of studying and reading. I enjoyed learning: whether it was working out mathematical or chemical equations or reading Portuguese literature or history, my life was focussed on the pursuit of all things mental and imaginative. I had girlfriends but our friendships stayed in the classroom. At home I was content to do schoolwork and read books that Padre António bought for me. Translations of Shakespeare, Tolstoy, and Flaubert— not always things a good Portuguese girl was supposed to be reading. I treasured those hours in my upstairs room, sitting at my desk by the window that went all the way to the floor, with a full view of the sea. I began to wonder what was out there. *Agua d'Alto* was getting smaller. There was no stopping the emigration. I didn't want to leave, but I started to see that the world beyond had much to experience. I never considered Canada or America. Lisbon and Europe caught my interest—university, monuments, places that I had read about.

Avó and I lived like mother and daughter. After my father had gone to Canada, tio Gabriel chose to cut her out of his life. She never set foot in his house again, although she would send me over with goodies—*arroz doce, massa sovada, fatias douradas*. I don't think it ever stopped hurting her, that she had lost both sons, but she learned to let them be. They were well into middle age and she had given them the best of herself. She accepted her fate and turned to what she had been given. I was her child. I lapped up her love like a hungry cat and rewarded her with complete devotion. We saw each other every day, but Sunday afternoon was a special time. Padre António visited, after he had celebrated the noon Mass, and she prepared a meal for the three of us. That is how I learned to cook. Measuring flour, sugar, spices for the cake. Marinating the fish in olive oil, lemon, garlic, pepper and salt, then grilling it on the fire, outside so that the kitchen wouldn't stink. The three of us ate and talked about what interested us—literature, what was happening in Portugal. When we finished the meal, I would clean up and the two of them would go and sit in the front room. After I had finished, I would go to my room and read. It was a habit that has stayed with me. When my sons were small and napped in the afternoon, I would close myself in my room and read. There were busy years when I did not have my Sunday afternoon pauses. Now that it is just Jorge and I, I never fail to withdraw into a book on Sunday afternoon. Some of the time, I forget that Avó is not somewhere else in the house, still with me.

Every few weeks I would visit Judite and Valentim in Ponta Delgada. They lived in a stately apartment on *Rua A.J. Almeida*, with ceilings as high as a church, cool marble floors, and antique furniture made of acacia. They had a maid, Maria dos Anjos, who had been with Valentim since his arrival on the island. They lived smack in the social centre of the city. A minute's walk to the Matriz, the main church, less than a minute to Café Central where Judite liked to take me for a *gelado*, and where I tasted my first espresso. It was two minutes to *Avenida Infante D. Henrique*, where we strolled along the wide cobbled sidewalk at the edge of the harbour. It was a good life for a mere government clerk and his teacher wife.

When I visited, Judite would take me out to a restaurant for *almoço*—the big meal, between noon and one o'clock. Sailors from all over the world, gleaming in their white uniforms and hats, strutted along *Avenida Gonçalo Velho* on the seafront; old men played dominoes in the middle of Praça Cabral while boys ran in circles around them. We strolled down to Hotel São Pedro, the oldest on the island. It had been built at the beginning of the 19th century in a George V colonial style, on top of a grassy mound landscaped with palm trees. Judite and Valentim had spent their honeymoon at the São Pedro.

The waiter, in a starched white cotton jacket and black gabardine pants, sat us at a table by the window, with a clear view of the blue crinkled sea.

I could smell the lemon trees growing in the patio just outside the restaurant.

"And what would the beautiful young ladies like today?" asked the waiter.

"Could I have *leitão* with *batata frita*?" I asked.

"Yes, of course."

"Then that's what I'll have."

Judite ordered the same.

We gazed out contentedly at the sea, like cats sitting in a window.

"Have you thought about what you're going to do when you finish *Colégio*?" Judite asked.

"I'll probably go to Teacher's College."

"You could go to university in Lisbon."

I looked at her in silence. The idea had occurred to me, but I couldn't imagine leaving home, leaving Avó.

"We're thinking...we're moving to Lisbon."

This announcement startled me. I was aware of the migration out of the island. My father. A number of my friends had fathers who had also emigrated to Canada. Inês, my first friend at school. The men who had stayed behind regretted it. I understood that there seemed to be no future. Anyone with ambition left for Lisbon for more education or opportunities. All that was just a couple of years ahead of me, but for the first time in my life I was content and settled where I was. I loved Agua d'Alto, but appreciated my visits to Judite's, where I was getting a small taste for the bigger world. I didn't want her to leave. I didn't want anything to change.

"Valentim has been offered a promotion. They're pleased with his work. He works very hard. It's all top secret. I don't understand the first thing about it." Judite laughed somewhat nervously.

"That's wonderful for you. Congratulations! You'll teach?"

"Oh yes. I love little children. Especially those who don't have much. I want to help them get a good start in school so that they'll do well."

I rose from my chair to hug her.

"I'm going to miss you."

"I'm going to miss you too. Isabel means well and I respect her very much, but she doesn't like coming to visit me. She thinks eating in restaurants is extravagant. A waste of money. She's so strict about life. Thank goodness I have you and David. It's been wonderful having him stay with us while he's at the *Colégio*. David always has so many friends and thinks nothing of bringing them all over for dinner without any notice."

"What does Valentim say?"

"Nothing. He's never home. He works late. By the time he comes home, everybody has eaten and left, and Maria dos Anjos has cleaned up everything, and he's no idea that we've fed five or six young men."

The waiter brought us each a platter—a slab of suckling pig in the centre, surrounded by thick potato wedges—and set it before us. I took the wine vinegar and sprinkled it over the potatoes. We drank red wine between bites of the tender meat and crisp hot potatoes.

"My brother David can charm anyone. Even Isabel." Judite threw her head back, sipped more wine and finished with a gleeful laugh.

"You wouldn't believe it," she whispered, stretching out across the table so that I could hear, "but she gives him a monthly allowance."

"Really!" I was aghast. Isabel's way with money was well-known to the family and *Agua d'Alto*—she would walk to and back from *Vila Franca do Campo* to save the postage on mailing a letter; she never bought any clothes for herself, but waited for Judite, who was shorter and had a rounder figure, to pass down hers, which had to be adjusted for the arms, length, and body—and often modified to be less frivolous. "How did he get her to do that?"

"David is going through a difficult phase. He threatens to quit school and be a beach bum. You know he's good friends with that horrible Pedro Santos who's always getting into brawls and doing these daredevil stunts. My mother is worried sick about him. And Isabel will do anything to keep him in school in Ponta Delgada, away from Pedro's influence. Father doesn't know the half of it. He's not been the same ever since that nasty business with the government."

Judite's face clouded over. For her and for all of us, the government was pervasive and frightening. Being married to someone who worked for the state did little to assuage that feeling.

When David visited *Agua d'Alto* on the weekends or holidays, things were different between us. We had grown into that awkward age where we felt socially and physically uncomfortable with one another. He no longer mussed my hair and I didn't bury my face in his chest as I used to. If he had been a girl, like Judite and Isabel, we would have kissed and embraced. Instead we stood woodenly beside each other, our faces covered in embarrassed smiles.

There were two Davids. He could be the life of the party, as he was whenever there was a crowd, all eyes on him. There is a later picture from near the end of his life. He is sitting on the floor without a jacket, holding a cigarette and a drink. His hair has begun to recede. He is laughing and close around him are his friends with drinks. He is like Frank Sinatra with the Rat Pack in the films we would watch later in the sixties. But there was also the hesitant, contemplative, vulnerable David, the one that was more like me. I loved both Davids, but only the one was close to me in return. The wild and rebellious one, Sinatra, was always running away.

I had heard of David's escapades. He and Pedro Santos had the reputation of being wild and glamorous. There is a picture—Isabel and Judite will come to it soon—of David standing beside Pedro's motorcycle, like Marlon Brandon, except that, being an Azorean, David is wearing a suit. There were limits to rebellion. Pedro was tall and blonde with green eyes—every young girl's heartthrob in *Agua d'Alto*, every parent's nightmare. Like most young people in the village he had done with school, had no trade, but was not going to work the land like his father and would emigrate to Canada as soon as he turned twenty-one. In the meantime he spent his days swimming in the ocean, hunting in the mountains, and drinking and carousing in the evenings. David was his dark-haired soul mate—with a smile that called out for fun the way drinkers call out for more wine. He moved with a swagger. Girls loved David. Parents considered him a potential worthy suitor for their daughters: he was educated, had good prospects for a career, and, when the time came, it was assumed, would settle down and make a responsible family man. In the meantime he was amusing himself.

Both he and Pedro were strong, self-taught swimmers. They loved the water—diving from cliff tops, swimming across *Lagoa de Fogo*, swimming out to the *Ilheu*, a tiny island about a kilometre away from the harbour in *Vila Franca do Campo*. They did that often, to see who could get there faster. One time they swam out in a rainstorm. What did it matter, it was all play for them. But the rain turned heavy and the sea churned dark and violent.

David and Pedro didn't return on the first night. Tia Teresa came wailing to Avó's house.

"David! My David! He's drowned. Why does God punish me so much? What have I done to deserve this grief?"

"He'll be fine," said my grandmother, although many times she had followed drowned men's funeral processions. "He's a strong swimmer. They're probably waiting for the sea to calm down before they swim back. There are caves around the cliff. They're waiting inside one of those."

Avó spoke tenderly and took tia Teresa into her arms.

Teresa did not return home that night so crazy was she with despair over her son. The next day Isabel came to take her home.

"How is your father bearing up?" Avó asked.

"He doesn't say anything."

Avó nodded in understanding. "Let me know if I can do anything, *querida*."

That day and the next were dark as night with rain beating down and the wind whipping over the sea. Men stayed home from the fields, children from school, and everyone in *Agua d'Alto* prayed for her two young sons. I sat in my bedroom facing the *Ilheu*, invisible in the dark storm, with my own fear. I couldn't bear the thought of losing David. He was my hero, brave and full of joy. He was so beautiful he made me want to grow up.

On the third day, the darkness began to lift. I could make out splotches of blue on the horizon.

"Margarida, Margarida," Avó was calling me, "the storm is over. We're going to *Vila Franca* to see about getting a boat over to the *Ilheu* to find David and Pedro." Avó spoke matter-of-factly, as if there was no doubt that the boys were fine.

A hushed group, family and friends, we walked to *Vila Franca*. Women mumbled prayers but no one dared to speak out loud.

The harbour was empty. Boats and nets were stacked against the stone retaining wall to keep them secure during the storm. Two boats were taken down and four fishermen volunteered to go in search of David and Pedro. The sky and sea rolled by peacefully, like someone sleeping after a fit of fever. We waited. The women prayed the rosary. The boats moved slowly out to sea, making their way towards the *Ilheu*, the fishermen scanning the waters for signs of the lost swimmers, or their remains. After a while, they were nothing but small black dots on the sea, then they were swallowed by the mouth of the *Ilheu*. On and on the women chanted Hail Marys and Our Fathers in one plaintive voice.

"They're coming back!" a man cried.

All eyes were on the distance as the two dots came back into view and grew bit by bit.

Halfway between the island and the harbour, someone stood up in one of the boats, waving his arms in the air.

The women stopped praying. Hope kept me from breathing.

Closer and closer to shore drew the boats.

"It's David! He's in the boat!" shouted one of David's friends.

The women now prayed the rosary in a loud, jubilant voice.

We were overcome with exultation as one by one we recognized David and Pedro with our own eyes.

When David and Pedro stepped out of the boat and onto the dock, we crowded round them in joyous celebration.

"My son, my son!" screamed tia Teresa, beating her arms like wings. Then she did what any good Portuguese mother would do— she collapsed in a faint.

When she came to, Teresa wept to remember she had thought David drowned and that she would never see him again.

"I'm going to die an old man," David laughed as he embraced his mother fiercely with both arms.

The walk back home was loud and jubilant. We sang and danced. Even the older people joined in the merriment. My heart was almost broken with relief. David was alive. I longed to bury my head on his chest like I used to do when we were younger, but instead I held on tightly to Avó's hand as we made our way back home.

Later David told me about the three days on the island, wet and cold with nothing to eat or drink. Pedro had cried for his mother and father, and David assured me he saw nothing shameful in that. He himself hadn't been preoccupied in that way. He'd thought of other things, other people, but mainly he'd thought about dying and wondered about the absurdity of a life wasted in such a frivolous fashion.

David spent the summers in *Agua d'Alto* because it had the best beaches. Every day he and his buddies swam. His skin was bronzed and his hair always moist and smelling of salt. Girls were only allowed to go to the beach on Sunday when families spread their blankets on the black sand and then they stretched out their legs to where the white foam licked their toes. Avó never went to the beach; she preferred to sit in the flower garden behind the house, but she encouraged me to go.

"David can take you," she said.

He would come for me and we would walk down to the beach together as we did when we were younger. Soon he would be leaving the island, to study at the university in Lisbon.

"I'll always come back to *Agua d'Alto* in the summer," he told me.

"There are lovely beaches around Lisbon. People from all over the world vacation there. At least, that's what I've read," I added.

He looked at me for a few moments and I felt my face turning red. I so wanted to make David notice me, to make him see that I was grown-up and knew things.

"The beaches in Lisbon could be a thousand times more beautiful, but I'll never have the same attachment as I do to ours. They're in my blood. The American poet Robert Frost writes about belonging to our roots. For me, it's the sea. This sea. That's my roots."

"But everyone is leaving," I cried.

"For now. But we'll always come back."

We walked silently for a few moments down the bamboo pathway to the water. The beach was full. Boys and men swam or splashed in the waves, while the women stretched out on blankets. Young children played where the white foam soaked into the sand. I had brought a book to read, but couldn't concentrate with all the noise and hot sun. David, as usual, was the centre of attention: racing his friends out to sea to see who was fastest; reciting Camões at the top of his lungs:

No more then of Ulysses and Aeneas
And their great journeys
No more Trajan or Alexander
And their famous victories
I sing the daring and renown of the Lusiads
Favourites of Neptune and Mars.
The old heroes are gone
And a great new valour has arisen!

Anyone who had studied at the *liceu* had committed to memory part of the epic, but even the uneducated who did not know the lines felt pride in our history. We had sailed the sea and conquered. We had brought Portuguese language and culture to places in Africa and India. The exploits of our ancestors in Africa and India were glorified in our poetry.

Only I knew that David wrote his own poetry, poetry that he would never recite to a crowd at the beach. He had shown it to me and I made copies and kept them in an album, mounted like a photograph. I will know them by heart forever:

It's smooth out where the boats are fishing. Lines
delicately cut the surface of the sea
with bloodless baits that will never return
to relate that world. But there are signs.
And what goes on beneath this opaque table
is told by knickknacks and souvenirs.
Shells are fledge souls that dictate to ears.
To eyes the green weed on torn anchor cable
reveals the fecund teeming downward incessantly.
The bay is never still.
The sand is always beating. The shrill
swimmer in the undertow is ever heard.

They weren't exactly "romantic," and I was nowhere in them, but I loved the soul they spoke from. Only I knew about the poems. Only the family, including Avó, myself, and Padre António, knew that David was contemplating the priesthood.

"I will pray for you, David. In the meantime, listen to what your heart tells you. You will know whether you have a religious vocation or not," Padre António advised him. Being a priest would not have been my choice for David, but I wanted him to be happy, and at least it brought out the contemplative side that liked to talk with me.

He wanted to help people and change the world. And he was in a hurry. And so the slow process of entering a seminary, being ordained a priest, and then following the orders of a bishop were rankling for him.

Then tio Gabriel died suddenly of a heart attack in his sleep.

Tia Teresa was demonstrably inconsolable.

"I'm a widow," she would whine. "I woke up a widow. What's going to happen to me without my Gabriel? Take me, Lord! Take me!"

David was defiant in his father's death. He would not wear a black suit.

"What difference does it make what colour suit I wear? My father is dead."

"Everybody will talk," warned Isabel.

"Let them talk. Our family has always given them lots to talk about. Father was a drunk and had a big mouth. They even talk about you, Isabel. You're too pious. You'll never marry. It's my duty to keep up the family notoriety. I'm wild. Everybody knows that."

"David, *querido*, wear the black suit for me," begged tia Teresa.

"Mother, you can't live through other people's approval."

"That's easy for you to say, David," scolded Isabel. "You're leaving São Miguel, but Mother and I are staying. We'll have to pay for your antics."

"You stay because you choose to, Isabel. You're intelligent and educated. You could move to Lisbon where people have better things to do than gossip."

"That's easy for you to say, young man," Isabel answered with deep scorn and contempt, enough to make most people wilt and give in. "You're the youngest and the only son. You're allowed to do as you please, but not if I had my way. I was raised to do my duty. *Agua d'Alto* is my home, not just a vacation spot full of beaches."

David stormed out of the house, leaving the family to worry he would miss the funeral altogether. He turned up, at the last minute, to walk behind his father's casket, still dressed in grey cotton pants and a short-sleeved shirt and wearing shoes without socks. His face was sombre and still. For once he didn't stop to chat as the procession descended the hill to the church.

He left *Agua d'Alto* right after the burial, straight from the cemetery. Pedro Santos drove up on his motorcycle and the two sped off to the city, leaving the mourners and tio Gabriel's body behind. His mother and sisters were aggrieved, but said nothing for fear of adding to the gossip.

"Goodness," moaned tia Teresa in the safety of her house. "What's he thinking of running off like that? They'll drag our name through the mud!"

Avó and I walked back home when the dark sky was heavy with stars.

We had come to Avó's house, the white paint fluorescent against the silhouettes of the hills. I put my arm around my grandmother's sloping shoulders.

"I was very young when I had Gabriel and ever since everything I've done was for him. For Julio too. I loved them both. And sacrificed. Now Gabriel is dead and I don't know whether I'll ever see your father again. My life as a mother is finished now."

"You have me," I cried.

"Yes." She stroked my hand, her touch as soft as her breath.

After the funeral, David lost interest in becoming a priest. It wasn't that Gabriel's death caused any great crisis of faith in him. Only a small part of David had ever been cut out for the priesthood. It was more that his father's death marked a new point in the rhythm of David's life. Like an alcoholic, it was time for him to fall off the wagon.

The last year before he left for Lisbon, David was full of rebellion. Tia Teresa and Isabel tried to coerce him into going to mass, but he was not to be swayed. He was at the beach when the rest of the village was at church. Padre António showed tolerance.

"It's better to come to church of your own free will than to be forced. David has a strong religious foundation. He'll come back someday, when he's ready." That wasn't to be quite yet.

The biggest scandal was when David didn't come home one night and was spotted with Pedro the next day coming out of a whorehouse on *Rua Do Beco*. Word travelled fast and those who were close to him were subjected to a long string of discomforting remarks. Isabel was mortified. My grandmother had Padre António sit down for a long talk with her grandson. I heard from a friend at school one afternoon. I felt inside hot humiliation and ugliness and (I hardly dared to admit) jealousy. I couldn't eat that evening or sleep that night.

In December the year before he left for Lisbon, David and I went up to *Três Voltas*, a few acres of mountain pine that belonged to Avó, to bring back Christmas trees. It was a tradition to cut one for my cousins' house and one for Avó's. Years back, tio Gabriel used to take charge of the task. Even my father had done it a couple of times. When we were younger, my three cousins and I would go along, singing as we climbed and helping to drag the trees down the mountain.

David talked about Lisbon as we walked up the narrow dirt road. The island was getting small and stale for him. The adventure of the wide world was calling him. A few times I slipped on the pebbles and he steadied me. His hands were strong. His skin smelled clean and warm. I loved being close to him.

There was a place where the soil was red. We used the red soil for the nativity scene under the tree. We dug some up with a hand shovel we had brought and put it into a burlap sack. I watched as David chopped down the trees with swift strokes of his father's axe.

My head was full of imaginings, of the past and future. I was caught up in the wonderful moment, being alone with David, but it was a moment with an imaginary undercurrent that took me out of the present into what might be. David continued to talk, his voice above the splintering wood and the refrain of bleating sheep. I heard him, but though he was very near to me, his words were far away.

Suddenly, he stopped and took me by the hand.

"Margarida, where are you?"

I looked at him for a second before casting my eyes down on the ground. I could feel the tears running down my face.

"What's the matter?"

"Nothing. Nothing. I'm sorry."

He held me to his chest.

"The beautiful Margarida has nothing to be sorry about. The beautiful Margarida who is so understanding, who knows what is in my heart."

I looked up into his eyes.

He kissed me.

In the summer, David graduated with great ceremony and festivity. The family attended the graduation ceremony at the school and then we all went together for *almoço*. There were presents for David and toasts to his future. Half way through, his friends strolled by and David could not be stopped from running off to join them.

After that it was an awkward occasion. Isabel and Tia Teresa kept saying they should go home.

"What's the hurry?" asked Judite, who had come especially for the occasion from Lisbon. "Enjoy the meal. We'll go for a stroll on the *Marginal* later."

The only ones she could convince to go for a stroll were Avó and I. It was a warm afternoon and the Avenida was full of strollers. Couples walked with their forearms linked together. Some of the girls looked younger than I. Usually I put my arm through Avó's, but on this occasion I felt awkward and kept my arms close to my side. Many of the students who had graduated with David were out and about.

There was a loud clamour of voices from the *Praça da República* in front of *Paço do Concelho*, the Town Hall. We turned into the square to see what was going on. A crowd had gathered to watch the spectacle. We saw a group of young men clustered below the statue of St. Michael the Archangel, hoisting someone on their shoulders. Up, up, the climber was standing on shoulders, his arms open wide as he embraced the stone feet of the statue, and then crawled his way up into a standing position beside St. Michael.

"*Viva São Miguel! Viva minha terra!*" He shouted in jubilation, his arms stretched in a salute.

"My goodness, that's David!" Judite cried out.

David's supporters standing beneath St. Michael were cheering him on.

"Let me hear your voices!" he cried out. "*Viva São Miguel!* We will always dream in Michaelense, no matter how many other accents and languages we learn!"

There were shouts of "Viva!" There was clapping. People began to sing "*Às armas*," and David conducted them.

Às armas, às armas!
Sobre a terra, sobre o mar,
Às armas, às armas!
Pela Pátria lutar
Contra os canhões marchar, marchar!

There used to be a photo of David this day on the statue. It was taken from below so that even the camera looked up to him. Many were the arms reaching to support him. He was triumphant. There used to be such a picture but I destroyed it.

Others were on the statue now and they had come to the final verse, the one that has always spoken to me most.

Salute the Sun that rises
On a smiling future:
The rays of that powerful dawn
Are like a mother's kisses
That protect us and support us
Against the insults of fate.

Suddenly David jumped down from the statue and he saw me in

the crowd. He was elated and flushed, as if drunk. He was the David who was always running away. But then I saw the other David peak out from behind his eyes and he rushed to me and took me in his arms. Both Davids were there and in that instant both were mine.

"Beautiful, darling Margarida, will you marry me?"

All my life, I had known this was what I wanted most of all.

"Yes! Yes! Of course, I will."

That was the happiest moment of my life.

Chapter Three

Isabel and Judite have now come to the pictures of Fatima.

The Easter holidays the year that David moved to Lisbon to start university, I visited him at the apartment of Judite and Valentim, where he was lodging. The family was, for the most part, quite pleased with our engagement. They took it as a sign that David was ready to settle down, and I could be expected to be a stable and responsible wife. Clearly I had deep feelings for him. I would stand by him, no matter what. Quiet Margarida, one of them, from their own village, from their own family. It was not that uncommon on a small island like ours for first cousins to marry, and besides, as everyone knew, but no one said, we were really only half first cousins anyway. So there were reasons to hope for the best.

They are looking at a photograph of Judite and me on the long stairway in front of the outstretched arms and great white tower of the basilica. Judite and Valentim insisted on taking me there on a day trip. David had refused to go to "that circus"—calling it this for Judite's sake but careful to do so when Valentim was not around. Besides, he was very busy with his studies and study groups and would not have endless time for me. So we went to the shrine without him.

There are photos of Judite and me, taken by Valentim, in front of all the great sights: before the holm oak and the Chapel of Apparitions where the Virgin showed the children, young as they were, a sea of fire with people burning like embers, shrieking and groaning in pain and despair, and told them that communist Russia was the problem; before the House of Our Lady of Dolours, where the sick came to be miraculously cured and many claimed they were; before the tombs of little Jacinta and Francisco—influenza took them as it had taken many in my own family; and before their simple houses, one-storey white stucco, such as poor people lived in on our own island. In all the pictures we smile respectfully, piously, dutifully. Judite bought us both rosaries.

I was a very young woman from a conservative society who had been given no forum in which to question her religious beliefs. Much of what I saw that day was undeniably and deeply compelling, but some of it left me confused. Judite was caught up in everything without ambivalence. Valentim hovered over us like a teacher who has taken his students on a particularly edifying field trip.

Over dinner we catechized about what we had experienced.

"Why would the Virgin show such innocent little children a vision of hell?" I asked.

"So that they would be driven to save themselves. None of us is truly innocent."

"But why did they die so young?"

"That was their reward."

"And why did she tell them to whip themselves? Is that really what God wants?"

"God wants us to be happy with him in heaven and to renounce the flesh."

I suppose I was too attached to the people, places, even the things, of this world to give the other world the due that the logic of belief demands. I didn't want to flagellate anyone including myself—at least not physically—and I was not ready to die. Valentim as well was ill prepared to give up his commitment to the things of this world.

"What Christ through the church has always taught," he said, "is respect for order. The family, the state, the leader—these are all manifestations of Christ's love for us. The role of those in positions of responsibility is to protect that love from those who do not respect it, especially the communists. This is why the Virgin appeared to *these* children—because of the rise of a godless Soviet Union. She knew that Christian Portugal would always stand firm."

There was no uncertainty in their answers. It would have been better to have had Padre António to talk with: he would have held firmly to his faith but understood my doubts and discussed them seriously.

When I tried to talk with David, he was just as certain from the opposite perspective.

"Why pick on the Russians? Why not Hitler? Or Franco? Or Salazar? Start by cleaning up your own house! Those of Lima's ilk have no respect for individual human freedom. It's all conformity with them. 'The individual must always be prepared to sacrifice his rights and privileges for the good of the community.' But who decides what is the good of the community? Really, the whole thing is absurd! The feverish imaginings of deluded children." I had never heard him say things like this before. It frightened me.

During the day, when I was going around with Judite, Lisbon smelled of sun, earth, and green, and not of the sea the way our island did. The houses leading into the centre were bright and many coloured—blue, green, yellow, pink. The heart of the city was a grid of wide avenues and open *praças*, leading down to the airy expanses along the river. Bright bouquets of fuchsia, yellow, red, orange, sprouted from the blue and white mosaics. But at night, when I went out with David to meet his new friends, especially up the hill to the old town, the city was a narrow and mysterious labyrinth, with people lurking in dark doorways who knew more than they said. Somewhere *fado* was being played. There are no photos of those nights.

David took me to Café Monaco, which the next year was destroyed by the police. It was hot, full of bodies, noise, and cigarette smoke. I clutched David's hand as I used to do when I was small. Most of the people there were men, only a few women. Many saluted David with embraces. I walked a step behind him.

He led me over to a group sitting at a table drinking wine and eating *chouriço*. Many of them were in a class with him on the history of the Golden Age.

"Meet my cousin, Margarida!"

I noticed that he didn't call me his fiancée.

He rhymed off their names as the strange, mainly bearded, faces turned to me. One man was black. I was relieved to see one other woman at the table. She had light hair, somewhere between red and orange, snipped close to the scalp and sprouting from it like grass. Her eyes were dark and intense. She was small and slender. Her tee shirt, not unlike those the men were wearing, was loose on her arms and chest. David introduced her as Evangelina.

I smiled and tried to catch her eye, but she turned partly away and lit a cigarette without looking at me.

"Let David's pretty little cousin sit next to us!"

The next thing I knew I was shoved and squeezed into a chair between two men, one with a beard and sullen eyes and another who blew cigarette smoke towards me as he turned and spoke.

"Pretty," Evangelina said to David, not bothering to look at me. I realized how I stood out from everyone else—hair long and wavy, silk blouse with ruffles around the neck and down the front, I was even wearing heels. I had taken great pains to look sophisticated but I had failed miserably.

I understood that Evangelina was not really complimenting me, but all I could say was "Thank you." I wanted to get up and leave. My eyes already stung with smoke and humiliation. David, who was sitting beside Evangelina, ordering a round of *aguardente*, brandy, for the table. The sullen man asked me how I liked Lisbon and then condescendingly imitated the way I pronounced certain words. It was embarrassing, as when waiters pretended not to understand what I was saying. I had noticed how both Judite and David very consciously strove to avoid sounding like Azoreans. In time I would do that too.

When someone placed a shot in front of me, I hesitated, then raised it to my mouth and drank it all at once. I had tasted *aguardente* before, to cure a cold or when I had bad menstrual cramps, but always in slow, measured swallows. This went down like sharp fire.

I was caught in a web of politics, *aguardente*, and cigarettes. On and on they talked, smoked, and drank. I was given another shot of *aguardente*, but this time I sipped at it slowly, sometimes only brushing the glass with my lips. David ordered plates of *chouriço* and *torresmos de molho fígado* and bottles of red wine. A couple of times I caught him moving his arm across Evangelina's shoulders, or putting his mouth near her ear as if he needed to speak to her in private.

"Let's do something!" said David. "Let's go to a film. Margarida likes American films."

"American films are mindless and commercial!" Evangelina exclaimed almost before David had finished, and glared at me.

David loved American films too, it wasn't just me. And who did she mean was mindless and commercial—Brando, Hitchcock, John Ford?

"American films are imperialist propaganda," declared the bearded student next to me, but he tried to say it nicely, as if he were tutoring me.

"I don't want to see a political film. I'm not interested in that. I'd like to see something by Hitchcock." My voice shook and I regretted speaking as soon as I'd finished.

"All art is political," Evangelina said, waiting to light another cigarette.

Was that true? Always? What did it mean? I wanted to see things that moved me or made me laugh. Politics. Politics. Politics. They never seemed to tire of it.

"But you Portuguese, you're as imperialist as the Americans," said the black man, whose name was Agostinho, and who was from Angola. Later he was put in prison. "You were the first of the slave trading nations and you'll be the last to let go of your overseas possessions. They'll drag you out kicking and screaming. You're *worse* than the Americans!"

"You're absolutely right, Agostinho," said the man beside me.

"I have to believe that my ancestors were less racist than the English and the Dutch," said David. "They intermarried when they colonized other peoples."

"And what does that say? The Portuguese have uncontrollable libidos and no fastidiousness. Besides, while Portuguese men had no difficulty marrying, or more often just taking, black women, no black man was ever allowed to take a Portuguese woman. And worst of all is your damn Camões! Remember how he talks about a white man taking a black woman: 'no crime of abominable incest, not violence on an innocent girl, not even foul adultery, for she is a brutish no-account slave.' How's that for great poetry?"

I knew how David loved, or used to love, Camões.

"And what of that other kind of bondage?" intervened Evangelina, with a voice higher than the men's but just as confident, just as sure of itself. "Portuguese men did no favour to black women when they married them. Marriage is just more slavery."

Why was marriage slavery? Sometimes it didn't work, as with my grandparents, but that wasn't slavery. And not all marriages were like that.

They decided they wanted to see a Brazilian film, *Orfeu Negro*.

"It won the Palme d'Or at Cannes," said Agostinho.

Evangelina quickly assumed the blank look on my face meant I didn't know anything about Cannes. She was right.

"Cannes is a town on the French Riviera," she lectured me. "It hosts the most important film festival in the world. American films do not do well there." I know now this last bit was untrue.

Orfeu Negro retells the story of Orpheus and Eurydice and is set during *Carneval* in the *favelas* of Rio. As always, he loses her twice. After the film there was more talk. They said it was about the dignity and oppression of the poor. They said it was an anthropological study of the way pagan myth informs Christian Lenten traditions. My head was buzzing. I thought it was a story about love and fate.

Later in the week we all went to see something commercial and mindless—*Girls, Legs, and Samba!* At least it wasn't American. Afterwards David's friends, shameless hams every one, danced as we ambled down the street. Evangelina, I noticed, moved like the cats I knew from my grandmother's garden.

David also took me back to Café Monaco another night, and again the café was full of loud voices and smoke. I thought about changing the way I dressed, maybe do something silly to my hair and smoke cigarettes, but I resisted the urge. This time I made sure David sat next to me.

Late, we stepped out of the café into the cool relief of the night. The sky was lit with stars. The air tasted clean and fresh. The city was quiet in sleep, with the occasional faint tinkle of glasses and cutlery. Below us the Tagus flowed gently. We walked home in silence. The street lamps through the leaves of the trees were like the embers of a green fire.

The apartment was dark and still. It smelled of pennyroyal tea and baking. David turned on a dim light and the marble floors, ceramic tiles, and high ceilings came out of the gloom, along with the silver crown of the Holy Spirit in the middle of the commode in the foyer and a red satin runner embroidered with the figure of Baby Jesus on the dining room table.

"I'm not used to staying up so late. Or eating so much spicy food."

"Do you want some tea?"

"That would be nice."

He lit the stove to boil water. When the tea was ready we sat in the open out on the balcony, looking down on the still streets.

"I like the quiet," I said. "It lets me think. About all the things I don't understand."

"And how do you like my friends?" David asked.

"I don't know them, of course, but they seem interesting." I thought they were full of themselves. They thought they knew everything. Little atheist popes. But that wasn't what he wanted to hear.

"I know sometimes they show off a bit, but underneath the bravado they're sincere about changing Portugal into a better place."

"Is that what you want to do?"

"Absolutely. It's all so oppressive here, especially in this apartment. I have no freedom. Religion and the status quo, that's all I hear about. Why can't I do what's expected of me? Judite and Valentim think they know everything. What we need is another Lisbon earthquake, on a Sunday morning when they're all at Mass."

"David, you don't really mean that." I would be one of those in the church.

"I don't know, maybe I do."

I smiled at him.

"You don't want to see people hurt, you just want everyone to like you."

"I know my sister means well and she's done a lot for me. I'll never be able to repay her. But I can't tolerate her trying to control me anymore. The way I see things is changing so quickly. I'm thinking of getting my own place."

"Can you afford it?"

"Not really, but I've got to get out. It would have to be a very modest place. I was thinking of writing Avó and asking for her help."

That was just like him—spending money that wasn't his.

"I don't fit in with your friends."

"How can you say that? You've just met them."

I waited before I said anything.

"David, are you sure you still want to marry me?"

"Of course, I do! Listen, I'm sorry I've been neglecting you. Whenever they start on their campaign to control me—what I say, what I believe, what I wear—I withdraw. It has nothing to do with you."

I began to cry.

"It has everything to do with me."

"No, Margarida, no!" He was holding me now. He turned my face up towards him and he kissed me. Between tears I kissed him back. I still remember exactly how that felt.

Both my sons have suddenly arrived with their wives and children. My once quiet house is alive with activity and noise.

"Avó, can I have some chicken soup right away?" asks my sweet little grandson.

"Of course you can, my little darling!"

His baby sister is crying because she's teething. The other two have already glued themselves to the computer and are playing video games. My sons Fernando and Tiago have always gotten along but now they only see each other when they get together at my house. They come in with their wives to greet Jorge and my cousins. There are embraces and kisses and compliments on how well everyone is looking. My sons are told how young and handsome they still are, and in response Fernando strokes his thinning hair. My daughters-in-law settle in. Gabriela goes into the bedroom to comfort her crying baby. Marta, who's an engineer, talks to Jorge. I go into the kitchen to make tea for my cousins and espresso for everybody else. It's quiet in the kitchen. I am not supposed to drink coffee. It affects my blood pressure and causes cysts in my breasts. But once in a while I indulge myself. Today will be such a time. By the time I prepare everything and bring it into the living room, my sons have slipped off onto the balcony to smoke and talk. I bring their demitasses out to them.

"Ah, thank you, Mãe, you're the best."

I stand outside and drink coffee with them and I can tell, by the way they talk and move and the looks in their eyes, that things are well with both of them. Not unexpected, but a relief anyway.

"How is the visit? Have they driven you crazy yet?"

"No. Actually, it's good to see them."

"Good. They're looking old, especially Isabel."

"Yes." After a moment I tell them that we really should go back in and visit.

"Of course," they say, putting out their cigarettes.

When we step back inside, Isabel and Judite still have the photo albums on their laps and beside them.

"Ah, all the family photos!" says Fernando.

"There used to be a lot more," says Tiago. "Mom got rid of them. We used to have pictures of *everything*."

Well, I think to myself, not quite everything. There are those things that were never photographed. Things that were not supposed to be known. People's secrets. I know of those unphotographed events, those things I was never meant to know about. Things that only I know now. Things that I'd be happier not to know. I leave everyone talking and go back into the kitchen.

In the summer David and I were married in a civil ceremony. The church wedding—the real wedding—would wait a year, till I was done with my schooling and ready to move to Lisbon. David went back to university, and I settled into school. I had decided to be a teacher. With this decision and marriage in place, I felt on the way to living my life. A life of love and happiness. David and I were a team now and whatever we did we would do together.

When David was back in Lisbon, he moved out on his own—presumably with financial help from Avó. Judite was very upset and begged him to come back. He refused. I was very much, as I often am, of two minds.

That was the year of political and student unrest, of riots and arrests. Of suppression.

In those days there were only letters. After David returned to Lisbon, we wrote each other often—well, I somewhat more regularly than he. When he did write, he told me about his classes and all the hubbub around the presidential election. I was somewhat anxious that he committed such things to paper and the post. David was always a bit reckless. He wrote little or nothing about his friends.

He wrote about General Umberto Delgado, who was running against the powers that be in the presidential election. Delgado wore two pearl-handled pistols and made bold pronouncements for the press. People called him General Cowboy and General Coca Cola. The communists said he was a fascist, but nobody else had a chance of going up against the state. He promised freedom of speech and no arbitrary arrest. He was running against Salazar's puppet, Américo Tomás.

"What of Prime Minister Salazar?" he was asked by a French journalist.

"Obviously, I'd dismiss him. We're tired of him."

There were illegal rallies and marches, often broken up by the police with tear gas, horses, and rifle shots. People were beaten and arrested. Rocks were thrown. On the whitewashed city walls was neatly and carefully printed political graffiti in red or green paint: *Viva Delgado! Viva a República Portuguesa!*" But it was quickly covered over.

On the island there was no Delgado campaign to speak of.

When the election finally took place, few voted, the government counted the votes, and Salazar's man won in a landslide. No surprises there.

David's letters, I couldn't help but feel, kept getting fewer, shorter, and colder.

He made a very brief trip home at Christmas but he was very distant from all of us. Avó had to ask a man from the village to go cut down trees for us.

In the new year, in the few letters I got from him, David never mentioned our upcoming wedding. His mother and sisters sent him ominous missives, admonishing him to think of his family, of what people would think, of poor Margarida, and threatening to cut off his funds, but they heard nothing back. Word travelled that he had been seen on the street in Lisbon kissing another woman in broad daylight. The winter seemed to go on forever and spring stayed cold and rainy.

I was depressed and anxious. Why was he doing this to me? Did he want me to end up like Isabel? That was unfair to Isabel, she was a strong and independent woman, but I never sought a life such as hers. I wanted to be with David, my husband, but I was afraid he would break my heart. There was nothing I could do to escape the prison he had put me in and only he could shorten my sentence.

Late in the spring, at last, and quite unexpectedly, David wrote that he was looking forward to our wedding in the summer.

David returned to São Miguel in a subdued mood. I couldn't tell what he was feeling; I didn't know how to talk to him. He said nothing more about the wedding. Everyone was happy that he was home but we treated him very cautiously as not to alienate him. When he had been home two weeks, one day when the family was sitting around the table, he suddenly spoke up.

"Well," he announced, "it's time we got on with the church wedding."

There was an audible group gasp, then smiles and laughter and exclamations.

The next day we walked up the hills behind our houses and sat on a mound of grass with a view of the sea. I kissed him on the lips and we slipped down from the mound into the privacy of the low field, hidden by the long grasses. There was no one around. I surprised him with my desire. I had never been with anyone before but my hands moved along his body with ease. He felt the fullness of my breasts as I lay on top of him. My mouth and sex opened up to him, moist and tender. My eyes leapt with pleasure when he gazed at my face. After he came, I embraced him with joy and triumph and kissed him softly all over his face. He was mine again.

He was quiet as we descended the hill but I bubbled inside like a glass of champagne.

Like those of all young women on the island my trousseau— *báu de felicidade*—had been made by the women in my family; my grandmother, aunt and cousins, and I myself had worked on it for years. It was stored in a chest made of acacia and everything inside smelled of moth balls. There was bed linen crocheted along the top edge. In the centre, below the crocheting, the letters M and D had been embroidered and crossed over each other in white silk thread. Forever inseparable, you couldn't remove one without unravelling the other. The M had been embroidered years ago, when I was little more than a girl. The D had been added since our engagement. There were tablecloths: white with crocheted edges; beige linen embroidered with fruits; a crocheted counterpane that had taken over a year to make (all the women had made the squares and together had stitched them into one piece); dozens of white linen handkerchiefs made from the leftovers and marked with my initials.

Judite gave me a piece of advice the day before the wedding.

"After you and David are married, I encourage you to learn to drive and to have your own income." She said the last in a soft voice, as if she were giving away a secret. "Valentim is a model husband and respects me, but how would I manage if I had to wait for him to drive me around and ask him for money every time I needed to buy something? That's the advice I give all my women friends."

On our wedding day the sky was the lightest blue. As the family expected, Judite and Valentim were maid of honour and best man, she soft and pretty in pink satin, he looking almost gay in a grey linen suit. I had chosen a dressmaker in Ponta Delgada to make my gown. Every day on my way to class I had admired the window display of Atelier Dona Ana. The skirt, of ivory satin, shimmered in waves with every step I took. The lace bodice was woven in a pattern of tiny, delicate roses. My curls were tied in a loose bun under the veil. Everyone said I looked beautiful and I believe I truly did. I beamed with the expectation of a glorious future. Avó, who could not hide her happiness for me, had given me her mother's shawl for something old. She had wrapped both my uncle and father in it when they were very young. When she gave it to me it was no more than a piece of frayed old cloth, like what's now left of a blanket my son Tiago dragged behind him for years when he was very young. The fabric was worn to translucence, as if it were the skin of an old person. Some things age sadly and tenderly, like people. I wore the shawl tucked inside my dress and have kept it stored away ever since.

My father came home to give me away. He brought photos of his apartment in Toronto. The electric stove. The refrigerator. The table full of beer and wine. His Chevrolet. Years later he would bring super 8 film and a projector with him from Canada to show movies of all the rooms of his house. He had to hunt all over to find the proper electrical adapter. He hung a white sheet in my grandmother's sitting room. When he was done with the photos, he pulled out his pay stub and bank book and showed everyone how much he had in dollars, their mouths hanging open when he converted it into escudos.

"Oh, Senhor Julio. You're a rich man."

"What type of work do you do, Senhor Julio?" the neighbours asked.

"I work in a factory that makes windows."

Years later, I learned that he had worked in many different factories and spent long periods without a job. For many years he was on medication for manic depression.

Late on the wedding night, after David and I had said our goodbyes and gone to bed, my father, drunk and not ready to retire, had gone into *Vila Franca* with a bottle of whiskey squeezed into the inside pocket of his suit. In town he bumped into a group of much younger men.

"Watch where you're going, you punks!"

"Go home to bed, old man, and sleep it off!"

My father hurled himself at the ringleader, missed, and tumbled onto the cobblestones.

"Hey, John Wayne! Don't hurt yourself!" They all laughed at him.

He managed to pull himself up, only to swing into the empty darkness and fall into some innocent shrubbery. He kept yelling and making a fuss even after the boys were gone.

The police arrested him and my father spent my wedding night in jail. The next day, of course, everybody knew, and his escapade, not my dress, was the talk of the village.

Chapter Four

When we first moved to Angola I sent my grandmother a postcard, which came back to me along with other mementos when she died. What you see is the long, seductive curve of Luanda's beautiful blue lagoon, the sand white in the sun, the palm trees along the shore, and the bright red roofs of the clean white buildings, all proudly facing the approach by water. This is the Angola that we thought of as ours, landscaped by God, rich in resources, ready for its glorious future. David and I had gone there, like thousands of other Portuguese, supported by the government, in pursuit of jobs that couldn't be found in Lisbon. We were attached to our language and culture and never considered immigrating to North America. There was a word for the exodus of Portuguese to Africa: Lusotropicalism—Portugal's sacred mission, a fusion of African and Portuguese that through miscegenation would produce racial and social harmony. Angola was not a colony, but an "overseas province," part of the fatherland. There were no Angolans, only Portuguese. We were all brothers, all equal. That was what we were told, what we tried to believe.

Luanda was the Paris of Africa, as Beirut was the Paris of the

Middle East, and Kabul, or Saigon, the Paris of Asia. Being the Paris of anything, it turns out, is a curse.

What the postcard doesn't show was everything that stretched inland from the sea: the tin-roof shanties that surrounded the city; the harsh plantations of the countryside; the impenetrable green forests that housed no one like us; the malnourished women and children, the forgotten but ever-patient landmines, the gunship helicopters, the burned villages and scorched earth. This was the Angola that we looked away from when we lived there. This is the Angola that the postcard helped you forget.

Now we are all around the table and all have filled their plates with food. The children make a mess until their mothers help them. My cousins sit and look a bit disapprovingly at the slightest thing, not asking for anything to be passed to them, but resentful if I don't make sure their favourites go around. My sons stuff their faces with quick big mouthfuls of everything.

"This reminds me of Angola," Fernando says while still chewing (Isabel sees this, I know). My sons have fond, indelible memories of Angola. For them Angola is about childhood and their father and innocent happiness—a strange but seductive place for that. Fernando, who was born in Lisbon and only months old when we crossed the Equator and landed in Luanda, will always consider himself Angolan, even though Angola has forsaken him, never wanted him, has orphaned him, so that he has never been, will never be, quite at home. Fernando, haunted by sadness and loss, will always be a citizen of a white, radiant paradise that doesn't exist.

"Remember when Pai used to bring all those guys home without telling you they were coming?"

"How could I forget?" I speak in my best (not so good) theatrical exasperation. "If it wasn't friends from work, it was someone from back home. He went out of his way to run into people accidentally."

"My brother was generous with everyone," Isabel states. "There was never anyone in the family like him."

A moment of quiet descends as each of us reflects on paradise lost. Except Jorge. Like the babies, he's very much in the here and now. Under the table I reach for his hand and squeeze it. I'm grateful to him. He keeps me away, usually, from the allure of the past, the way you keep a child away from the edge of a swimming pool. He helps me sweep the dust out of our life and refills it with the gadgets and concerns of the present. Still, sometimes, one needs to remember.

Paradise was so hot, so humid, my skin and my clothing were rarely dry. Plants liked it. Yellow, purple, turquoise, crimson, almost fluorescent. Insects liked it too, especially in the early evening. Best, kindest, was always the morning. Good and bright and not so horribly hot. I woke early and prepared breakfast. We ate on the veranda outside the kitchen, under the canopy of bougainvillaea, at first David, myself, and baby Fernando, then later Tiago joined us. Fruit juice and coffee and bread. I left for school before eight, but David lingered over his second and third cups of coffee. He wrote for *Jornal das Notícias* and liked to write his stories at home, when he wasn't travelling.

I learned to drive and we bought a second car. We hired a young girl, black of course, Josefina, to clean the house and look after the children while I was teaching. She lived with us. Her family was from a village in the north, near São Salvador. She was young, not more than fourteen, but mature and responsible. The children were very fond of her. Every morning she took them for a stroll in the baby carriage and later, when they could walk, she took them out holding their little hands in hers. She was a good companion and we grew attached to one other.

We were happy. I was part of a family such as I had never had before. I wrote to Avó and encouraged her to visit and sent her pictures of our baby boys, our house, Angola. At first, the photographs were black and white. Me, my hair cut short and wavy, wearing a sleeveless dress with princess seams to hide the pregnancy or the fleshliness that lingered afterwards, standing before a baby carriage with

Fernando sitting in it, holding his baby brother in his lap. A little later, there was one of David, holding a child on each arm, standing in front of palm trees, the three of them in their own world of delight. Then came colour. The four of us sitting on the front porch, potted hibiscus on either side of the steps. The boys and David crisp and clean in white, I in orange and turquoise. We took the photos on Sundays, after *almoço*, the day of the week when we were all home, sacred family time. Sunday afternoon we would drive along the coast and stop for a picnic. We wore sun hats and drank lemonade in the shade. Fernando and Tiago dozed off on a blanket, Josefina curled up near them, while I read a book with my back against a tree. David went off for a stroll, his camera around his neck. Sometimes we went to the beach, the boys coated in sand as the water lapped their little legs. Later in the evening, when the temperature and humidity had dropped, but there was still plenty of light, we would play tennis at Coqueiros, a site, we were told, that had once been a slave market. In photographs we all looked so happy. David and I were in our prime, on our own and prospering, our relationship having endured. We had left the island forever. We had left our shadows behind in Lisbon.

My world was all about children. My own little boys. My young students, most of them black. I washed and dressed my little boys at home and kissed them to sleep. I taught my children at school to read and write and hugged them when they did well or scraped a knee at recess. I had found my calling. I enjoyed teaching but always yearned to be with my sweet babies. I taught Josefina to read as well.

I took her under my wing in other ways. I decided that she would look good with a haircut and took her to the hairdresser. She closed her eyes when the hairdresser snipped away at her thick, tight curls. When the hairdresser was done, we beheld a new Josefina. She was almost too surprised to recognize herself at first. I thought she looked beautiful and modern. After that, I started to take her with me whenever I bought fabric for dresses. We would choose material and take it to the dressmaker to order our outfits. Josefina appeared to be happy. She began to look very stylish and European.

This led to a rather unsettling incident. Although we were all supposed to be in principle equal, indigenes—blacks and mulattos— were regularly shooed away from shops and restaurants meant for the white Portuguese. One day I was out with Josephina, both of us in our stylish haircuts and new dresses. We wandered into a jewellery store to have a look around. The proprietor gave us a puzzled stare, as if he couldn't quite size us up, then, past hesitation, he said in a loud voice, "You two, get out of here! You're not allowed in here, you should know that." Rather than protest, I led Josefina out the door. My attempts to make her more like me had backfired: in the shopkeeper's eyes, I had become more like her. It was an honest mistake—I suppose. I was dark, but not, I would have thought, that dark.

It was not a mistake that ever happened again, but the possibility was there in the back of my mind and made me slightly self-conscious when I was out with Josefina. I was angry with the shopkeeper, and with the system that he was part of. But wasn't I also secretly angry at Josefina, and even at my own skin?

Teaching days, I was home from school in the early afternoon and Josefina and I prepared dinner while the boys played or napped. I most enjoyed baking. Stirring the flour and butter, the way it made the house smell sweet. But I wouldn't do it as much as I was tempted because I didn't want the boys to eat too many sweets. David looked after the fun and I looked after everything else.

He often came home late. The boys loved the songs he made up for them. I can hear David singing to Tiago:

I love my Tiago's bum bum,
It's such a wonderful sight!
I wonder where it comes from
When he farts in the middle of the night.

I haven't thought about that song in a long time. No one ever wrote it down of course, but I remember it clearly. I can hear him singing and the boys clamouring for more. Of the two of us, he was the indulgent parent. Always bringing them candy and sweets.

"They'll spoil their dinner," I would say.

He did it anyway.

As much as I loved my husband and my family—and I loved nothing more—I have always needed a place inside to which I could retreat and be alone. In Luanda I had a real hiding place. There was a small alcove under the mottled and chipped cement of the veranda, and if I sat right at the back in the dark, no one could see me, even if they peered in from a metre away. When I needed to, I would stash myself in there. Sometimes the children or David would come calling for me, but I never gave myself away. At dusk I could sit and watch the black silhouettes of the birds against the glowing red sky. To this day I have never told anyone about that place.

After dinner, when the children were asleep, David liked to go out for drinks at friends' houses. I went along with him, but by ten o'clock I was tired, and ready for bed. I would slip away and drive home by myself. David stayed on and wouldn't get back until early in the morning. I was a sound sleeper and seldom woke up when he came to bed. On weekends there were parties. They never meant much to me. David, on the other hand, came alive when he was surrounded by an audience. Wherever he was, that was the centre of the excitement. He would say something witty or funny or merely exuberant, and everyone laughed. David, like many others, often drank until he was drunk. I was content to stay in the background with the canapés and table settings. I noticed women flirting with him, asking him to light their cigarettes, smiling at him with their eyes, brushing up against him with their bodies. But of course I'd been through this before and I wasn't really worried. Because I was often standing alone, I sometimes got unwanted attention myself. I remember an American oilman from Texas with a big smile and a big hat who asked me to dance and then tried to kiss me on the neck.

"When you people are done dealing with your niggers," I once heard him say, "maybe you can come on over to the States and help us deal with ours." Some people laughed.

Not all Portuguese who came to Angola were very cultured or educated. Some came for rather menial jobs that otherwise would have been taken by young blacks who streamed to the city from the desolated countryside. Sometimes such people made it to our parties. Living closer to the indigenes, in competition with them, these Portuguese were harsher and more openly intolerant. There were groups of vigilantes who attacked black people in the city night. They had nothing good to say about the natives. They were stupid, lazy, savage, unappreciative.

"They hate us all. You can see it in their eyes. They'd slit our throats given half a chance." Later I would read in the poetry of Agostinho Neto of the death of hope and "the tired footsteps of the servants / whose fathers were also servants." I thought of my darling Josefina. She didn't think like that, did she?

There were heated discussions. Some people blamed the Soviets and the communists for the problems, for supplying the guerrillas with guns. There could be no peace or prosperity, especially for the blacks, as long as the fighting went on. And the guerrillas had to be defeated—they were communists themselves with no respect for Portugal or its mission. All the Americans wanted was to get their hands on the oil off the coast. Others said there would be no peace until we beat all the blacks into submission.

"But it's their land."

"It's Portuguese land! We've been here for 500 years! Should we fight for it or just throw up our hands in surrender like women, like we did in Goa?"

In Canada, my father had a black co-worker. When my father told him that he had family in Angola, the co-worker said we were there to kill black people. My father wrote indignantly to tell us this, as if it simply wasn't true.

Life in Luanda was quite safe for us whites. But few of us ever got into the countryside. David, as a journalist, made trips there, although he was quite restricted in where he could go. He caught glimpses of the destruction and the death, the bombing, the strafing, the napalm, and the starvation.

His job, ostensibly, was to report the truth, but at that time freedom of expression was not exactly a national ideal. Many of the stories he wrote he never expected to see published, and he filed the pages away in a drawer. In this way he wrote about the slave trade and its lingering effects, about the struggles between white landowners and black labourers over fair treatment that often broke out in violence initiated by the landowners, about the struggle to be master in one's own land and the various factions that this struggle bred, about the UPA, the *União das Populações de Angola*, and the MPLA, the *Movimento Popular Para a Libertação*, and Neto, who had been flogged in front of his family and dragged away to the Cape Verde Islands, where he was jailed without charges, about uprisings and retaliations, and always about more deaths, most of them among the blacks. He wrote about how the other European imperial powers were dismantling their empires, about Angolan similarities to the Americans in Vietnam. He wrote about young Portuguese soldiers—hardly more than boys, poorly educated—from our island or Madeira, or small towns on the mainland, with no real understanding of what they were doing, many of whom would die in that ignorance or in a growing inchoate disillusionment. Mainly he didn't share these stories with me, and I didn't ask him to.

The stories that were published were more innocuous and deceiving. I remember he reported on the awarding of a medal to a young lieutenant. In the photograph he took, an officer in a white uniform is pinning the medal to the chest of the lieutenant in camouflage fatigues and a beret. Behind them rows of soldiers stand at attention. It so happened that the decorated soldier was from our island, and this photo was a big hit back home for a number of years afterwards. I don't really know how David felt about this. Was he ashamed, proud, amused? We should have talked about this more.

Sometimes late at night, when the boys and Josefina were asleep, we would argue about money. We were always in debt, despite earning two good incomes. I never knew what to expect from David's paycheque every month. He kept what he needed for personal expenses, the rest he was supposed to give to me as his contribution to our common expenses—rent, food, Josefina's wages, car payments. He only ever gave me a small amount, some months nothing. We might have managed if it had stayed that way, but he regularly took loans to cover his excess expenses. David loved being the bon vivant. He always paid for the fun. Restaurant bills, bottles of good wine, flowers to celebrate some happy occasion, he never hesitated to pick up the tab. Whoever needed money could rely on David to help out. I don't think he gave it much thought. It was no different than when he used to spend the money Avó gave him on treats for himself and his friends.

"David, why did you borrow this money from the bank?"

"I can't remember. I must have needed it for something." He shrugged his shoulders as if it meant nothing.

"They're charging us interest! The longer we wait to pay them back, the more they'll take. You'll have to start paying the bank from your money. I have nothing extra."

"Sure. Whatever. Don't worry about it."

"Somebody has to worry about it, since you won't."

We never sat down and planned a future. David was so preoccupied with work, his many friends, the present, that I don't think it ever occurred to him. Should we think about buying a house? Should we consider going back to Portugal? We never discussed any of that. As the boys got older we would need money for their education. I arranged to have David's pay check deposited in the bank so that at least I could know what he was spending. He grumbled, but he accepted the new regime. I would give him an allowance every week and more often than not he would ask for more, but at least I knew what was going on.

Despite whatever worries I might have harboured, those years when I went to bed I slept pretty well. And in the morning all was fresh again.

In Angola government employees were entitled to a paid six-month leave from work, provided they left the country for that period. It was a chance to get away from the various tropical diseases to which we were exposed. When we became eligible for the leave, we decided (it was David's idea) to travel through Europe. Fernando and Tiago were too young for the grind of travelling, so we would leave them with Avó in São Miguel. She would get to know her great-grandsons and we would be reassured that they were in the best of care.

But what to do about Josefina? It would be very expensive to fly her to the Azores and pay her salary, especially when we had someone there to watch the boys. The island was not the most accepting place for black people—although my grandmother would have made her feel more than welcome. Besides, the boys were getting older and would both be in school full time when we got back and we wouldn't be needing someone home for the whole day. So I thought Josefina might be better off if we let her go. The decision felt a little cold blooded, but it seemed the wise thing to do. David said I was a heartless bitch even to think about it, but I was just being the practical one as usual. He said the boys would never forgive me. In the end, I just couldn't bring myself to do it. Josefina had become part of my family. So we found a temporary position for her while we were away and would take her back on our return. We all had a good cry when we parted.

We hadn't been to São Miguel in many years. How small it looked from the plane on our approach: a scrawny little thing in the middle of endless sea. Avó met us at the airport, with a smile of unalloyed and undisguised joy. She had aged: her hair was all white and she used a cane for walks of any distance. She seemed sadder than I remembered her being in the past. In the house David and I were put in the room that had been mine all my childhood. How strange that was! The boys slept in the room that had been my father's. All our bed sheets smelled of soap and there was a sweet fragrance coming from the cedar branches scattered in the corners.

Friends and family came to visit us in the sitting room of my grandmother's house. I told them about life in Angola and they told me rumours about my father—things that he wouldn't mention in his letters but that inevitably made their way back to the village. He was constantly losing one job and finding a new one. In between he was kicked off the dole for not cooperating with the officials. He got into fights and trouble with the police. He kept a handgun in the glove box of his car and, as protection against rising prices, stockpiled enough gasoline in an old tank in his garage to blow up a city block. I was happy to be living on another continent.

We visited tia Teresa and Isabel at their house. Teresa, naturally addled, had become more so with age. Isabel, stern and demanding, was the *grande dame* of the *liceu*, terror and inspiration to generations of students. She taught them rigid and unforgiving propriety and an almost religious devotion to Camões.

Teresa blathered on about her grandsons while Isabel corrected them on their manners and diction. David amused himself by doing and saying things that would rub her the wrong way.

Often David ran off with the boys, eager to share with them the things he himself had known as a child. They hiked up to *Lagoa de Fogo* and down to one beach or another. I made him promise they wouldn't swim out to any islands.

"I promise. And if we run across any dead bodies washed up on the shore, I'll say, 'Sorry, *compadre*, but we can't have anything to do with you.'"

"Sorry, *compadre!*" echoed the boys.

On Sunday we all went to Mass, except for David. There was a new priest, António having died the year before.

We stayed only a few days to settle the boys, before flying to Lisbon. David was adamant that he had no interest in seeing Lisbon or staying with Judite and Lima, so we went right to the train station and headed out of the country.

Western Europe was an eye opener. Everywhere seemed more free and more advanced than we were. On the beach in the south of France, there were women with their breasts exposed—I myself wouldn't have done that in a million years. When we got back to the pension, David was so randy and flushed with sun that he made love to me like a steam engine. I was appalled by the prices of hotels and restaurants. We often fought over food. I was happy to save money and buy simple things we could put together ourselves. David wanted to sample the fine cuisine. Inevitably, one of us would have his way and the other would pout.

The French were very rude and condescending and made us feel inferior. At the Follies Bergères the woman sitting in front of David refused to remove her hat and he had a hard time seeing anything (more bare breasts). I had always thought of him as a tall man, but it was hard to do so after that and after meeting deep-voiced Germans who were as big as the statues in our village squares. The English were rude and tried to cheat us with their ridiculously complicated system of coins. In London young people wore outlandishly colourful clothes and sometimes you couldn't tell the boys from the girls. David said the boys must all be queers. We saw signs promoting birth control.

We visited many museums and art galleries, the Prado, the Uffizi, the Vatican, the Rijksmuseum, and I fell most deeply in love with the statue of Cupid and Psyche in the Louvre—if I were ever to harbour lesbian desires it would be because of the awful, perfect beauty of Psyche's bum. We crossed into East Berlin at Checkpoint Charlie to see the museums there. Given our anti-communist upbringing, this journey carried the frisson of travelling to the heart of darkness. The border guard was very friendly and joked with David about how hot it must be in Angola. David was always striking up conversations with strangers in whatever languages were available. He especially liked talking with the hip, young ones, especially the women. Near the Brandenburg Gate there were red banners the length of tall buildings with communist slogans and policeman who made us very wary of doing anything wrong. Of course that's all gone now.

In Paris we saw Charles Aznavour in concert—*Hier Encore, Tous les Visages de l'Amour*. Beautiful songs. And my favourite, *Il Faut Savoir*—"*Mais moi, je ne sais pas!*" In London it was Dusty Springfield:

> *Left alone with just a memory*
> *Life seems dead and so unreal*
> *All that's left is loneliness*
> *There's nothing left to feel.*

Later I found out this was originally an Italian song—hence my Mediterranean connection to it. David took me to Vidal Sassoon and I got my hair cut in a bob like London girls. He wanted to buy me an Yves St. Laurent shift dress, Mondrian-inspired, in colour blocks of white, red, blue, black, and yellow. I wouldn't allow him to spend the money. Instead we found a similar dress but without a designer label. Seeing me in it aroused him sharply, and when we got back to the bed and breakfast it was like he was making love with Petula Clark.

I wrote a letter every other day to Avó, telling her where we were and how she could contact us, what we were seeing and eating, how much I missed my boys. Her letters were much less frequent. She had to mail them to designated *Poste Restante* addresses, which I sent to her in advance. Her letters were full of the boys. There were usually a few words from Fernando, a picture by Tiago. I sent postcards—of the Eiffel Tower, the Beefeaters at the Tower of London, the Pope—

to Josefina.

I promised myself that I would spend more time with Avó on the return trip.

David wanted us to go to North America. New York. California. My father in Toronto. But I missed my boys and after four months I yearned to see them.

"Let's go back to the island and stay a few weeks. We still have another month after that and if you still want to go to America, we can go then," I promised.

We returned to São Miguel to find Fernando taller, with a longer face so that his eyes didn't seem as big. He was a proper boy now, not a baby any more, and I had not been there to witness the change. Tiago, thank goodness, still had the soft body and round features of a young child—but without his front tooth! He had lost his first tooth while I was away. The boys made strange with me. When I covered them with hugs and kisses I could feel their bodies stiffen.

I was being punished for abandoning them. Fernando didn't speak. Tiago said, "What happened to your hair? And where did you get that silly dress? You look like a clown."

Even my grandmother, who was always anything but censorious, looked askance at the way I was dressed. Obviously the London style did not travel well. So the dress went into the bottom of the suitcase.

"I can't leave them again, David," I confessed that night. "If you really want to go to America maybe you should go on your own." He wouldn't hear of it, so we decided to stay on the island until it was time to return home. I could tell he was disappointed: he loved his sons, but he would have liked the adventure to go on forever; he'd had enough of the island and didn't relish the return to Angola. He was suddenly slightly less joyous.

One afternoon when we were alone, my grandmother brought me up to her room and showed me a large stack of books.

"António wanted you to have these," she said.

There were translations of *Wuthering Heights*, *Great Expectations*,

War and Peace, and many other books I remembered reading with him when I was a girl. It was touching that he had left them for me.

"I learned so much from him." I said.

There was a pause. Then my grandmother spoke.

"I know you saw him in my bed the night of Judite's wedding, although I suspect you've tried not to remember."

I said nothing. She continued.

"For a long time life was not kind to me. I was very young when my mother died. I have no memory of her. Only a photograph of a beautiful young woman. My father loved me deeply—that I remember. But he was often ill. He would take to bed for long periods of time and then he died too. And I was an orphan.

"I was hardly more than a girl when I met Manuel. He was older, but in our own ways neither of us knew much about love. He was handsome and strong and he made me desire him and want to love him. We had a son together and I was able to love my boy and dedicate myself to him. But Manuel took him away from me and that wounded me deeply. I was sure I would never see my child again. I took up with a boy, a very nice boy, whom I had known my whole life. Armando had always loved me. I loved him too, though more like a brother. I became pregnant with your father and I settled down into a marriage for the second time in my short life. But always there was the loss of my first born.

"Then after years of nothing, Manuel wrote and asked me to join him. What else could I do? He had my son. I was a mother with a mother's loyalties. So I ran away from Armando with your father and came here where I knew no one. That was very hard. People shunned me and told stories behind my back. Manuel had never loved me, but now he despised me. He called me a whore. But he couldn't send me away and he needed my money. The worst was that my little boy didn't love me any more either. He never would. He hated me no matter how hard I tried. And poor little Julio, he was lost. He was a loving child, but Manuel and his brother could never love him. He succeeded at nothing. I like to remember him the way he was before, not the way he has become.

"Life was not kind to my sons, but also they were not kind to themselves. They drank too much. They refused to forgive. One refused to be tender and one refused to be strong. I had given up my home and a man who loved me to come here where everything was cold and broken. But I would do it again. I cannot regret that choice. They were my sons and I had to try.

"So for a long time I was not a happy woman. It broke my heart the way my sons turned out. I had hoped for happiness, but there was none whatsoever. Things only got worse. And that went on a long time. I came to expect nothing else.

"But then two things changed. There were grandchildren. Isabel, Judite, and David, who loved me very much despite their father's coldness, and especially you. Poor little Margarida whose mother died like my own had, and whose father abandoned her. Then you were my own child, and I loved you and you loved me in the way I had always wanted things to be. I am so sorry about your mother, yet I cherish having had you all those years, as if you were my own daughter.

"And then there was António. At first he was my spiritual adviser. Then for a long time we were just friends. He was a priest and I was a married woman. Even when we realized we loved each other, nothing happened between us, not while Manuel was alive. But after that we broke God's rules and he was my lover. I loved him like I had loved no man before. He was kind and thoughtful and we saw things eye to eye. We didn't hide ourselves from each other. We never took each other for granted. We were both middle-aged so there was no wild passion, but I loved being intimate with him all the same. I, who had come to expect nothing, found myself happy, with a husband and a child who loved me and whom I loved with all my heart. I don't know if God was rewarding me for all my unhappiness or waiting until I die to punish me in hell for my transgressions. All I know is that life *has* been good to me and I have been very, very happy. António and I found each other, even though we weren't supposed to. And I know with my last breath I will feel the anguish of my sons' lives, but I will also feel António's love for me.

"Still, it is so terribly sad," she said, "now that he's gone. I was there with him at the end. I sat there for a long time after he died. I talked to him and made believe he was still with me. It was the last time I could have him to myself. After all, he was *Agua d'Alto's* priest, and I was just one of his parishioners."

For a while we were silent, afraid that we would cry if we tried to speak.

Of all the things she had told me, there was only one about which I asked her.

"What happened to my grandfather? Armando."

"Yes, Armando was your grandfather. António encouraged me to write to him and I did. I told him about Julio and I asked him to forgive me. He wrote back and was very kind. Armando was the kindest person I ever knew. He said he would welcome Julio in his home. He said I had been a wonderful mother and it broke his heart to hear that my sons had such unhappy lives. He had married and had four children. His mother—her name was Nanette—had lived to enjoy her four grandchildren. I stole Julio from her too. And Armando said he was happy, but that I would always be the love of his life."

"Is my grandfather still alive?" I asked.

"No. He died five years ago. His widow returned my letters to me and sent a photograph of their family. That was a gracious thing for her to do, one that I did not deserve. I didn't recognize Armando—I don't know if he would have recognized me either. He was an old man. Bald, his shoulders stooped, his face dropping down with jowls. But I could see that he was a happy man. I could see that they were a close family, the way they were together, Armando and his wife sitting in chairs, surrounded by their children and grandchildren.

Seeing that he had been blessed with a loving family, that was as close to forgiving myself as I ever came."

She told me that she would keep Padre António's books, her father's diaries and letters, and her own papers in the walk-in closet in her bedroom. They were my inheritance.

"Someday, you'll come back for them. They belong to you. And I hope they'll help you love where you came from."

"I promise you I'll cherish them, and they'll make me think of you."

If anyone deserved to be happy, it was my beloved grandmother, and I was happy to see that happiness could come to someone after a long time in a way that had not been foreseen. I also saw that nothing, either good or bad, lasts forever.

It was time to go home. Living away and out of a suitcase for a long time is very draining. So is being in a place that no longer feels quite like home. We found the island narrow and closed-minded and irritating. We were bothered by the way people spoke, in an accent that had once been our own.

We were all very happy to be reunited with Josefina. I felt badly that I had ever considered letting her go. I could see in her watery eyes that as much as we loved her, she loved us back—maybe more so, and more than we deserved.

The trip to Europe left us in worse debt and we returned to a mountain of bills.

"David, we have to start to be more frugal about things. We're spending more than we make."

"You worry too much" was his response.

"Look at all these bills! How am I going to pay them off?"

"We'll take another bank loan."

"We can't keep doing that! We both make good money. There's no reason why we can't live within our means."

"What do you suggest we do?"

"For one thing, you can stop picking up the restaurant tab every time. Let someone else take a turn."

"Sure, if that's all it takes, no problem."

He kissed me and promised to try harder, but the next month was no better. I wrote to Avó asking for help, which, of course, she gave us.

Meanwhile the war dragged on with no end in sight. It would drag on long after we had left—the last time I saw images of the place was the English Princess Diana on television talking about landmines. David told me nothing was improving and that we might consider the possibility of leaving. But where could we go? Where could we find jobs? This was our home now.

And so years passed, in denial, in work, in family life, in spending. The parties continued, with David at the frolicking centre of things.

One day we received word that Valentim was coming to Luanda on official government business. I wrote back that he must stay with us, although David seemed none too happy about this.

"He is your brother-in-law, you know."

"Alas!"

"I don't know why you dislike him so much."

In her letters Judite couldn't stop boasting about her husband's advancements. He was a man of great responsibilities. He had never lacked for confidence and correctness. He wore a suit when all the other men were in short sleeves and casual trousers. Most unusual was how dry his skin was when everyone else's glowed with sweat. The only thing shiny about him were his buffed, paired nails.

Valentim stayed with us about a week and David gave him the cold shoulder the entire time. One evening towards the end of his stay, after a difficult day at work and a particularly frosty evening meal, I needed to retreat to my hideaway under the cement veranda. After a while in the dark, I heard someone come outside, then I smelled cigarette smoke and knew it must be David. Some minutes later, I heard another person come outside.

"Where is Margarida?" Lima asked.

"I don't know. Sometimes she just disappears and nobody can

find her."

We were all silent together, listening to the night.

"You still act so cold towards me, David, even after all these years."

David answered with a short harsh laugh.

"Yes, well—"

"Everything has turned out for your good. Look around, you have a wonderful wife with beautiful sons. You live in paradise."

"A paradise of napalm and butchery."

"Some force is always necessary. Besides, it won't last forever, and in the end Angola will be a better place for it. You have been placed on the winning side. You should appreciate that.

"We got your man Delgado," he announced coolly.

It was February, the heat was sweltering. It rained frequently, but the humidity never broke. I felt bloated, sticky, and tired. I was always tired.

"What are you talking about?" asked David.

"We lured him out of his hole and cornered him like a rat on the Spanish border. That blowhard would believe anything that made him think he was Julius Caesar, so it was easy to convince him that Portugal was finally ready to embrace him. Once we got our hands on him, we shot the traitor and strangled his Brazilian whore. We dumped the bodies in a ditch on the side of a dirt road and covered them with quicklime and rocks. Then we put out that he'd gotten it in infighting among the communists. And so ends his inglorious chapter in Portuguese history."

"Why should I believe you?"

"You know why."

"And why are you telling me this?"

"To keep you in the loop, my dear man! I say, where is that wife of yours?"

I was shocked and troubled by this conversation. I had never heard Valentim, who was always so proper, speak so crudely and so cruelly. He had always been such an upright gentleman. What role had he played in the terrible things he talked about? I had never quite known what his role in government was, though David seemed to have known more and never told me. Why would Valentim reveal these things to David? To keep him in what loop? Something troubling had been kept from me, something that had troubled the relations between the two men for some time. I didn't tell David what I had overheard (in part because I didn't want to give away my hiding place), so I waited for him to come to me with it. He never did. I tried not to think about all this too much. After all, there were other concerns.

Suddenly David bought himself a sports car. I couldn't believe it!

"But it's used! You don't realize how much I've saved."

"When are you going to grow up? We're living beyond our means and I don't see how we're going to get out of debt unless you change."

"Look Margarida, I've got a headache. This isn't the best time to hit me with one of your sermons."

"You don't have a headache, David. You have a hangover. I'm not giving you a sermon, I just want to discuss our debts. The bills from the restaurants haven't stopped. And now this car! Nothing ever changes."

"We'll get help from Avó."

"I can't go to Avó for more money!"

"Why not? She would be happy to give it to us."

"You're being incredibly selfish. What about Isabel and Judite?"

"They don't need Avó's money. Isabel lives at home like a nun and stuffs every escudo she makes into her mattress. Judite and Lima are doing fine. And the two of us deserve a double share—more if you count the kids."

"And what are we going to do when Avó's inheritance runs out?"

He laughed. "How far away is that? Why would you worry about something before it happens?"

"Why do we have to live on the edge?"

"We're hardly living on the edge. Why are you afraid of life,

Margarida?"

"I'm not afraid of life. I'm just tired of looking after all the problems while you pretend that there's nothing to worry about."

"Here we go again! Poor you. You can't do this. You can't do that. Life is hard."

"Life isn't hard, it's just out of control. Can't you learn to scale stay back a little bit and save something for the boys and me? Do you have to go to parties every night?"

"I don't go to parties every night! I'm tired, Margarida. We're going around in circles. I work hard for you and the boys, but I have to be myself. I thought you understood that. I haven't changed. I'm the same David I always was." With that he went upstairs to the bedroom.

I spent the rest of the night sitting in the wicker rocking chair, smoking cigarettes and drinking tea. I felt burdened and anxious with my responsibilities, and slightly sick to my stomach. The smoking settled my nerves and the nausea. I watched the ribbon of blue smoke curl off the end of the cigarette and the browner stream that I exhaled.

A few weeks later I found myself bleeding on the way home from work. I drove myself to the hospital. I had been pregnant without realizing it and had just miscarried.

I mourned in a way I would not have expected for a child I had never known, that would never be. Still I felt the loss—of part of me, part of David, part of our family. I needed understanding and comforting of a kind that no one knew how to give me.

"You're young and healthy," said the doctor. "You can have another child." But that was hardly the point.

David took me home and he tried to be nice, but he couldn't say what I needed to hear—whatever that was. I didn't have anyone to turn to for help. Another child wouldn't make any difference to David's life. He would go on the way he always had. Joyously and carelessly, never bothering to check whether his actions might be harmful to his family. He had married me for that. I would look after things. Deal with the bank. Look after the house. Yet he never appreciated me for those things. He took me for granted. He was disappointed when I wouldn't go to the parties with him, when I sat quietly while other women flirted and laughed. But it wasn't entirely David's fault. I, like everyone else in the family, had always loved him despite or because of the way he was. We had spoiled him. He would never change.

"We'll have another baby," he said, trying, as hard as he could, to be kind and understanding. Then I said things I shouldn't have.

"But I don't want another baby! Not with you. You'd never be able to feed it."

He paused. I had hurt him.

"That's absurd and cruel."

"Is it? I have nothing more to give."

"I'll leave you to rest. We can talk about this later."

"Sure. Run away. Have a good time."

When he was gone I wished I'd kept my mouth shut, or said different things, more positive things, how I loved him and our boys and would like to have more children if only we could manage things better, how sad I was at the loss of our little one and how tired I was of quarrelling.

I put the boys to bed and waited for David to get home so we could try and make things right. Eventually it got late and he wasn't home yet. There was nothing particularly startling in that, but I was disappointed nonetheless. Eventually I gave up on him and went to bed. We'd talk tomorrow. I fell asleep. Very late there was a knock at the door. Two policemen asked me if I was Senhora Aguiar.

"I am sorry to have to inform you that your husband has been killed."

"What? That can't be! There must be some mistake."

There was no mistake. His red sports car had gone off the road and hit a tree.

The policemen stayed with me for an hour to make sure I was alright. I remained very calm in front of them. Numb and stunned with grief. (Why must I remember this!) They asked if there was anyone close they could call to come over. No, just people at the school and people from the parties. Eventually I said they should go; there were no doubt important duties to attend to and there was nothing more they could do for me. Josefina was sobbing and trying to restrain herself. It was a loss for her too. She was part of the family now more than ever.

In the morning I had to tell the boys. I remember Fernando weeping and clutching a crucifix and saying he would do anything if God would give his Daddy back. But that was not a bargain God was interested in making.

It was a closed casket.

Chapter Five

The little one has just vomited all over her mother, my upholstered dining room chair, and the carpet. There are gasps and oohs and an insuppressible chuckle or two from those around the table.

"I'm so sorry!" says my daughter-in-law, starting up and catching the remnants from her baby's mouth in her hand.

"It's nothing," I answer. "She's a baby. This is what babies do."

We take the child to the bathroom together, while my sons and other daughter-in-law see to the rest of the mess.

"I'm so sorry about your chair and your carpet!" says Marta. "What if they're stained?"

"Oh, I'm sure we can clean them. And if we can't, then we have a souvenir of this lovely day together."

We take off the baby's soiled clothing and wipe her face and hands.

"Let me dress her while you clean yourself up," I say.

I take the baby into my bedroom where her parents have put a bag with clean baby clothes. I lay her on my bed and put a new clean outfit on her.

"There, isn't that better? Avó's poor little darling isn't feeling well."

I take her in my arms and hold her gently, stroking her hair, only slightly wary that she might spew forth again.

"Too much excitement for my poor darling, with all those people. We like it quieter, don't we?"

We sit softly together in the dark and she begins to suck her thumb, which Marta, I know, is worried about, but which at a moment like this I think is just fine.

The shutters are shut tight. I realize I'm losing my bearings. I'm alone, slipping down the edge of that vast hole that I carry permanently inside me.

Marta returns with her dress damp from wiping.

"How is she doing?" she asks.

"I think she's better. It's just all the excitement."

"Why don't you go back and join your guests and I'll see if I can get her to go to sleep."

"Can I bring you anything?"

"No, thank you, I'm fine."

When I arrive back in the dining room, I am asked about the little one.

"She'll be fine. Her nasty old grandmother gave her something that disagreed with her."

"You're not nasty," says my grandson very earnestly, "you're nice."

"Well thank you!" I say.

Fernando declares, with a flourish toward the chair and carpet, "Look, Mãe, as good as new! No signs of puke!"

"Fernando, you're bad!" says Judite.

"But why? Puke, that's what it is! And the other end is shit!"

He hasn't had too much to drink, I can see that. He's just trying to get a rise out of my cousins, the way his father used to do. But his father was more playful and had a lighter touch.

The newspaper articles when David died lamented the loss of a new voice that spoke compassionately about what he had observed. In his picture he was handsome and frozen in youth, eyes smiling and alive.

There have been no more horrible days for me than in the months following David's death, so many days not worth living. He left me to go on alone, burdened with his responsibilities, when so often it would have been far easier to die, responsible for two young boys with their spirits shattered, their suffering dwarfing my own endless suffering, with nothing but duty driving me, the wounded attending to the wounded, day after harsh day, night after disquieted night. The mornings, which I had always loved, were now joyless and brittle and my evening hiding place too much like a tomb, the red of the evening sky too much like fire and blood.

There were nightmares and sick days and sullen self-protection, signs of the open psychic wounds that Josefina and I had to nurse the boys through. But through to what? There are ways I see even today they have never recovered, especially my sweet, scarred little Fernando holding his crucifix. Josefina helped me through it, with love and duty. Of course, she had lost him too and seen the home we all shared shattered, but she refused to indulge herself in that way. I think she showed more strength than I did. It might have been because for her something horrible had happened but nothing had changed at the heart of things. Life was still life, promising good things and bad. For me it was much more that the emptiness and loss that had always been a tenor of existence had finally been fully revealed.

I had bad dreams. I would see David in the morgue. He was covered in blood; it had dried and was dark brown, thick, mixed with soil and plastered on his skin, over his clothes. His shirt was torn and in the cuts on his chest the flesh was pulp. His legs were spread to the side, as if they had come out of the hip sockets. One foot was bare, clean and swollen; the other had been severed at the ankle, the front dangling loose from his leg. My eyes travelled up his body, to his neck, which had been wrenched open, exposing the dark inner throat. His face was squashed flat, sockets where his eyes had been, his mouth an empty dark cave.

Did I blame myself for what had happened? Had I pushed him to this? I didn't buy the red sports car; I wasn't at the wheel; if I had angered him it was only after showing almost endless patience. No, I am not a person who grasps after irrational guilt. But I did regret that our last words together were what they were. Most of all, I was overwhelmed with black feelings of loss.

What was there to do that wouldn't be futile, that would make things the slightest bit better? It quickly became apparent how isolated we were. We had no family in Angola but ourselves. My colleagues at school liked and respected me, but we weren't close. Most of our social acquaintances had been David's friends much more than mine. I had thought of this place as home, but now that illusion was gone. It was as if I was revisiting a place where I had once lived: all the things that used to be rich with quotidian purpose now held nothing.

I began to think that we needed to go somewhere where there was family, somewhere we wouldn't feel we were so on our own. It wasn't at all that I was prescient about the future of the Portuguese in Africa—as far as I knew, the empire might last for hundreds of years. Moving was not a political decision. But where to? My father was not the kind of family I was looking for. My grandmother was old and there was something too humiliating about returning in defeat to the island. So I wrote and broached the idea with Judite: if we moved to Lisbon would they help me find a job and settle in. She wrote back promptly and said of course we would stay with her and Valentim.

I never felt about Valentim the way David did. He had always been kind to me, a bit stiff and omniscient (in his own mind, at least), but that I could live with. He had always done what he thought was best. I tried to put the overheard conversation with David out of my mind. Judite and Valentim had no trouble with the idea that Josefina might come with us, and when she did, he treated her with respect and good will. To this day, I have never heard her say a harsh word against him.

Before I knew it, Judite and Valentim had used their influence to find me a position in a school on the outskirts of Lisbon. It would be a new start, one where everything was not on my small tight shoulders. I began to arrange for the move.

There was so much we owned and only so much we could take with us. I needed to be ruthless in my discarding. Eventually I had to go through David's things. Clothing—things I'd seem him wear a thousand times, now all utterly changed. Rings and pens and small things I knew deeply or had forgotten or didn't know he had. There were so many papers and photographs, stories he'd never filed, negatives and contact sheets. Books and records, shaving things, broken watches, glasses and sunglasses, an old guitar. A small pillbox with locks of the children's hair, birthday cards the boys had made him and a pencil holder Tiago had decorated. I wanted to keep it all.

In a box of letters that had come to him over many years I found an old leather notebook. It was a diary. I didn't know that David had ever kept one. There were no other volumes, only this one. Nothing before and nothing after, something he'd started but dropped. It began when he went away to University in Lisbon and stopped two years later.

I read for a while before I realized what I had in my hands. Then the story came over me wave after wave. None of this did I want to know, all of it sending me into round after round of turmoil.

When she heard that he had gotten married to me in a civil ceremony, she mocked him relentlessly. He was a man of property, she said, a slave owner, a cradle robber, the family pet, a trained monkey, a dog with its bone, a civil servant, a silhouette, a puppet, a figure on a cake, an altar boy, a Portuguese Youth. He took it all silently and sourly. They sat apart in the classroom and across the table from each other in the café. Whenever he expressed a position on the presidential election, which was all the talk, she dismissed him outright.

David started missing most of his classes, which suddenly seemed irrelevant and hardly to matter. He dedicated his time, that not spent in listlessness, to the Delgado campaign, and watched her in steely silence.

In October, after the phony election had gone to Salazar's man, on the anniversary of the founding of the lost Portuguese republic, there was a protest march with thousands of people. They gathered in front of the statue of António José de Almeida, and people spoke in praise of Almeida and other republican leaders, especially in contrast to the thugs and goons who ran things now. When Delgado appeared to speak, people cheered uproariously. He said the election was a fraud and his fight wasn't over. When he was finished a group of men hoisted him on their shoulders and went to carry him away. They were P.I.D.E., as treacherous as ever. The crowd wrestled the general out of their hands. He disappeared and then reappeared in a window overlooking the street, gesticulating to his supporters and renouncing the regime.

That's when the police moved in on horseback, dispersing the crowd and beating those who tried to slip away at the end of the street. David was in the crowd, as were his university friends. He wasn't standing with Evangelina when the police attacked—she had continued to shun him—but they were both part of the group that ran up the street. When they tried to break through the police line, one of them seized Evangelina. David, who was coming up behind, saw this and ran to help her, pulling her free. A cop hit him across the shoulder with a club, but David stumbled away with the redhead.

They made their way through the streets. People were running, there were sirens and shouts, and sometimes police came storming by and everyone ducked or tried to hide. The closest place to get to was David's room, so they made their way there as quickly and as stealthily as possible, even when they were inside the building.

Up the stairs and in his room, they both breathed heavily with fear and excitement.

"Are you alright?" he asked her.

"Yes, but what about you? How's your shoulder?"

He went to move it and flinched in pain.

"Let me look at it."

"Are you a nurse?"

"Just let me look at it."

She lit a cigarette while he took off his jacket and unbuttoned his shirt. When he dropped his shirt off his shoulder she could see a huge red and blue bruise going across his back.

"My god!"

When she touched it he flinched again.

"Sorry. He really gave it to you. Thank you for coming to my rescue."

"It was nothing."

"On the contrary."

She kissed him gently on the bruise and this time he didn't flinch. He turned to her and for the first time they looked at each other without hiding anything. He kissed her.

"Fuck me!" she said. He had never heard a woman talk that way before.

They stayed in his room for two days. She even let him come in her mouth.

He loved her small breasts and stiff nipples, the mole in the middle of her white back, the freckles across her shoulders, and the red hair pointing down between her legs.

One warm sunny day in early December, they took the ferry across the river and a bus to Costa da Caparica. They drank *vinho verde* and ate grilled chicken with olives and cornbread on the front patio of a restaurant on the beach. Afterwards, they walked along the sand and hid themselves in between rocks to make love. His penis stood shamelessly in the bright sunlight. Late in the afternoon, shoes full of sand, drowsy and flushed, they made their careless way back to the city.

"I want to get divorced and marry you."

"I don't believe in marriage. I believe in a love without chains."

"I don't want to be without chains. I want you to chain me."

"That's a problem. As you can see, I have no chains."

"Your eyes bind me."

"No they don't. You bind yourself."

After a while, she kissed him and said, "Lovers of the world, unite. You have nothing to lose but your chains."

When they got back to his room, they made love and passed out rolled together. In the middle of the night they reached for each other and made love again.

In January the country slipped back into secrecy and hiding. Opposition leaders began to leave the country. David and his lover enrolled in classes, but stopped going to lectures after the first week. They often spent the day in bed, sleeping or making love. The nights they prowled around the cafés that were still open, huddled at tables, smoking, talking and planning the revolution.

"Cunhal and the communists understand what has to be done," she declared. "We have to start from scratch. Tear down the past, all the institutions, and build new ones. Salazar's is a brutal regime and the only way to defeat it is to be equally as brutal."

Early one evening late in the winter David came back to his room alone to find Valentim sitting in a chair in a dark corner waiting for him. Startled, David took a moment to recover.

"What are you doing hiding there like that?"

Lima stared at him for a while before he spoke.

"I have come here for several reasons, my dear brother-in-law, all for your benefit."

"And how is that. I'm not moving back in with you."

"We'll get to that. But let me go through things with you one at a time. First, I want to confess something to you, something I fully expect, once you've heard everything and thought it through, you'll agree to keep in the strictest confidence."

"I make no guarantees. What is it you have to tell me?"

Lima paused again, for effect, not out of any hesitation.

"You'll remember when your father was arrested and detained for three months by the police. I led your family to believe that I did everything I could to secure his release. I'm afraid that's somewhat inaccurate. The truth is I am the one who instigated his arrest and who made sure that he was detained a sufficient length of time."

"Why would you do that?"

"I did it for his sake and for the sake of the family that I was about to marry into. He was a drunk, out of control, with no discipline or respect for society. Given my position, it would have been irresponsible not to have done something."

"And exactly what is your position?"

"There's no need to go into those specifics with you. Suffice it to say I monitored your father's treatment and progress very carefully. I decided how harsh his treatment was to be. I wanted to break his spirit but not crush the entire man. I was quite proud of my success. To see him walk on his knees on *Senhor Santo Cristo*, to drive him home in my car, to see that he never touched a drink again—it was all very gratifying."

"So why not tell everybody about it?"

"I'm afraid people—even you, David—might misconstrue things. They would not understand with full sympathy the justness of my actions."

"And I won't tell them all because...?"

"You bring me to my second purpose in coming here this evening. I want to warn you that you are now in the position your father was in. You are out of control. You have no respect for the things that are important. It is my duty and responsibility to put an end to this."

"Are you going to arrest me and have me tortured?"

"Don't get upset. No need to panic. We're a long way from resorting to such measures. You, David, are not so much like your father. You are not a brute. You are a man of reason. It is perhaps not necessary to work so much on the level of the flesh. That is my third reason for being here: I come to present you with a certain scenario to which I expect you to acquiesce. That way we can avoid physical unpleasantries."

"What scenario?"

"Simply to do what you have planned to do. This summer you will marry your cousin, you will finish school, and you will take up your duty as a responsible member of your family. No more politics, no more rebelliousness."

"And if I refuse."

"Well, I can and would have you arrested. But before that I think it would be more effective to go after your little communist friend, Evangelina."

"Leave her out of this!"

"She's already in it. She'll most likely be arrested even if I do nothing. You've both been extremely careless and irresponsible. Don't you think we know? It's not nice when women are arrested. Sometimes they are, unfortunately, molested. Raped. Even the whores like your little friend don't like that so much. I can see you getting angry. I can see that you want to attack me. You don't understand that I'm here to help you. Your little friend doesn't have to be arrested. There are other possibilities."

"Like what?"

"She can leave the country and never come back."

"No!"

"David, there is no choice here. It has to be this way. When you reflect you'll see that. You'll see that what I propose is for the best."

"What you propose, as in my father's case, is to break the spirit. Freedom, human dignity, love, these things mean nothing to you. I despise you for that and everything you've said to me today merely deepens my feelings. I look forward to the day when you and your kind are swept away on the ash heap of history. And that will happen. Because of strong people, glorious people, such as Evangelina!"

"And I'm offering her the chance to do so. We can throw her in prison now, and that will be the end of it, or she can run off and fight another day. I'm not afraid of that. My real concern is you and our family. If you were anyone else, I would have you taken care of without a second thought. Right now you despise me and everything I stand for. Someday you'll do what is right because you have come to believe in it. Until then you have to be made to obey as if you were on a leash. Anyway, I've taken up enough of your time. I think we've understood each other. Now I leave you to do what you have to do. She has forty-eight hours."

And with that he stood up and left.

That night David went to see Evangelina. He told her what Lima had said to him.

"We have to fight them!"

"Fight them how? Even Delgado can't fight them."

"We'll go into hiding."

"They'll find us."

"Then we can leave together."

"They'd arrest us before we got to the border. And then we'll be imprisoned and tortured. Besides, I'm not as strong as you. I'm Portuguese. This is my home. I'm not ready for a life of exile. No matter how much I love you, inevitably I'll disappoint you. Remember my chains. You have no choice but to go alone."

Evangelina left everything behind and fled the country. Eventually she joined Cabral in Czechoslovakia.

We were a society and a state very accomplished at curbing rebelliousness. Slowly, David came out of himself and started going to classes. By then Delgado had fled to Brazil and in time there was a purge of faculty at the university. It was a relief for David to do nothing but listen to someone lecture about philosophy and history. In the evening he stayed at the library and worked on his assignments. When he finally wrote to me, he said he was looking forward to our wedding in the summer. And so, although I didn't know it at the time, I owe my marriage to the secret police.

David kept one photo of her, a picture of just her face in golden evening sunlight. The picture was the product of one of those serendipitous moments when the camera captures something unexpected and wonderful. She was smiling, lovely, even sweet. This was not a side of her I knew, but apparently it existed.

I read all this in his office, then took the diary with me. I refused to keep it in our bedroom, or anywhere in the house. I put it deep in my hiding place, in the darkest part where no one could find it, a mesmerizing and deadly spider.

Why had he kept it all those years? Had he carelessly forgotten about it, the way he was careless about so many things? Or did he hold onto it because he could never let it go? It was the life that had been denied him, the love that had been denied him. Would he have been happier, better, more of a man, if he had been free to roam the world in exile with her or would he have regretted it the moment that such a life showed its discomforts? Why was I left to wonder these things? Why leave this for me like a land mine when everything had been mangled already? How dare he leave me with this too! The eternal carelessness, the money, the car, the children. How dare he! I wished he'd gone with her, the red devil, she would have shown him a thing or two, and not just how she could suck his cock. They deserved each other. I'd given him everything I had and he'd thrown it away over and over until the last time behind the red wheel. Did he ever think of me? Did he regret having chosen me? He was the love of my life, but maybe I meant almost nothing to him, a servant and a womb. Did he ever write about me the way he wrote about her, even think about me that way, or was I completely taken for granted? I enchained him, but not with love, with lethargy and tradition and comfort and cowardice. Where was my freedom? Where was my life? What was I left with but responsibilities, his responsibilities, responsibilities we should have shared. I hoped he had suffered when he thought of her. I hoped he had felt loss the way he made me feel loss. Bitterness, anger, resentment, I had never before felt these things so fiercely.

He had so loved life, but not enough to take care with it. Maybe he deserved to have it taken away.

Now I wanted to destroy everything of his. Not a shirt not a letter not a memory remaining. We had to leave things behind, that went without saying, so now I had warrant and motive to purge more thoroughly. I burned so many letters, some that were dear to me, fresh in my heart. One moment they were there and the next they were black nothing and it was as if they had never existed.

Only a chosen few things would go with us, a few things to remember Angola and David by: some but by no means all of our photos, a camera for each of the boys to be given when they were older. I thought of selling David's wedding ring, but in the end I kept it. Years later, after another move, it went missing and I never found it. Nor do I know whatever became of our marriage licence.

As far as I know, the spider is still in its cave, in my dark hiding place. But I look back on it now with much more equanimity and I have long since abandoned my anger and resentment, if not my sadness. It was an upsetting thing, that goes without saying. But why had it hurt me so profoundly? Would it have bothered me as much if I had discovered it while David was still alive, or would I have forgiven him and gone on with our lives? After all, for whatever suspect reasons he had chosen me. It had mattered so much, I think, because I found it when I did, and because David was not there to mitigate and delimit the betrayal. But now everything that happened—whatever happened—is a long time ago. As if to make the point, my cousins are saying things about the priesthood they never would have said back then.

"Celibacy is a great deal to ask of a man," admits Isabel.

"Let them marry!" says Judite.

"Why not let women be priests?" asks my daughter-in-law.

"I wouldn't go that far," says Isabel.

"Why not?" declares Judite.

When I was a child I would see my cousins every day. When my sons were young I would see them most hours of every day. It seems natural now that I see my sons once a month at best. I wouldn't have believed it if someone had told me that when they were babies. It's the same thing when someone dies. You don't believe that it will become natural not to see them anymore. When you are shattered into pieces, you don't believe you'll be whole again, or even close to it. But life can be strong glue. I've had a full and rich life, which has kept me together, despite the cracks. There are still times when I feel everything breaking inside and I feel smashed to bits all over again. It began to happen just now, in the bedroom. But my family called me back.

"You're just like your father," Judite is saying to Tiago's little boy. "He was just a little older than you are now when he, your tio Fernando, your Avó, and tia Josefina, came to live with me and my husband."

My eyes search out Judite's and for a few moments we connect and I thank her for the thousandth time for taking us in and helping us build a new life.

Lisbon felt very cramped after Angola. We would live with Judite and Valentim until we felt settled and I could find an affordable apartment.

"Margarida, you're too thin," Judite would remind me every meal and then add more food to my plate.

I had forgotten how bossy she was. How she liked to control people. I was used to living under my own roof and didn't appreciate her interference, especially when it came to my sons.

"Fernando, your shorts are all grass stained," she reproached when he came in from playing football.

I didn't have the nerve to disagree with her while I was living in her home. At night, when I put the boys to bed, I would whisper encouraging words to them before I read to them.

"Tia Judite is kind. She means well. She doesn't understand that it's natural to get dirty when you play."

"When are we going to get our own place?" Fernando wanted to know.

"First, I have to save money, and then we'll get an apartment. After that we'll get a car and we can go for Sunday trips like we used to in Luanda."

"Will Pai come with us?" asked Tiago.

"Pai is dead, he can't come back," Fernando told his brother firmly.

"I have a new book I want to read to you. It's by an Englishman who wrote many stories about young boys. Charles Dickens. The one we're going to read is *David Copperfield*. It's very long and will take us a while to finish. We'll probably be in our own place before that."

After dinner I would take the boys for a walk. On Sundays we would go down to *Praça de Comércio*—they liked to look at the ships on the Tagus. Walking up the steps to *Alfama* or strolling in circles around the *Rossio*, it was our chance to be alone. Judite was gracious and kind, but she simply didn't know how to let us be ourselves. Worst was when we sat down for meals.

"Tiago, don't open your mouth when you eat."

"Fernando, pull your chair closer to the table. You're too far away from the table. Make sure your bread crumbs fall on the table, not the floor. That way Maria dos Anjos won't need to sweep."

Sometimes the boys played ball when we took our evening stroll. I let them run ahead of me and I could see with pleasure passers-by smiling at my beautiful children. The parting sun flickered gold in their chestnut hair.

"You're late," Judite would say, when we quietly slipped back into the apartment.

"It's good for them to get exercise," I told her as I whisked them away for their bath.

Smelling of warm water and soap, the boys would kiss everyone goodnight: Josefina, who sat with Maria dos Anjos in the parlour learning to crochet; Tia Judite who was reading her prayer book.

Valentim was usually still at work.

"Good night, my angels. Let's pray the Our Father together."

Judite would make them kneel down with her as they prayed. She would always end with a prayer for the soul of David.

Josefina slept with Maria dos Anjos and the boys and I shared a bedroom. I knew Judite wanted me to put them to bed, turn off the light, and join her, but I preferred to stay in the bedroom and make believe it was our own little house. The three of us squeezed into the armchair away from the door, so that she couldn't hear me reading. I covered the space between the door and the floor with a dark blanket so that she couldn't see that the light was on. The boys fell asleep in the chair, first Tiago, whom I would scoop in my arms and put to bed, tucking the sheet and blanket tight around him. Fernando waited for me in the chair. It would not do to read anymore for that would mean leaving Tiago out. Instead Fernando would tell me about school.

"Dona Julia is nice. But I liked Luanda better."

"It will take a while, but you'll grow to like it in Lisbon. Don't forget you were born in Lisbon."

"Tiago was born in Luanda."

"Yes, but he'll like Lisbon too."

"He doesn't remember as much as I do, does he?" His voice was heavy with sleep.

"Not as much."

His little head bobbed back and forth before it landed on my shoulder. I gathered him in my arms and laid him beside his brother.

After that I sat back in the armchair, wrapped warm in a shawl, and drifted with my thoughts. I liked to have the light on so that I could look at the children sleeping soundly to remind me that I had much to live for. Later, I would hear Valentim come in, his steps light across the floor. He went to the bedroom first. I could hear his and Judite's voices, like soft bubbles. The soft click of their bedroom light was the signal that they were done for the night.

I fought to keep back sleep because I hated waking to the realization that David was dead. I was falling asleep into the warm past, when he was still alive, which in itself was deceptively comforting, but waking always hurled me back unprepared into the present. So in the quiet stillness of children breathing in sleep I pampered myself with memories of our lost life in Luanda until I lost the struggle to keep my eyes open.

Somehow Isabel and Judite have come round to arguing about the lattice doors on the elevator again. This time Tiago pipes right up.

"Those doors on the elevator? They've always been there!"

"That's impossible," declares Isabel.

"Tia, I remember them when my mother first moved in! Right, Mãe?"

"Hmm" is all I say.

Isabel looks resentful and only somewhat crestfallen, but Judite is silently, smugly triumphant.

More than places, more than things, people, as long as they last, have supplied the constant bearings of my life, as far as such bearings have existed. These two old sisters are the last of those who were there from my beginning. And they've changed so little, essentially. They would have fought this way over nothing seventy years ago and they do it today. But soon one of them will not be there to fight with anymore.

The day of our liberation came one grey morning late in April, a day that was expected to be more or less like any other day. I woke at the same time as usual and as usual found that Valentim had already left for work and Judite was making coffee for me in the kitchen. I sat with her at the table to drink my coffee before I woke the boys. It was a cold morning and I rubbed my hands together in my lap and shivered.

There was a quiet but rapid knocking at the apartment door. Judite went to answer it. It was our neighbour.

"Senhora, there's something happening," she said. "Turn on your radio."

"What is it?" I asked.

"I don't know. Let's find out."

Judite turned on the radio. After she fiddled with it for a few moments, she came across a strong, eager male voice. "The *Movimento das Forças Armadas* appeals to all the inhabitants of Lisbon to stay at home and to remain as calm as possible. All medical personnel, especially those in hospitals, should hold themselves ready to give help, though it is hoped this will not be needed. It is not our intention to shed blood unnecessarily, but if we meet provocation we shall deal with it."

"What is the *Movimento das Forças Armadas*?"

"I don't know. Let me see if the neighbour knows anything."

Judite went out into the hallway. The neighbour was standing in her open apartment door.

"What is it?" Judite asked. "Is it the communists?"

"I don't know. The schools and the banks are closed."

"I don't like the sounds of this," said Judite.

"Best just stay put inside," said the neighbour.

"Yes,"

Judite and I sat listening for more news from the radio but there was nothing else. Soon the boys and Josefina were up and I told them there was no school today.

"Why not?"

"I'm not sure. It appears to be a holiday."

"Hurray!"

I asked Josefina to take the boys to play in our room and Judite and I stayed listening to the radio. After a while there was another announcement. "People of Portugal, our intent is to free you from those who have oppressed you for so long." Someone in the army was staging a coup.

"I knew it!" said Judite. "How dare they try this! The fools are bound to fail."

From the balcony we could see that people were not heeding the call to stay inside. Many were taking to the streets, not yet sure of any aim or direction.

"Viva Portugal!" someone shouted, but no one responded. Judite insisted we go down into the street to see if there was any more news.

"There are tanks in the *Praça do Comércio*," someone said.

"But whose?"

"That's not clear."

"It began at midnight," said another. "There was a song on the radio. That was the signal." And he began to sing:

Land of fraternity
It is the people
Who rule the city
On each corner a friend
On each face equality.

"We have to get to Valentim!" said Judite.

"It's too dangerous to go downtown," I said. "If we stay home like we've been told, this will all blow over."

"Valentim is in danger," she said.

"We don't know that."

"They will accuse him of bad things."

She looked at me and didn't elaborate. I didn't know how much she knew.

"You must come with me!" she said.

Someone behind us shouted, "Down with Fascism!"

And some cheered.

We went upstairs and made sure that the children would be alright with Josefina and Maria dos Anjos.

"Don't leave the apartment and don't let anyone in unless you know who it is. Tia Judite and I will be back as soon as we can."

It was pointless to take the car. Streets were jammed with people and blockaded by military vehicles and soldiers. Even navigating by foot was difficult and there were many detours. It took us several hours. Eventually we made it down to the wide expanse of the river, hoping to come at the city centre along the waterfront. The closer we got to the heart of things the thicker was the throng. There were soldiers everywhere. They had smiles on their faces and people were cheering for them and shaking their hands.

"Viva Portugal! Long Live the Army! Long Live the Republic!"

Everywhere were red carnations. Pretty young girls were putting them into the barrels of the soldiers' guns. Someone handed carnations to us, but Judite wouldn't take one. I stuffed mine deep into my pocket.

There was a warship at rest in the river and people were watching it.

"They've trained their guns on the city!" said someone. "Those pricks, they want to fire on their own people!"

We pushed on into the centre. We came across people with newspapers that had appeared with more details about the coup. It was led by leftist junior army officers. They had Caetano holed up in the police barracks near the *Igreja do Carmo*. Forces loyal to the government were refusing orders to fire on the rebels. By the time we made it to the *Rossio* it seemed that everyone in the city had gathered there. At that time we saw the ship in the river raise its guns and turn them away from the city. People cheered like crazy.

Canvas banners appeared.

Estado Novo e morto.

Viva Liberdade!

Hands raised in the air—V for victory—car horns honking, chants and cheers, wild and joyous, swelling over and over in the air.

Viva A República!

Viva!

Morto o P.I.D.E.!

We had to make it to *Rua António Maria Cardoso* where Valentim's office was. It took forever to move a block, squeezing through the tightly packed crowds. More and more all indications were that the government was falling and that a new freedom was upon us. Judite was anxious and terrified, while the crowds around her were jubilant. And me? Part of me was caught up in the spirit of revolution, like someone thrown high in a blanket. I thought how David would have taken this day, waving a banner and shouting poetry from atop a statue, as he had once done, like these students many years his junior. This was a great day for Portugal, something to rejoice in. But love and loyalty to my cousin, who had done so much for me, made me push all that underneath.

"Victory! Victory! Victory!"

As we jostled our way block by stubborn block up the narrow streets, a warplane roared by just overhead and I got a quick vision of its hard belly. No one knew which side it was on or what it was going to do.

When we made it to police headquarters there was a very angry crowd out front in the street.

"*Morto o P.I.D.E.!*"

"What's happening?" I asked someone.

"The bastards have shot at us from inside the building! There are a couple of people dead over there! They won't go down without a fight, but we'll give them a fight if that's what they want!"

Judite was half out of her mind with terror.

"I have to go and find him!"

"Judite, you can't do that. If they don't shoot you from inside, the mob will kill you! Listen, Judite, we have to stay here and be patient!"

There was another shot from inside and the sleeve of a man's coat was suddenly red with blood.

"You goddamn bastards!"

I remember a newspaper photograph that appeared over the next few days. A middle-aged agent of the state police was surrounded by young men with rifles. The hunched, defensive stance of the agent was full of fear and shame, as if he'd just been caught coming out of a whore house. Valentim was not like that. As I look back now, I don't think he was afraid that his deeds would come to light. Certainly there were things that for strategic reasons he wouldn't want known and things out of tact and sensitivity he had always kept from Judite, but I believe he was proud of what he had done. He felt no guilt or shame. He was a different kind of evil—a principled, true believer. Among all the deserting rats he was more like a captain going down with his beloved ship.

Over a loudspeaker there was an announcement: Caetano had surrendered. There was an enormous cheer. There was laughing and weeping. It was over. Portugal was free! We were beginning again. The future shone like the buttons on a soldier's jacket.

It must have been just around that moment that Valentim, in his office just above us, took his pistol out of his desk, put the barrel behind his ear, and very efficiently and effectively blew his brains out.

Chapter Six

The house is quiet. The family is sitting around after dinner. Isabel has fallen asleep in her chair. Judite's eyes are open, but still and far away. It is time to take photographs.

Tiago brings out his digital camera. Jorge asks him about megapixels. Tiago says three point five and Jorge looks suitably impressed.

"Let me get my tripod," he says. "That way we can put it on the timer and we can all be in it."

"Tia Isabel, wake up. We're going to take a picture of the whole family," Tiago announces.

Isabel smiles quietly as she shakes herself awake. Then she remembers she has brought her own camera.

"Take a picture with mine too," she says, digging into her bag. "Here's some film."

Tiago takes her camera with a look of bemused inconvenience.

"Does this thing still work? When was the last time you used it? Tia, this film is four years old; it's probably no good anymore!"

"Why not? The package has never been opened."

"Why don't we send you one we take with my camera? Do you

have a computer? Do you have email?"

"Why would I have a computer?

"Well then, we'll mail you a copy."

"Yes, but take one with my camera too."

Jorge returns with the tripod and sets up Tiago's camera, while Tiago makes faces loading the film into Isabel's jalopy.

My daughter-in-law comes out from the bedroom with the little vomitty one rolled up in her arms, her thumb in her mouth, peeping warily out at the world.

My cousins, Jorge and I sit on the couch, Fernando stands behind us, and Gabriela and Marta sit at our feet, holding their children on their laps.

"Make sure you get the flowers," Marta tells Tiago. She points to the vase of mimosas on a side table, to the right of Jorge.

Tiago composes the shot. He reminds me of his father when he takes photographs, although here too he lacks David's grace and ease.

"That's it. No one move. Your best smile." He adjusts the camera to automatic timer and runs into the picture to sit beside his wife and children.

We're all frozen together for a moment waiting. Then there is the flash and the click.

"One more!"

Tiago jumps up and resets the timer and we freeze another time.

"Now mine," says Isabel.

"Yes, Tia," says Tiago with more than a hint of impatience.

With no timer Tiago won't be in this one. Isabel seems untroubled by his absence. He frames the shot without a great deal of care.

"Everybody smile."

This will be our last picture together. We are old. Judite, as if thinking this too, squeezes my hand just before the flash.

Most people didn't know what a revolution would be like—how would we? As revolutions go, ours was a good one—democracy and freedom with very little bloodshed. The Portuguese were not so stupid after all. But it was nothing like the Second Coming or the birth of a new world. Many things changed profoundly, but much remained essentially the same. The sun rose each morning on a world held down by gravity. They changed the name of Salazar Bridge to 25th of April, but it's the same bridge. In Angola they're still fighting.

After the big day there was the continuing revolutionary process. I was forced to stand in front of my class and denounce my colonial past and imperialist complicity. How I had exploited and oppressed Josefina. Today she's married to a dentist in Sintra. She has two beautiful children, a boy and a girl, almost full grown with skin the colour of cinnamon. The girl, Marina, is a fashion model. They would have been here today but they're at one of his conferences in Paris. Judite had to move back to the island, where the revolutionary fervour was decidedly more tepid. People there would rather gossip about you behind your back than denounce you to your face. She stayed there three years.

When the colonies were given independence, there was an influx of refugees and ex-soldiers. Each street corner had its beggars, amputees many of them. There were strikes and constant shortages. Everybody, rich or poor, had to manage the daily inconveniences. No water after nine o'clock in the morning and before six o'clock in the evening. I filled bottles to use during the day. Often the electricity went out. When that happened at night I kept an oil lamp so the boys could do their schoolwork. Food was rationed—cod, milk, olive oil.

I, like most others, was an observer, not a maker of history. In the face of tanks, elections, and shortages, I went home and made dinner and put my children to bed. For Judite, on the other hand, history pulled the carpet out from under her, the nice carpets of a nice apartment she shared with a husband who cared for her and protected her. She hasn't really been able to recover. She dresses in black or white, although she does so more fashionably than the widows of old. She has built little that is new and the last decades have been for her a long period of mournful stasis, time to kill. Her life has undergone a premature stunting, her losses coming at an age when she felt too young for them and too old to start again. Others, of course, might have started over at her age, but Judite is Judite, and I understand.

At her worst, Judite is one of many who long retained their sympathies for the past, its order, efficiency, and predictability, a time when the trains ran (though no Portuguese ever expected them to run on time). Strong men and rigid regimes have their sympathizers, and Judite's sympathies were more personal than most. Salazar was no Hitler, they say. We were not among the great villains of history— whatever consolation that might be to the bombed out villages in Angola and Mozambique.

My own story has gone somewhat differently than hers. In the ten years before I met Jorge I grew in strength and independence. I became more outgoing—although to this day it would be a dull party indeed that I was the life of. I was fortunate to have a secure job, albeit one with a modest income. I was very controlled in my spending. I had chosen our apartment carefully—close to my school, the boys' school, and with all the conveniences of living in the city centre. It wasn't necessary to have a car, and we didn't for many years. By the time my sons were ready for university, the economy was much stronger and we could afford small luxuries.

Eventually freedom became a settled and expected component of our lives. Women, even, or especially, enjoyed new liberties—our own jobs, our own money, our own pleasures—as we modelled ourselves after our sisters in northern Europe and America.

From time to time now I see Evangelina in Lisbon. Her hair is still short, but grey now, and her body has thickened with age, so that she doesn't look that different from other women of her generation. She is a law professor at the University in Coimbra and a regular television commentator on political issues, especially those relating to women. She has earned her success. Evangelina's choices have proven her right in many ways—government, women's rights, marriage, there have been so many changes in those things. We never acknowledge each other when our paths cross, but I'm sure that she recognizes me. We are old now and at any rate I have long stopped thinking of her as a rival.

Also still living in Coimbra is little Lucia, who has just revealed the third secret of Fatima. It has something to do with the pope being shot—I didn't pay close attention, I'm not very religious anymore.

Sunday afternoons I would drive with my girlfriends—I had my own friends now!—along the coast to Cascais. On the beach the boats were turned over on the sand and the fishing nets were spread out as the scruffy and wizened fishermen repaired them. You wouldn't know it was the twentieth century. On the other side of the road there were a handful of cafés. A little further along the road was the casino at Estoril with its fancy gardens. Whenever we went there men would flirt with us shamelessly, which had its appeal, but we usually preferred to sit at an outdoor café with the palm trees flickering and shielding us from the sun, as we sipped Nescafé, smoked cigarettes, and shared our little intimacies before the relentless and hypnotic sea.

My life was quiet: teaching and raising two adolescent boys who didn't give me problems. I had little to say. Anyway, my natural preference was to listen.

"Silvino is so tight with money. When I buy a new dress I have to hide it for months so that he won't notice and lecture me about spending."

"Vasco has a lover. Sometimes I wish he'd just leave."

"I'm so tired at night and Manuel just wants to have sex. New things he's seen in movies. He's obsessed with staying young."

"António wants his mother to live with us! She's impossible! What am I going to do?"

Theirs were marriages of many years and habits, heavy with responsibilities and chores, and more than a measure of doubt and disappointment. The passion had waned or completely died, and they felt the gnawing realization that the best times were already behind. David had been the love of my life and I had no thought of replacing him. I came from a tradition where women took on widow's weeds and not a second husband. I missed so much about my married life, but in other ways I had to admit life without a man was good, the independence, the control, the even keel. I was content to stay in the safe territory of friendship, intimacy that went no further than conversation, secrets that were comfortably expressed over a coffee table rather than in the dense jungle of a bedroom. I didn't expect passion, had lost touch with it, and happily settled for the pleasure of my girlfriends' company.

"What was your husband like?" they asked.

"He was a lot of fun," I said. "A real extrovert. Always the centre of the action." But what would have been a proper answer? He shone in the sun. He wanted everything. He embraced it all. His ambition exceeded his strength. He was the father all boys crave. He thrilled me and cut me. The red sports car.

"Wouldn't you like to meet someone? You'd have no problem. Francisco has a friend who's divorced. No kids."

"Fernando and Tiago are too young. It would be too difficult for them. Maybe when they're older."

When we drove back home along the coast, the sea quiet and calm, I felt more or less happy and couldn't wait to prepare dinner for the boys.

One evening the phone rang and Isabel was on the line. They had received word from my father's landlady in Toronto that he was in the hospital. He had inoperable cancer and was not expected to live very long.

"Avó's here," Isabel said. "She wants to speak to you."

There was that long pause that comes when old people pass the phone.

"Hello, my darling."

"Hi, Avó. How are you?"

"Isabel told you about your father?"

"Yes."

"I want to go to him. I need you to come with me."

I hadn't heard from my father in many years, perhaps not since David died. When the boys were younger I used to write regularly to him, letting him know how his grandsons were doing and getting them each to write a few childish sentences. But there were no letters in return, no acknowledgements of holidays or birthdays, no interest expressed in our lives. Now I rarely thought of him and never with affection. For me he had already been dead a long time. I had no need to say goodbye to him. Taking time off work and travelling all that way would be a major inconvenience. Who would watch the boys? But my grandmother was asking and nothing in me could deny her.

The boys insisted they were fine on their own, but I asked Josefina to stay with them. I flew to São Miguel to pick up Ávo, and together we went to Toronto. Ávo looked no bigger than a child; her body was bent and twisted like a shrub roughed up by the wind. You could almost see through her translucent skin, hair white, as if she were already in the process of becoming spirit. She was quiet, almost still, during the flight across the Atlantic, even when the plane shook and was knocked about with turbulence. It simply didn't disturb her. I suppose that nothing would have at this point in her life. She was going to bury her son.

"It should be the other way around," she said. "The way it's meant to be." But there was no distress in her saying this, just sadness and resignation.

We were arriving in the middle of January. Neither of us had ever experienced anything like this. So cold, I never knew the earth could be so cold. It was really all very shocking. From the airport we took grey busy highways into the flat city. As far as I could see the land stretched flat and grey forever. There was nothing pretty about the place. Already at four o'clock in the afternoon the sky was turning murky. Winter back home was grey like this, but here everything was covered in snow, white and shimmering, or dirty and grey, powdery or hard like meringue. In the streets cars had churned it the colour and consistency of cookie dough. Other times it turned into dirty, salty slush. We could see high rise towers in the distance. We drove into the city, a hodgepodge of mismatched buildings, and the taxi pulled up in front of a faded and dirty yellow brick house on Margueretta Street—almost my name. This was the house where my father had been boarding, and we were going to stay in his room while we were in Toronto. When we stepped outside, not properly dressed and shivering, our breath congealed into fog in front of our mouths. With one hand around Avó and the other pulling the suitcases, I walked slowly up the sidewalk, afraid we might slip in our dress shoes on one of the icy patches.

I knocked on the door and a short fat woman answered and greeted us in Portuguese.

"You must be Senhor Julio's mother and daughter. Please come in, it's so cold out there!" And she made a gesture of shivering.

"Thank you, Senhora."

"You've come such a long way. Would you like some coffee? Something to eat?"

"We don't want to bother you and we must get to the hospital to see my father, but maybe something small would be good. But could we first put our bags in his room?"

"Yes, of course. His room is in the basement." She pointed to the side of the house and steps that led below the ground.

We made our way carefully down the narrow steps into the darkness of his home. There was an unmade single bed and a small partition separating it from a toilet and shower, a short counter about an arm's length covered with pots and dishes and a hot plate next to a water tap that ran into a deep wash basin. Near his bed was an armchair that faced a television on a small table. The place badly needed cleaning—obviously a skill that my father had not quite perfected. There were many books, most of them in English—novels and books of poetry and books on a variety of topics that had no connection: history, automobiles, travel, medicine. Most of them, we would discover, were overdue library books.

"Oh yes, your father is a real reader. His English is very good, everyone says."

Down in the corner a small white cat hid itself.

"That's Coconut," she said, using the English word. "He's your father's cat. They're always together. It's a real love affair between them!"

The litter box needed cleaning. I'd have to see to that.

After she left us alone, we freshened ourselves up ever so slightly and ascended to join her in the kitchen. She fed us with a generosity befitting far-travelled guests and spoke of my father.

"It is so terrible and sad about the cancer. He's only been with us for three years but I've grown quite fond of him. He's such a nice man—not very tidy, as you can see, but very nice nonetheless."

Dona Teolinda called a taxi to take us to the hospital where my father was staying.

At the hospital I asked for my father in my halting English and we were directed to his ward. He was in a room with three other dying men and when we stopped in the doorway we had to look around carefully to see which one he was. Avó saw him first, recognized the son she knew behind the slow withering of years and the sudden heavy ravages of terminal illness. His eyes were closed and sunk in his long face—he was already on a moderate dose of morphine—and his arms atop the covers were pale flabby sticks.

Avó walked to his bed and without taking off her coat sat on the mattress and took his hand. Roused from sleep, he opened his eyes and saw her.

"And who are you?"

"Julio, it's me, Mama."

"Mama! You're so old, what are you doing here?"

"I've come to see you."

"That's very nice of you."

"And here is Margarida."

"Margarida who?"

"Your daughter Margarida."

"My daughter?" he said, amused and bemused. "But my daughter is very young."

"Not any more, Pai."

I think he thought he was in a dream.

"This is a pleasant surprise," he said and nodded off again.

According to the nurse in charge he had a month or less to live. Apparently he had been in pain for some time but had never seen a doctor.

We sat with him until late. Then Avó kissed him on the forehead and told him we would see him tomorrow. He smiled faintly.

The whole day had exhausted her physically and emotionally and when we got back to my father's room she fell right asleep. I sat in the chair and looked around. There was no sign of any drinking. Maybe the landlady had removed the bottles before we arrived. Coconut came and jumped up on my lap. It seemed to like me.

The next morning I did some cleaning before we set out for the hospital. That day my father was more fully conscious, but mostly he lived in a confusion of different times and places.

"It's so good that you've come," he said. "I don't deserve such kindness."

"Everyone deserves kindness."

When I showed him a photo of my sons, he looked at it appreciatively and attentively and said, "They're wonderful boys! David must be very proud."

We joined Dona Teolinda and her husband for meals. Every few days I would go out to buy food with her. Her husband would drive us to the hospital whenever he could. She decided my coat and shoes wouldn't do for winter and took me to a large store with a great wall of flashing lights on the outside, Honest Ed's, where there were bins full of cheap clothes. I bought a warm black coat and knee high snow boots.

Avó talked to my father about his childhood in Brazil and he liked that and seemed clearheaded in remembering. Sometimes he corrected her.

"No, the swing was on the other side of the flowerbeds!"

On other times and places he was not so clear. In an attempt to connect with him I reminded him about my first hot dog on Terceira.

"I ate it starting in the middle, so it came apart in two halves."

"That's funny, but I don't remember. Are you sure it was with me?"

Was I more hurt or more sad that he had forgotten?

One moment when we were sitting with him, after a long period of silence in which he drifted in and out of being there, he looked at me and said, "There's a poem I wrote I want to recite to you."

"I didn't know you wrote poetry."

"It's in English. It goes like this:

Lake Erie, Lake Erie,
Don't you get weary
Making waves all day?
It must be nice
To crawl under the ice
And sleep the whole winter away."

I wrote down the words and later asked Dona Teolinda to translate. She could tell me what each word meant, but she didn't really understand the poem.

I realized I didn't really know this man—although in hindsight there was nothing surprising about that: I'd hardly seen him since I was a child. He was not what I expected. Certainly the process of dying must have made alterations to him, but even the accounts Dona Teolinda gave us of him before the illness were not what I might have expected.

"He's been with us three years. At first he was more outgoing and he had friends over."

"Did you have problems with his drinking?" I asked.

"Drinking? I've seen no drinking. No, he had a woman friend but he knew I didn't allow that sort of thing in my house and she never stayed overnight. But in the last year he's kept more to himself. I think maybe he was in pain. But he didn't say anything. Often he would eat with us, until a month ago. I began taking a tray down to him."

So he had stopped drinking? Had he abandoned the anguish and desperation that had always been so unmistakeably part of him? When? How? Do wounded people of his ilk ever change? Unfortunately he wasn't in any condition to explain things to me.

Did I feel guilty that I had not given him more of myself? Did I feel resentment that he had so completely abandoned me? I am a creature of calculation. I measure out my duties, first to my husband and children and my grandmother, with only so much left for others. I am not an endless reservoir of caring and I know it. Nor will I expend too much compulsive concern on things that have not gone as one might have wished. I have mourned deeply for David. That was enough. As a child my father had etched sadness on my heart. But that was long ago and I wasn't going to dwell on it.

One day he took a turn for the worse and they increased his dose of morphine. After that he was mainly unconscious. He rarely spoke and when he did he didn't make much sense.

"Where are the rabbits?" he asked anxiously.

"What rabbits, Pai?" I replied.

But my grandmother just told him, "The rabbits are safe."

When he died we sat with him late into the dark morning. His mother held his hand and whispered comforts to him. At times he seemed almost to smile and my grandmother claimed he tried to squeeze her hand once or twice. When his breathing got very shallow and the nurses told us the end was near, I leaned close to his ear and spoke to him.

"Pai, I wish I could have known you better. I hope you've been happy."

I don't know if he heard me. I began to cry.

Dona Teolinda said she would be happy to take Coconut. She asked if we intended to bring my father's body back to the island.

"That would be Margarida's decision," said my grandmother, "but the island was never his home. I believe he would be happier here."

I begged Avó to come to Lisbon with me, but I couldn't convince her.

"I have so much to do at home," she insisted. "Maybe in the summer if you visit, I'll go back with you..."

I called her every Sunday night at eight o'clock without fail. Sometimes she was tired and there was little to say. Sometimes she entered more fully into conversation. Sometimes she came alive with the enthusiasm of the past.

"The carnations in the garden are in bloom when I sit outside to take my coffee!"

She died before the summer. Isabel, who looked in on her every day on her way home from school, found her in bed, cold and at peace. I returned to the island for her funeral and walked behind her coffin, up the hill to the cemetery that faced the sea. This place had truly become her home in a way that it had never been my father's, or mine I suppose.

I stayed in her house for a week, packing the mementos—the diaries and letters and photos that she wanted me to have. Some of the pictures were ones I used to have but had destroyed when we left Angola. Now they had found their way back to me and it seemed like fate that I should keep them. In the evening I sat in the back garden and looked to the darkening green mountains fading away before me as they had when I was a child. Except for some old houses that had been torn down and some new ones that had gone up, the vista was as it had always been. Cows that had been grazing on the grass were about to make their way home for the night. I almost felt that I was still that young girl and this was still my home.

I slept in the bedroom that used to be mine. The sheets smelled clean and fresh. Avó had kept the bed prepared for me and an unexpected visit. The scent of cedar branches still haunted the corners of the room. Through the open window, I heard the waves rolling in to shore and before dawn the fishermen going down to the sea.

Now I was truly and finally orphaned.

Judite came for the funeral and stayed at her mother's house. She, Isabel and I inherited Avó's house and savings. Judite remained after I left and considered buying Isabel's and my share of the house, but decided against it.

"Lisbon is home for me now."

So we sold the house. I will never go back there. When I married Jorge, we went to Barcelona for our honeymoon. We've been to California and New York and all over Europe. We both love North Africa.

Isabel is getting up to go now. She is leaving and I will never see her again. Here she is for the last time, grey and stooped over her cane, almost unrecognizable from the young girl I once knew. The grandchildren will not remember her.

"And who is this?" they will ask when they look at old pictures.

"That's Isabel. You met her."

"Did I? I don't remember."

And soon there will be no one left to identify her.

She is going like so many have gone before. When she arrived the other day I caught myself wanting to ask her about people who have been dead a long time already. "And how is your mother?" I wanted to ask. And even, "How is Avó?"

Isabel is leaving for São Miguel early in the morning.

We embrace.

"My dear, sweet Margarida! It has been so good to see you again!"

"You too, Isabel. Will you come for Christmas?"

She shrugs her shoulders with doubt. "It would be wonderful to see you on the island."

"We'll have to see. Take care of yourself."

Everybody kisses everybody else goodbye. My sons and their wives have to get their little ones home to bed. They have to get back to their own lives. Judite and Isabel have to catch a few hours' sleep.

"Goodbye, tia Isabel, we'll send you our pictures," says Tiago.

"And I'll send you mine," answers Isabel.

"Terrific!"

This parting for me is soft and sharp, like a cat: tenderness and the opening of a wound.

"So long, Mãe, we'll see you soon," says Fernando, kissing me on each cheek.

"You take proper care of my grandchildren," I say.

"I will."

Jorge closes the door and everyone is gone. We can hear them chattering as they make their way down the hall. The elevator comes, they all get in, the door closes, they are gone.

Jorge heads for the dining room to bring dishes to the kitchen.

"Tiago is going to show me some new software," he tells me.

"That's good," I answer, sensing his interest, happy that he has something in common with my son.

"He's doing some exciting work."

I am happy he takes an interest in my boys. It has taken many years. There's respect, not love, but that will do.

"The meal was fantastic, by the way."

"Thank you. I think everyone liked it. Except my poor little one."

"I'm sure it was just the excitement."

We store the food in plastic containers, the bread and cake in bags, stack the dishes in the dishwasher, and sweep the crumbs from the tablecloth and the floor.

So here we are alone again, Pierre and Natasha. Often there is silence between us, because we know what the other is thinking, or we've said everything we want to say, or we're bored with talking to each other, or there is something we don't want to share. Sometimes it's awkward, like a married couple eating silently together in a restaurant while around them at other tables everyone is effusive, but mostly it's just the way it is.

"Let me do the rest in the morning," he considerately suggests.

"Your wish is my command, kind sir."

At first and for a long time I felt he was so good at cleaning up in the kitchen as a rebuke to my sons, who, he believed, didn't do enough to help me, and whom, he believed, I did not push enough in that direction.

"How about a nightcap?" he asks, using the English word.

"Yes, a little glass of port, maybe?"

"Coming right up!" Again in English. He likes to speak English. Before I knew him he worked for several years in California, after his short first marriage ended. Later he used his connections to get Fernando a job over there. I was not necessarily happy about that, afraid that my son would never come back. But he did, and he married a Portuguese woman, and now they have children, and I don't worry about them going away.

I don't think my grandchildren will leave Portugal. Things have changed. We are part of the European Community and while we're not as prosperous as North America, there are opportunities here and it's appealing to be close to other European cities. Paris. Berlin. Rome. Amsterdam. Madrid. These are all seductive places. As for the government, it's not perfect, it never is, but it's no better anywhere else. So, I don't think my grandchildren will leave, but anyway, by the time they reach that age I'll be dead.

While he's getting us a nightcap—even I use English now—I bring two glasses of water and put one on each of our night tables. I put his pills next to his water and my pills next to mine. Then I go to join him on the sofa.

"I don't think Isabel has long," I say.

"No. But she's not really that old."

"Old enough. People in my family don't live that long."

"Except your grandmother."

"Yes." He never knew my grandmother. That always strikes me as strange. "And Maria de Deus. She's going to set a record."

"Too bad she won't be aware enough to celebrate it."

"Be nice."

"I am nice."

"Yes, I suppose you are. Give me a kiss."

Sometimes we read in bed before sleep, I a novel, or much more rarely now, a book of poetry, he something about business or technology. Once upon a time I used to read to him, a poem or a paragraph of fiction, but it was like speaking into a void, so I stopped.

When we turn out the light we begin by trying to fall asleep in each other's arms, but eventually we turn away from each other so we can point in our own directions.

Before long he's sleeping, his breath whirring around in his nose. I lie here thinking about the day. I wander over snippets of conversation, the food, feelings and impressions, and back again. Isabel really liked the soup. I must make sure that Tiago sends her a photo. Why does he have to tussle with her the way he does? Was I in the photograph? I don't remember. Isabel liked the soup. It was very good soup. Where's Coconut? I have to mail Coconut some soup. I realize for a moment that the quality of my reasoning means I'm falling asleep, but almost as soon as I can think that, I've completely passed over into the realm of dreams.

I will remember relatively little of this. I am in a huge hall with crowds of people milling around or seated at long tables. It is a convention of everyone who has ever lived. We are divided into groups and seated according to who we essentially were or are. I have been put with the serious family members, although I don't really have a sense of any other people in my particular group. At the next table over are the *Fado* singers. The musicians are tuning up. I think they're going to play something for all of us later. A woman with braided hair holding a violin cranes her neck and closes her eyes and moves her bow back and forth. A black man sits quite still, his eyes shut tight, as he fingers the valves of his trumpet. Other obscured musicians devote their attention to their instruments and don't notice me.

"But where is Amália Rodrigues?" I ask.

"She's not part of this group," I am told.

"But how can that be?"

"It's just the way it is. She's with the famous people."

"I'd like to see some famous people," I say.

Someone suggests that I might like to see the saints and I'm eager to do so. I am led to a table where old women are sitting placidly, some knitting, most just quietly doing nothing. I look for Mother Teresa and my grandmother, but I don't see them. It's not a very exciting group, actually. Not much to see. I notice stands with signs here and there designating different groups, but I can't read what they say—they are almost, but not quite, legible.

There is a podium on a stage at the front of the hall. A man stands at it. I think he might be the head of the United Nations. He has a proposition he wants to float by us. If everybody was half the size we are now, we could fit twice as many people in the world, or have the same number and live twice as long. He wants us to have a discussion and debate about this. I think about it for a moment and it seems to make sense.

The keynote speaker at the convention is Sister Lucia from Fatima. Everybody is very anxious to hear her and what she will reveal.

"The third secret of Fatima," she announces, "is that there is a fourth secret that no one can ever know."

Someone asks her, "Is it a good idea that we whip ourselves?"

"Each person will have to decide that individually."

Next is supposed to be the musical entertainment, the greatest *Fado* performance of all time. I am looking forward to it. But instead

I find myself outside in the bright clear sunlight. There are white peacocks and trees cast deep sweet shadows in the thin air. Japanese tourists are taking photographs. They want the peacocks to spread their feathers, but the birds scatter away from the cameras' clicking. I'm high up the hill, looking down from inside the walls of the *Castelo São Jorge*. Below me the white buildings of the city are like winding rows of teeth. Far down below, many kilometres it seems, in a soft, hazy light the wide Tagus, disconcertingly wide, runs to the sea.

Someone is sitting beside me. I glance over. Although it looks nothing like her, I realize it is Lucia. She resembles someone else I know, someone from the past, but at the moment I can't place her. If I remember this, it might come to me later. Her presence makes me uncomfortable.

"What did you think of my speech?"

I realize I don't remember much of what she said, but I'm afraid to tell her.

"I'm not sure what to think. I'm a bit confused."

"That's because you're lacking in faith."

I become angry at this.

"How can you say that? You don't even know me! What gives you the right to judge?"

"Did I say faith was a good thing?"

"Well, isn't it?"

"That's something each person will have to decide individually."

Now there are many people from the convention on the castle grounds and I realize all my family is here, generations of them, although I can't distinguish anyone in particular in the crowd. All around the long lost are finding one another, husbands and wives, parents and children, embracing, crying for joy. The sky is very, very blue.

Suddenly I see my boys in the crowd. They are as they are now but also younger somehow, still children, as if they had been frozen in the past. I call out to them, but they don't hear me. Then I see that Fernando is looking at someone who is looking back. They walk slowly toward each other.

"Papai, it's been so long!"

"I know!" David sobs.

"You don't know how much I've missed you. All these years!"

"I've missed you too! But now I'm back."

"There's so much I want to tell you. So much has happened. There was a revolution. We have democracy now, and computers. I'll show you everything."

"I'd like that very much."

Fernando embraces his father and they hold each other, each shaking with tears. Watching them I have a sense of great goodness and my oneness with everyone.

Where the peacocks stood are now angels with flaming swords they hold outstretched before them. Something bright, someone bright, appears in the air above the trees. I sense it is my mother. Behind her the sun pulses, as if it is about to explode, and fills the hilltop with blinding light. An airliner roars out of the light falling towards us and I am about to die.

When I wake in the morning Jorge will be doing the last of the dishes, there will be fresh coffee, and I will go on with the life that has been given me to finish.

Glossary of Portuguese words
with English meanings:

Adega, wine cellar

Aguardente, type of brandy

Almoço, lunch

Arroz doce, rice pudding

Avó, Avô, grandmother, grandfather

Azulejo, glazed tile

Batata frita, fried potato

Chouriço, pork sausage

Caboclo, person of mixed Brazilian Indian and European ancestry

Comadre, Compadre, godmother, godfather

Dom, Dona, sir, madam (title preceding proper name)

Fado, fate, destiny; Portuguese folk song

Fatias douradas, French toast

Favela, shanty town

Festa, feast, festival, or party

Gelado, ice-cream

Igreja, church

Liceu, secondary school

Leitão, suckling pig

Patrão, boss

Praça, square

Querida, Querido, dear

Senhor Santo Cristo dos Milagres, feast of Christ of Miracles, largest
   religious celebration in the Azores

Tia, Tio, aunt, uncle

Torresmos de molho fígado, marinated pork pieces with liver sauce

Graziela Pimentel was born
in São Miguel, Azores,
where she has a home.
She lives in Toronto, Canada.

Mark Fortier has two Portuguese
daughters and lives in
Guelph, Ontario.